Sabre

James Follett
SABRE

HEINEMANN : LONDON

First published in Great Britain 1997
by William Heinemann

3 5 7 9 10 8 6 4 2

Random House UK Limited
20 Vauxhall Bridge Road, London, SW1V 2SA

Random House Australia (Pty) Limited
20 Alfred Street, Milsons Point, Sydney,
New South Wales 2061, Australia

Random House New Zealand Limited
18 Poland Road, Glenfield,
Auckland 10, New Zealand

Random House South Africa (Pty) Limited
Endulini, 5a Jubilee Road, Parktown 2193, South Africa

Random House UK Limited Reg. No. 954009

A CIP catalogue record for this book
is available from the British Library

Papers used by Random House UK Limited
are natural, recyclable products made from wood grown in
sustainable forests. The manufacturing processes conform to
the environmental regulations of the country of origin.

ISBN 0 434 26767 8

Printed and bound in Great Britain by
Mackays of Chatham PLC, Chatham, Kent

Part One
A Perfect Bomb

1

It was all so bloody unfair!

The sound of the four Rolls-Royce engines rising from a muted whine to a dull roar had the same effect on the crowd of hardened plane-spotters in Heathrow's Terminal 6 public observation dome as the whinny of a mare on heat summoning a clamouring herd of eager stallions.

'I was here first!' Jeremy Moreton yelled indignantly. But no one heard him in the stampede. This was the first take-off of a Sabre spaceplane from a civil airport, therefore this was war. He was swept aside and bowled over by the pushing, jostling crowd of plane-spotting anoraks muscling their way to the rail, every one of them grimly determined to get the best position – the position young Jez had just been occupying. He crouched his diminutive body over his dad's Sony Memcorder (if anything happened to that it wouldn't be safe for him to return home), and an oaf built like a bison trampled on his shoulder and broke the strap on his kitbag.

'Bastards!' Jez spat in spirited fury. He scrambled to his feet, his body still question-marked protectively over the Memcorder, and tried to dive through the tangle of legs. Some of the plane-spotters popped electronic flashes, bouncing light off the windows and arousing the wrath of the video camera owners.

Half Jez's vision went blurred.

Left contact lens gone. Scrabbling on floor. Fingers trodden on. Shit! Shit! Shit!

'Not your day, young man,' said a friendly voice.

Jez blinked forlornly around as the uniformed Terminal 6 security officer helped him to his feet.

'I used to be a plane-spotter when I was your age, young man.'

'I am *not* a plane-spotter!' said Jez hotly, loathing the man's patronising attitude. 'Planes belong in the past. I've come to see the Sabre!'

Jez had no interest in aircraft but he was space-mad. His bedroom was filled with models of spacecraft, from one of Yuri Gagarin's cannonball capsule to the giant Airfix model of the production Sabre that he had been given for his birthday. Also, he had the Sabre's flight sim proggy on his computer, and his dressing table was piled high with technical material that he had badgered out of Sabre Industries' press office. There wasn't much that young Jeremy didn't know about the spaceplane.

'And I was here first!' he continued. '*And* I had the best position!'

The security officer nodded sympathetically. 'Aren't you the one who was at the front of the queue all night?'

Jez agreed that he was and peered at the floor in the hope of spotting the gleam of his missing contact lens, but it was hopeless. And cycling home to Richmond with a broken kit-bag strap was going to be a pain. The day he had been dreaming about was turning into a disaster.

'Thought so,' said the security officer. 'Saw you on the monitors. Kept an eye on you. Funny people in all-night queues.' He beckoned Jez to follow him. 'If you come through here, you'll get a better view of the take-off.' The official pressed his forefinger on a security door's ID pad and pushed it open. The balcony on the far side of the door was exposed to the elements – none of the usual grimy panes of glass that characterised airport observation lounges and which had infuriated Jez. TV cameramen, wrapped in heated Yeti suits, were pointing their zoom lenses at Runway 27R. The press balcony was packed, but not as crowded as the public area. Normally Jez resented being patronised, but this sort of condescension was tolerable. His thanks were polite and profuse as he took up a position alongside a Cable News Network cameraman. She flashed

Jez a warm smile and heeled her gadget bag under her tripod to make more room for him. His fingers shook as he checked the Memcorder's video card. It had enough memory for twenty minutes of deep-vision colour recording or forty minutes of ordinary 2-D recording.

'Plug this into your video input, kiddo,' said the CNN cameraman, giving Jez a spare output lead from the optical fibre spaghetti sprouting from her camera. 'Take advantage of the best long lens money can buy. You'll be able to count the rivets on that bird's wings when I tighten.'

Kiddo! Jez could cheerfully have throttled her with one of her video leads. Well – it wasn't her fault that he was fourteen and looked twelve, and one didn't pass up a free feed from CNN.

'Thank you – you're very kind.' His voice let him down and went high. He plugged the lead into his Memcorder and marvelled at the pin-sharp close-up. The detail from her lens was stunning. He could even see the familiar face of his hero, Len Allenby, at the left-hand controls.

'Actually,' said Jez, managing to screw his voice down an octave as he feasted his eyes on the wondrous delta-wing machine, 'there aren't any rivets in her skin at all.'

'You don't say?'

'All the fuselage and wing sections are flow-moulded and spark-eroded from solid billets of aluminium alloy, and RF pressure-welded together.'

'Really?'

'Frames, stringers, skin – all machined in one go. The Airbus's wings were made like that. With the Sabre, it's the entire airframe. You should see the flow-moulders and shapers they use at St Omer. Huge.'

'Sounds like it's carved rather than built.'

Jez nodded emphatically. 'That's exactly right. It saves on assembling hundreds of components, and you end up with a totally stress-free airframe.'

'Amazing. Shouldn't you be at school?

'An embarrassing question but one that Jez didn't have to answer because the cameraman was listening attentively to instructions in her radio earphone. 'Oh, Christ,' she muttered.

Jez looked at her expectantly. 'What's the matter?'

'Sabre Industries have been keeping something to themselves. Their press office have just announced that it's not going to be a short demo flight after all. I've got to stay for its return which means being stuck here all bloody day.'

2

At 09:58 Central European Time, Captain Len Allenby swung Sabre 004 off the taxiway and on to the runway. An early December sun etched the shadow of the Concorde-like delta-wing on to the dirty white slush that lined the runway.

He had tower clearance so there was no delay. He applied power smoothly and progressively. The sudden acceleration provoked a murmur of appreciation from the army of pressmen recording the take-off of the world's first passenger-licensed spaceplane, even though many of them had covered the extensive test flights of Sabre 002 and 003 at St Omer.

Sabre 001 had been the original mock-up in plywood and fibre glass. Sabre 002 had been the prototype – designed and produced in record time specifically as a flying testbed for the engines, and tested almost to destruction. 003 included passenger life-support systems. It too had been flown to near destruction. And now this one: 004 was the pre-production model – fully equipped and licensed to carry passengers. 005 and 006 were still being built in Sabre Industries' giant construction shed at their complex near St Omer in northern France.

Ten hundred hours. Vee One was achieved with 900 metres of concrete to spare. Sabre lifted its nose. Its main-gear cleared the runway. A perfect take-off. The heartbeat of Len Allenby and co-pilot, Simone Frankel, dropped back to normal. They were a politically ideal pair – an Englishman and a Frenchwoman on attachment from British Airways and Air France respectively. Very professional. And discreet enough for no one to have the slightest inkling of their developing personal relationship.

Paul Santos, chairman of Sabre Industries, closed his eyes and savoured the massive surge of power as his dream child climbed. The suborbital Sabre passenger spaceplane was his blinding obsession, brought to fruition by ten years of gut-grinding effort that had destroyed his marriage and estranged his two sons. Behind him in the main cabin, where 200 fare-paying passengers would be sitting in the six-abreast rows a year from today, were forty specially-selected VIP guest passengers, and behind them, aft of the mid-cabin zero-gee toilets, racks of computers recorded information from the thousands of sensors in the aircraft's engines, flight-systems and airframe. Lashed along the length of the hold below were several hundred small sacks of sand to simulate the weight of a hundred passengers and their baggage. Not a full payload, but fifty per cent because Sabre was still suffering weight problems. Kristy Wood of *Time*, looking cool and elegant in a black Gabbana Nycra suit, was sitting at the opposite window seat. She and Paul were the only occupants of the front row.

Ten-o-one.

Forty thousand feet. A noise abatement turn. Power, ninety per cent. Heading 000 – due north.

So far, a normal take-off. But the Sabre didn't level off and reduce power at around 37,000 feet like a normal air-craft. The delta-wing kept climbing and accelerating. Paul twisted around to survey his guest passengers. He noticed that their eyes kept returning to the bulkhead flight inform-ation screen. It weighed ten kilos and represented a major battle with Ralph Peterson to retain it.

Fifty thousand feet . . . 60,000 feet . . . 100,000 feet . . .

The screen observed the international civil aviation con-vention of measuring height in feet. And then it changed to the metric system because the new height bore no relation-ship to the old days of commercial flight.

Thirty kilometres.

The acceleration was gentle but constant.

Ten twelve. Sabre was now at a height over Scotland that could not be reached even by military jets. And it was flying at 3,000 knots – nearly eight times the speed of sound. The atmosphere the spaceplane was flying through was too thin to generate a sonic boom – a problem that had prevented Concorde flying supersonic over land.

And Sabre kept climbing and accelerating through the rarified air. Canards extended from the fuselage to help the engines claw in the last vestiges of atmospheric oxygen. Drag-reducing ionisers accelerated the incoming air to match Sabre's speed before it was drawn into the engines. At this height the problems of atmospheric drag and the high skin temperatures due to trying to fly an aluminium-skinned aircraft above Mach 2 did not exist. In the 1960s and '70s such problems had dogged Concorde and spiralled its development costs.

Ten twenty.

Even after having flown on ten test flights, Paul could not help cupping his hand against his window and marvelling at a sky that was merging from a cloud-streaked rich indigo to the blackness of space. Venus shone like a beacon. Sixty kilometres below were the frozen north polar wastes. The graceful curvature of the earth was plainly discernible with the naked eye. There was a buzz of excitement from the hard-nosed journalists and cynical airline executives who had been invited on this passenger maiden flight. Those in the outer seats had their faces pressed eagerly to their windows. That pleased Paul: he had been right to overrule Ralph Peterson and insist on that design feature. To venture into space was a spiritual adventure that many would want to share; windows would be a major passenger attraction.

Ten twenty-five.

Len Allenby flipped down the safety guards and touched the fuel change-over controls when the flight management system computers okayed the next phase. Liquid oxygen and hydrogen flowed through the Plessey motorised regulators and boiled into the combustion chambers of the engines so that they could continue to provide thrust in space. It was the brilliant concept of the Rolls-Royce Sabre engine that had made the spaceplane a commercial proposition. The Sabre – an acronym for Synergic Air-Breathing Rocket Engine – was three engines in one. In the atmosphere it used ordinary air as a combustor and propellant mixed with kerosene like a conventional jet engine; over 80,000 feet and 8,000 kph and the incoming air by-passed the turbine compressors – the engines became ramjets, using the spaceplane's tremendous velocity to force rarefied air into their combustion chambers. And in space, liquid oxygen and liquid hydrogen was mixed for burning as a rocket engine. There was no need for separate rocket engines and jet engines which had led to the Americans junking their commercial suborbital flight (SOFT) project although the huge amount of research that they had put into their SOFT had not been lost because much of their airframe design work had been incorporated in the Sabre. What the Americans had lacked was an engine.

Ten-thirty. Altitude 150 kilometres. Speed 22,000 kph.

'Ladies and gentlemen,' Allenby announced over the passenger address system. 'We are about to close down our engines. We will be experiencing weightlessness so please ensure that your seat-belts remain fastened. Please read your briefing card on zero gee and relax. If you need to move about, please wear your Velcro overshoes.'

The VDU displays in front of Len Allenby and Simone Frankel changed to show the passenger seating plan. Computer-generated graphics indicated that all the seat-belts in occupied seats were secure.

Ten-thirty-five. Altitude 160 kilometres. Speed 25,000 kph.

Simone Frankel called up the graphic displays of the fuel systems and touched the controls for a throttle-down. In the lower hull the Plessey motorised regulators whirred softly, progressively closing down the liquid oxygen and liquid hydrogen feeds to the engines.

Despite their pre-flight briefing and the information in

their press packs, there were gasps from the passengers. None had ever experienced total silence aboard an aircraft when in flight, nor the strange sensation of their weightless bodies nudging gently against their seat-belts. The Spaceqel tablet that each passenger had been required to swallow on check-in ensured that their stomachs did not rebel at not knowing which way was up or down. The drug also contained a mild urinary suppressant. That, coupled with the zero humidity of the Sabre's internal atmosphere to stimulate dehydration of the passengers, ensured that their primary fluid losses were by means of perspiration, thus reducing their need to use the zero-gee lavatory. Human sweat extracted as distilled water by the dehumidifiers was useful for keeping the fuel-cell coolant tanks topped up – it saved weight – whereas droplets of urine floating around the cabin as a result of passengers not following the lavatory instructions were of little use to anyone.

Paul released his seat-belt and stood in the centre aisle, pushing his Velcro overshoes firmly on the carpet so that he could adopt a casual stance. Such was his eye for detail that he was wearing a normal-looking business suit that had been specially tailored to look good on his slight figure in weightless conditions. One of his guiding principles to gain passenger acceptance of the Sabre was that suborbital flight should be as similar as possible to ordinary flight. For that reason the interior of the Sabre looked no different from a conventional jet. All the fittings – seats, overhead bins, et cetera – were ordinary to the point of blandness.

He was uncomfortably aware of Kristy Wood's green eyes watching him carefully. It irked him that she was the one passenger who was not so interested in pressing her face to her window. It was some moments before he commanded full attention. There was the distraction of a BBC newsman who was gaping in amazement at his camera which obligingly remained hanging before him when he took his hands away. Several of his colleagues laughed and did likewise. The press conference was being broadcast live. The founder of Virgin hung his A4 day book in front of him and gave it a tumble. His bearded face creased into an impish grin. He was seventy now – still fit and trim, and still with that irrepressible sense of humour cloaking a driving force that had enabled him to build Virgin into the world's sixth largest airline. During the world recession of 2010–15, Virgin had been the only major airline to increase its market share.

'Ladies and gentlemen,' said Paul in English when enough faces were turned towards him. 'Welcome to space. Not only are you recording history today with this live broadcast, but you are also making history: you are the world's first commercial passengers to journey into space . . .' His smile broadened. 'But you are not, regrettably, fare-paying passengers . . .'

Some laughter. He had their full attention now. The strange quiet meant that he could speak in his normal voice without PA aids.

Paul Santos was fifty-four. A grave, diminutive Frenchman with perfect English, who exuded confidence and an unconscious charm that had resulted in this extraordinary aircraft. Almost single-handedly, this former chairman of Airbus Industries had channelled his ferocious energy and remarkable vision into welding together the expertise of all the member nations of the European Union to form Sabre Industries, and he had cajoled the European Central Enterprise Bank in Frankfurt into bankrolling fifty per cent of the venture. The ECEB had been established to finance ambitious projects such as this, to provide employment for Europe and to keep such projects free from political interference. The other fifty per cent had been snapped up eagerly by Europe's stock exchanges as a part-paid rights issue. Paul had performed a near-miracle in turning Airbus Industries into the world's biggest civil aircraft builder. In his last year with them, AI's turnover had outstripped the Boeing–McDonnell-Douglas axis. He was still young, therefore Europe's eager fund managers saw no reason why he shouldn't do the same for Sabre Industries. The reticence of those with serious money to invest in advanced technology during the 1980s and 1990s had largely disappeared in the

11

new, buoyant mood that was gripping Europe. Paul Santos was the right man in the right place, with the right ideas at the right time.

Paul adopted a crestfallen expression as he faced his passengers. 'I have an apology to make, ladies and gentlemen. This flight won't be the brief few minutes in space we promised as a demo – it will be slightly longer. Nor will there be a champagne lunch at St Omer followed by a guided tour of Sabre Industries this afternoon. There's been a slight change to our schedule due to technical reasons.' He grinned at the airline VIPs. 'How many of you have inflicted that excuse on your passengers, I wonder?'

That produced laughter. Kristy Wood's eyebrows arched.

'Nevertheless,' Paul continued, 'I can promise you an interesting day, and we will be returning you to Heathrow at the scheduled time.'

He went on to outline Sabre Industries' brief history, concluding with: 'I know many of you have grave reservations about our ambitious time scales. But I would remind you that from our leasing of the Hermes plant at St Omer to putting the prototype Sabre into space was four years – 1,401 days to be exact.

'Almost sixty years ago, in 1961, an American president committed his country to landing a man on the moon and returning him safely to earth by the end of the decade. Afterwards he said that the best way to keep down the cost of a major project was to do it quickly. He was right, of course. There is a self-limiting factor in what can be spent in a given time . . . That is why I am now giving you and the world a solemn undertaking that such is our commitment to the Sabre, that even if you drag your feet on exercising your options, a Sabre spaceplane will fly its first fare-paying passengers exactly one year from today . . .' He added with a mischievous grin: 'And if BA and Air France pull out of the loan deal we did with them, then we'll set up our own airline. But come what may, fare-paying commercial flight will start in one year.'

His candour went down well and few doubted that he

meant what he said.

His sad gaze moved from face to face. 'So . . . Any questions?'

A barrage of technical questions followed that Paul handled succinctly, with the skill of a born communicator. Some were not so technical – not all the journalists were knowledgeable air correspondents.

'Mr Santos. Forgive me if this is a stupid question, but if our engines are closed down, why aren't we falling?'

'But we *are* falling,' Paul answered. 'That's why you're weightless — just as you would be in a falling lift with a broken cable.' He gestured to the information screen on the bulkhead behind him. 'As you can see, our forward velocity is nearly 28,000 kilometres per hour, but we are nevertheless in free fall, following a downward curve towards the earth's surface. But the earth is round, of course – its surface is falling away beneath us at a rate equal to our rate of fall. Therefore our height above the surface remains constant. We are in orbit, and weightless, of course. Most people have experienced suborbital flight and weightlessness at some time.' That caused a few ears to prick up. 'Those who have driven fast over a hump-backed bridge. It's exactly the same thing that we're experiencing now, except that it's lasting longer.'

'So if we did nothing, we'd orbit the earth?'

'Precisely.'

'And go on orbiting the earth?'

'Yes. The fuel used is the same for a 12,000 mile flight half-way round the world as for a 24,000 mile flight right round the world. Should a Sabre be unable to land at its destination, it can continue its orbit and land at virtually any suitable airport along its orbital path. Most of our test flights from St Omer have been complete circumnavigations of the globe simply because that's the easiest way to bring a spaceplane back to where it set out from. And, of course, compared with conventional jets, we use less fossil-based fuel. I note that oil went up another five dollars a barrel yesterday.' The latter comment was aimed at the airline accountants among his passengers. The twenty per cent production cut by the League of Gulf Oil Producers the previous week had led to light crude reaching $45 a barrel on the Amsterdam spot market. And it looked set to go even higher. China's thirst for oil following her spectacular economic growth since the turn of the century had seen to that.

There were the inevitable questions about things going wrong.

'Well, apart from the fuel savings, being able to close down our engines in flight gives us a huge advantage over conventional aircraft,' said Paul smoothly. 'We have access to most systems and the engines via the service bay in the lower hull. We can change a spark plug or a flint in flight . . .'

Laughter. Paul believed in keeping the press happy with quotable quotes.

'. . . and we can even carry out external EVA repairs – extra-vehicular activities – spacewalks. On the prototype we once changed an undercarriage wheel in flight. All Sabres have three lightweight spacesuits in their flight deck emergency gear.'

He explained that for strength and integrity, Sabre consisted of two separate hulls. The upper passenger hull; and the lower hull which contained the freight and baggage hold and the service bay housing the fuel, electrical and all other systems. Both were independently pressurised. Access to the lower hull was possible in-flight through a hatch in the flight-deck floor. In an emergency the flight-deck itself served as an airlock.

The questions went on for forty-five minutes. Pocket recorders dumped the exchanges into their memories; copy was written and revised on computer memopads anchored to laps with Velcro. Kristy Wood was scribbling rapidly, her handwriting being converted to neat rows of Times Roman text as it flowed from her stylus. Had she been alone she would have used the machine's voice-type facility and dictated her copy. She stopped writing and regarded Paul thoughtfully before adding a few notes on his appearance.

14

Greying hair swept straight back; height – no more than five-four. Sombre, wide-set, brown eyes . . . Strange to think that this seemingly mild-mannered man had instilled near-panic in US civil aviation when he was boss of Airbus Industries. Would he do the same with Sabre Industries? She underlined the question carefully so that her memopad wouldn't think she was deleting the sentence. The underlined text was converted to italics.

No – there would be no in-flight meals, Paul was saying. Many airlines were cutting out meals on short flights and the weight saving in galley equipment was considerable. Self-heating, suck and squeeze bulbs containing tea or coffee would be available from compartments in the back of each seat above the video screen. Yes – the zero-gravity toilets left much to be desired but no one had come up with a better idea.

A camera drifted out of its operator's hands and had to be recovered by a technician. But no one's attention was ever far from the windows and the heady realisation that they were actually in space. As a finale, Len Allenby rolled the Sabre 'upside down' so that everyone could get a good look 'up' at the earth. The Sabre's delta-wing configuration gave poor downward visibility. The chorus of gasps delighted Paul. Luckily the northern Pacific was largely clear from the west coast of America to Japan. The entire ocean shone with the blue-green intensity of a laser-illuminated emerald. As Paul had expected, the distortion due to the earth's curvature caused land masses to appear very different from the shapes people were used to seeing on maps therefore the guesses from the passengers as to what they were seeing were wildly inaccurate.

'Fifty years ago as a kid, I watched Neil Armstrong and Buzz Aldrin hopping about on the moon,' breathed an awed Qantas executive. 'Never in my wildest dreams did I ever think that one day I would go into space.'

'I thought exactly the same thing on my first trip in Sabre 003,' said Paul. 'I had to keep pinching myself for about a month afterwards.' He looked inquiringly at each passenger

15

in turn. 'So, if there are no more questions, the view outside is much more interesting than listening to me. So please enjoy your flight and thank you for flying Sabre Air.'

Even Kristy Wood laughed at that. 'Congratulations,' she said as Paul was about to resume his seat. Her accent was British, which had surprised him when he had first heard her speak. 'Won't you join me?'

Paul moved to the seat beside her. He smiled self-effacingly, uncertain how to handle this woman with such disturbing green eyes. 'Thank you, Miss Wood.'

'In a few words you explained something I've never understood and never had the guts to ask. I've always wondered how orbiting bodies stayed up. Now there's an admission from an aerospace correspondent.'

'I cannot imagine you lacking the courage to ask anything, Miss Wood,' said Paul, aware that he sounded stiff and formal. 'I trust you are enjoying the flight?'

Kristy glanced out of her window. 'Not as much as I've enjoyed watching my Sabre shares go up over the last six months.'

'Ah,' said Paul with mock servility. 'A shareholder.'

'Sure. I don't suppose the Sabre will make me rich, but it is going to change the world.'

Paul looked sharply at her, thinking she was being facetious, but her expression was serious. 'Well,' he said carefully. 'It will certainly revolutionise long-haul civil aviation.'

The journalist shook her head. 'The Sabre spaceplane will change the world, Mr Santos. Change it irrevocably and, hopefully, for the better.'

'Oh, I can hardly see—'

'Of course you can't see, Mr Santos. You're a technocrat. Technocrats can never see beyond the ends of their noses. They usher in the new, which they see as mere improvements on what already exists, and never think through the consequences. Look out of the window and tell me what you see.'

Paul disliked games. 'The earth.'

'Can you see national frontiers?'

'Of course not.'

Kristy smiled and glanced down at her memopad. 'A year after going into scheduled service, about 400 people will have flown in Sabres – perhaps more. Within another two years that figure will have risen to a quarter of a million. A million after five years. And maybe as many as ten million by the end of the decade.'

'I wish all our shareholders had your confidence, Miss Wood,' said Paul ruefully.

The journalist studied Paul earnestly, tapping her stylus thoughtfully on her teeth. She could sense his energy and found it sexually exciting. 'The people who will be flying in these spaceplanes will be politicians, journalists, financiers, fund managers, heads of industry and so on. Men and women with influence on world affairs. Day after day they'll look down on earth and see it as a single, finite body drifting in space. They may not realise that it is affecting them, but it will. Little by little their perspectives and values will change – they will come to see national frontiers as an irritating irrelevance. Patriotism will eventually be seen for what it is even by the most hardened zealots — neolithic tribalism. This change won't happen overnight, but it will happen, and when it does, the world will start moving, one cautious step at a time, towards a single government and a single integrated economy. The social revolution that the Sabre will trigger will be the most profound change in history, even more significant than the invention of writing.'

'Will that be the gist of your article?' Paul asked casually.

Kristy smiled archly. 'Possibly.'

Paul met those green eyes head on. 'Your argument is attractive. But I fear that the world's falling oil reserves will be a powerful wedge against a unified world economy. Poor countries are continuing to get poorer because they're paying more for their oil. As for political unification, I've heard similar from people who've been up to Earthport 1, Miss Wood.'

She shook her head. 'You're still missing my point. Those who visit the space station are mostly technicians, and relatively few of them at that. The difference with the Sabre is that it will open up space to millions of men and women from all walks of life.' She smiled suddenly. 'You've been described as a man of vision, but you're not. You see the Sabre as nothing more than an improved aircraft. When the electric lamp was invented it was nothing more than a better candle, therefore its power was measured in candlepower. The internal combustion engine was seen as an improved horse – and was measured in horsepower. Back in the 1980s, computer messaging systems – the forerunners of the Internet — were called bulletin boards. In other words, we can never see the future because we insist on looking at it through a rear-view mirror. Marshall McLuhan.'

Paul was about to say something when Len Allenby's voice came over the PA.

'It's 11:19 Central European Time, ladies and gentlemen. Re-entry will commence in five minutes. Please stow all equipment and fasten your seat belts. All floating objects must be retrieved and secured.'

A flight attendant wearing a tight-fitting grey trouser-suit moved along the aisle to ensure that the skipper's instructions were followed, her Velcro overshoes making soft tearing noises with each step as they separated from the carpet.

Small vernier retro rockets turned the Sabre through 180 degrees so that its nose was pointing back along its trajectory. The Rolls-Royce engines spewed gases at full thrust, killing its enormous velocity. Allenby again turned the Sabre so that it was pointing forward. The five minutes of deorbit burn had been sufficient to slow the Sabre and send it skimming through the upper reaches of the atmosphere, trading height and velocity in exchange for heat that was reflected by the paper-thin coating of 'Super Starlite' on the Sabre's underside. The material was a development of an invention in the 1990s by a British hairdresser, Maurice Ward, that did away with the need for a thick heat shield such as the heavy tiles that the NASA shuttle employed.

The heat shield glowed cherry red as the Sabre plunged earthwards, the spaceplane's nose held high to present its

18

protected underside to the atmosphere. The manoeuvre used a minimum of fuel: gravity and air resistance did most of the work. The Sabre was merely getting back a small return on the energy it had invested getting into space. There are no free lunches in the laws of physics.

Weight and noise returned. The sky changed colour from black to blue, and the Sabre became a conventional jet, buffeted by conventional winds as it descended. The sun sank in harmony with the spaceplane and the atmosphere darkened. Clouds whipped past the windows. The wings warped to increase lift in the manner of flaps. Then the most enjoyable part of any flight: the sensation of anticipation of a journey's end heightened by the leisurely, sinking glide above now recognisable marks of man on the landscape in the fading twilight: roads snaking across the terrain, the blue confetti of swimming-pools sprinkled across dense residential zones; a glimpse of lights twinkling in a crowded harbour. The whine of main-gear being lowered and suddenly the objects on the ground took on human proportions: approach roads jammed with stationary vehicles, headlights flashing furiously; crowds thronging perimeter fences even though radio and TV stations had announced the electrifying news of Sabre's pending arrival only an hour before.

A bump. The howl of reverse thrust. A recorded voice requesting passengers to remain seated until the spaceplane had come to a complete standstill. Doors opening. The heat of a hot December evening unexpectedly invading the Sabre's interior. On terminal roof-tops just about every TV news camera that could be mustered at such short notice was trained on the sleek delta-wing as the mobile escalator was wheeled into place. For this arrival Paul Santos, with his showman's eye for detail, had rejected a normal jetty docking. He wanted the TV cameras to capture the drama of his bemused VIP passengers, blinking in the floodlights as they disembarked 12,000 miles from where they had expected to be.

Paul stood at the door and shook hands with each guest

as they stepped on to the moving stairs. Jack Helmann, the vice-president of Eastern-United was looking shaken and excited at the same time. He was probably a lousy poker player.

Kristy Wood gave Paul Santos a dazzling smile. 'Brilliant,' she said. 'Maybe you've got the knack of looking around that rear-view mirror after all.'

But best of all, the boss of Virgin, no mean showman himself, returned Paul's handshake with a joke about kidnapping old age pensioners being no way to run an airline.

It was Paul's shock announcement shortly after Sabre had come to a standstill on the apron that had done it of course: 'Welcome to Sydney, Australia, ladies and gentlemen. After the press call, we've laid on some limousines for a brief sightseeing tour of the city while we check and refuel Sabre for our return. A light snack meal at Doyles has been arranged for you. We'll be back at Heathrow on time, and in time for tea.'

His rider that the purpose of the escorted tour was to ensure that no one stuffed a heavy dinner inside them provoked laughter.

The flying time from London to Sydney had been exactly ninety minutes.

Paul's huge gamble in kidnapping some of the top names in civil aviation had paid off, and Barnes Wallis's concept seventy years before of suborbital passenger flight had become a reality.

3

It was the Darwin's tenth dive, its deepest and most important.

Alec Rose's original name for his strange, bullet-shaped pump was Deepwater Alluvial Recovery Widget, which led to Christine dubbing it 'Darwin'. It was hanging from ten kilometres of Plastronic flat-wound hose and had taken two hours to reach the floor of the Banda Trench, and a further two hours for its contra-rotating nose cutters to help ease the device through a kilometre of the yielding, three-kilometre-thick layer of alluvial ooze that covered the floor of the trench.

The latest sonar and seismic resonance measurements indicated that the ocean depth here measured 10,900 metres from the surface to the bedrock beneath the 2,000-metre layer of unconsolidated sediment. Thus the Banda Trench was the world's deepest spot although the area of this extreme depth, 300 miles south of Indonesia, covered less than 400 square kilometres.

The Darwin's mother ship was the *Ben Gunn*, a well-maintained 500-tonne schooner that had spent most of its seventy-year working life as a squid jigger. There was little squid left now, although the smell still permeated the *Ben Gunn*'s timbers, but there were other treasures locked in the depths that Alec and Christine Rose were seeking.

This was their third consecutive charter of the Darwin-registered schooner from her owner-skipper – Gus Newton. She was not Alec's and Christine's first choice as an oceano-graphic research ship but it was all their struggling company could afford, although they now had a backer for this latest charter. But the elderly 1950s-built two-master had a number of pluses. A generous keel gave her reasonable stability and she still had her big power capstan, formerly used for lowering and raising the racks of halogen lights that had been used to lure squid. Gus had kept the unwieldy capstan because the day-dreaming treasure-hunting scuba loons always imagined that they would be needing a derrick capable of raising a cannon. Handling the twelve-kilometres of hose that was normally coiled in the aft hold was no problem for the capstan.

But the biggest plus factor was Gus Newton's superb sea-manship. The *Ben Gunn* was his home and business, and he bullied his six-man Filipino crew day and night to keep it shipshape. The down side was his brand of racist bigotry and his dinner-table diatribes about wops and wogs and what they were doing to his beloved Australia.

21

Alec and Christine crouched in the converted midships fish hold that served as their laboratory and control room. The downwash from a watching Hovercam's wire-caged rotors provided some air movement, but the suffocating heat was forgotten as they peered with suppressed excitement at the monitors that would tell them when the Darwin had penetrated the ooze to its target depth. If Alec's thermocouple electric pump worked when buried in sediment at this immense depth, they would soon begin the crucial stage of the experiment. The pump was Alec's invention. While there was nothing new in using the temperature difference between the ocean's surface and the depths to generate electricity, Alec's ingenious design, to mould the electronics into the wall of the hose, was brilliantly original. For every metre of pressure-flattened hose snaking into the depths, an average of 125 milliwatts of energy could be produced – a tenth of the power output of a small torch battery. But the total power capable of flowing down to the pump added up to a kilowatt – more than enough for the task that the high-efficiency electric pump would soon be called on to perform. The wall of the hose, now crushed flat by the enormous pressure of 1,000 atmospheres, also carried the optical fibre telemetry signalling lines that controlled the Darwin's systems.

As the pump sank through the primeval ooze, so it was reaching back into prehistory: through the Tertiary period of sixty-five million years ago when the continental land masses looked very much as they do today; through the Cretaceous period when birds first appeared, and deeper yet, back 180 million years into the Jurassic – the so-called Dinosaur Age when the mighty reptiles roamed the new earth that was being created as the great southern land mass of Gondwanaland was breaking up to form the continents of Australia and Antarctica.

The Jurassic period was the Darwin's destination as it sank deeper into the alluvial sludge than any man-made instrument had ever reached and remained working.

The sediment penetration display registered 1,200 metres.

Alec caught his wife's eye and gave her a broad, exultant

grin. 'Stop boring, Chris.'

Christine hit the escape key on the cordless keyboard. 'Auger stopped,' she confirmed. She leaned back in her chair and watched her husband check the readings. The film of gleaming sweat clinging to her olive skin suited her admirably. It heightened her dark, un-English looks – high cheekbones, a wide, generous mouth, and large, serious eyes that conveyed vulnerability. But there was nothing vulnerable abut Christian Rose.

'Mr Newton!' Alec yelled. The *Ben Gunn* didn't have an interphone system.

There was a *clock-clock* of flip-flops on the teak deckhead and Gus Newton's leathern features appeared at the open hatch above the couple. He had a face that was held together by scar tissue. His nose and ears, recognisable as such only by their position in relation to each other, bore witness to a lifetime of waterfront bar brawls, usually as a result of his loud-mouthed comments about wops, dagos and bush bunnies. He tipped back his battered Akubra and glowered down at the couple. His quick, cunning gaze noticed the way Christine's sleeveless T-shirt clung to her breasts as she stretched and yawned.

'Yeah?'

'We've stopped boring, Mr Newton. The sampler's in deep enough to hold, so pay out all the surplus hose – let it all drift free – the current should keep it clear of the props.'

Gus's gaze lingered for a moment on Christine's graceful bronzed legs and moved aft to yell orders at the two Filipino crewmen who were using long bamboo boathooks to keep the hose clear of the sterngear. The small satellite communication dish that Alec Rose had clamped to a derrick mounting for this charter was whirring back and forth continuously as its servos fought a constant battle with the swell to maintain a private communication link. Why the hell couldn't they use the Iridium global phone system like everyone else? And where had these Pommies got their money from? They hadn't had two cents to rub together on their previous charters. Now they had equipment which he

23

guessed was worth at least a couple of million dollars, and this latest version of their Darwin gizmo was the biggest yet. And this time they weren't content with getting muck samples from 4,000 metres, oh, no. Twelve kilometres of their weird flat hose in the hold this time and its weight when stowed in the aft fish hold had made the *Ben Gunn* roll like a pig in a mud bath.

Gus wasn't happy about this charter. Not only had they messed up his beloved boat with all their new gear, but this time he was uncomfortably close to Indonesia. Okay, so they were in international waters, but the Indonesian navy regarded this as their patch. They were a touchy lot and were capable of taking a dislike to the idea of an Aussie boat hoovering muck samples off the floor of a trench.

Like many Australians, Gus was edgy about Indonesia, and with good reason. It was the world's fourth most populous country; two million men under arms; a large and modern air force and navy equipped with the latest gadgetry, courtesy of the arms factories of Europe, and a willingness to use them, as had happened in the last century when they had overrun east Timor. And now they had done the same with south Borneo and grabbed its new oilfields. There had been United Nations resolutions but nothing had been done. Indonesia's emerging democracy was sure to be stillborn. President Sulimann's plans to axe half the armed services and withdraw from south Borneo had turned General Oman Putriana into a dictator-in-waiting, nursing ambitions about the Australian continent. Most Aussies believed that if Putriana got control again, and Indonesia did to Australia what they had done to Timor and south Borneo, the West would look at the logistic problems of mounting a military operation in the Antipodes, shudder, and turn its back. Australia was on its own.

Gus returned to the hatch and stared down at Christine. 'How much longer do we have to keep up with this fucking station-keeping shit?' he demanded. One could be forgiven for thinking that Gus had been trained by the Serbian diplomatic corps.

'About another eight to ten hours,' Alec replied, not looking up. 'Is that a problem?'

Gus shrugged and jammed a cheroot between yellowing teeth. 'You're paying for the diesel we're burning up going nowhere, Mister Rose. Went up another ten dollars a tonne this morning.' He glanced at his wrist global position indicator and moved off to harangue the helmsman. The twin diesel engines had been running at slow ahead to counter the steady one-knot thrust of the South Equatorial Current. They picked up 100 rpm, setting up harmonic vibrations in the transportable analyser and cracker behind Alec and Christine. The two cabinets had been bolted to the bulkhead – another thing Gus had moaned about.

Alec sensed that Christine's volatile temper was about to explode. 'Don't let him get to you, Chris,' he warned. He spun his swivel chair to face the Hovercam. As a Shell senior geo-engineer, he had had to put up with these damned things peering over his shoulder. He thought that he had seen the last of them when he and Christine had set up on their own.

'Mr Shief – we're about to start pumping.'

Christine frowned at the deferential tone in her husband's voice but said nothing.

Twelve thousand miles away in London, on the twenty-second floor of the Canary Wharf Tower, Joshua Shief motioned the members of the board of Avanti Oil to silence and turned to Alec's unshaven, hawklike face that was filling the wall screen monitor. He gave the voice recognition instruction that enabled the *Ben Gunn* to hear him.

'Any problems, Alec?'

The digitalised videofone link was routed through two satellites, resulting in a second's delay before Alec's reply was heard in the boardroom.

'Sweet as sin, Mr Shief. Strain load at the capstan is twenty per cent under redline and we've got nearly all the hose out.'

'HC1 loosen,' Shief ordered the Hovercam. The shot widened to take in Christine at her console, intent on the information being sent from the Darwin. The intolerable

25

heat had led to her bobbing her rich tresses of coal-black hair, giving her a slightly boyish look, although there was nothing boyish about the second-skin effect of her drenched T-shirt. The male members of the board watched her appreciatively. The exception was Alain Colgate, the company's technical director, absorbed in his memopad that was relaying the Darwin's telemetry data from the boardroom's comm links. It was he who had listened to Alec's ideas and had persuaded Shief to finance this survey.

'Concentrate on your work, Alec,' said Shief, his florid features as impassive as ever. 'Don't take any notice of us. We'll just watch with great interest.'

The Hovercam backed off and settled on top of the cracker cabinet to conserve its battery, its transmission indicator diode a glowing pinpoint in the stifling air. The couple ignored it and went through the litany of the pre-operation check menu, verifying each other's work, checking and double-checking as each stage was completed.

Alec's finger hovered over the 'enter' key on the cordless keyboard. 'Well – we're about to learn if we're paupers or plutocrats,' he joked to hide his nervousness. He kept his voice low so that it wouldn't be picked up by the detested Hovercam.

Christine pumped her T-shirt. 'The idea isn't to make us filthy rich,' she said reprovingly.

'Just rich?'

'Perhaps,' said Christine dismissively. Alec's enthusiasm for wealth irritated her.

'But it will.'

'Just get on with it!'

Alec punched the key. The ammeter digits raced up and settled at 400 milliamps. The first hurdle was over: the Darwin's pump motor was free-running at 10,000 rpm. Alec moved the scroll bar down to the 'gearbox clutch – engage' menu line and pressed 'enter'. Over ten kilometres below the *Ben Gunn*, in the eternal darkness of the awesome depth that the Darwin had reached, a clutch solenoid whirred and engaged the pump. Alec's and Christine's attention was now focused on the ammeter display. If the pump's 2,000–1 reduction gearbox couldn't cope with the staggering pressure, the electric motor would draw an abnormally high current load and probably burn out. But the reading stayed at a safe level and showed that the pump was starting to draw sediment through its intake. The big question now was whether or not it had the power to thrust the ooze into the hose against the pressure of 1,000 atmospheres . . .

The flowmeter digits remained stuck at a string of zeros but the readings provided evidence that the pump was now fully primed with the thick, alluvial ooze. As long as the motor kept turning, the system had to work because the final stage used positive displacement – similar to hospital plasma pumps – in which rotating jockey wheels mounted in massive bearings, squeezed the gunk into the hose, pushing it out from flat to round, like cake icing being forced through a piping bag.

Alec offered a silent prayer.

Despite their different backgrounds, he and Christine had turned out to be surprisingly well matched. Their marriage was into its twelfth year; both were in their mid-thirties. The seams of their relationship had been stretched on many occasions but had never come apart because Alec preferred to give way to his strong-willed wife – not out of any weakness of character but because he loved her and recognised that her sharper business sense was the means of turning his talents into real money.

Christine came from a wealthy landowning, racehorse-training family – old money which she inherited on the death of her mother while Christine was at London University reading economics. She decided to let her younger brother run the family business. Peter lived and breathed horses. She gave him a free hand, with the proviso that their land was no longer to be used for hunting. She joined Shell as a PA and met Alec at a seminar in New York. Amid a sea of respectable grey suits, the geo-engineer caused a stir by turning up to give a presentation on sonic drilling techniques wearing a water-cooled bushsuit, complete with calf-length boots and a floppy sun-hat. The suit's conditioner on his belt whined all through his spiel, its electronics interfered with the overhead projection system and there was a poorly disguised hostility in his answers to questions about sonic drilling techniques falling into the wrong hands – i.e. Third World countries. Christine decided that such a man was worth cultivating. They were married a year later. After five years they had chucked up their jobs and set up a business venture using Christine's money.

Their objective in founding Triton Exploration was to exploit an idea that Alec had been nurturing for years: the dream that could lead to cheap energy for poor countries and wealth for him. The three versions of the Darwin that Alec had designed had swallowed nearly three million dollars of Christine's money. One million dollars had gone into the purchase of a laser lathe and mill from Shaeffers of Geneva to achieve the close tolerances that the moving parts of the Darwin demanded. Christine's insistence on the use of top agents to protect the thirty-two patents that had gone into the Darwin took the R and D bill to just over the three million. The economics of this latest expedition to Indonesian waters and Alec's blunt refusal to allow Christine to pump any more of her money into the firm had resulted in their accepting an exploration contract with Joshua Shief's Avanti Oil Corporation. They were the only company prepared to back Alec's theories with money and equipment, and they had major investments in Indonesia. According to Shief, not even the Indonesian government were interested in Alec's ideas. Christine mistrusted Shief and suspected that he was lying; she was nursing an idea of her own about making a direct approach to the Indonesians if this survey proved successful.

'Flow!' Christine snapped, her voice brittle.

Alec opened his eyes. The flowmeter digits were clocking furiously – sediment was rising in the hose at nearly one metre per second. The Darwin was working.

'She's working, Mr Shief! We have positive flow.'

'So I see,' Shief's voice replied from London. The

Hovercam's oversize rotors became a disk of light. The machine lifted and moved in for a closer look. 'How long before you have an analysis for us?'

'Three hours before the sample reaches us,' Alec answered. 'We should have something for you in four hours.'

Shief thanked Alec and closed the circuit. He glanced at his wrist-watch and noted that the gold strap was cutting into his flesh again. A course of Leptin tablets should cure that. He looked up at the expectant faces of his directors. 'I think we should adjourn this extraordinary meeting for three and a half hours, ladies and gentlemen. I'm sure that won't inconvenience you and that you'll all be able to return.' It was an order that they would all obey. They depended on him for their jobs. There were no non-executive directors on the Avanti board; Joshua Shief didn't believe in carrying dead wood.

'Come on,' said Christine, dragging Alec to his feet. 'It'll look after itself now. Let's get out of this hellhole for a couple of hours and grab some zeds.'

Gus Newton watched the couple through the wheelhouse window as they settled under an awning. The wheelhouse TV was tuned to Southern Cross. The station had abandoned its outpourings of non-stop pop to carry a report on the Sabre flight. London to Sydney in ninety minutes. Jeez . . . The world was shrinking fast. A journalist on the flight was talking to the camera, saying that the smaller the world got, the less room there was for wars.

Gus snorted. Try telling that to bloody General putrid Putriana and his two million uniformed murdering bush bunnies.

4

The long wait at Heathrow Airport for Sabre's return from Australia was over.

Jez could have hugged the CNN cameraman for her generosity. His Memcorder's lens was good, but its low-light

29

performance was nowhere near as good as her lens when it came to zapping glare and turning night into colour-corrected day. He got a perfect shot of Sabre 004's touchdown. Jesus H – if only he could show that herd of oafs in T6's public gallery the quality of the shots he was getting. As the space-plane swung on to the taxiway, he was disappointed that the tailfin illumination lights weren't working. Then he remembered a Sabre Industries' press release saying that the designers had scrapped them in their unremitting battle against weight. Pity – the Sabre logo shining out across Heathrow would have made a great shot.

Suddenly there was orderly pandemonium as the press crews began stowing their gear in aluminium cases.

'What's happening, Ross?' He had befriended the CNN cameraman during the wait and had been pleased to keep her and her colleagues supplied with coffee and make himself useful running errands. He could see better now, having found a contact lens vending machine that read the prescription data off his battered identity card on its third attempt.

'Press conference in the VIP lounge, Jez,' said Ross as she stowed her camera. 'Grab that case, stick with me, and I'll do my damnedest to smuggle you in.'

Ross was as good as her word. In the seething lounge Jez did his best to look indifferent to what was going on – as though he had seen it all before. But his excitement was tempered with anxiety. His original plan had been to go to school in the afternoon and return home at the normal time. If news of this latest escapade got back to his parents . . . He simply couldn't leave this room packed with so many of his heroes and yet he knew that he must. At that moment Len Allenby and Simone Frankel came in and sat at the conference table. Jez's worries were cast to the wind. He stood rooted, his thoughts a whirl. This was too much. Autograph books were for kids. Bugger that. He delved frantically into his bag. Radio scanner; memopad; portable phone – the usual paraphernalia of high-tech gadgets that a fourteen-year-old boy considered indispensable. His rummaging fingers closed thankfully around the tattered volume. Thank God he hadn't thrown it out.

The questions being fired by the journalists and the euphoric replies from the passengers, still on a tingling high from their two trips into space in a day, seemed to go on and on. Jack Helmann was almost shaking with excitement.

'I still don't believe it,' he told a BBC correspondent. 'I board a plane here in London just after breakfast, I fly to Sydney, Australia, go on a tour of the city, have a bite to eat at Doyles and I'm back here in London in time for an English tea.' He beamed at the chorus of laughter.

'Will you buy the Sabre spaceplane, sir?'

Paul decided not to intervene. Someone had to ask outright the one question on everyone's mind despite the statement by the passengers that morning that they were not prepared to answer such questions.

Jack Helmann's expression became serious. 'Like most airlines these days, we don't buy – we lease through a holding company.' He smiled. 'All I'll say on that is that it is the policy of Eastern-United to lease the best planes for its passengers that money can buy.'

A similar question was directed at Yuri Segal, the chairman of Commonwealth Air. In twenty years, the burly Slav businessman had welded together the 400 or so airlines that were the loss-making fragments of the once-mighty Soviet Aeroflot. He had head-hunted ruthlessly for talent, creaming off the best men and women from the world's airlines, and had confounded his critics by turning Commonwealth Air into the first great commercial success story of the twenty-first century. At any hour of any day, there was a Commonwealth 950-seater theatre-body Tupolev TU1000 giant, either landing or taking off at all the world's major airports.

Luckily the canny Slav always pondered his replies at length. Paul rose unhurriedly to his feet, smiling as always. The taciturn Segal was too important a prey to be pounced on by a pack of press pumas. He thanked the journalists for their long wait and stressed that the next great event would

31

be the roll-out ceremony of Sabre 005 in June, followed by the start of scheduled services in one year. It was the signal that the conference was over. The press crews didn't need much prompting – it had been a long day. Lights were switched off and there was a swirl of activity as cameras and equipment were dumped in cases.

Jez saw his opportunity and closed in on Len Allenby and Simone Frankel but was too late – Jim Curtis, Director of Terminal 6 Plc, moved more quickly and engaged the Sabre's flight-deck crew in earnest conversation. But there was someone else . . .

Paul Santos was exhausted, anxious to avoid off-the-cuff interviews. He was about to summon his car when the boy he had noticed earlier spoke to him.

'Mr Santos?'

Paul regarded Jez and decided that he looked in need of regular meals. He adopted a pleading expression but his tone was firm. 'Please forgive me, but no more questions. I've had a most tiring day.' As always, he was extremely polite. This youngster was probably the son of an airline VIP.

'Could I trouble you for your autograph please, sir?'

For once Paul's customary poise deserted him. He actually looked surprised. 'My autograph?'

'If you could sign it 'To Jez' that's J-E-Z, I'd be very grateful, sir.' Jez could match politeness any day.

'Does your father work for an airline, er – Jez?'

It was Jez's turn to look surprised. 'No, sir – a bank.'

'Are you sure you don't want Sir Richard's autograph? He's now the oldest man to go into space.'

Jez glanced across the lounge at Sir Richard Branson. His retine were gathered around him, listening with interest to his account of the flight.

'Jets belong in the past,' said Jez dismissively. 'The Sabre is the future.'

Paul smiled. 'I don't think he'd like to hear you saying that. The Sabre is practical only for long-haul flights of 8,000 to 12,000-miles. Eighty per cent of airline passenger journeys are less than that. The conventional jet will be with us for many years to come.'

'But that twenty per cent extra-long-haul traffic represents a twenty billion a year market,' Jez pointed out. 'And you only have to sell twenty-five Sabres this year to break even. From Sabre 030 onwards you'll be running into profit, provided you get those orders in now. And I'm sure you will.'

'Only twenty-five!' Paul echoed. He looked hard at Jez's earnest young face and put his age at about twelve. But this wasn't a case of a space-besotted youth; this lad had made a real study of the Sabre. Good for him. 'I only wish others shared your confidence, Jez,' said Paul regretfully.

'I've got the Sabre flight simulator program on my computer,' Jez blurted, not wanting this conversation with the great Paul Santos to end.

'Ha . . . Which version?'

'Six, sir.'

Paul smiled and tried not to sound patronising. 'You need version seven, Jez. There's been a lot of design mods over the past year.'

'Oh, I know,' said Jez enthusiastically. 'Mostly to do with weight reduction. I've flown London to Sydney thousands of times when I'm supposed to be doing homework.'

Paul chuckled. He produced a Sabre pen, signed the offered autograph book with an expansive flourish and gave the pen to a delighted Jez.

5

In Seattle, former union boss Joe Yavanoski switched off his lathe, bit down angrily on his cigar, and glowered at his workshop TV. He punched the control box. God-damnit, even the local cable feeds were carrying stories and interviews about the flight of the Sabre. It had finally happened: the god-damned thing had been test flying for years with hardly any press coverage and had suddenly grabbed everyone's imagination by unexpectedly flying a load of passengers from London to Sydney and back in a day.

Hadn't he warned those blind, do-nothing cretins in Washington that this would happen sooner rather than later? How many committees had he gone before and laid it on the line that giving the Euros virtually unlimited access to all the design work on the defunct SOFT project as part of a trade deal amounted to signing away the future of commercial airplane construction in the US? If successful, the Sabre would eat into traditional US markets, just as the Airbus had. What was needed was the funding to develop an engine like the Rolls-Royce Sabre. But the blinkered old men who advised the president didn't think the time right for commercial suborbital space travel – they didn't think the technology was ready. Once, at a top-level White House meeting, he had even pounded the table and declared that if prehistoric man had refused to have anything to do with fire after burning his fingers once, we'd still be living in caves.

There were grounds for Joe's fury. Twenty years ago there had been 40,000 members in his union. Now there were less than 20,000,and the plant was shedding a steady hundred jobs a week. Twenty thousand hard-working, skilled Americans tossed on the scrap-heap. Joe had been one of them four years ago when he'd hit seventy. It wasn't the company that turned him out but his own union. Joe, who had spent all his life bending rules, came up against the one rule that they weren't going to let him as much as flex a little.

'Sorry, Joe,' said the union president, 'but there's no way we can work something around that Seven-O. Give you more time in that workshop, eh?'

At the 'Farewell, Joe' dinner in his honour he overheard one grey-suited munchkin say to another: 'Thank Christ we've got the little shit off our backs at last.'

That decided Joe. He knew exactly what he had to do. He rented a cheap office near the complex, hired a secretary, hooked into the Internet and set up a relocation bureau for the plant's cast-offs.

With his boundless capacity for hard work, his knowledge of the industry and his huge circle of contacts, AeroSpace Talent was a success right from the start. Joe employed his union negotiating skills to fix up good deals for his clients, while the union's relocation bureau was still pratting about with the paperwork. He would think nothing of phoning the president of a corporation if he reckoned he had the right employee for them. As always, his judgement was as sound as the huge database he had built up. After two years he moved to larger premises and took on more staff. Eventually executives started coming to him – munchkins who didn't know the nose of an airplane from the tail. They got looked after by Joe's growing army of assistants. But those off the shop floor, men and women who shaped metal and plastics to make airplanes, got Joe's personal treatment.

Joe had a deep-rooted love of engineering – not merely for the joy of making things useful to one's fellow man, that was reason enough, but because he believed that making things was the only real way of creating wealth. You took a piece of metal costing ten cents, put ten cents' worth of labour into stamping it, shaping it and spraying it, and ended up with a piece of metal worth a dollar. That was wealth creation in a nutshell. Not chasing bits of paper up and down Wall Street. Which was why, despite the demands of his business, his great love was to spend his weekends in his fully equipped model engineering workshop. At first he had made real toys for his grandchildren, but the death of his wife, Judith, after forty years together left a huge hole in his life which he filled by building models of great American airplanes. His latest and most ambitious project, now nearing completion after two years, was a twenty-fourth scale model of Howard Hughes's *Spruce Goose* – the biggest twentieth-century airplane ever built. Accurate right down to the markings on the flight instruments.

Howard Hughes . . . Now there was a guy who understood the importance of making things, whether it was movies, airplanes, or semiconductors. When the *Spruce Goose* was finished, Joe's next project would be the *Spirit of*

35

St Louis – although Lindbergh was one of his lesser heroes.

Joe's love of aviation was, literally, in his blood. His parents had lived and breathed airplanes. In early 1939 the newly married couple had packed their lives into two cheap fibre suitcases, taken one last look at the Sena-Warsaw Aviation plant where they worked and left for France. At Cherbourg they boarded the *Queen Elizabeth* and sailed into New York six days later. Joe was born in 1945, after they had moved to Seattle and secured good jobs in the design office.

At first Joe hadn't wanted to follow his parents into the company. The exact moment when he changed his mind was still thrillingly fresh in his memory after more than half a century. On 9 February 1969 he had accompanied his parents to the plant to watch the unveiling of the project that they had been working on for three years: the roll-out and test flight of the world's first Jumbo jet – the mighty Boeing 747. Along with thousands of employees and press-men, he stood rooted in an agony of suspense as test pilot Waddell nursed the thing into the air, almost burning the tail on the runway after rotation because the giant refused to 'unstick' until most of the runway had been used up. After a few fly-pasts, Waddell had done something that had caused a gasp of amazement from everyone in the crowd: he barrel-rolled the prototype monster over Lake Washington. The sheer iron nerve and chutzpah it took to do such a thing with an untried aircraft had left Joe speechless with admira-tion. He decided there and then that he wanted to work with people with the nerve and guts of that test pilot. For a few stunned seconds the future of the company had hung on the guy levelling out after that spectacular manoeuvre. That's what American aviation lacked these days – men and women with guts to take chances, with a dash of showman-ship thrown in to let the world know what they were doing. They were around, but they were all in Europe. That was where the confidence was now.

Paul Santos appeared on the TV screen. Joe had seen him before. The guy was good. No ... fuck that – he was brilliant. After five years of test flying in which the world had largely forgotten the Sabre, he had suddenly kidnapped half the world's top airline big shots . . . If that little stunt had gone wrong, Sabre Industries would've been sued into oblivion, and even then the lawyers would've kept going. But then, if that 747 had fallen off the sky over Lake Washington all those years ago . . .

In answer to a question, Paul Santos stated that the first fare-paying passengers would be flying in exactly one year. The news caused Joe to chomp down hard on his cigar. A cutaway shot of a grinning Jack Helmann and Sir Richard Branson decided him. Without bothering to check the time he muted the TV, snatched up a phone and called Senator Mayhew on his private Iridium number.

The sleepy voice that answered at the other end did not belong to a happy man. 'For Chrissake, Joe! It's five in the morning!'

'CNN-World,' said Joe brusquely.

'What about it?'

'Take a look.'

'Look—'

'Take a look, senator! This is fucking important.'

With anyone else the politician would've hung-up. But that would be dangerous with Joe Yavanoski. The pugnacious former union boss still wielded a lot of influence. Whenever the networks needed some informed acerbic comments on America's civil aviation industry they called in Joe. 'Give me a minute,' Mayhew muttered. 'I'll go downstairs. I don't want to wake Ann.'

There was a pause, then the TV sound that Joe had killed came down the line.

'Yeah – I've got it, Joe,' said a weary voice. Another pause, then an awed: 'Holy shit . . .'

'Exactly,' said Joe evenly. 'Santos keeps a press low profile on his spaceplane during its test programme and then pulls this out of the hat. That's Yuri Segal of Commonwealth. And the guy behind him is Matthew Holden of Qantas.' Joe filled him in on the background to the story.

'Listen, Joe,' said Senator Mayhew when Joe had finished. 'Just because a few civil aviation bigshots get themselves a free trip—'

'Trip?' Joe echoed angrily. '*Trip!* Listen, senator, those guys have just flown from England to Australia and back again this morning! Twenty-four thousand miles. Just think about that.'

'Yeah – I'm thinking, Joe . . .'

There was a pause as both men watched the report.

'Listen, Joe,' said the politician at length. 'It's Concorde all over again. We sit back and scrape omelette in five years.'

'It's *not* Concorde!' Joe yelled. 'Concorde was a techno blind alley. The fastest you could push an aluminium skin through the air without it melting. No scope to go faster. These Euros have short-circuited all the design problems of supersonic air transport by hopping straight into space! And they've done it with an airframe design that's fifty per cent American! That's what really sticks in my craw!'

'Would you want to go into space, Joe?'

Joe thought about the hours cooped up in a Boeing on his annual vacation to Hawaii. He thought about all the businessmen and women flying the Pacific between Asia and the West Coast. There were 30,000 of them airborne at any one time. Millions of expensive man-hours wasted every year. He thought about the prototype 1,200-seat theatre-body monster taking shape on the plant floor not ten miles away – a lumbering leviathan of an airplane designed by short-sighted accountants who didn't think that oil prices could do the same thing that they had done in 1970s.

'The Sabre is a dead duck, Joe,' said the senator dismissively. 'Spaceplanes – it's new technology. Theatre bodies are the future.'

Had Senator Mayhew been with Joe, the chances were that he would have planted one on the politician. 'Space technology is not new!' he stormed. 'It's as old as me, for Chrissake! German V2 rockets were raining down out of space the year I was born and I'm seventy-five! It's half a century since we landed men on the moon!' In his anger he bit the end right off his cigar. Jesus Christ! This shit was one of the president's top advisers on aeronautics. He was typical of the current bunch of dinosaur Republicans now garrisoning the Senate. Mayhew and creeps like him had about as much vision as a rancid cowpat; they couldn't see the future even when it twisted their heads off and crapped down their necks.

'Tell you what, senator,' Joe snarled down the phone. 'It just so happens that I'd love to go into space. And if I'm any judge of character, so would millions of Americans. Only they'll be doing it in airplanes carrying "made in Europe" tags because you and your let's-sell-our-country-down-the-river cretins handed them the airframe design!' He slammed the phone down and immediately regretted his actions.

Shit. What good had the call done? Fuck all. His tirade hadn't even made him feel better. He unwrapped another cigar and stared moodily at the *Spruce Goose*'s fuselage. The flying boat's hull dominated his workshop. 'Come back, Howard,' he muttered. 'Jesus, do we need you.'

The phone rang. It was a radio station asking for Joe's views on the spaceplane. They received a five-minute diatribe that would need editing.

He turned up the TV sound when he was through with the radio station. The Sabre story had finished. He channel-hopped and settled on World Business who were carrying an interview update with Jack Helmann of Eastern-United before he boarded his flight back to Washington.

'Look at it this way,' he was telling the reporter. 'This morning I had breakfast here at Heathrow. I've been to Australia, toured Sydney, seen the opera house, seen the earth from space, and here I am back in London waiting to board a flight that's going to take longer to cross the North Atlantic than it took me to fly right around the world. I've just been talking to my colleagues and I can tell you that we're going to exercise our options.'

'For five Sabres?' the interviewer pressed.

'For seven,' said Helmann without hesitation. 'We've

39

decided that this time we're not going to sit back and wait for the technology to mature. As far as we're concerned, it is mature.'

Joe recalled that he had met Helmann at a seminar some ten years back and that the airline boss had struck him as a shrewd operator. Helmann taking such a positive line would be certain to underpin the confidence of smaller airlines who might be considering Sabres.

The story was capped by a Wall Street transport analyst saying that Sabre Industries' break-even point was twenty-five airplanes and that the price of Sabre Industries shares had nearly doubled that day despite a pending final payment on part-paid stock that would fund them for another year. Those part-paid shares were zooming.

He rounded off: 'For seventy years civil jets have been flying at 500 miles per hour and now Sabre has broken out of that rut with speeds twenty times that. World trade is booming. More people than ever are flying long-haul therefore the demand for shorter-duration flights has become a clamour. Unless public confidence in suborbital flight is badly shaken, names like Boeing and McDonnell-Douglas risk being pushed to the sidelines in the harsh world of twenty-first century commercial aviation.'

The analyst's words brought Joe's blurred thoughts into sharp focus.

Unless public confidence in suborbital flight is badly shaken.

A year to the first scheduled flight.

Joe's cigar went out as he sat deep in thought.

Unless public confidence in suborbital flight is badly shaken.

The British had a phrase about dropping a spanner in the works. Joe reckoned he could forge a pretty mean, drop-forged, case-hardened, vanadium-toughened, chrome-plated spanner within a year.

6

'*Shit! Shit! Shit!*'

Christine sat up, wide awake in an instant and frantically shaking Alec's shoulder. The couple gaped in horror at the spectacle of a loudly cursing Gus Newton and two Filipinos trying to catch the flailing end of Darwin's hose as it vomited black gunk and thrashed about like a demented sea serpent. Ozzy's head bobbed up through the galley hatch to see what the commotion was about and caught a delivery of foul-smelling ooze full in the face. He fell on to his stove with a loud yell and an even louder crash.

'You grab it! I'll turn it off!' Christine yelled, and dived down the hatch into the Darwin control room, narrowly missing a gout of airborne mud-bath as Alec and Gus threw themselves on the thrashing hose.

'Sample drum!' Alec panted, half blinded, pinning the hose to the deck by its coupling nut. 'Quickly!'

The stuff was icy cold. It drenched his shorts, stung his genitals and smelt like a million canned camel farts. One of the sterilised oil drums that wasn't supposed to be needed for another hour was dragged into position by its cradle. Helping Alec wrestle the hose coupling on to the drum's thread produced a black rose spray that reached all the parts of Gus that hadn't been reached so far. His stream of sulphurous expletives directed at Alec grew in volume and general awesomeness at the terrible visitations he wished not only on Alec, and successive generations of his family, but all Pommie bastards as yet unborn. He managed to wipe his eyes when Alec spun the coupling home. His sustained broadside of invectives stopped abruptly when he fully comprehended the state his beloved boat was in. The bleached, holy-stoned teak-planked decks were smothered. Thick, black goo dripped from the masts and running rigging. It glurped obscenely through the scuppers and down the side of the hull. It streamed down the wheelhouse and caked the lifeboat. He spun round in the forlorn hope that the after-deck had been spared, but nothing had escaped the evil black onslaught from 5,000 fathoms. He espied three of his crew who had evaded the worst by yanking a canvas dodger around them. Two were doubled up, helpless with laughter, and the third had had the presence of mind to grab a Memcorder and record the scene for posterity. Gus's wild gesturing and bellowed abuse as he launched himself at the men and promptly skidded on to his back bore all the hall-marks of one who is very pissed off indeed.

7

It was midnight when Paul returned to St Omer where he had an apartment on the top floor of the Sabre Industries' administration block.

He parked his car and swore softly to himself when he saw Ralph's car in a parking slot. Normally, he prided himself on his approachability. Being approachable meant receiving early warning of impending problems and consequently having more time to deal with them, and dealing with them before they posed a financial hazard. But on this occasion he was exhausted – it had been a long day and the last person he wanted to see was Ralph Peterson. He glanced up as he got out of his car and saw that his apartment's lights were on. Apart from his private secretary, the chief designer was the only member of his staff whom the apartment's fingerprint ID lock was programmed to recognise.

In the lift he rehearsed what he was going to say. Ralph jumped up hurriedly when Paul entered the spacious living-room. Sabre's chief designer was a heavy, thick set man, not over-endowed with a sense of humour, but he was totally dedicated to the project and had no concept of time or the necessity to eat and drink when immersed in his work. The papers he had been studying were spread across the coffee table. That and his shambling presence made the otherwise

42

tidy room look a mess.

He was about to speak but Paul held his hand up for silence. 'I know exactly why you're here, Ralph. I had the car on auto most of the way and read the preliminary flight analysis reports. Just give me five minutes to have a quick shower. You can be an unlikely fairy godmother and make me some coffee.'

A few minutes later, wearing an elegant silk dressing gown and sipping coffee, Paul began to feel more civilised, or he would have, if only Ralph had known how to use an AutoChef – the coffee was frightful.

'Something strange happened today at Heathrow,' said Paul conversationally. 'Did you see a kid talking to me in the VIP lounge?'

'No,' said the chief designer, sorting through his papers.

'He asked me for my autograph. First time that's ever happened.'

Ralph found the flight analysis printout he was looking for. 'Diversion fuel fell ten per cent below flight-plan outbound,' he reported bitterly. 'And eleven per cent inbound. Had he had a maximum passenger load Allenby wouldn't have had enough fuel to meet a diversion to Manchester or Stanstead.'

Paul stared at Ralph in dismay, his exhaustion forgotten. Three years before, the European Aerospace Authority had decided that Sabres should have sufficient kerosene in their tanks for a further eighty minutes conventional jet flight at the end of their journey to enable them to divert to another airport. The requirement was sensible in the case of conventional civilian aircraft because fog could sock in a northern airport in an hour, but it made little sense in the case of the Sabre because the spaceplane could select an alternative airport before re-entry. It was a ruling that had accentuated the problem that had come to dominate his life and that of everyone else on the project.

Weight.

Meeting the diversion fuel requirement had taxed the best brains in European aerospace. The Sabre was safe, yet according to EAA requirements it was still too heavy to carry its designed capacity of 200 passengers and their baggage. The graphs would have been radio-faxed to the EAA during the flight. For once Paul regretted the degree of openness that had characterised his running of Sabre Industries.

There was a silence apart from the ticking of an ornate longcase clock that had belonged to Paul's parents.

'Is there any scope left to increase the kerosene fuel capacity?' Paul asked tentatively, even though he knew what the answer would be.

Ralph snorted. 'Fuel capacity isn't the problem. Any increase in uplifted fuel weight would only lead to us burning more rocket fuel to carry the jet fuel, and we'd end up right back at square one. The three problems are weight, weight and weight.' He looked sideways at Paul. 'More properly, the real problem is this crazy diversion fuel requirement. You'll have to go back to them. Lay it down hard. Tell them that it's crazy to apply to a spaceplane the old jet concept of having an aircraft carrying enough fuel to divert to another airport on arrival at its intended airport. The Sabre is not designed to go crawling around the atmosphere looking for places to land. It has to be committed to one airport from before deorbit burn. Good God – we can choose from any airport anywhere in the world before DOB and land twenty minutes later. A conventional jet is committed to landing on final approach and flare. With the Sabre, it's before re-entry. That's the only difference. They've got to be made to see that.'

Paul recalled his conversation with Kristy Wood. 'We can never see the future because we insist on looking at it through a rear view mirror,' he murmured.

'What?'

Paul smiled at Ralph's startled expression. 'Something someone said to me today . . . I think it sums up the attitude of the EAA rather succinctly.' His smile faded. 'They won't budge, Ralph. We've won a lot of waivers out of Madame de Vere. I know she won't give way on deviation fuel. She and her authority see it as a safety cornerstone. In the face of new technology, they feel safe in clinging to the standards of the past.'

'The whole sodding mess is their fault anyway,' Ralph muttered, running stubby fingers through his unkempt hair. 'They were the ones who wanted those fucking great crease beams under the flight deck floor. Half a tonne of unnecessary metal. We design a geodetic laminate you could drop a bus on and those silly buggers don't trust our compression-distortion tests. God give us strength.'

Paul suppressed a yawn. His body was screaming for sleep, and he was in for a busy time tomorrow teleconferencing with the VIPs who had flown that day. 'So how much weight have we got to shed?'

'Five tonnes,' said Ralph abruptly.

Paul was silent. Five tonnes didn't sound much, but it was a lot coming at the end of a gruelling twelve-month weight reduction programme that had seen Sabre lose ten tonnes. Over a thousand points had been identified by computer analysis throughout the airframe where a few hundredths of a millimetre of skin and frame could be shaved off without sacrificing strength or integrity.

Ralph intruded on his thoughts. 'We're slap up against the law of diminishing returns. For a year we've been spending more and more money to lose less and less weight.' The chief designer looked speculatively at his colleague. 'We need a drastic change in philosophy. There is one thing we could do that would slash two tonnes at a stroke without costing a penny.'

'No!'

'For Chrissake, Paul – we've reached the end of the road. If you don't consider it now, we don't have a spaceplane.'

'We won't have any buyers if they have to say to their passengers, yes – we'll fly you half-way around the world in ninety minutes but, sorry, sir or madam – your baggage limit is ten kilos.' Paul's tone was mildly reproving, an indication of his anger and how strongly he felt on the matter. From the outset of the Sabre development programme he had clung grimly to a key objective: user confidence. Passengers

45

boarding a Sabre should feel like airline passengers and not pioneer astronauts. They should check in at a normal desk with a normal baggage allowance, board a normal-looking aircraft, enter a normal-looking cabin and sit in normal-looking seats. The battle to get him to accept that every passenger would have to take a Spaceqel anti-spacesickness tablet before departure had been particularly hard-fought. As for the horrors of the zero-gee toilets ... he had been forced to accept them because it wasn't possible to invent gravity. The in-flight meals battle had been easier. Paul had never liked airline food. Now he was fond of saying that no one would ever complain about the food on a Sabre flight because there wouldn't be any.

Ralph stood up and stared down at his boss. 'There's something I'd like you to take a look at in 001.'

'Now?'

'It's important.' Ralph's voice was ice.

Paul was too tired to argue. Besides, he saw the grim determination in his colleague's eyes. His one sleepless night was nothing compared with what Ralph had been through recently to get 004 passenger-licensed in time for yesterday's demonstration flight. He climbed to his feet.

'Okay. Let's go.'

The two men took the lift down to the ground floor and sat on an electric golf cart – the most practical vehicle for getting around the sprawling complex. Ralph pressed the symbol for the mock-up shed. The electric cart hummed along silent corridors, past the drawing office, crammed with computers and draughtsmen's boards, past several machine shops, and through a breezeway that connected with the vast construction shed where Sabre 005 and 006 were being built.

The entire plant had been constructed fifteen years earlier for the ill-fated Hermes/Skylon programme when the French and British governments had nursed grandiose ideas about going it alone with a spaceplane. The project had floundered because the British government decided that the French government had seen it primarily as a means of creating

46

vote-winning employment. The cost of the design study alone went up tenfold. Paul's approach was very different and owed much to his experience with British industrial practices which he had used to cut serious overmanning at Airbus Industries. Sabre Industries employed less than 2,000 – a remarkably low figure. There was very little piece-part manufacture in the St Omer plant: what could be bought in was bought in. Wherever possible, standard space-qualified components were used. In-house research was cut to the minimum: design problems were hived off to universities where the best brains were able to solve them at fiercely competitive rates. This British approach had led to universities across the channel becoming R and D hubs for many multinationals, and many had set up profitable companies, particularly in bio-sciences.

Drawings, specifications and the many thousands of documents associated with such a project existed in digital form, and were transmitted over the telephone network. In answer to queries from visitors about the apparent smallness of the Sabre design offices, Paul was fond of pointing out that the whole of the European aerospace community was the Sabre's design office. As for the unused sheds, they had been profitably sub-leased as bonded warehouses to take advantage of the tight security at the complex and would be used when the spaceplane went into main production. There was even a visitors' centre and conducted tours hosted by aircrews. In the souvenir supermarket, visitors could even buy shares in Sabre Industries without incurring dealing charges. Despite the early reservations of the French government towards a project on their soil that was free of control from their ponderous bureaucracy, they had been only too pleased to lease their white elephant to Sabre Industries and didn't much care how it was used. The subsequent aggressive commercial exploitation of the project was incorrectly attributed to the considerable British influence in the project.

The golf cart entered Construction Shed A where 005 and 006 stood – looking in opposite directions, wings dovetailed, nearly touching, to make best use of the space. A small night-shift team were working against the clock to install the ten kilometres of optical fibre harnesses in each Sabre. They took little notice of the electric cart that scuttled between the two spaceplanes along a designated forklift truck lane. Autosensors recognised the signals transmitted from Ralph's security badge so that doors opened and closed automatically.

They entered a much smaller shed that housed a dummy section of the Sabre's fuselage mounted on scaffolding. All that was left of the original 001 plywood and glass fibre mock-up was rarely referred to by the design team now and had been pressed into service for cabin crew training. Paul followed Ralph up the steep ramp and through the gaping tail opening. The interior lights were already on. Despite his exhaustion and the fact that this was not the real thing, Paul still experienced a tingle of excitement whenever he boarded a Sabre and saw the orderly rows of cushioned seats waiting for eager passengers to sink into them.

Ralph stopped at two rows of seats that were alarmingly different from the others. Paul stared askance at the twelve moulded seats. There were no armrests, no video screen built into each backrest, no safety card pockets because all the safety instructions were printed on the back of each seat, no back recline or in-flight entertainment controls, not even trays. Just single-piece moulded shells with slender T-shaped headrests. They looked as inviting as village hall seats set out for a public inquiry. And what appeared to be cushions turned out to be textile hologram patterning that had been cleverly printed on to the surfaces. In short, the seats had the grace and charm of plastic garden furniture.

'What', said Paul slowly, 'the hell are these?'

'How many guesses would you like?' Ralph countered.

'They look like canteen chairs.'

'Much more comfortable and much stronger.'

'Who made them?'

'Malaga University. Try one.'

'How much?'

'Please, Paul, just try one.'

Paul felt anger rising unbidden in his throat. He came perilously close to losing his tight control. 'The answer's "no", Ralph,' he said quietly. 'Ordinary seats or . . .'

Ralph's response was characteristically harsh. 'Or what, Paul? Nothing? Is that what you were going to say? Now listen – we've all gone along with you on this weight reduction so that your precious ideas on cabin fixtures and fittings could go unscathed. Well, we've reached the end of the road. The EAA's stupid crease beams under the flight deck floor are the last straw.'

'I did my best to persuade them otherwise, Ralph.'

'And now there's nowhere else to go, Paul. You've now got to start listening to your designers or this thing never gets off the ground. Either that or a new chief executive will have to be found because it's crazy that we should still be grappling with this problem when we're on the verge of main production. An extraordinary board meeting could be convened in seven days. If it comes to having to make a choice between loyalty to you or loyalty to the spaceplane, I can tell you now which way my vote will go. And a few others as well.'

The colour drained from Paul's face. In the ten years of their association, these were the strongest words that Ralph Peterson had ever used in many, often acrimonious, discussions. Never before had there ever been a hint of a challenge to Paul's leadership. The Frenchman *was* Sabre. Without Paul Santos's dedication and vision, they wouldn't be where they were now. A palace revolution was unthinkable.

As if realising that he had gone too far, Ralph's tone was suddenly conciliatory. 'This whole thing's too big now for one man's views to prevail, Paul.' He had nearly said 'ego'. 'You wanted it to be owned by the public and that's what you've got. You've always got your own way because you've always been right. But this time you're wrong . . . Please, Paul, just try them.'

Paul gave a characteristic French shrug and lowered himself into an aisle seat. To his surprise the plastic felt warm to the touch, not unlike the feel of cotton, and the unyielding-looking moulded seat and back contoured themselves to his shape like well-made cushions. The result was a surprisingly comfortable seat. He moved about experimentally and felt the seat, backrest and elongated headrest adjusting smoothly to the changes.

'Pressure-sensitive flo-plastics,' said Ralph. 'Long chain molecules that permit three-way movement.'

'They're space qualified?'

Ralph knew his chief too well to scent victory. Logic didn't necessarily win arguments with Paul – he was too much the stubborn Frenchman. 'Approval came through yesterday. They passed on everything: deceleration, shock and gee-tests; strength; distortion; flame-resistance; toxicity. The lot. Okay, so they may not look much but there's a choice of six colours and they're easy to clean. The important thing is that the passengers are going to be weightless for most of every flight. They don't need deep cushions, padded back supports and armrests.'

Paul remained silent. It was an argument he had dealt with before.

'The weight-saving on seventy racks of these seats amounts to nearly four tonnes,' Ralph continued. To prove his point, he moved forward, picked up a spare rack of three of the new seats and hung it from a stubby forefinger. He returned it and rapped his knuckles on the overhead stowage bins. 'And replacing all these with vinyl fabric pockets or netting will give us another half tonne. Scrapping the lining panels—'

'For God's sake – you'll have her looking like the inside of a bus!' Paul protested.

Ralph ignored the outburst. 'Replacing the carpeting with spray-on Velcro compo only where passengers will be placing their feet will give us about fifty kilos – not much, I grant you, but with all the other weight savings in fixtures we've identified in the main cabin we can win six tonnes at little cost and without any airframe mods. Scrapping the lining panels will save two tonnes.' He chuckled. 'Scrapping the

50

safety instruction cards saves two kilos.'

Paul sat in silence, trying to visualise Sabre's bleak, spartan interior if the chief designer had his way.

Ralph dropped his bulk into the aisle seat opposite Paul. 'Has it ever crossed your mind that your passenger philosophy about suborbital flight might be wrong? Maybe passengers do want something original. Maybe they'll get a buzz out of saying to their friends that going into space is very different from ordinary flying. That they're restricted to ten kilos of baggage and that the seats don't look like any airline seats they've ever sat in. It could be a form of one-upmanship.' He chuckled to himself. 'If train designers hadn't changed their ideas, the Eurostars would be fitted out like Victorian salons.'

Paul remained silent, turning over his chief designer's words. Kristy Wood's phrase returned to mock him: *We can never see the future because we insist on looking at it through a rear view mirror.*

But it did more than merely taunt him: it propelled him forcibly to the edge of an abyss. It revealed to him with awesome clarity that what he had always seen in himself as a strength was a deadly weakness that could destroy his beloved project. It was some seconds before the turmoil of his thoughts calmed sufficiently for him to utter the fateful words of capitulation.

'You're right, Ralph. You've been right all along and I've been wrong . . . So very wrong . . .' His exhaustion made the climb-down easier . . . And the seat was deceptively comfortable.

Not believing that he had heard right, the chief designer turned to Paul. 'What was that?'

There was no answer.

Paul Santos was asleep.

8

The infrared bug Jez had planted outside his bedroom alerted him before he heard his father's heavy tread on the landing. He switched off the miniature projection television that was playing his recording of Sabre 004, shoved it under his pillow, hid the earpiece and feigned sleep. The door opened, spilling light and his father's shadow into the bedroom. Jez was uncomfortably aware of a suspicious gaze raking the room. The door closed. Darkness returned, but Jez waited – he knew his father. The bug's warning LED continued to glow. Sure enough the door flew open again after two minutes.

Silly old fool, thought Jez with affection when he heard his father eventually close the door and move away.

Relations between Jez and his parents, never very good at the best of times, were particularly strained tonight.

While preparing dinner, his mother had seen her son on television in the Terminal 6 VIP lounge at Heathrow and had hit the TV's video buffer. His father arrived home ten minutes later and she showed him the recording. A phone call to Jez's class teacher established that, yet again, Jez hadn't been to school that day. Something told Jez when he arrived home an hour after his father that somehow this row was going to be on a par with the time when he had manufactured a huge crop of realistic measles spots the night before his Bar Mitzvah. In that respect, he wasn't disappointed: the row had been a one-sided two-hour flaming that had crisped Jez's hide and ended with his banishment to his room without dinner.

What they would really like, Jez had thought as his father set about locking his treasures in the spare bedroom, was for me to be turning in crap work at school. But Jez had denied his parents that because his school work was consistently good. Maths, science and technology, English, and several other subjects – all top grades, and he had scored an impressive list of credits in his last mocks. Instead his father had to content himself by seizing Jez's mains TV, his stereo and his computer, and placing them under lock and key. All the other stuff – the books on space, the stack of Sabre Industries press releases and the models of spacecraft – he left because there was so much of it. Naturally, his mother consulted her books on parenthood to determine whether such a move would have a damaging, long-term effect on her son. She was a model mother: careful of Jez's diet; went to every school open day; made sure he had a clean shirt each day. Jez's unjustified view was that she was always so busy being a mother that she had little time for her son.

Jez considered that his friend, Chris Fallon, had the ideal mother. Their house was a tip and Mrs Fallon a cheerful mess; she sprawled on her stomach on the living-room carpet, sharing six-packs of lager, and playing a mean hand at poker with her son and his friends on Saturday afternoons. It never occurred to Jez that his mother went out to work to save the extra money that would be needed to send him to university.

He nursed his hunger while waiting for the next stage of the banishment ritual. A few minutes later his warning LED glowed. He heard his mother's step outside and the clink of a tray placed on the floor. Ten minutes on he was tucking into a huge triple-deck hamburger and a mountain of chips while reliving those blissful moments when he had recorded Sabre 004's departure and return at Heathrow.

9

Midnight. It had been dark for six hours when Gus Newton declared that he was satisfied with the *Ben Gunn*'s clean-up operation. To be fair, the two Poms seemed keen to get the boat hosed down despite their obvious exhaustion. As soon as the bow floodlight went out, Christine peeled off her clothes and she and Alec took it in turns to use the hose on each other. Gus realised what was happening and switched the light on again but Christine, imbued with that remarkable sixth sense that women acquire when naked, had whipped a towel around herself before he got a good look at her.

'No point in getting my ship clean if you go and hose it off yourselves on to the decks again,' Gus observed from the wheelhouse door.

Christine ignored him and went to work with a scrubbing brush, holding the towel in place with one hand, while Alec wielded a mop.

'I'll get the boys to finish up,' Gus offered.

Christine stormed across to him. 'I said that we'd do the cleaning up, Mr Newton. And that's what we'll do. All things considered, we've done a good job.'

Gus's reply was to jab a thumb in the direction of the open hatch over the Darwin's control room. 'Your comm system's been squawking. Whoever they are, I reckon they ought to buy that satellite – the hours they spend on it.'

Leaving Alec to finish, Christine went down the companionway into the brightly-lit control room. The Hovercam backed hurriedly away from her like a startled insect. Bugger the thing! She couldn't get changed.

'Still awake then, Shief?'

Joshua Shief's voice answered from London. 'Alain and I are still very much awake, Mrs Rose. I've sent the others home. Perhaps you would be good enough to explain what happened.'

'Well, we've finished cleaning up,' Christine replied, knowing full-well that that wasn't what Shief meant.

'I was thinking more along the lines of a solution to a puzzle. The puzzle being that sediment has come up the hose at a faster rate than the Darwin pump could possibly pump it.'

'Expansion, Mr Shief,' said Alec, clattering down the companionway.

'Please explain, Alec.'

Alec flopped into his swivel chair, ran his fingers through his hair and regarded the Hovercam. 'It's only a theory, Mr

Shief, but as the tests – ecoskeletons – came up the hose and the pressure on them dropped, they either expanded slightly, or released a gas that caused a massive increase in buoyancy. The result – vroom – the stuff came up like a rocket.'

'Excuse me a moment please,' said Shief.

The channel went dead. The Hovercam settled on its favourite perch on top of the analyser. Christine pulled on a long T-shirt.

'That's given them something to think about,' Alec commented, swinging his chair back and forth and yawning. 'Christ, am I beat.'

There was a faint click as the channel opened. 'Alain favours your gas-coming-out-of-solution theory, Alec,' said Shief. 'He thinks it most unlikely that tests would expand sufficiently to go from negative to positive buoyancy, despite the considerable pressure change.'

'Tell Mr Colgate that he and I are in agreement for once,' said Alec. 'If their specific gravity was less than one when they were alive, they wouldn't've fallen to the bottom in the first place.'

'It's certainly unexpected,' said Shief. 'A phenomenon that may have considerable implications for large-scale extraction. Your analysis will answer the question.'

'That'll have to wait until morning, Mr Shief. We're both dead. We've had a helluva long day. Why don't you do what we're going to do, and get some sleep?'

The Hovercam's rotors spun faster. It rose and closed purposefully in on Alec, getting as near as its infra-red proximity sensors would permit.

'The test results are vital, Alec,' said Shief quietly. 'Alain and I have an important meeting in a few hours. We need those results and we need them now.'

'Look,' said Alec in a reasoning tone. 'If we start work now, we'll make mistakes.' He added in mocking tone: "Ave a heart, guv – me and the missus are done for.'

As always, Shief's tone was mild. 'All that is required is for you to load test samples into that very expensive portable analyser we've loaned you. Considering our backing for this expedition, and considering our possible future investment, I don't think my request is unreasonable.'

'Well, I think it is unreasonable,' Christine countered. 'We've been hours cleaning up.'

'I take it you ensured that no one kept a sample?'

'Jesus Christ – you should smell the stuff. It stinks like shit.'

'I appreciate that you're tired,' said Shief. 'Nevertheless, an early report—'

'An analysis won't take long,' Alec intervened quickly, seeing that Christine was about to erupt. 'Let's get it out of the way and get some sleep.'

'As sensible a suggestion as I've heard in many hours,' Shief commented acidly.

Christine knew when she was beaten and besides, she was secretly burning with curiosity about the results. Watched by the Hovercam, she and Alec went through the simple check list to initialise the analyser. Alec checked that the analyser's magnetrons, which would be evaporating the sample in stages, were capable of delivering full power while Christine sent some test readings to London.

'All received okay, Mrs Rose,' Alain Colgate reported.

Christine had met the Avanti technical director several times in London. A cold fish, she had decided, but on this occasion she was certain that she detected a hint of excitement in his voice.

The analyser's ready light came on. Alec flipped up the guard on the start button and pressed it. A pump hummed, drawing ooze from the barrel. After a few obscene glugs and burps as the viscous ooze was squeezed past the pump's impellers, the big machine settled down to its work of breaking the sample down into its component molecules and examining their structure.

The deep sea sediments covering the floors of the world's oceans consist primarily of calcium carbonate and silica. The carbon content comes from the steady rain of tests – the ecoskeletons of diatoms, plankton and myriads of other sea creatures deposited over two hundred million years. The silica and calcium content is the accumulation of billions of shell creatures over the aeons. Earlier deposits had led to the huge chalk deposits in southern England and northern Europe. In geographic terms, the floors of the oceans, such as the deep trenches that Alec and Christine were interested in, are much younger.

The formation of deep-sea sediments is the same process as that which formed the world's oilfields. In the case of the three main types of oilfield – fault trap, anticline trap and salt dome – the oil deposits are sandwiched between strata of impervious cap rock and igneous reservoir rock, thus retaining the oil's carbon content which gives it its volatile nature and usefulness as a fuel. The enclosing strata of impermeable rock also prevents the oil from migrating away from the oilfield. With deep-ocean sediment the material is not so contained; the carbon content of the ooze's organic material is leached out by the action of seawater, leaving largely useless silicates and calcium deposits. Below 1,000 to 2,000 metres, referred to as the Carbonate Compensation Depth, the perceived wisdom had been that the carbon dissolution effect of seawater was so high that no carbon fraction whatsoever was retained in the sediment. This had been largely proved as a result of many thousands of sediment samples removed from the floors of the world's oceans.

As with all seemingly sound theories, there are always a few perverse individuals who think otherwise. In the case of carbonate dissolution of deep-sea sediments, one such person was Alec Rose whose views were largely ignored because he wasn't an oceanographer or a marine biologist.

Alec's belief was that the lowest layers of sediment at extreme depths in isolated trenches, which had never been sampled, may have retained their carbon content because the layers had been formed during the Jurassic Period when it was believed that ocean salinity had varied markedly. He maintained that subsequent deposits of primary silicate and calcium material would have had an isolating effect on the lower layers in the same way that cap rock isolated oilfields. Also the extreme pressure may have served to consolidate the carbon and slow down or even stop the carbon dissolution effect. He had based his theory on some curious gravimeter readings that the Scripps Institute of Oceanography had obtained from the Banda Trench, indicating that the composition of the lower sediment was very different from the upper sediment.

The analyser's first results started scrolling on to the Darwin's control console. It was raw data after the seawater separator had done its job: the identification of skeletal fragments. Phytoplankton, zooplankton, foraminifera, and pteropods seemed to make up the bulk of solid material. No surprises there.

Christine and Alec sat forward when they heard the magnetrons switch in. Radio frequency energy was now pouring into the sample, breaking it down for spectral analysis.

The screen glitched and went blank. The analyser hummed. And then the results began in alphabetical order. The high traces of argillaceous material were unexpected.

BAUXITE: 21 PPM.

Well – forget alluvial ooze for aluminium production.

CALCIUM: 249K PPM. As Alec had expected – the damned sludge was mostly tests anyway.

And then the information they had been waiting for appeared.

HYDROCARBON: 320K PPM.

'Bloody hell,' was all Christine could think of saying as she gaped at the screen.

'Oil,' Alec whispered. 'I was right . . . There must be billions of barrels of oil locked up in that sediment.'

'More than the Gulf fields?'

'Far more. This is going make Indonesia the richest country in the world.'

Alec suddenly hit his armrests, gave a loud whoop and jumped up. He dragged Christine to her feet and danced her around, kissing and hugging her. They crashed into the console and fell, laughing, in a heap on the floor.

'I was right!' Alec cried. 'I was right all along!'

Gus Newton heard the commotion. He kicked off his flip-flops to avoid making a noise, left the wheelhouse and stared down at the celebrating couple through the open hatch. Stupid bloody Pommies. Or maybe not so stupid. So what was it with ocean muck that they were prepared to spend so much money? Not research like they claimed, he was certain of that. He saw that one of the big cabinets they had brought aboard for this charter was lit up. First time that had happened. He had wondered what was causing the extra load on the batteries.

Deep in thought, he padded aft where four of his men were neatly stowing in the hold the coils of hose that the capstan and winch was bringing aboard.

'Another thousand metres and it's all in, boss,' his bosun reported.

'Good job too,' Gus growled. 'I'm fucked off with all this bloody station-keeping. Which one of you scum has the video camera?'

'How's that, boss?'

'One of you has a video camera. Someone was waving it about when that shit was flying everywhere.'

'That's Billy, boss. He'll be asleep.'

Gus grunted and slid down the companionway rails that led to the crew's quarters.

In London Joshua Shief sat quietly in his chair while Colgate worked on some figures. It took considerable effort for the oil chief to avoid drumming his fingers. Spread out on the boardroom table were sonargraphs of the Banda Trench that Colgate was constantly referring to. The side scan images showed a huge, horseshoe-shaped depression in the ocean floor that was three kilometres high in places and twenty kilometres wide. If Alec Rose was right, the fault had acted as a huge scoop over a period of two hundred million years to trap the steady rain of decaying marine organisms from above. The wall screen showed Alec and Christine similarly engaged after their bout of euphoria. Information was still flooding in from the analyser. A printer had taken over from the memory in Colgate's memopad and was silently feeding pages filled with tabulated columns of data into its collection bin.

Colgate raised his head from his memopad. His voice was strained. 'You must understand that these are very provisional figures.'

Shief looked sharply at him: he had omitted the customary 'Mr Shief'. 'Okay. So how much?'

'Five cubic kilometres.'

'I can't visualise that. Give it to me in barrels.'

Colgate looked on the point of fainting. He stared down at his figures as though they were a particularly despicable traitor. 'Well . . .' he began. 'One cubic kilometre is a billion cubic metres, of course. That's a volume of 1,000 metres by 1,000 metres by 1,000 metres. At five barrels per cubic metre, one cubic kilometre equals five billion barrels.'

Shief allowed his fingers to drum. 'Twenty-five billion barrels total?'

Colgate's face was white. 'Yes.'

Shief broke the silence that followed. 'I'm right in thinking that's more oil than has been produced since man started pumping the stuff out of the earth's crust?'

Colgate nodded. 'I think so.'

Shief never swore but on this occasion he permitted himself a soft, single word expletive: 'Fuck.'

'Mr Shief!'

Alec's face was filling the TV screen. Shief opened the audio circuit. 'Yes, Alec?'

'We reckon around ten cubic kilometres. After separation, that'll be around five cubic kilometres. We're going to bed now.'

An hour later Christine lay awake in her bunk, unable to sleep despite her exhaustion as she turned over the consequences of their remarkable discovery. Indonesia did not have the money or the expertise to develop the huge resource on their doorstep. They would have to depend on oil companies – people like Shief who put profit above everything else, and who would use Indonesia's endemic corruption to further his own ends without any consideration for the well-being and prosperity of that country's teeming millions. True, Triton Exploration owned the crucial patents that held the key to large-scale extraction of the oil, but would someone like Shief allow a few pieces of paper to stand in his way when the prize was what could be the largest oil deposit ever found? No. Furthermore she had no doubt that he would distort the results of this survey to shaft Indonesia. The sooner she made direct contact with the new government in Jakarta, the better.

The sleep that eventually claimed Christine was troubled by a deep sense of foreboding that their discovery would unleash dark forces.

10

Three hours later the *Ben Gunn* was underway, heading south under the blazing constellations of a clear sky, marking her passage across the limpid surface with a glowing luminescence wake that stretched to the horizon. There was a knot of burning cigarette ends and murmured conversation from the bow where the off-watch crew were enjoying the breeze after the three hellish days of station-keeping.

Gus gave a curt order to the helmsman to distract him and slipped the Memcorder into his shirt pocket. He pulled on soft shoes and went quietly down the companionway into the control room. Lights were unnecessary – he knew his way around the *Ben Gunn* blindfolded.

He listened carefully for the regular breathing from the aft end of the former hold that told him the two Poms were asleep in their bunks. There was that fucking flying bug gizmo to look out for. He wouldn't be surprised if the bloody thing could see in the dark. He located it plugged into its charger, its transmission LED extinguished. Gus was about to switch on his flashlight but the husband stirred. He froze. Shit! He needed the torch to use the Memcorder. The breeze through the deckhead ventilators caused something to rustle. He felt around. Papers! Normally they cleared them away every night. Gus grudgingly admitted to himself that they kept everything shipshape, but not tonight. He gathered up as many of the documents as he could find and stole away as silently as he had come.

Once in the security of his tiny cabin-cum-office under the wheelhouse, he switched on his desk lamp, made room on the chart table and studied his trophies. He could make no sense of the columns of strange names and figures. What the fuck did 'cosmogenic sedimentation' or 'phosphatic skeletal remains' mean?

The tables of compounds and elements ran to three pages. Well, maybe this crap would mean something to someone. He fumbled with the Memcorder's unfamiliar controls. The autofocus feature gave him a sharp image of the first document and he pressed the record button. Two seconds ought to be enough. He repeated the process until he had captured all the documents on the Memcorder's card. He pulled the card out of the camera and slid it into his TV's reader. The images were fine. Every word and figure perfectly legible. Clever little buggers, the Japs – the camera had even averaged out his handshake so that the pictures were steady. He returned the papers and decided that tomorrow, while the Poms were having lunch, he would take some single-frame video pics of their equipment.

11

Paul Santos loathed video conferencing. There was none of the good-natured ambience of a face-to-face meeting which his natural charm could always generate even under the most adverse circumstances. He couldn't swing his intuitive audio beam and intercept those snatches of conversation between others that told him how the meeting was progressing. He couldn't direct his remarks to the most receptive person present or catch for whom a telling glance or gesture was intended.

And now he was having to cope with something far worse, a Technicolor nightmare in fact: The holographic conference.

Instead of being confronted by his office wall screen subdivided into smaller screens, each bearing an image of a person taking part in the discussion, his desktop merged eerily into the different desktops of four bland, woodenly smiling senior members of Japan Air International's board, each bland, wooden smile sitting in a different office with a different background that created a hellish clash of materials and hues. To make matters worse, the positions of those taking part could be switched around at will. Paul had fiddled with the controls at the beginning of the meeting with the result that when one person spoke, the others looked in the wrong direction. It was like holding a debate with a gang of grinning ghosts. Right now everyone was respectfully silent because the chairman of JAI was talking.

'We believe a US shuttle compatible docking facility is essential,' Asamu Kwashina was saying from the head of the table. Japanese protocol decreed that this was his position and Paul couldn't move him about like the others. 'You already have a conventional emergency hatch in the flight-deck roof of the Sabre, therefore our engineers cannot see that there is a problem installing such a docking facility in place of it.' The actual words were spoken by the JAI interpreter to Paul's left but the others were looking to Paul's right. It was all hideously confusing, and particularly annoying because Asamu Kwashina spoke perfect English – Paul had got on well with him when JAI had bought thirty Airbuses, but the airline had an expensive interpreter for their board, therefore protocol dictated that she should be used.

Paul leaned forward. He wanted to look Asamu straight in the eye but he suspected that, to the others, he was looking at a coffee maker he couldn't see.

'Asamu . . .' To hell with protocol. He had been saying 'Mr Kwashina' for the best part of two hours. 'Fitting a shuttle-compatible hatch would be crazy. Even if a Sabre did get stranded in orbit, the Americans would need at least two

63

weeks to prepare a shuttle for a rescue.' He paused to allow the interpreter to catch up.

'Could a rescue be staged with another Sabre?' the airline chief ventured.

'The Sabre isn't designed for complex manoeuvres once in space. To be blunt, it doesn't have the fuel capacity for the orbital jockeying that a space docking would need. The design doesn't include such a hatch for the same reason that you don't give your passengers parachutes. It simply isn't practical.'

While he was talking, Paul was repeatedly touching Ralph's call panel. Where the hell was he? And how many other nit-picking points did Asamu have on his memopad? The strain was beginning to tell on Paul. The tiny sensor under his left armpit would have noted the increase in his heartbeat and blood pressure and would have signalled the monitoring system in the St Omer BUPA hospital. The hospital's rapid response paramedic team prided themselves on their efficiency. No doubt they were now checking with his secretary. Three months previously, they had noted a sudden change in his blood-sugar level while he was swimming in the social club's pool and had got to him before he had a minor heart attack.

The Japanese airline chief smiled at Paul's last comment without waiting for the interpreter. The screen set into Paul's desk glitched and Ralph's face appeared. He was in Italy visiting a subcontractor. The note he was scribbling appeared on Paul's screen:

Sorry. Been following this in car. Hatch no problem. NASA design royalty $10,000 per hatch but will do deal. EAA type approval already exists. Suggest you back down on this but don't budge on ten-kilo baggage limit per passenger – we still need that weight saving.

'The hatch would not require a separate airlock,' Asamu Kwashina pointed out. 'The flight-deck itself serves as an airlock, is that not correct?' He spoke in English which completely threw the interpreter and she automatically repeated his comment in Japanese. The ghosts thought this particu-

64

larly funny. Paul joined in with the laughter. At least it finally broke the ice, which he had been struggling to do since the conference started.

'Our chief designer has just told me that a shuttle-compatible docking hatch is no problem,' said Paul. He glanced at Ralph's screen to ensure he was paying attention and made an immediate decision. 'We'll fit it to all Sabres, therefore it won't go on your customising bill.' His fingers moved quickly on the memopad to send a message to Ralph.

That okay?

Fine, Ralph replied.

Asamu beamed and reverted to Japanese. 'That is excellent, Mr Santos. The last point concerns pooling the refuelling and servicing facilities at LA and London with other operators. Paragraph 233 on the draft contract is not clear on the question of facility sharing.'

Ahh . . . All the nasties coming thick and fast now.

'We're still trying to dovetail refuelling and maintenance operations to single facilities at all the major airports,' Paul replied. 'If it doesn't go smoothly, then Sabre Industries will set up a separate company to offer such services to Sabre operators. I'm sorry I can't give you a more positive answer at the moment, Asamu, but we can't make definite plans until we have definite sales. But I give you my personal guarantee that operators such as yourself will be looked after.'

The Japanese scribbled a note to a colleague on his memopad and awaited a reply before looking up at the gathering. Paul had learned that the chairman was addressing him when his gaze was directed to the left. 'That is good enough for us, Mr Santos. We will go ahead with final contract negotiations on the basis of eight Sabres. Thank you for your patience.'

It was as simple as that. Paul scrambled to his feet and returned the bows and goodbyes, reserving the deepest bow for the airline chief. The desktops and grinning ghosts disappeared. Paul opened the audio circuit to Ralph.

'Sounds like it went well,' the chief designer commented.

'Well enough. You were right about the seats and the ten-kilo baggage allowance. They skipped right past them. They weren't even discussed.'

Ralph wasn't the type to gloat. He merely nodded and said that he would be back tomorrow. Paul cleared the line and sank into his chair, utterly drained. Sophia, his Swiss secretary, glided into the office with the sinuous grace of a cat, bearing a cup of strong black coffee. She had been with Paul fifteen years: a tall, striking brunette approaching fifty with disturbing, wide-set dark brown eyes that missed nothing. They had once consoled each other when their respective marriages had broken up. Their relationship was back on its mature, professional level, but was now tempered with warmth and understanding, although neither had forgotten the tempestuous days and nights of ten years ago when Paul had resigned from Airbus Industries and the time when his wife had left him. Paul longed for a return to those days. He longed to see her lovely hair spread across a pillow again, her divine body covered in a film of sweat, her arms and legs hungrily around him, her whole being making demands on him that his wife had never made. But Sophia always smilingly and gently resisted him, fuelling his hunger for her, while using his craving for her to make her position unassailable within the company.

Paul's driving ambition and dominant personality were too strong for him to see Sophia as a formidable power behind the throne, but in her quiet, unobtrusive way she had imposed her Calvinistic thrift, the consequence of an impoverished childhood, on the running of Sabre Industries. The strict controls on expediture and the company's eagerness to capitalise on every opportunity to make money all stemmed from Sophia; her influence over Paul's decision making, although always seemingly unobtrusive, was more persuasive than he sensed he ought to allow, but he valued her judgement and that she always stayed out of the company's internal wrangling and politics. He downed the coffee in one gulp.

'It went well, Paul,' Sophia observed. Not once in fifteen

years had she ever slipped and used his first name in company.

'Damned hologram conferencing,' Paul complained. 'I didn't know where I was. I hate all this new technology.'

'That's rich, coming from you.'

He smiled at the incongruity of what he had said. 'Well – space technology isn't new. It's just that we're late using it.'

'*Paris Match*, last June,' said Sophia. 'You are now quoting yourself.'

'How long were we?'

'Two hours, three minutes.'

Paul groaned. 'And I've got another one tomorrow with Virgin. Ordinary screens, so it won't be so bad.'

'It's been cancelled.'

Only when he was with Sophia did Paul allow it to show when he was rattled. 'What! Why? Did they give a reason?'

Sophia moved behind Paul's chair and massaged his temples gently with her fingertips, knowing full well the effect it had on him. 'They didn't cancel. We did. I played a hunch and called Dan Robertson to ask him if he hated video conferencing as much as you did. He does and will be happy to meet you in Calais at one o'clock.'

Paul took hold of Sophia's hands and squeezed them affectionately. 'I won't tell you how wonderful you are because you'll want a rise.'

'You'd be surprised at what I really want, Paul. But I'll wait until you've sold twenty-five Sabres. The company has to come before us.'

'Does that mean what I think it means?'

She gave a sexy little laugh that he remembered so well but hadn't heard for years. And then she was pressing her cheek against his temple. 'Perhaps, Mr Santos. But those sales must come first.' She resumed the gentle massaging.

Paul leaned back in his chair, savouring the erotic touch of her long, sensuous fingers. 'Eight today. Another ten tomorrow. We're getting there, Sophia.'

'Wait until you've got Commonwealth in the bag,' she said reprovingly.

Her words had a salutary effect, coming on the heels of his euphoria at closing the Japanese deal. She was right, of course.

There was a long road ahead.

A hell of a long road.

12

'The licence debit for your journey is two dollars, seventy cents,' Dickhead advised Joe Yavanoski when he parked his car outside his office on Tacoma Drive. 'This message is brought to you by Peugeot Electric City Cars – easy on the pocket; easy on the environment.'

'Waddya mean?' Joe snarled. 'It's always seventy cents!'

The driver information computer remained silent. Joe rephrased his response so that the Dickhead would understand him. 'D.I.C. query. Charge is normally seventy cents.'

'Low-wind speed surcharge invoked,' advised the computer's friendly female voice. 'State pollution control authorisation issued at o-eight-thirty today. Do you require hard copy?'

'Negative,' Joe muttered. He pulled his driver's licence card out of its reader slot and climbed out of his Chevvy. A sunny morning which meant that his knee wouldn't give him trouble today. But a windless day which meant that the pockets of millions of Americans on their way to work in real cars, not those crap little Euro electric bugs, would get plenty of grief from the state. The windless days of last summer when the temperatures passed ninety and the pollution count climbed had resulted in five dollars per journey penalty charges. A big money spinner for the state, but did they invest the proceeds in the American car industry to help it produce electric cars? Did they hell. It went into public transport. And who ran the buses and trains? Immigrants. Plenty of jobs for them. None for Americans.

The short walk across the sidewalk to his office suite over Benny's Bar was long enough for his thoughts to have worked him into a black mood by the time he had unlocked and was sat at his desk.

He heard Maggie Harriman come in. She put her head cautiously round the door. 'Morning, Joe. Coffee?' She was scared of her employer; this part of her daily ritual was to gauge his mood rather than meet his needs.

Joe grunted an affirmative. One day he'd surprise her and say 'no'. 'God-damned low-wind penalty,' he growled when she placed the coffee before him.

She nodded sympathetically. 'My husband said that it was only a matter of time before they'd bring in winter charges the way pollution is going up all the year round.' She gestured to the screen moulded into Joe's desk. 'It's a bad one today, Joe. They came in yesterday after you'd left.'

Alone with his coffee, Joe voice-activated the screen and tabbed through his mail. At least the software read it first and dumped the junk under the appropriate heading. Minutes of meetings. Details of the latest Washington State retraining schemes – skill reprofiling programs they were called now. Joe wondered how much all this distortion of language led to distortion of understanding of the under-lying social problems that led to such schemes. He came to the latest lay-offs and swore at the length of the list. There were over one hundred of them, sixty-seven from the plant. This time the axe was falling on the design shop. Jesus – the munchkins were ripping the heart out now to save the body.

All the applicants for Joe's services had given their consent for his company to access their personal records. He went through them one at a time, checking on specialist skills and voice-assigning each one to the right placement counsellor on his team. Most of them worked from home. Joe's actions dumped the details into their terminals so that they could begin work as soon as they signed on. The two catering managers were routed through to Jilly Hawkes – a smart operator who could land a skunk a job in a BurgerKing. She'd have them fixed up by lunch-time. Accountants, clerks, cleaners – all were dropped in someone's capable lap. Joe dealt with the engineers himself. He was about to give the assign command to dump a technical author on Mike

Stenning's terminal but paused for thought. Technical authors weren't the usual paper-pushing munchkins – invariably a solid engineering background was an essential requirement for their job.

Jean Lesseps. Sounded French.

He called up more information. French-Canadian. Forty-five. The colour pic showed a sallow, drawn complexion, lank hair. Technical author and a yard of qualifications. Practical experience included five years as an instrument engineer for Maple Aviation — just across the straits in Vancouver.

Christ, thought Joe, he must've been good to have lasted so long with that hire 'em and fire 'em outfit. A note from a previous employer: Jean was obsessed with flying . . .

So what was wrong with that? Joe wondered.

. . . but first class at his job. Divorced. No children. Bilingual: French and English. County entailment orders on his paychecks for his ex and creditors.

Fully expecting that this Jean Pierre Lesseps would have blocked disclosure of further information, Joe ran a credit check and found that Lesseps had given AeroSpace Talent access to the main state online credit service. Jesus Christ, the stupid guy had debts to the tune of over half a million bucks! He had everyone snapping at his heels from the IRS to a TV repair shop. How could such a nondescript-looking guy run up that level of debt? A check on cars that he had owned showed nothing exceptional.

Joe called up the usual video bite. Personnel departments hardly ever looked at them but recording them had become *de rigueur*. A self-conscious, smiling face appeared on the screen: wide-set eyes hiding behind heavy spectacle frames; the lank, dark hair now brushed straight back. Looked younger than forty-five. He cleared his throat. That should've been edited out. Some people had no idea how to sell themselves.

'Hi. I'm Jean Lesseps. I was born in Quebec 1975 and obtained American citizenship when I was thirty.' The accent was West Coast. 'My interest in aviation started when my father taught me to fly when I was twelve. I now

70

fly around a thousand hours a year and I own a Cessna—'

Joe cut the audio. Oh, Christ – the guy was selling his interests before his qualifications. He loosened the shot to a head and shoulders. Jean Lesseps's hands were clasped together on his desk, maybe to hide his nervousness at recording his CV, but there was no hiding the cheap suit and the general air of unkemptness.

While the video rolled in a window on the desktop screen, Joe took a snoop at the FAA database and found that Jean Lesseps owned a twin-turbine Cessna Cayman. Holy shit! No wonder the guy was broke. One database led to another. By the time Lesseps's qualifications captions were rolling across the foot of the window, Joe's experienced trawling had unearthed the fact that before the Cayman had been repossessed, Lesseps had been refused non-emergency use of over a hundred airfields across the North-West, and that his outstanding servicing and hangarage bill was over $50,000. The stupid guy was air crazy. A hundred per cent ownership of a Cayman on his salary! Most people would settle for part ownership. The guy was clearly insane, as were the finance company. Okay – let's see if anyone was interested.

A few word commands were all that was necessary to transfer Jean Lesseps's data to the Joblink database to search for a match or near match. Not likely. What was the demand for aviation technical authors these days?

He got a match immediately that scored enough points for the Joblink computer to clock a $100 charge on Joe's account.

Sabre Industries of St Omer, France, wanted a bilingual technical author to work on the documentation of their spaceplane.

Sabre Industries!

The hated name seemed to jump off the screen at Joe. He was about to wipe the data when the vague outline of a wraithlike, unbidden idea entered his mind. He stared down at the screen, thinking hard and then, not really sure of what he was doing or why he was doing it, he compiled the data on Jean Pierre Lesseps into a report and job application, first

71

erasing details of his client's debt burden. It was unethical but a European outfit such as Sabre would be unlikely to have the sort of gateways to US databases that Joe's company had. He e-mailed the report. Sabre Industries' autoresponder acknowledged receipt of the application a minute later, and a positive reply came just after lunch with a videofone call from Sabre Industries. He checked the time in France. Christ – they were keen.

Claudia Picquet introduced herself as the Director of Documentation Support Services at Sabre Industries. A grey-haired, fiftyish woman, hollow-eyed from lack of sleep, fighting hard to look bright and alert, speaking slow but good English. 'We've just read the application from Jean Pierre Lesseps, Mr Yavanoski. And we have watched his CV. It is possible that we may be interested in making him an offer.'

'That's fine, Miss Picquet,' Joe replied, nearly mis-pronouncing her name. 'I'll put you on the end of the list. Match his existing salary with twenty per cent over and above and I'll move you up the list.' Nothing about his manner betrayed the rage that churned within him at this dealing with a senior employee of the company that threat-ened to destroy his beloved country's civil aviation industry. His years as a union negotiator had honed his acting skills.

The woman nodded. 'And the other jobs on the list would be cleaning posts, Mr Yavanoski?'

Ha. No fool, this one. Joe decided. He summed people up fast and decided that he could talk straight with Claudia Picquet. 'He'll go soon, Miss Picquet. Bilingual techies with my client's qualifications aren't too common.'

'That's why I'm calling.'

'And because you're overworked. You've got an airplane going into production and you haven't got the documentation moving that you're going to have to deliver with the air-planes because your accountants decided that cutting pits in CD ROMs didn't put rivets in aluminium. Am I right?'

The Frenchwoman smiled. 'There is an apt English phrase about nutshells, Mr Yavanoski.'

72

'Believe me, honey. We have the same problems here. Accountants are the same the world over. Okay – you've seen the guy. You've heard him. You've seen his experience and qualifications résumé. So let's talk.'

They talked for fifteen minutes.

As soon as he finished, Joe put a call through to Lesseps on his Iridium number. 'John? Joe Yavanoski – AeroSpace Talent. I think I may have a job for you with a big raise. Can you drop by our office on Tacoma Drive?'

The French-Canadian's delight was genuine. 'So soon? That's fantastic, Mr Yavanoski. Would tomorrow some time be okay?'

'Make it this afternoon some time,' Joe replied bluntly. 'These sorts of jobs don't wait.'

'I'll be with you in thirty minutes,' Lesseps promised.

It was twenty-nine minutes to be exact. Joe was chancing a chill by standing at his open window smoking a cigar when a battered pick-up slid into a parking bay. Jean Pierre Lesseps was tall – about six nothing. Medium build. Wearing the uniform of a filling station attendant and the haunted expression of one who has just realised the extent of the hard times that lay ahead.

Well, that suited Joe.

It suited him very well indeed.

Maggie showed him into Joe's office. He refused coffee and sat abruptly in the offered chair, perched stiffly on the edge and staring hopefully at Joe.

'You have a job for me as a technical author, Mr Yavanoski?' he blurted after the introductions.

'Call me Joe. John okay with you? Nothing is fixed . . . yet. An inquiry. But first a few questions . . . How would you feel about working in Europe?'

Hope flared in Lesseps's eyes like gasoline thrown on a dying campfire. 'I would like that very much indeed, Mr— Joe.'

'How about family ties?'

'None. I could leave tomorrow.'

Joe relit his cigar and took care to hold it near the extractor set into his desktop as he talked. One whiff escaping under the door and he'd have a staff rebellion on his hands.

'They're offering twenty per cent over what you were getting. But there's a catch: you'd have to work your ass off for the next year. Forty-eight hours a week because they're badly behind.'

'I'll take it, Joe.'

'Not so fast. Firstly, they haven't offered you the job yet. Secondly, you don't even know what country it's in.'

Lesseps smiled suddenly. 'I don't have to be very clever to guess France.'

'You guessed right. Sabre Industries.'

The French-Canadian was suddenly alive. 'The spaceplane! Christ – I'd love to work on that. I nearly cried when they did that flight to Australia. It's what we should be doing. We should never have handed over the results of all that SOFT airframe research.'

'Guess I'll second that,' said Joe suavely. This guy was identifying himself with the United States. Good. 'Okay. You'd better talk to them. They're expecting to hear from you.' He called Maggie and instructed her to show Lesseps to an interview booth for a video conference with Sabre Industries.

'Stick to your experience and qualifications,' was Joe's parting instruction as Lesseps was shown out of his office. 'Don't talk salary, and for Chrissake don't mention anything about any financial commitments you may have. Don't volunteer anything unless they ask. Borrow a jacket. Comb your hair. See you in thirty minutes. That's how long these interviews normally take.'

Joe settled down to some figure work and checking on state law. After five minutes he listened in to the interview for a few seconds, but they were rattling away in fast French. He was surprised when Claudia Picquet paged him after only fifteen minutes. Shit – they had bounced the guy.

'Mr Yavanoski,' she said when Joe opened the line and her face appeared on his desktop screen. 'We like your client and we wish for him to start as soon as possible.'

74

That meant that they had run their security checks on Lesseps's qualifications while waiting for him to call them. They were keen.

'He's a great guy, Claudia,' said Joe affably. 'You've made a good choice. So let's talk.'

They talked turkey for ten minutes. Claudia Picquet's toughness didn't come naturally but was imposed on her by her budget.

For once Joe gave way on more points than he would normally have done. The offer of $10,000 relocation expenses was a joke but he went along with it. The deal was closed on a two-year contract. Joe promised to process all the relevant documentation immediately.

Lesseps was a changed man when Maggie showed him back into the office. He punched the air and pumped Joe's hand, beaming, not bothering to brush away the hair falling over his eyes. 'Joe – I just don't how to thank you. This morning I was seriously thinking of ending it all . . . And now—'

'Sit down, John.'

'And to think I'll be working on the spaceplane! I never dreamed that—'

'I said, sit down.'

Lesseps sat and stared anxiously at Joe. 'Is there a problem?'

'Sure there's a problem. A big problem. I ran a check on your credit rating while you were talking to Sabre. It made unhappy reading. You owe over half a million bucks and the county entailment orders against you amount to $30,000 a month.'

Lesseps swallowed and combed his fingers through lank hair. It had a tendency to flop over his eyes. 'You don't have to tell that to Sabre.'

'We're not bound by state disclosure laws with overseas outfits, but there's a Fed agreement with the European Union that's been in force five years now. Your earning entailments and civil liabilities would apply in Europe. The world's shrinking. You can't run out on your debts no more.'

The light died in Lesseps's eyes. 'My salary would be stopped?'

'Just as it is here. But it would never come to that. Thirty thousand dollars a month is gonna frighten Sabre Industries – frighten them bad.'

'But why should that worry them so long as I do my job?'

Joe had worked out a convincing answer to that. 'For Chrissake!' he exploded. 'Look at it from their point of view. They'd be giving unlimited access to confidential industrial information to a guy who's vulnerable. They'll see your monthly entailments as a form of blackmail. You're not the first guy who's over-reached himself and gotten himself up to his skull in debt. I've got over a hundred on our database. Software engineers, mask designers, draughtsmen. You name 'em, we've got 'em. You know what they've all got in common? Earnings entailments. Mostly not in your league. But despite their skills they're unemployable because outfits don't like taking on staff who might be tempted to sell their secrets. It's as simple and as brutal as that. The spaceplane is the world's biggest capital commercial project. Hundreds of valuable patents are being registered every week. European universities are working flat out – their ideas the property of Sabre Industries because that's how the Euros work over there. Do you think they'll let a guy into that chain who's having thirty big ones sliced off his paycheck every month? Will they hell. Once the first check-docking order comes through, your ass will burn a groove between their plant and Charles de Gaulle Airport.'

Joe broke off. He was good – the poor sap was sweating diluted shit and looked utterly crushed. Joe felt sorry for the guy. No criminal this. Just a poor sap scoring bottom grades at running his life. The trap was yawning open.

Lesseps's voice was a whisper. 'Joe – even with a job, this last year has been ... I can't tell you what I've been through.'

Joe was tempted to make a cutting comment about the stupidity of guys who committed themselves to buying twin-

76

turbine light aircraft, but running the agency had taught him some diplomacy when dealing with clients. Besides, alienating this Lesseps didn't fit in with the plan that was now taking on a definite shape. Time to wind the trap open a little more.

He said non-committally: 'Maybe something could be fixed.'

Lesseps leaned forward, pleading almost. 'I'd be eternally in your debt.'

Joe pretended to think hard, aware of the renewed hope that had suddenly gripped the other man. 'I've got a lot of contacts in this business . . . Some big names.'

'You mean a job with someone else?'

'I wasn't thinking that . . .'

Pleading now. 'What then, Joe?'

Joe was tempted to put the idea to Lesseps right there and then but decided that he was cooking so nicely that another twenty-four hours' simmering wouldn't hurt. Besides, he needed time to arrange the encashment of an insurance bond. Tough on his grandchildren but what the hell – let them work for their money as he had done. This was for their future and the future of America. It was time to put his money to work. 'I can't promise anything, John. I'll have to make a few calls.' He produced a business card and scribbled on the back. 'That's my private address. Come and see me tomorrow evening at nine.'

Lesseps almost snatched the card out of Joe's fingers in his eagerness. 'I'll be there, Joe. Please do your best for me.'

The trap was open. Lesseps was in it, but the jaws had yet to be sprung.

'I'll try,' was Joe's curt reply.

A few moments later he was standing at his window, watching the pick-up reverse out of its parking slot.

The first step in the forging of a chrome-vanadium spanner to be dropped right in the heart of Sabre Industries had been taken.

13

The sun beat down on Darwin's Clarence Marina with unremitting ferocity. Christine had been working an hour in the drenching humidity to clean out the last of the oil drums that had been used to store sediment samples. She asked Gus to turn the deck hose on her and twisted her lithe body gratefully in the cooling stream, knowing that her T-shirt and panties were turning transparent and not giving a damn. Gus played the hose up and down her, allowing the jet of seawater to pluck revealingly at her panties. From aft came the sound of hammering as the Filipinos stowed the Darwin in its shipping and storage crate for air-freighting back to England. The two big cabinets had already left that morning, as had the twelve giant reels, each one containing 1,000 metres of the strange plastic hose. Even the satellite dish had been crated up.

An electric minicab bumped over the pseudo-cobbles of the fake nineteenth-century street-cum-quayside with its neat lines of phoney gaslights guarding equally neat lines of genuine money-spinning apartments. Alec paid the driver and raced nimbly up the *Ben Gunn*'s gangway, his hawklike features hard and drawn. Gus shut off the hose and Christine grabbed a towel.

'I've squared everything with the shipping agents, Mr Newton,' said Alec without preamble. 'They're coming for the Darwin this afternoon. I was hoping to strip it down but there won't be time now.' He saw the oil drums. 'Are they clean?'

'Spotless,' Christine replied, rubbing herself down.

'Dunno why you bother,' Gus commented. 'Bit of muck inside ain't gonna do much harm.'

'We might need them again,' said Alec. 'We don't want to risk contaminating samples.'

Gus felt in the hatband of his Akubra for the remains of a cheroot. 'You figure on chartering me again this year?'

'It's very likely, Mr Newton,' Alec replied. 'In about seven months' time, if we can get a new sediment sampler finished in time.'

'I'm booked for June.'

'July and August will be fine.'

'I'll want a deposit.'

'Don't you always. Okay – let's settle up now.'

The two men went below to Gus's cabin, leaving Christine to supervise the unloading of their personal luggage. She was looking forward to returning to England. The sooner she was behind her desk, the sooner she could get busy with facsimile machine and telephone to work on making solid contacts in Jakarta.

She was grimly determined to sabotage Shief before he screwed Triton Exploration and, more importantly to her, the people of Indonesia.

14

As soon as he had shaken hands with Alec and Christine and seen them off in their taxi, Gus returned to his stifling cabin. He switched the electric fan to full blast and sat at the chart table, contemplating the Memcorder's memory card and wondering what to do next. In a bulkhead pigeonhole in front of him stood a vacuum flask containing a litre of the strange muck that the couple had recovered from the Banda Trench. Getting hold of it had involved another nocturnal visit to the converted hold while they were asleep. He doubted that they would've given him some had he asked for it openly. They had been so damned possessive about the gunge. He reckoned that when the filthy stuff had gunked all over the *Ben Gunn*, their eagerness to help sluice down with the hoses was because they wanted to make sure that no one got hold of any.

He was convinced that he was sitting on sensitive information that was worth money. Big money. But to whom? The oil companies? Chances were that a big oil company was behind the Roses. How about his own government, even though he detested them? Anything to do with Indonesia would make them jumpy and maybe open a wallet. Trouble was that he didn't know any big shots in the government. He had an idea and took down a grubby five-year desk diary that contained names and addresses of clients. There was a city-suit government guy from Canberra who had chartered the *Ben Gunn* to take a scuba-diving party out to the Japanese submarine that had been found off Croker Island. The navy cutter that was going to be used had had engine trouble. What the hell was his name? He hunted through the pages, knowing that he'd recognise the name when he saw it. Maybe it was as long ago as three years? He searched back and there it was in sweat-smudged pencil: William please-call-me-Bill Honicker. A clean-shaven city type. He had been seasick most of the trip and complained endlessly about the *Ben Gunn's* lack of air-conditioning. But the guy knew his engineering and the problems of deep scuba diving.

No address but a direct-line Canberra telephone number. Yeah – he remembered now. The whole party had been government officials. They had always clammed up whenever Gus had gone near them but he had overheard enough snatches of conversation to catch on that this Honicker was a big wheel. Once the party had discovered that there wasn't a trace of Japanese human remains in the sub that might cause problems with the Japanese government, the interim war-grave ban had been lifted and the thing was open to any scuba diver prepared to risk narcosis and oxygen poisoning by diving to a hundred metres on compressed air. By the time the Darwin authorities had discovered that the sub had been involved in the Japanese bombing raid that devastated the town in 1942 – a radio beacon had been the theory – it had been stripped by souvenir hunters and wasn't worth raising.

Gus called the Canberra number and asked to speak to William Honicker.

'I'll check if we have anyone of that name,' said the girl.

Gus recalled that he had had this hassle before. 'Mr Honicker will remember me. Gus Newton – owner of the *Ben Gunn*. He chartered my schooner a couple of years back out of Darwin. You got my number on your screen?'

'I have indeed, Mr Newton.'

'Well you give Mr Honicker a message from me. Tell him that I've just finished a deep-water charter and that I may have found something a helluva lot more important than a Japanese submarine. You tell him that, honey. Okay?'

'If we have anyone of that name, I will see that he receives your message,' said the girl frostily.

Gus remained deep in thought after the channel had been cleared, wondering if he ought to turn the problem over to the local police. The trouble was that the Poms had done nothing illegal. If anything, he had acted illegally in video-ing their papers and equipment. There were several bastards on Darwin's force who'd think all their birthdays had arrived together if they could pin something on Gus. He decided to leave it twenty-four hours. If he heard nothing from this Honicker guy in Canberra he'd look up his home number. And if that failed . . . Well – what the hell – he'd done his best to make himself a few extra bucks.

The answer came quicker than he anticipated: four hours later when he was inspecting a cracked liferaft buoyancy chamber and wondering if a coating of resin would fool the licensing inspectors. He took the call in his cabin.

'Mr Newton. You called this office about a deep-water find. Would you care to enlarge please?'

The voice was too young to be Honicker. 'Would you care to tell me who you are?' Gus countered.

'I will see that your report is routed through to the appropriate department,' said the voice smoothly.

'Why can't I speak to Mr Honicker?'

'An appropriate official is listening to this conversation at the moment, Mr Newton. I assure you—' His patronising tone annoyed Gus. That was a good enough reason for him to clear the line.

He waited ten minutes. The phone warbled. He picked up

the handset and recognised Honicker's friendly voice immediately.

'Hi there, Gus. Bill Honicker. How are you doing up there?'

'Scratching a living despite the taxes you bastards are laying on me,' Gus growled, resenting the guy's familiarity.

Honicker laughed easily. 'If that's the problem, you're through to the wrong department, Gus.'

'What department *am* I through to?'

'Are you on a ship-to-shore?'

'Digital,' Gus replied, guessing that Honicker would be worried about their conversation being picked up by scanners had he been using the analogue ship-to-shore radio-telephone.

'Fine. So what's all this about a discovery, Gus?'

'If it's important, there'll be an invoice for my time.'

The good humour faded from Honicker's voice. 'Let's hear what you've got to say first.'

Gus talked for five minutes. Honicker interrupted him when he described how he had made a video recording of the equipment and the papers in the Darwin's control room.

'Hold on, Gus. Is this recording on a standard memory card?'

'Sure. About five minutes.'

'Does your phone have a video reader?'

'Sure. The only way to get decent movies these days with you bastards censoring everything.'

'Do me a dump.'

'I reckon that'd be worth a thousand bucks,' said Gus, knowing that he was pushing his luck.

'You do me a dump and we'll decide what it's worth.'

Gus slipped the video memory card into the telephone's card reader. 'I'll send you the first sixty seconds. Shows the shit flying all over the place. Ready when you are, Mr Honicker.'

'Standing by.'

The tones told Gus when both ends of the line were in sync and the data transmission had started. He talked for another ten minutes while the video recording was multi-

82

plexed and sent on the same channel. The slight loss of audio quality that the transmission caused lasted less than ten seconds. He answered Honicker's searching questions as best he could.

'Sure. They had a constant link with whoever was paying them. Had one of those little helicopter camera things buzzing around them all the time.'

'A Hovercam?'

'That's it. Expensive, I guess.'

'Very,' Honicker agreed. Nothing in his tone betrayed what he was thinking but Gus fancied he could smell the tension when he described the two big pieces of equipment that the Roses had been using.

'And you've got a sample of this sediment?'

'About a litre. They sure were anxious to clean up.'

'Processed or unprocessed?'

'Unprocessed. Just as it came off the ocean floor.'

'And the stuff came gushing up the hose to the surface?'

'Saw it with my own eyes. You will too.'

'You logged the position?'

'Sure.'

'Which is?'

'Another thousand bucks. Let's say Indonesia way.'

Honicker changed tack. 'Who else knows about this? What about your crew?'

This time Gus didn't need a sixth sense – there was an unmistakable note of urgency in Honicker's voice. 'Only my crew,' he answered. 'But they just think it's a seabed sampling charter. The Poms have used us before. I can tell my boys to keep their mouths shut.'

'Best not to draw attention,' said Honicker. 'Don't say anything to them. Okay, Gus. We'll take a look at the video recording and come back to you.'

'A thousand for the full recording,' Gus reminded him before the line went dead.

He cracked open a can of beer and waited for it to chill. He didn't really expect that any money would be forthcoming as a result of the information he had supplied. He

grinned to himself. It was just that he was a grasping oppor-
tunist. Condensation formed on the outside of the can as the
chemical reaction forced it to surrender its heat. He sipped
slowly, wondering what they would make of his video
recording in the corridors of power.

What Gus didn't know was that serendipity had played a
major hand when he had plucked William Honicker's name
from his diary. Honicker had moved on since the days of the
Japanese submarine. The engineer turned civil servant was
the industrial consultant on the prime minister's secret
advisory group: SETAC – an acronym for Serious External
Threats Analysis Committee.

SETAC's number one target was Indonesia.

Had Gus been aware of the consternation his one minute
of video recording was causing at that very moment, as
Honicker and a colleague played it in a Canberra office, its
price would have been more than a thousand dollars.

A lot more.

15

Lesseps turned his attention from the *Spruce Goose*'s hull
and picked up a model marine steam engine. It was perfect
right down to the non-slip embossing on the catwalks
around the double-action cylinders. Its polished brass fly-
wheel shone like gold under the workshop's fluorescent
lights. 'This is nice turning, Joe,' he said admiringly.

Joe jabbed a thumb at an old Southbend lathe. 'I like to
keep my hand in.' He watched his guest carefully as the
French-Canadian looked around the workshop. He could
almost see the unasked questions crawling up and down the
poor guy's throat as he made small talk.

'A mill, a jig-borer, a gear-cutter. You're well set up, Joe.
This Perrin must've cost several thousand.'

'Five-fifty in an auction when Tacoma Industries went
under.'

'A good company.'

'Two hundred and forty-nine skilled men and women thrown on the street,' said Joe evenly. 'Over a hundred on our books still without jobs. Guess they'd be unemployable now even if jobs did materialise.' His expression blackened with rage as he stared at the Perrin jig-borer. Lesseps thought he saw a hint of insanity in his enraged eyes. 'That machine used make parts for airplanes. Now look at it – sitting in a old man's workshop, not earning its keep.' He was silent for a moment and the hatred became sorrow. 'They'll all go in the end.'

'What will, Joe?'

'The plants. Renton, Everett, Kent. The skills are leaking away. Seattle will become a lumber town again unless something is done. Boeing was a lumber company once. That's how it started, that's how it'll end.'

Lesseps looked at the craggy face. 'You're being a pessimist, Joe.'

'You think so? The industry that Bill Boeing built in his lifetime because he didn't like the family's lumber business could be gone in five years. It's easy to get out of something – god-damned impossible to get back in again. Talents like you – once they leave Seattle, will they want to come back?'

Lesseps saw the opening and grabbed it. 'But will I be leaving Seattle, Joe?'

'Sure you will. You want the job, don't you?'

'Yes – but after what you said . . .'.

'Your debts can be taken care of if you're sensible,' said Joe abruptly.

Lesseps stared. 'How?'

Joe picked up a micrometer and cleaned it carefully. A mechanical micrometer – he disliked the electronic gizmos. 'I know some big noises in this business – people right at the top who would be interested in monthly reports on Sabre Industries. Technical reports. Real hard information.'

Lesseps swallowed. 'In return for what, Joe?'

'In return for a wipe-out of the half-million you owe and maybe some more after that.' He looked up in time to catch the sudden flash of greed in Lesseps's eyes. 'You'd be starting clean at Sabre Industries. Nothing docked off your paychecks.'

'Expensive industrial espionage,' Lesseps observed.

Joe shrugged and laid the micrometer carefully in its case. 'The going price. You'd be the right man in the right place at the right time.' He added that the information was owing to America because America had helped out by handing over so much work on the SOFT.

There was a long pause before Lesseps replied. 'Seven hundred and fifty thousand up front,' he said.

'Forget it,' was Joe's brusque reply. A quick glance at his visitor was rewarded by his catching a flash of panic.

'Six-fifty.'

'I said, forget it.'

'But—'

'You're a fool, John. A greedy fool. Half a million puts you in the clear in a new, well-paid job. Six months of shoulder to the wheel and maybe you'd be able to buy a small airplane.' If that didn't spring the trap, nothing would. He started rounding up the twist drills on the bench and placing them in their stand.

'Okay,' said Lesseps hoarsely.

Snap! Gottcha . . .

'There're a few things you'll have to watch for your own protection,' said Joe casually. 'Don't send nothing from France. I've been warned that their security services are hot. Don't use e-mail or any network. Don't use computers. Take the train to England once a month and post me a hand-written report from there. Ordinary letters don't get logged.'

After a few minutes discussing details the two men shook hands and Lesseps left.

Joe stared at the *Spruce Goose*, admiring the fine lines of the flying boat's graceful hull. Getting hold of the raw material for his spanner had been easy, if expensive. Moulding it into shape would take a little longer.

16

Luckily the snail mail arrived late which meant that Jez, usually first home when he wasn't playing truant from school, was able to intercept it. He hotfooted upstairs to the security of his bedroom clutching the familiar blue envelope from Sabre Industries' London PR office. He loved letters – real letters with embossed company logos and the names of directors and lists of awards. E-mails were deadly boring. People collected letters now. He placed the envelope reverently on his dressing table and stared at it, his heart thumping. They would've said no. A personal letter of regret from the manager rather than the usual e-mail message that would be awaiting Jez when he switched on his computer. To open the letter would merely confirm the agony. Eventually he nerved himself to slit the envelope open. The words on the blue headed notepaper jumped off the page:

Dear Mr Moreton,
Thank you for your application for a ticket to attend the roll-out of Sabre 005 at St Omer next June. Normally visitors tickets for roll-outs are sold only to the press and families of employees. However, in view of your long and continuing interest in the Sabre programme, a ticket for the roll-out will be sent to you upon receipt within ten days of the amount shown on the enclosed invoice.

Jez looked at the amount in dismay. That and the Eurostar rail fare would leave his savings account in a sorry state.

In ruins, his voice corrected.

God – Sabre Industries were a tight outfit. They gave nothing away. Even the public tours of the complex were charged for. Jez's first visit to St Omer had been a school trip when he was eleven. It was that visit that had fired his burning enthusiasm for space and the spaceplane, and had led to his father complaining on numerous occasions since then that the outing had been the worst investment in his son's education that he had ever made.

Since that day Jez had learned the hard way just how cost-conscious a big organisation could be. It had taken several pleading e-mail bombs from him before Sabre unbent and put him on their distribution list for free reports and press releases.

There was another problem. Hitherto he had never told Sabre Industries his age. So how was he to pay for the ticket? His junior credit card worked only with emergency purchases. Turning up at their London office with a bag of money would be a bit of a giveaway, as would sending them a postal order. They'd realise that they had been conned by a kid and would promptly expunge his deceitful name from their mailing list.

He checked the date of the roll-out. Oh, bugger – a schoolday. That would mean having to stay well hidden in the crowd. To venture near the Sabre would risk being picked up by those damned long lenses that the TV news crews used, or their inquisitive Hovercams. The event was certain to be on TV. 005 would be in British Airways livery – the first spaceplane to carry fare-paying passengers when it had completed its pre-delivery trials. Jez shivered at the consequences of being caught playing truant again. But that wasn't the immediate problem. First of all he had to get this money to Sabre Industries for the roll-out ticket.

Just looking at the letter gave him an idea.

He went downstairs to his father's den and rummaged in a stationery drawer. The blank paper he found wasn't the right weight but the colour was a good enough match. He waited for his father's photocopier to warm up, while listening carefully for his mother's car turning into the drive. It was a simple matter to photocopy the company's heading on to a blank sheet of a blue paper. He made several copies to be on the safe side and returned to his bedroom just as his mother arrived home.

The rest of the operation was completed on his own computer and printer. He finished the work just as his mother called him down to dinner. The last stage was more a case of careful timing than careful typing.

He entered the den that evening when he knew his father would be enjoying a smoke and a read. Jack Moreton loathed television.

'Dad. Would you do me a big favour please?'

'If I can.' Jack Moreton was a kindly man. Despite their frequent rows, Jez was fond of him. He held out the envelope containing the forged letter.

'It's from Sabre Industries, Dad. They're selling off some PR models of the spaceplane. I said I'd like to buy one.'

'But you've already got several models of the damned thing.'

'But this is special, Dad.' There was pleading in Jez's voice and eyes.

Jack groaned. 'How big?'

'That's not the problem,' said Jez quickly to forestall objections. 'I need you to write a cheque for them and I'll give you the money. If I send them a postal order they rumble my age and stop sending me press releases.'

His father grinned at that. He took the letter and read it. 'Good God, Jez – what's it covered with? Gold leaf?'

'I don't know.'

'You could buy a woman with this.' He chuckled. 'You know, you might have to one day. The way you're going about your life, you're never going to meet girls in the ordinary way. When I was your age I was lusting after everything in skirts.'

Jez did plenty of lusting but he kept it to himself. It had become his father's favourite theme of late. His second favourite theme was the apparent failure of Jez's hormone factory, assuming he had one, to spring into life and stimulate some growth. Jez remained silent. His heart gave a surge when his father produced his cheque-book and wrote out a cheque.

'Thanks, Dad, that's great,' Jez blurted, taking the cheque. 'I'll get the money out of my account on Saturday.'

'No you won't. You leave it in there. Look upon that as an early birthday present, and not a word to your mother.'

Jez thanked him profusely and shot up to his bedroom, almost hugging himself in delight. In any other circumstances he would have felt guilty about deceiving his father, but not where the Sabre spaceplane was concerned.

17

Paul Santos was never one to thump the table at a meeting, but there were times when those who had to deal with him wished that he were a little more demonstrative and a little less intransigent. When Paul refused to budge on a point his customary charm disappeared, his French bloody-mindedness surfaced and he could be as unyielding as the Arc de Triomphe.

'No,' he repeated.

Sir Andrew Hobson, chairman of British Airways, was always ill at ease when having to deal with this disconcerting Frenchman who spoke English as though he had been to Sandhurst. He looked to his colleagues for support, but they studiously avoided his gaze. It was their way of telling him that he had picked this confrontation with Paul Santos and he could pull his own chestnuts out of the fire. Outside the office, London traffic went about its droning bustle.

'Mr Santos, it is customary for the passengers on an inaugural service's first flight to be specially invited. Heads of the big travel companies; tour operator chiefs. People who are important to the future success of the Sabre.'

Paul shook his head. 'The people who are important to the success of the Sabre, Sir Andrew, are the bourgeoisie – the millions of ordinary men and women who will choose to fly in it over the next two decades. Not a handful of worthies and members of the aristocracy. I have said all along that I do not wish the Sabre to become a plush conveyance for privileged merchant princes as happened with Concorde.'

Hobson grunted dismissively. 'There was no choice with Concorde, Mr Santos. Air France and BA had to operate within a restrictive framework of international air fare agreements.'

'Which, thankfully, no longer exist,' Paul pointed out.

Hobson nodded. 'True. But whatever happens, all Sabre operators will have to offer a one-class first-class service. We've agreed that.'

'That I have accepted,' Paul replied. 'But for the inaugural service I must insist on the appropriate contract clause being adhered to.'

Hobson's eyebrows signalled a message across the table to David Morgan, his recently appointed manager of space-flight operations: what contract clause?

Paul saw the gesture and interpreted it correctly. 'I'm referring to the clause that says the inaugural flight shall consist wholly of fare-paying passengers.'

Hobson shrugged. He disliked this sort of lawyer-mentality nit-picking. 'All that means is that *we'll* be paying their fares. So what?'

Paul was unperturbed by the other man's hostility. 'The French and English contracts have identical meanings, Sir Andrew. Fare-paying passengers means that each passenger pays his or her own fare at the normal rate for a first-class London–Sydney flight. This is something that I have insisted on as part of the loan contract. It is not an unreasonable clause, bearing in mind that you and Air France have yet to place definite orders.' He smiled, his charm breaking through. 'Sabre Industries does what it's good at – flying VIPs around on free trips to sell the Sabre. And you do what you're good at, which is selling seats. You'll have to forgive me, Sir Andrew, but I've given way on so many issues lately. For example, much against my instinct and wishes, the Sabre's cabin is going to look like the interior of a school bus. Therefore please understand if I refuse to give way on this. It is very important to me.'

The chairman of the world's favourite airline wasn't going to give in that easily. 'But this is ridiculous! So what do we

91

do? We advertise the flight and you know what will happen? We'll be flooded with people wanting to buy tickets. Our agents and offices will be inundated with needless and expensive work! For every seat we'll have to cope with a thousand applications!'

'More like ten thousand,' said Morgan, and received a baleful glare as a reward for his observation.

'That would be excellent,' said Paul. 'With a little showmanship, you could turn the problem to your advantage. Hold a big gala draw for the seats. Sell the rights to a TV company. You'd get more publicity that way, and you'd be earning revenue from day one.' He smiled and glanced at his watch. 'You must forgive me, gentlemen, but I have a meeting at St Omer in three hours. Thank you for your patience and hospitality.' He shook hands warmly all round and left.

'Damned socialist frog telling me how to run my business,' Hobson grumbled.

'He's right,' said David Morgan unhelpfully.

The chairman glowered at his subordinate. 'I'm considering changing my policy on yes-men and surrounding myself with them. I'd get lousy decision making, but it would do my ego a power of good. Right about what?'

'Concorde *did* become a plush conveyance for wealthy merchant princes.'

Hobson passed a photograph across the conference table that showed a computer-generated model of the Sabre's spartan, redesigned cabin. 'Tell me what's plush about that,' he invited.

18

Gus's stuffy, claustrophobic cabin on the *Ben Gunn* was not the best place for a conference at any time, and definitely not when the temperature was 36 Celsius. But it suited Gus. His visitor was sweating in more ways than one. He liked that.

Bill Honicker ran his finger around the inside of his collar and wished he'd thought to pack some casual clothing before jumping on the flight to Darwin. He was a tall, fair-haired, forty-year-old career scientific civil servant of Germanic stock, used to an air-conditioned office, an air-conditioned car, an air-conditioned home and smart, house-trained girl-friends – all of which suited his fastidious habits. Sitting arguing with Gus in this oven was close to his idea of hell. And this uncouth, money-grubbing bastard hadn't even offered him a drink. There was an untouched vacuum flask between them on the chart table – probably brimming with chilled drink. He decided to play tough.

'Well, if you won't give your boat's position when—'

'I didn't say I wouldn't, Mr Honicker,' said Gus mildly. 'For five thousand bucks you can have everything. The sample, the position. The full video recording. You get the works.' He grinned slyly. 'And if you hadn't been so fucking slow off the mark, you could have got to those Poms and their sampling gear before they skipped out of the country.'

Honicker said nothing. The prime minister had made a similar comment when he had been briefed that morning. Gus lit a cheroot, filling the cabin with smoke, adding to Honicker's discomfort. The civil servant believed that to be within ten kilometres of anyone smoking was courting imminent death. An irrational view for a rational man like William Honicker, but probably not in the case of Gus's cheroots.

'Now, Mr Honicker, you're not going to tell me that five is going to break the bank, are you? All that heavy welfare that's thrown at immigrants.'

Honicker was tempted to throw the vacuum flask at his host. 'You're being unreasonable, Gus. We could get a court order to impound your boat, your log, everything.' He realised that he had played a dud card the moment he finished speaking; the damned heat was warping his judgement.

Gus leaned back and laughed. 'Sure you could. Take a few days. And what do you reckon you'd find? A blank video card. Log pages missing. Sample accidentally tipped over the side.' His face darkened. 'And don't you go trying patriotism on me, Mr Honicker. I know those Poms are up to something big because there's big money behind them now. And I'm still an Aussie through and through. It's not me that's letting wogs swarm in by the million, but I'm one of the millions of Aussies having to find these new taxes you bastards have dreamed up to pay their welfare.'

'Okay – five,' said Honicker tiredly, not wanting a political argument with this racist cretin, but wanting out of this cabin, out of the cigar smoke and out of Darwin. A stinking hole in his opinion, long overdue for another cyclone like 1974.

'Not a cent less,' Gus stressed.

The civil servant dropped the banknotes on the table one by one. Gus scooped them up and stuffed them casually in his shirt pocket.

'The sediment sample first please, Gus.'

Gus grinned and pushed the vacuum flask across the table. 'Have a drink, Mr Honicker.'

19

The crowded visitors' walkway above the construction shed floor provided the best view of 005. The tour guide urged his charges along but many wanted to stop and stare at the stunning, end-on view of the spaceplane's needle-like nose that seemed poised to launch itself straight at them. Those who had bought photographic licences at the beginning of their tour were allowed a few seconds to point their cameras at the spaceplane before being requested to move on. The guide ignored the couple wearing staff security badges who were leaning on the rail.

Lesseps was overwhelmed. '*Magnifique*,' he breathed, his professionalism forgotten. 'It looks so . . . so . . .' He was lost for words. He loved all aircraft but never had one gripped his imagination at first sighting to this extent. None of the sequences he had seen on TV had conveyed the awesome power and dynamism locked into the graceful curves of this beautiful creation.

'Right?' Claudia Picquet prompted.

'It's the best word,' Lesseps agreed. He was uneasy with his new boss. She had a penetrating gaze that seemed to strip away his secrets, and she wore a severe business skirt, short enough to accentuate her good legs, and a jacket that looked well on her but reminded him of a schoolteacher who had once caught him masturbating.

She nodded sagely. 'Of course, it doesn't have be so streamlined. It travels quite slowly in the lower atmosphere. When you call up the original designs you'll see that it was going to be very chunky, rather like the American SOFT air-frame. But Mr Santos insisted that it should look like this. He said he wanted a bird to sell to the public, not a brick.'

Lesseps laughed. 'A wise man.'

'A great man,' the woman replied.

A second party of tourists made their way past the couple.

'It's making money before it goes into service,' Lesseps observed. 004 was standing outside on the apron. He had been surprised at the length of the queue of those prepared to pay to walk through it.

'Exploitation makes a valuable contribution to the running costs of this complex,' Claudia replied. 'EuroDisney offers make-believe – we offer reality.'

The French-Canadian contemplated the Sabre in silence. This was the finale to his half-day orientation tour of the complex. He had been shown everything: the shaping shops, engine testing facilities, workshops, the 001 mock-up, the huge runway, and had even spent thirty minutes in the simulator watching an Air France flight-deck crew coping with an engine close-down and an emergency landing. And now this. Apart from the Sabre itself and the colossal shapers, there was nothing new here. It was all much the same as Seattle but on a very much smaller scale, and without the usual facilities such as wind tunnels because the research was either carried out by universities or using computer modelling. Giant wind tunnels were a legacy of the 'suck-it-

95

and-see' approach to research; there was little of that at Sabre Industries. Also the conveyor-belt tourist facilities were better organised. But there was one fundamental difference here that shone in the faces of everyone he had been introduced to that morning. Three things in fact: dedication, loyalty and pride.

There had been none of that at his last employers. There had been once, according to an old-timer he had chatted to under Seattle's Space Needle, but it had all gone now. And yet those still in employment in Seattle had more secure jobs than these people. There would always be a demand for fighters and bombers, whereas the entire Sabre project was balanced on an economic knife-edge with no military safety net. The overhead monitors that hung everywhere like Damoclean swords bore the same message that said it all:

TARGET FOR THIS YEAR: 25. SOLD SO FAR: 18.

Dedication . . . Loyalty . . . Pride . . .

Lesseps reflected wryly that it could be the subject of his first report to Joe. The sort of information that could be obtained by flying to France and shelling out $200 for a tour of Sabre Industries. Best not – Joe wanted real information.

His new boss touched his arm. 'I will now show you your work station.'

They returned to the corridor and took a golf cart to the documentation department. High screens around the various terminals created a feeling of isolation so that each employee felt alone. Lesseps' work station was near a window with a commanding view of the main runway. Claudia was showing him a map of the room's layout that bore the names of his new colleagues and their functions, but his attention had been captured by a row of twenty or so light aircraft in a neat line near a huddle of buildings against the far perimeter fence. One of the aircraft stood out from the rest: a bright yellow Mistral – a racy two-seater jet – waiting for its owner like a loyal woman.

'Who do those aircraft belong to?' he asked.

'We have a flying club and some are owned by senior employees.'

'No executive aircraft?' Lesseps asked.

'None.'

'How does the boss cat get around?'

She stared hard at him. 'If an executive aircraft is needed, Mr Santos charters one,' she said huffily, clearly resenting her hero being referred to in this fashion. 'Mr Santos does not believe in unnecessary expense. You said that you were interested in the living accommodation available.'

Twenty minutes later Claudia Picquet was watching Lesseps perform the mandatory experimental bounces on the bed.

'Well used,' he remarked.

'We work hard and play hard,' said Claudia drily.

Lesseps chuckled politely and avoided her secret-gleaning gaze. It was not easy to imagine her 'playing hard'. He rose from the bed and looked out of the window. There were at least 200 of the tiny prefabricated terraced apartments inside the northern perimeter fence. The blocks were grouped around a small square that contained the only remaining pear trees of what had once been two thousand hectares of orchards. A group of employees, well-wrapped against the biting north wind, were playing boules on a patch of grass outside the staff restaurant. He opened the window and craned his neck when he heard a light aircraft. The ancient single-seater Turbulent rocked in the wind as it began its final approach to the 4000-metre runway of which it would need less than a hundred metres. A gnat landing on a motorway.

'Will it be possible for me to join the flying club?' he asked.

Claudia made a note on her clipboard. 'Of course. I do not have the scale of charges for membership but I will see that you receive the application forms. But do you not think a decision on your accommodation is more important?'

What could be more important than flying? thought Lesseps. He had poured over some flight magazines in his hotel room the night before and had already decided on the aircraft he was going to buy. He moved into the living-room.

'It's small,' he complained.

Claudia shrugged. 'It has everything. Also it is the only one left. Most new employees occupy them when they start. But if you leave early and rent somewhere in the town, you will still have to pay the rent until the end of your lease period.'

Lesseps had seen the terms. Sabre Industries charged a market rent for their apartments. There was no such thing as special rates or discounts for their employees. He nodded. 'Okay. I'll take it.'

'You will have to sign these papers.'

Lesseps scrawled his signature on her clipboard documents.

'The electricity meter is read once a month. Also, if you keep a car on the complex, there is a small additional charge.'

Lesseps laughed and reverted to English. 'Christ – you run a tight ship.'

Claudia's English was good but she lacked the colloquial skills that came from living many years in an English-speaking country. 'It is not permitted for any employee to be drunk on the premises,' she said primly. 'You may collect your baggage from my car and move in now. I will see you at your work station at 16:30.'

'You mean I have to start work today?'

She paused at the door and gave him a hard, disconcerting stare. 'But of course, Mr Lesseps. You are being paid from today.'

As Lesseps unpacked, he reflected that working for Sabre Industries was going to take some getting used to. He got bored with hanging clothes in the tiny built-in wardrobes and sprawled on the bed with the aviation magazines, day-dreaming about his next aircraft: a sexy little bright-yellow Mistral.

20

Paul Santos sat alone in his office, drumming his fingers on his desk and attempting to be kind to his heart by trying not to worry, but it was proving impossible.

The noon deadline for the final payment on several million part-paid ordinary shares had passed an hour ago, but the flow of figures coming in from the merchant banks across Europe who were handling this last stage of the flotation was agonisingly slow. The tension was bad for Paul's blood pressure. Maybe he should've listened to the wise counsels on his board and hired a financial director to shoulder the responsibility. No – that wouldn't work. Even if he had the best financial whizzkid on the payroll, he'd still be sitting in his office, staring at his wall screen and fretting. Besides, Sophia's acumen was worth ten financial directors.

Billy Allison's lugrubious face reappeared in one of the screen's windows. Had the London banker been a stock-broker, his gloom and doom expression would be enough for any big investor who didn't know him to take an immediate dive out of a twentieth-floor window without waiting for him to speak.

'Hanson are in,' the banker announced sorrowfully. 'Prudential; MAM; Argent; Dune Holdings.' He went on to intone the names of a further forty major UK investors, making the list sound like the roll-call of the dead after a disaster.

Paul checked his memopad and saw that all the major UK investors had come across. Why couldn't Allison have said so at the beginning instead of ploughing relentlessly through the list?

'That's excellent news, Billy,' said Paul trying to sound enthusiastic. It was expected news. It was most unlikely that the big funds would forfeit their holdings. If they had wanted to dump their part-paid shares they would have leaked them on to the London stock exchange over the last few weeks in the run-up to the deadline. But the part-paid price had been creeping steadily up, indicating that no one had been doing any serious unloading and that demand for stock was staying ahead of supply. The sudden surge after the surprise December flight to Australia had led to a dip due to profit taking the following week, but the overall trend had remained solidly upward.

But the matter close to Paul's socialist heart were the millions of ordinary men and women whose holdings across Europe in Sabre Industries averaged thirty per cent of the issued share capital. Their continuing support was vital and they were the ones most likely to baulk at this call if they thought they were throwing good money after bad.

'How about the private investors?' Paul ventured.

The London banker's face lengthened. As far as he was concerned private investors were the ultimate in low forms of life and spelt instability in the market-place.

'Ninety-one per cent so far, and late payers are still trickling in.'

It was too early in the afternoon for Paul to feel elated. He thanked Allison and took a call from Paris, followed by one from Frankfurt. The picture was much the same as London – confidence was holding and the money was coming in. Milan was a disappointment: an eighty per cent take-up and the fully paid stock was taking a hammering. Paul wasn't unduly worried; experience had taught him that the volatile nature of trading on the Milan stock exchange rarely had a long-term effect on the other European markets.

The long afternoon wore on. Paul remained hunched at his desk in his darkened office, intent on the screen, not noticing Sophia's endless cups of coffee that he drained in single swallows lest he missed anything. His eyes started to smart from the concentration of reading the figures that scrolled along the bottom of the screen. Although his memopad was capturing everything and distilling the information into a few lines on a graph, he largely ignored it, preferring to wrestle with the raw data as it came in.

And then the eastern market reports started.

Prague: 70 per cent.

Warsaw: 75 per cent.

Budapest: 60 per cent. Rather than stump up, Hungary's leading investment house had lost its nerve and tried to sell their entire holding an hour before the deadline. They had unloaded forty per cent, knocking the price badly, and had so far defaulted on the balance.

By 5.00 p.m., with one report still to come, Paul was engulfed in a black cloud of despair.

And there it was on the screen:

Moscow: 65 per cent.

His last hope dashed.

He told Sophia that he was taking calls and sat staring at the plunging lines on his memopad, trying mentally to convert the percentages into hard cash because he had forgotten the software commands. He recalled them after a few moments but too late to prevent the flood of self-doubts. They came muscling in like a gang of thugs terrorising a respectable bar. How could someone who couldn't even remember a few simple voice commands be considered capable of running a project such as the Sabre? His chief designer had come perilously close to throwing down a direct challenge to his leadership because it had been found wanting. And now his insistence on a public rights issue across Europe was going to lead to a severe cash shortfall.

The screen glitched. The heavy-jowled face that appeared belonged to the last person Paul wanted to talk to at that moment. But Heinrich Kluge was important – Sophia was right to have put him straight through. The genial president of the European Central Enterprise Bank in Frankfurt was a valued confidant and had proved himself a good friend of the spaceplane. His remarkably tough hide had taken a lot of sniping from his political enemies over his warm support for the project. He had gone up in Paul's estimation when he declined to go on the VIP passenger flight, saying that the seat should not go to one of the converted.

'Hallo, Harry,' said Paul tiredly in English because it was a language they had in common. 'I take it you've been following the débâcle?'

The German chuckled richly. 'That's not a word I would use. Setback . . . perhaps.'

'A one point six billion shortfall,' Paul muttered. 'That's what I call a débâcle.'

'Nearer two billion,' the banker observed.

'Thanks.'

'It's your pride that has been hurt, Paul – not the Sabre. You were warned of the risks of going to market but you have this idealistic dream of the citizens of Europe having a stake in the spaceplane. But private citizens are greedy, just like the big institutions. They want a quick profit. And with only eighteen orders in the bag, they no longer see that quick profit being so quick.'

'Your words are a great comfort to me in my hour of need, Harry.' Paul's words were flat, without rancour.

The German banker grinned wolfishly. 'You still have your big preferential shareholders: British Aerospace, Thomson, Philips—'

'I'm not risking a call on them,' said Paul bluntly. 'That would see the value of private investors' stock go down, as well as a dilution.'

Heinrich sighed. 'You must forgive me for saying this to you, Paul, but if I don't, no one else will dare to do so. You are not a victim of the markets – you are a victim of your outdated political views.'

Paul did not respond. His unspoken thought was that if the value of Sabre Industries stock went down, it would be easy for Heinrich's bank to acquire one per cent and so gain complete control. The ECEB hadn't been set up to control big concerns, but then neither had it been set up to risk so much money on one venture. They had poured money in for ten years, and now they were in the year when the forecasts had predicted that money should start coming in.

His anger welled up although he was careful not to show it. My God, how he loathed the stock markets. They always had been gambling dens, now they were much worse. The British short-term quick-profit disease had spread through-out Europe. The days when people invested in companies

102

because they liked them and their products, and looked to dividends for a secure income, were over. Shares in a company could go up one day on the strength of a good report, and plunge the next because the short-termist snouts in the trough sold out *en masse* to grab a quick profit. Even more insane were those prudent companies that built up cash reserves to fend off predators and saw the value of their shares go down when the snouts realised that there wouldn't be a nice boost to prices because there wouldn't be any take-over bids. On the other hand, the prices of badly run companies went zooming up when they were stalked. There was no stability – only money madness.

'I hear what you say, Harry,' said Paul at length. 'If I have to go to the preferential holders with rights issue proposals at the end of the year then I will do so.'

'Even that might not be enough if the orders stay at eighteen for that long,' said the banker seriously. 'How's TranAsia?'

'They'll be signing for their five tomorrow.'

'Leaving Commonwealth's ten. Any idea why they haven't signed up yet?'

Paul shook his head. 'I've no idea what Segal's game is. He's cancelled two meetings now.'

'You need his ten to put you well in the black, Paul.'

'You think I don't know that, Harry? For God's sake, I go to sleep and wake up with a giant "25" dangling before me. And my employees have to live with it every working minute.'

This time the German banker didn't smile. 'As I said, Paul, it's a setback – a serious one, maybe. But it isn't a disaster. You've got just enough funding in hand to see you through to December. Eleven months. Start next year with firm orders for twenty-five plus and your credit and future are secure.'

'December is when the scheduled services start,' Paul remarked, surprised that he felt little gratitude for the banker's bullish comments.

'If that goes well, with plenty of the positive publicity

you're so good at, it may be all that's needed to tip Segal into making a decision. And others will follow.'

'If that goes well,' was Paul's uncharacteristically pessimistic reply. As he cleared the line he realised that he was coming dangerously close to losing his nerve.

21

Christine was adamant. She squared up to Alec, her eyes blazing. 'I don't interfere in the way you run your workshop,' she declared, 'so you don't interfere in the way I run the office.'

Alec gave a sudden grin. 'But you do interfere. You're always telling me to look after the Shaeffer.'

'Because it cost a fortune!'

'There's no point in me looking at the Darwin until we've cleared this backlog of paperwork,' Alec reasoned. 'Two of us will clear it in a couple of days, otherwise it'll take you a week.'

'I can manage!' Christine snapped.

Concern at the work facing his wife had been Alec's first reaction when he and Christine had arrived back in England and surveyed the mountain of mail that was awaiting them. To save money, their home at Walton-on-Thames also served as Triton Exploration's office and workshop. It was a rambling nineteenth-century mansion overlooking the River Thames which they had purchased with Christine's money a year after their marriage. The converted stables served as a workshop and the servants quarters as the offices. Change of use consent had been obtained from the local authority, provided no external alternations were carried out.

Alec sat at a side desk and opened his laptop computer. Christine glared at him. 'Now what are you doing?'

'I promised Mr Shief that the first thing I would do was prepare a précis of the sediment analysis.'

'Bugger Shief,' said Christine succinctly. 'He's had a verbal report and all the instrumentation data. His minions can write it.' She went on to say that if the little wanker started grizzling, she would tell him to do something to himself which, were it physically possible, would guarantee that the oil chief could earn a respectable living doing a floor show in an Amsterdam night-club.

Alec laughed. Sometimes it was hard to believe that Christine was a product of Malvern College. Nevertheless her attitude to a major backer worried him.

'We don't need him,' Christine answered when he expressed his concern.

'But he's the only one who's been prepared to back us.'

'There'll be others when we start whispering in the right ears about our findings.'

Now Alec was really alarmed. 'The information isn't our property, Chris. Shief financed the expedition. There's a whole string of clauses in the contract—'

Christine's answer was to spin Alec's chair around and plonk herself on his lap. 'Do you know what I would like right now?' she said seductively, grinding her buttocks against his groin. 'Right this very minute?'

Had Alec been a romantic individual he would have returned his wife's nuzzling attention to his earlobe in kind. But he wasn't. Instead, he looked at the cheap cord carpeting and said that the floor wouldn't be very comfortable.

'I want a separation,' Christine announced.

'What?' Alec looked at her in astonishment.

She put her arms round his neck and pressed her breasts hard against his chest — tactics that guaranteed she would get her own way with her husband. 'I want you downstairs in your workshop doing what you're good at, while you leave me alone to deal with this mess — which is what I'm good at. If you don't, I shall invoke a few contract clauses of my own.'

'Such as?'

'Cold suppers and no nookie for a month.'

'You wouldn't?'

'Try me.'

'You're a cruel woman, Christine Rose.'

'A bitch is the word,' said Christine. She jumped up and bundled Alec from the office.

Safely alone, she sat at her terminal and logged on to the Net. Within minutes she was trying to make sense of the thousands of badly maintained sites run by the Indonesian government. To her dismay, the search menus were not properly cross-referenced and there seemed to be enormous duplications. Somewhere among the three million civil servants in a ramshackle collection of over thirty ministries, no doubt all insanely jealous of each other, was the one person who would be interested in what she had to say and with the authority to do something about it.

Finding him or her was going to take a long time and starting at the top might alert the wrong people. She had no doubt that Shief would have several influential Indonesian civil servants in his pay.

22

Triton Exploration's large, modern workshop was a shrine to Alec's remarkable inventiveness and industry, and his monumental untidiness. Breadboard working models of various versions of successive Darwin mechanisms were strewn everywhere. The workbenches lining the walls were broad but they fulfilled the adage about junk expanding to fill the space available for its storage. The worst area was the wood-machining end where Alec built full-size working mock-ups of his ideas. A wood-turning lathe protruded from a heap of sawdust like a desert artefact partly exposed by a sandstorm. The opposite end of the workshop was the drawing office. It consisted of a computer, an expensive plotter, a drawing-board and piles of grubby drawings. The exception to the pervading chaos was the workbench along the main wall where the Shaeffer laser lathe and mill stood underneath its dust cover. The area was spotless because the computer-controlled machine, capable of working to tolerances as close as a thousandth of a millimetre, represented a huge investment and Christine therefore insisted that it should be cosseted. She was right, of course. Triton's possession of the machine had brought in a considerable amount of subcontract work which had helped with the company's frequent cashflow problems, although Alec had always resented work which took him off his Darwin project. To comply with their insurance company's requirements to protect the machine, Alec and Christine had been obliged to have the entire workshop fitted with an expensive steel lining, and to install air-conditioning, internal security doors and an alarm system that a wandering stag beetle could trigger. Christine's view had always been that the drawings associated with Alec's Darwin patents were worth more than the Swiss machine and had willingly gone along with the expense.

Alec winched the Darwin's two-metre-long bullet-shaped bulk on to a servicing trolley and began dismantling. To minimise the risk of distortion, the many recessed tungsten bolts around the rim had to be slackened off half a turn at a time in the reverse order of tightening. The two halves of the shell separated easily. There was no internal damage. Had there been even a pinhole leak, water rushing under such pressure would have destroyed everything inside.

After another thirty minutes he had the pump and gearbox assembly on a cleared area of workbench. At no time did his impatience prompt him to take short cuts; his dismantling of the pump was meticulous. He even took photographs at the end of each stage. Two rotary solenoids had failed. Nothing to do with their working environment – just perverse mechanics. They had simply decided that they didn't want to be solenoids any more and had turned up their toes. He found the main damage without trouble: his beautifully machined jockey wheels which forced the sediment into the hose had been distorted by the enormous back-pressure surge when the sediment had unexpectedly gushed up the hose. The phenomenon had also led to stripped helical gears in the gearbox. He stared at the damaged components laid out on the bench. Instead of reflecting on the hours of work on the laser lathe that had gone into their manufacture, his fertile mind sought solutions. An automatic bypass was needed once the flow had started. He was one of those remarkable individuals who occurred once in every 10,000 of the populace: his brain worked intuitively so that he could submit likely solutions to thought experiments without the need for expensive manufacture and testing. He could 'see' mechanisms working and anticipate how they would fail or succeed. When called upon to explain his reasoning he was usually stumped for an answer, which was why he had had trouble earlier in his career getting his ideas accepted.

He mulled over the drawings of the pump, thinking through several modifications in his strange manner, discarding ideas that he sensed were not the answer. Eventually he settled on a solution – not with any great enthusiasm because it added considerably to the Darwin's size and weight. Weight was the bogeyman. He could not afford to make the Darwin excessively heavy, even when fully submerged, otherwise it would not be possible to use the Plastron tubing to raise and lower it. Having to add the huge weight of ten kilometres of steel cable would cripple the entire design concept.

It was past midnight when Christine entered the workshop, having deliberately not disturbed him until now. She found him slumped in front of his computer monitor, surrounded by sketches and sound asleep.

She picked up the drawings and looked through them. She was not an engineer but she knew enough about the Darwin, and the way her husband worked, to see that the problem had been licked.

23

The views of the harbour, the opera house and the botanical gardens were superb from the Fisherman's Restaurant in Sydney's Inter-Continental Hotel. The food was pretty good and the prices on the menu best described as having more sauce than most of the dishes. But Honicker's reason for choosing it for this meeting was the air-conditioning. It wasn't ordinary air-conditioning but, so it was rumoured, a private large-bore subterranean pipe laid at enormous expense that connected the hotel with Antarctica where a series of giant wind traps across the ice-cap ensured that a continuous blizzard blew into the hotel.

Honicker liked that. He liked the way his fingers didn't stick to the leather-bound menu when he returned it to the waiter, or the way his underwear stopped itching whenever he entered the hotel on his frequent missions to Sydney from his beloved, orderly Canberra. On the other hand, his guest was not so happy.

Professor Lionel Shawcross was a local. A hard-working, down-to-earth outdoor type with a deep-rooted dislike of fitted carpets and air-conditioning. He was also a noted marine biologist and a trusted government adviser with a reputation for keeping his mouth shut tighter than the clams he liked to prise off reefs. Right now he would rather be eating mushy peas and meat pies at Harry's Café near the dockyard, where he could smoke his pipe without receiving assassination threats from other diners.

'So what happened to the tasty brunette that used to hang on to your arm?' Shawcross asked.

'She used to leave the top off my toothpaste.'

Shawcross threw up his hands in mock horror. 'God – how you must've suffered.'

'And her underwear on the bathroom floor. She had to go.'

'You should've sent her round to me for retraining.'

'You have the report?' Honicker asked as soon as the waiter had withdrawn with their order.

Shawcross nodded and gestured to their elaborate surroundings. 'I hope all this isn't in lieu of my fee? Had I known we'd be eating here I would've brought a sweater.'

Honicker grinned. 'You're lucky they let you in wearing casuals.'

Shawcross felt in his jacket pocket and passed a two-page document to his host. 'That's the only copy, just as you said. I prepared it myself. No one else has seen it or knows what I've been up to.'

Honicker glanced quickly through the papers while Shawcross sipped an orange juice. The marine biologist was fifty-five and had spent too many years scuba diving, pushing his body to its limits. After a mild HA his doctor had told him to cut down on alcohol or women. Which was why he was sipping the orange stuff ... and still pushing his body to its limits.

'Hell, Lionel, I don't understand a word of this,' said Honicker, flicking the pages back and forth in the hope of finding a sentence that made sense.

'Biogenic sedimentation is a complex subject,' said Shawcross. 'I know bugger all about it myself. A lot of those big words I copied out of books.'

'Then why did you take on the job?'

'Because I've got a decent library in the uni and you haven't. Where the hell did that sample come from, Bill?'

'Classified information.'

'God preserve us from civil servants. How the hell can a sediment sample be classified, for Chrissake?'

'Because it is, Lionel. Trust me.'

'Never.'

Honicker grinned. He folded the report neatly and zipped it into his inside pocket. 'So *you* tell *me* where it came from.'

'A fucking deep trench. Over 8,000 metres at a guess. That was my first thought. It's Jurassic. 150 to 200 million years old. That's old material for sediment. Full of the usual crap with some more recent tests of pteropods and coccolithophorids. Try saying that during the soup course.' Shawcross paused and chewed thoughtfully on his lip. He leaned forward confidingly. 'I don't suppose you've ever heard of the Carbonate Compensation Depth?'

'It sounds like a lawyer's expression,' said Honicker carefully, not yet prepared to admit that he had seen the term on the papers that Gus Newton had recorded on the *Ben Gunn*. Another government adviser had been called upon to examine stills from the recording.

'It's a term used by oceanographers to indicate the depth at which the carbon content of organic material is leached out of sediments,' said Shawcross. 'Your sample shouldn't contain a hydrocarbon fraction – maybe a few parts per million. Nothing more . . .'

'But it does?' Honicker prompted.

Shawcross nodded. 'A helluva lot more. That's why I checked the age and fractions several times. I didn't believe the results I was getting. And I still don't.'

'So what is the content?' Honicker asked.

They stopped talking when the waiter arrived with their first course.

'Thirty per cent,' said Shawcross when they were alone again. 'It's crazy. It shouldn't be there, but it is. If I were in the government's shoes, I'd want to carry out a proper sonar survey of the area where that sediment came from. Get the size of the deposit pinned down.'

'Why do you say that?' Honicker asked indifferently, seeming to be more interested in his soup. Shawcross chuckled. 'You could do all sorts of things with it if you found a bright spark to come up with a way of pumping the stuff up in commercial quantities. Of course, ocean sediment hasn't been subjected to the geothermal cooking process of normal oilfield deposits, but that could carried out as part of the processing. The hydrocarbons are there.'

Honicker lowered his spoon and met Shawcross's gaze. 'What are you trying to tell me, Lionel? That it might be possible to refine the stuff into oil?'

The scientist chuckled at a private joke. He felt in his

pocket and gave Honicker a glass phial containing a clear, golden liquid. 'There's no *might* about it, Bill.'

24

Lesseps had to work so hard during his early days at Sabre Industries that he had little time to think about flying or the next aircraft that he intended to buy. Most of the work was catching up on the neglected bytework – Sabre's term for paperwork.

'I did warn you that the documentation is in a mess,' Claudia sympathised when he complained that it would need an army of clerks to sort out. 'But it is something you must do yourself. It will give you an insight into the way we do things here.'

Lesseps set to work, reluctantly at first, then with steadily increasing enthusiasm. By the third day he discovered, much to his surprise, that he was enjoying himself, despite the long hours. But what was getting to him was the atmosphere of the place. There was a heady sense of infectious urgency and nervous tension that was impossible to ignore. It was like being caught in the rush at a busy station when you weren't in a hurry. You were ensnared in the vibrant flow of energy and became a part of it.

There was little time for private life. He was working round the clock from eight until eight. He had never slogged so hard in his life, but there was the benefit of a three-day weekend if he put in the hours. He managed to book an hour's flying on his second Sunday, having had his application for membership of the Sabre Flying Club accepted. As expected, he hated flying the club aircraft. His emotions were even sharper than those of a motoring enthusiast towards a rented car. Unlike a car, which could only follow the preordained course of a road, an aircraft could move anywhere in three dimensions. It was an extension of the human body and a moving platform for the launch of those emotions which to Jean Pierre Lesseps were more important than sex. For him, flying was an unconscious escape from an emotionally impoverished childhood that had been dominated by poverty, a harsh, overbearing father, a fiercely possessive mother and a later failure with women. The desire to have his own aircraft had once again become a burning obsession that came to a head during his third week, when he learned that the little yellow Mistral that taunted him each day from his work station was for sale.

He turned from the flying club's notice board and tracked down the chief flying instructor to his usual spot propped against the bar with a group of cronies. The CFI was George Campion, who was also the club secretary.

'The Mistral?' he said in answer to Lesseps' inquiry. 'English guy owns it. Johnny Moore. He was posted to London a year ago and never gets a chance to use it. There's a flyshare group interested in making an offer but they need another two members. Shall I put your name down? I warn you, it won't be cheap, even split four ways.'

Lesseps promised to think it over. No wonder he had never seen the Mistral move from its parking spot. He left the clubhouse and spent thirty minutes admiring the aircraft. The swept-wing monoplane had speed written into every line.

That evening he checked the aircraft's registration and traced the owner. He was talking to him after two call diverts.

'Right now I'm in Cape Town on holiday,' said Johnny Moore. 'George Campion is handling the sale on a commission basis but I'm back in London next Saturday for two days. Any chance of getting over to discuss it?'

Lesseps thought fast. His first monthly report to Joe Yavanoski was due to be sent the following weekend. That would mean having to leave France to comply with Joe's instructions. He could easily combine the two tasks and arranged to meet the Mistral's owner at his London flat on the following Saturday.

He was unable to concentrate on his work the next day.

His gaze kept returning to the Mistral. She was standing there patiently – a mistress awaiting her new lover.

25

'Trouble,' said Christine from the office window, having heard the crunch of tyres on gravel.

Alec looked up from the estimates he was studying. 'What sort of trouble?'

'Chauffeur-driven Rolls-Royce trouble. Joshua Shief has decided to tackle us lions in our den. Hide those drawings.' She went down to greet the new arrival, her fixed smile concealing the concern she felt at this visit. Last week Shief had made an offer for a percentage of Triton Exploration which, to Alec's mortification because he saw it as a generous offer, she had rejected out of hand. Also she wondered if news of her many fruitless searches of Indonesian government Net sites had got back to the oil man. All such accesses were logged, but she doubted if anyone seriously monitored the many thousands of calls that were made each day to the Jakarta databases.

Alec had stuffed all the new drawings in a filing cabinet when Christine showed Shief into the office. He declined an offer of coffee. 'Forgive me, Christine, Alec. But I'm visiting Shell so I thought I'd drop by,' he said without preamble, refusing to surrender his camelhair overcoat to Christine. 'Congratulations on solving the problem with the Darwin.'

Alec looked puzzled. 'We haven't said that we've solved it.'

Shief's florid face broke into a smile. 'But you've been working on the surge problem for three weeks now.'

'True.'

'Then if I know you, Alec, you've solved it.'

'Your confidence in Alec's ability is touching,' said Christine frostily.

'It's founded on experience.'

'Thank you for the final payment,' said Christine. 'I take it you were happy with your samples and Alec's reports?'

'I would've been happier with more samples taken from the entire area. The lack of verification is worrying. Nevertheless, I'm prepared to take a chance and substantially increase my offer for a stake in Triton Exploration.'

Alec caught Christine's eye but he knew better than to say anything. Their last row had left him wounded. The glance didn't escape Shief's experienced eye. He had found out that Christine was the main source of Triton's income and not their subcontract work. He guessed that Alec wasn't happy with the arrangement.

'What sort of increase did you have in mind, Shief?' Christine asked.

'Double,' Shief replied genially, watching Alec carefully.

'For a thirty per cent holding?'

'And use of your patents,' said Shief evenly. 'That's an extremely generous offer considering that one sampling doesn't prove the deposits.' He saw that Christine was about to speak and held up his hand. 'Please don't decide yet. Talk it over for a few days. But do consider that my buy-in will still leave you as majority shareholders . . . And you'll both be very comfortably off. I imagine that there would be more than enough to pay off any debts that the company may have incurred.'

'We don't have any debts,' said Christine evenly. 'Alec's machining work with our laser lathe and mill generates a healthy income.'

There was a heavy tread on the stairs. A rap on the door preceded an aristocratic-looking young man. 'Sorry to trouble you, sir.' His cultured voice had been forged in the workshops of Eton and Cambridge. 'But your next appointment is in forty-five minutes.'

'Thank you, Ian,' said Shief. He turned to Christine and Alec, flashing them a warm, predatory smile. 'Forgive me, but my diary calls. Please give my offer careful consideration.'

Alec was the first to break the silence that followed the oil chief's departure.

'Double his previous bid,' he breathed. 'Wow. We'd be rich.'

'It's a lousy offer and you know it,' Christine retorted. 'Once he has his thirty per cent foot in the door, he'd strive day and night to drive a wedge between us. One of us siding with him would give him total control. And even if that didn't work, he'd still get the right to exploit a set of patents that gives him access to the world's biggest oil deposits.'

'We don't know that, Chris.'

'We know enough to be ninety per cent certain. If Shief gets control of the patents then Indonesia will get a raw deal.' Christine's lips set into a hard line. 'Alec – it's time we took the initative with Indonesia.'

He looked quizzically at her. 'How?'

'We've got to go to Jakarta. We'll take all our data, drawings, a working model of the Darwin – everything. We'll bang on government doors and make such a thorough ongoing nuisance of ourselves that eventually someone will have to listen to us.'

Alec looked worried. 'You mean the data we've just collected on the Banda Trench?'

'Well of course I mean that!'

'But as I keep telling you – Shief paid for that. It's his information.'

'So let the bastard sue us if he finds out!'

26

'Well, Ian?' Shief queried, settling into the Rolls-Royce's deep cushions as the vehicle moved off down the drive. He touched the control that polarised the windows to opaque black from the outside.

'No surveillance devices that I could see, sir. A lamentable lack of security if I may say so.'

'Enough of a lack to persuade you to change your mind?'

Ian looked at his boss in the mirror. 'That's all behind me now, sir.'

'That wasn't what I asked. I suppose you're waiting for me to offer you a little bonus?'

The chauffeur grinned and turned the car into the road. 'No, sir. I'm waiting for you to offer me a large bonus.'

Shief nodded. He liked Ian. A man who put price before principles. If only there were more like him doing business would be so much simpler.

They swept past a nondescript rental Ford tucked into a lay-by. Honicker reached for his memopad and made a note of the Rolls-Royce's registration number.

27

London was providing a particularly hot spring day, which did not please Honicker. Despite his love of espionage novels, he wasn't enjoying his assignment although he had insisted that his expenses should cover staying at the Savoy Hotel – which was where all the best spies had stayed. The trouble was that he wasn't a spy – there were professionals to do what he was doing – but Don Houseman, the prime minister's mole-like personal secretary had been adamant: 'The prime minister wants to keep this a low-key operation until we're a hundred per cent sure of our facts. Only the three of us know what's going on. You don't even report this to your committee. He trusts you, Bill. You're a smart operator and a good engineer. This job needs engineering know-how for a proper assessment. All you've got to do is some nosing about. Nothing illegal. You're a journalist working on a story.'

All very well for Houseman to talk, thought Honicker gloomily as he worked at the business terminal in his hotel room, but journalists had a back-up organisation behind them. He had nothing except access to a number of data-bases. His seven days in London had been a waste of time. Apart from keeping the Roses' premises under surveillance – and even that close approximation of cloak and dagger work had become deadly boring after a while – all he had uncovered so far could have been done from his office in Canberra.

He had tracked down Alec and Christine Rose through the European Union companies database in Brussels without leaving his room. Both were listed as directors of Triton Exploration of Walton-on-Thames. The articles of association were vague. The company had been set up as a consultancy specialising in the design and development of low-cost mineral extraction equipment. A recent amendment included specialist machining activities.

The name Alec Rose cropped up on a surprising number of databases. The earliest reference was twelve years old and was cross-referred to the *Geological Review*. The journal was owned by a large publishing group whose on-line database demanded a credit card number before allowing him unrestricted access to the back-numbers area. Fortunately the database was well indexed. Tucked away on a back page, Honicker found the article in which Alec Rose, a geo-engineer with Shell, had outlined a theory concerning the possibility of processing alluvial sediment into low-grade fossil fuels by third world countries. In the same article he had challenged the perceived wisdom of the time that all deep-ocean sediment contained little or no carbon fractions or hydrocarbons.

Honicker read the 1,000-word piece in mounting dismay. Not only was Rose's theory public knowledge, but it had been for twelve years! He reproduced the article on his printer and toyed with the idea of faxing it straight through to Houseman, but decided first to round up all the references to Alec Rose. The index showed further mentions in subsequent issues of the *Geological Review*. He accessed them, but they were readers' letters – all from worthy names in marine biology, and all launching attacks on Alec Rose and his bizarre theory, ranging from the mildly abrasive to the sulphurously vitriolic. Either the editor had had no correspondence in support of Rose or he regretted his decision to publish the article and had decided to throw the author to the wolves.

On a hunch Honicker logged into the European Patents Register. More trashing of his credit card but it did throw up a whole string of patents registered to Triton Exploration. He downloaded the description précis, logged off and printed them. The forty pages that hissed out of his printer were a credit to the agent who had prepared the descriptions. They were all concerned with the mechanics of deepwater sedimentation sampling, and skilfully worded so as to volunteer no more information than they had to. The accompanying drawings, all bearing the signature 'AR', were likewise as vague as was legally permitted.

Next on Honicker's list was the registration number of the Rolls-Royce that had visited the Roses. The UK government's Vehicle Information Computer demanded a charge card number. Honicker provided VIC with the information it needed and a description of the Rolls appeared on his screen. Colour. Year of registration, but not the hard information he needed.

OWNER: LONDON CARRIAGE LEASING.

CURRENT KEEPER: PARTICULARS WITHHELD.

Damn. Well, maybe this was an opportunity to do some real espionage by tracking down a seedy private investigator to his equally seedy premises over a butcher's shop in South London. It was an opportunity he didn't take up; electronic yellow pages did a better job of cruising the phone numbers of private eyes and their specialist abilities. He found one and this time got through to a human being.

'Good afternoon, sir,' said the girl, her face smiling brightly at him from the screen. Nothing seedy about her surroundings: a modern office and a row of cacti on the window-sill behind her. 'How can I help you?'

Honicker gave her details of the Rolls-Royce and asked if it would be possible to obtain the name and address of the vehicle's keeper. The girl's fingers danced on an unseen keyboard as he spoke.

'Yes, sir. I have that information for you.' She reeled off a list of charges. Honicker inserted his credit card in the reader.

'And your fingerprint, please, sir,' the girl prompted.

'It's one of the old cards,' Honicker explained.

The girl checked the card's number and smiled sweetly. 'So it is, sir. I'm sending the information now. Thank you for using our services.'

The telephone's fax printer delivered a whole screed of information on the Rolls-Royce. And there it was:

CURRENT KEEPER: AVANTI OIL CORPORATION.

Avanti Oil: that would make Houseman jump.

The rest was easy. From that lead Honicker was able to delve into several databases – each one providing pointers to another. Eventually his printer was delivering facsimiles of newspaper cuttings. One bore a photograph of Joshua Shief. There was no mistaking those florid features. It was a man whom Honicker knew well from reports he had seen. Shief was known to have business connections with General Oman Putriana, the ambitious commander-in-chief of Indonesia's armed forces. Avanti had a liaison bureau in Jakarta which was believed to be nothing more than a bribe-paying centre. He sat back, staring at the papers strewn across the desk, and began dictating a report. After a few edits to correct the software's voice-recognition errors, he e-mailed the whole thing to Houseman in Canberra.

The rest of the day was his. A visit to the Science Museum to look at Charles Babbage's mechanical calculating engines was in order, and then a concert at the Queen Elizabeth Hall. Frederick Delius – now enjoying a well-deserved revival.

He returned to the Savoy after midnight with the English composer's lovely nocturnes playing in his mind.

'You have one message,' said his portable fax machine when he pressed his forefinger on the ID pad to unlock its memory. A single sheet of paper hissed out of the machine. It bore a telephone number which Honicker recognised as Houseman's Iridium number. He called it, using his own Iridium Klipfone.

'I've been trying to get hold of you,' said Houseman without preamble.

'I've been to a concert. I didn't take my phone with me.'

'Mode E.'

120

Honicker pressed the 'E' button on his telephone. Unfortunately it stood for 'Encryption' and not 'Espionage'. The button introduced a second level of encryption to defeat digital scanners. It was not a device fitted by an Antipodean version of Ian Fleming's 'Q' character but a business service provided by Motorola.

'Your report has been read,' said Houseman tersely. 'The involvement of the oil man you mentioned is a major concern. His Indonesian connections and his association with your flower people is ringing many alarm bells here.'

Flower people? Ah – the Roses. It was Houseman who ought to be doing the spying.

'Therefore', Houseman continued, 'a decision has been taken regarding removal of the threat that your flower people pose.'

A serpent of fear twisted in Honicker's stomach. He didn't like the sound of that. 'Removal of the flower people won't achieve anything,' he observed. 'What they've done, others will—'

'I didn't say anything about their removal,' Houseman snapped. 'I said removal of the threat that they pose.'

'And how do *you* propose doing that?' Honicker's emphasis ensured that responsibility was passed back to Houseman.

'We buy them out.'

'The oil man has probably already done that,' Honicker reasoned. Despite the security of the satellite telephone system, Houseman's habit of avoiding names was infectious.

'Not according to company records.'

'Which may not be up to date,' Honicker pointed out.

'That's something you have to find out,' Houseman shot back. 'If the flower people still have control of their company, you're to make them an offer.'

'What's the point? They've designed and built an extraction system that works. If they can do it, others will do the same eventually. All we buy is time.'

'Time is the one thing we need above all else,' said Houseman. 'They'll be ahead of everyone else in the development of commercial systems. Things are moving fast in our friends' camp.' At all meetings the Indonesians were always referred to as 'our friends'.

'Any pointers on what's happening?' Honicker asked guardedly.

'Something's given our much-medallioned friend a confidence fix. A big one. You've put two and two together and now we think there might be something in your nasty four – that this could make them the richest country in the world within ten years. If that happens we'll be in serious shit. So your job is to buy out the flower people. We need those patents.'

'I just walk in and offer to buy their company?' said Honicker sarcastically, feeling that all this was becoming unreal.

'Why not?'

'So how much do I offer them?'

'Ten million US dollars. But you can go to fifteen. But they must be retained in their company. Buy fifty-one per cent and keep them in under a five-year management contract or whatever. We don't want them using the money to set up again.'

The figure astonished Honicker. 'For God's sake – we've got an overseas trade department for that sort of negotiating.'

'They'd take too long. Start at five million, stick at ten and only go the rest of the way if that's what it takes.'

'Fifteen million dollars!' Honicker muttered.

'The price of a Churchill tank,' said Houseman curtly. The channel went dead.

28

The entire management team of Sabre Industries had turned out to welcome 004 back to St Omer. They stood on the apron in a small knot near the mobile steps, overcoats flapping in the icy wind that was sweeping across northern Europe from the Steppes. The flying club's windsock stood rigid and nearly horizontal from its pole like an inflated condom. Old technology, Paul reflected, and wondered if Allenby and Frankel would refer to it on their final approach. He was about to ask Ralph but the chief designer was busy stabbing at his memopad when he wasn't scanning the leaden sky or listening on his earphone to the exchanges between the tower and 004.

'Fifty-three minutes since take-off,' he announced to no one in particular. 'They're reporting severe buffeting.'

Paul pulled up the collar of his overcoat and wished he had a heated Yeti suit like the news crews crouched behind their cameras. But a bloated children's monster shaking hands with Allenby and Frankel wouldn't look good on TV.

'Fifty-four,' someone muttered behind Paul. 'They're not going to make it.'

The tension had even got to the newsmen. All their cameras were aimed at the northern sky where Sabre 004 was due to appear.

The wind whipped away the smoke of a newsman's cigarette.

Outwardly Paul remained stoically indifferent to the mounting tension around him. Inwardly he was desperately willing his heartbeat to stay normal. The last thing he wanted was for his underarm health sensor to scent a heart attack in the offing and to signal the rapid-response paramedics to come after him.

Fifty-five minutes.

'They're going to need a miracle,' said the voice behind Paul. He wanted to turn round and tell whoever it was to keep his mouth shut. Instead he looked at his wrist-watch and pressed the button that opened a window on the display showing the view from 004's forward TV camera. The postage-stamp-size screen showed nothing but ugly cumulonimbus racing past, giving the effect of plunging down a fog-filled tunnel of darkness. There was no sign of the ground. Ralph called out the spaceplane's range and height.

The digits on Paul's wrist-watch above the TV picture passed fifty-six minutes and clocked relentlessly towards fifty-seven.

And then everyone heard it at once: a dull rumble of distant thunder reverberating around the sullen sky. But unlike thunder, the sound grew steadily in volume until it was of such intensity that it seemed his skull was resonating in sympathy. This was no throttle-back, noise abatement approach.

Fifty-seven minutes.

'There she is!'

The TV cameras swung and zoomed on the shape that had broken through the cloudbase. The thunder bore down relentlessly on the watchers like a monstrous herd of stampeding bison.

Fifty-eight.

The rapidly approaching shape became the outline of his beloved Sabre – landing lights blazing and sonic howlers working flat out to frighten off birds. Paul could see that something was wrong with the Sabre's wing configuration. Ralph was frantically waving his arms as though his gestures possessed a divine power that could ward off the inevitable disaster.

'He's coming in virtually clean! Only fifty per cent warp!' the chief designer was yelling, barely making himself audible above the terrible roar.

Unlike conventional aircraft, the Sabre used wing-warping instead of flaps to increase lift and decrease speed on landing. The technique saved on weight and moving parts. It was nothing new: Louis Bleriot, the first man to fly across the English Channel, had used it in 1909. But Len Allenby was hardly using it now: 004 was coming in at a frightening speed.

Fifty-nine minutes since take-off.

On the far side of the complex, George Campion and Lesseps were sitting in the Mistral's cockpit going through the light aircraft's sale contract and finance documents when the Sabre appeared. Lesseps had now witnessed enough test flight arrivals to know that something was seriously wrong. Both men jumped from the aircraft's cockpit and stared at the rapidly swelling blaze of lights in the sky.

'My God!' Campion breathed. 'He's coming in too fast!'

But the expected landing abort never happened. 004's tyres hit concrete at 250 knots – well within their design tolerance but way outside the nerve tolerance of those watching on the ground. The screech of tortured rubber was drowned by the shattering roar of maximum reverse thrust. It shook the giant sliding doors of the construction shed but seemed to have no effect on the frightening rate at which the hurtling Sabre gobbled up the runway. Paul closed his eyes, his heart steam-hammering as he braced himself for the inevitable crash. The part of his mind that was not numbed by the appalling noise held an image of his cardiac paramedic team piling aboard their helicopter at the very moment that it lifted off. The noise suddenly subsided. He opened his eyes and saw that 004 had swung off the taxiway and was heading, serene and unconcerned, towards its mark on the apron. For a moment he thought his legs were going to give way.

'Fifty-nine minutes and fifty-eight seconds! We've done it! We've done it!' Ralph exclaimed, dancing around like a demented bear. The crowd broke into cheers and hugs. Passionate kisses were exchanged regardless of gender. Paul's hand was pumped furiously as he was pushed towards the steps that were quickly wheeled into position even before 004's engines had closed down. Simone Frankel and Len Allenby appeared side by side as soon as the door opened, punching the air in triumph and hugging each other in delight.

Paul raced nimbly up the steps, pursued by a Canal Plus Hovercam, to meet the two heroes half-way. More kisses, hugs and handshakes.

'You're two seconds early and your landing unnerved us,' said Paul to both of them.

'Blame Simone,' said Allenby, deadpan. 'She was flying.'

Simone raced down the steps and set off towards the main building. She called out over her shoulder: 'Sorry if we frightened everyone but I hate using zero gravity toilets.'

125

The remark was picked up by the Hovercam's microphone and became a long-remembered quote.

Lesseps and Campion returned to the Mistral's cockpit to complete the sale formalities. The flying instructor wanted to discuss the Sabre's remarkable flight, but Lesseps was anxious to get the sale formalities out of the way.

'Do you also get a commission from the finance company, George?' he asked, signing the documents after only a cursory glance.

Campion gave no sign of resentment at the question. 'Sure. It's no secret. It's in the small print if you read it.'

'Small print,' said Lesseps dismissively, impatient to own this wondrous creation he was sitting in.

'This is the last one,' said Campion, handing a contract to Lesseps. 'I think you should read it.'

'I've read through the originals.'

'Even so, I think you should read it. The finance company are understandably uneasy. It's a big loan. The six-month default clause has been amended to three months. Page 3. You'll have to initial it.'

Lesseps had only to look at the gleaming array of instruments before him to suppress the tiny warning voice telling him that he was making a big mistake. He was about to sign the final form, but Campion stayed his hand.

'Listen, Jean. I don't care about my sale commission or the finance commission. That's not why I'm in this game. I'm in it because I want people to enjoy their flying and to get a good deal at the same time. What I don't like to see is people being carried away and getting into debt. I've seen it happen before. After all, it's only an aircraft.'

Lesseps laughed good naturedly to hide his impatience. 'I promise you I can afford this little beauty, George – I have private means.' He signed the last form with an air of casual bravura.

Here we go again, said the little voice.

But Lesseps ignored it.

He became the new owner of the bright yellow Mistral just as Paul Santos returned to his office.

126

29

Paul Santos sat at his desk and unwound for a few minutes, watching the price of Sabre Industries stock edging upwards, while dwelling on the flight. Like the other stunts, this one had been his idea. But there had been nothing impetuous about it.

Firstly, its purpose was to pump the price of Sabre Industries' shares on the eve of a release of a further ten million shares from the unissued share capital. Well it had certainly done that all right, as the upward movement on his screen showed. The major investors would complain about the dilution of their holdings, but they were getting respectable growth. The move had been forced on Paul by the continuing reluctance of Commonwealth to confirm their option, and mounting labour costs to get 005 and 006 ready by the end of the year. Already he had cut back on the man-hours going into Air France's 006 so that it would be a month late on delivery. There would be no penalties because, like 005, 006 was being loaned.

Secondly, every aspect of the record-breaking flight had been planned and tested on the simulator and subjected to intense computer modelling. By using a low orbital trajectory and careful fuel-loading 12,000 miles away to ensure minimum take-off weight, coupled with an eastward take-off to get an initial 'kick' from the earth's rotation, the near impossible had been achieved. The venture was of no commercial significance because the payload had been nil – the cabin and cargo bay had been stripped. But the record-breaking flight was a resounding public relations success:

Sabre 004 had flown from Sydney to St Omer in under one hour.

30

A stunt, thought Joe Yavanoski angrily, tossing the *Tacoma News-Tribune* across his desk.

The other bad news was that Airbus Industries had won another big order, and Arianespace was celebrating the successful launching of its three hundredth commercial satellite from their spaceport at Kourou in French Guiana.

What the hell was it about the French?

Joe had been reading a lot about France recently; it was becoming an obsession. A country with a sixth of the population of the United States and yet they challenged America on every front, smashing their way into traditional US markets. Space: they had grabbed just about everything off NASA with their series of Ariane rockets. Arms: France was now the world's biggest exporter and had been since the 1990s. Agriculture: the second biggest producer after the US and the gap was closing. His local supermarket was crammed with French wines and cheeses. How many American wines and cheeses would he find in a French supermarket? The French were the world's largest producers of nuclear power and they had just finished a massive tidal power station on the River Rance in Brittany. In oceanography France had always led the world. They had invented the scuba. Their TGVs were the fastest trains in the world – faster than the Japanese so-called 'bullet' trains. Their god-damned Renault and Peugeot electric bugs were everywhere, cluttering up shopping mall parking lots. On his last visit to France he hadn't seen one American car with a French plate.

They and the Germans had even invented cars. The words were French: automobile, limousine, chauffeur, garage, chassis. Those who invent a technology name the technology. Henry Royce had gotten started in England by copying French car engines because they were so quiet and refined. The first men to fly were French brothers over a century before Wilbur and Orville. And again, much of the terminology of flight was French: aviation, fuselage, aileron. Almost every unit in physics had the name of a French physicist hung on it. The French had invented photography, the facsimile machine, motion pictures, radar and the metric system that was now taking over America.

All America had left was software and movies, and even they were under threat from the French. Canal Plus was continuing to buy its way into the TV networks – it already had huge stakes in cable and satellite TV – and Microsoft, right here in Seattle, was battling with French companies that were nibbling away at its traditional world markets.

And now the spaceplane – based on designs that were the result of the hard work of many American research centres. As always, just thinking about it turned the running sore in Joe's mind to a festering wound that distorted his reason into a blinding hatred.

That Sabre Industries was, like Airbus Industries, a consortium of backers and manufactures from many countries didn't count with Joe. Nor did the fact that many of the huge improvements that Sabre Industries had made on the original American airframe designs were available to the United States if required. And he ignored the simple fact that the Sabre was named after the British-developed engines that had made the European venture possible. As far as Joe was concerned, the French had mugged his beloved United States, and Paul Santos was French through and through.

The rage burning within him made his hands shake as he picked up the last report Lesseps had sent him by snail mail. He took care to handle it by the corners. Like the earlier reports, Lesseps' notes accompanying the packet of drawings were handwritten in accordance with his instructions. Over fifty documents – a mass of commercial secrets and sensitive information concerning the Sabre engine. Enough to earn Lesseps fifteen years under French law, and the greedy sap didn't know that the US, Canada and the EU had extradition agreements.

The reports were better than he had hoped for. They gave

him a lever that was long enough to use as a club if necessary.

Or a wrench.

31

Christine liked Honicker. Unlike Joshua Shief, there was an
engaging openness about him. He was neat, well-educated,
well-scrubbed. A man who liked order and truth. Not a
natural-born liar. Nevertheless, she was blunt. 'If you won't
tell me who these mysterious principals are that you
represent,' she stated, 'I see little point in continuing this discussion.'

The Australian placed his hands palm up on the desk and
looked at Alec and Christine in turn. Well, he had done
what Houseman had suggested. He had phoned Triton
Exploration, made an appointment and walked into their
office with a bold offer. As expected, he had met with
guarded suspicion, but it was early days yet.

'I'm sorry, but all I can disclose at this juncture is that it
is an Australian concern.'

Alec laughed. 'I think we had worked that out, Mr
Honicker.'

Christine regarded their visitor steadily. Her initial con-
viction that this was another of Shief's ploys was fading. She
sensed that this man would never work for someone like
Shief, or fit in with his business methods. She prided herself
on her ability to sum people up and recognise integrity when
she saw it. 'Why should you think that fifty-one per cent of
Triton is worth five million dollars, Mr Honicker?' She
gestured around the shabby little office. 'Do we look like a
ten-million-dollar company?'

'We've done some scratching around,' said Honicker. He
nodded to Alec. 'Research. Nothing underhand. Public
domain material. Starting with an article you wrote twelve
years ago for the *Geological Review*.'

Alec chuckled. 'No one took that seriously at the time.'

'We do now,' Honicker replied, comfortable that he was being mostly truthful. 'We've also taken a look at your patents. They don't say much but we've deduced that you've either solved the problem of commercial extraction of deepwater sediment, or are well on the way to solving the problem. Australia's population is burgeoning. It's going to have to expand its agriculture rapidly over the next ten years to keep pace. Millions of cubic metres of soil conditioner will be needed to bring enough hectares under cultivation. Seawater silt, suitably washed and filtered, is ideal. The alternative is to ship peat half-way round the world. The price of good-quality sedge has rocketed.' Well that bit was true enough.

'Registering a few patents doesn't mean we've solved anything,' said Christine, watching Honicker carefully. She glanced quickly at Alec – a warning to keep quiet. 'I'm sorry. But we're not interested, Mr Honicker. Triton Exploration is our life.'

'You would still have management control. In the day-to-day running of the company, everything would be much the same as it is now. In many respects you would have even more freedom because you would be able to draw on a research and development budget.'

Christine shook her head regretfully. 'Sorry, Mr Honicker. Thank you for your interest in Triton. I'm only sorry that we can't respond with the same interest in your offer.'

'I can go to seven,' said Honicker flatly. He made a move to stand. 'I can always wait in my car while you talk it over.'

Alec signalled to Christine that he wanted to talk. 'All right, Mr Honicker,' she said. 'Give us ten minutes please.'

As soon as they were alone, Alec felt down the sides of the chair cushions where Honicker had been sitting. He even crouched and peered along the underside of the desk and checked outside the door. 'Clean,' he announced. 'I watched him all the time. He didn't plant anything.' He looked questioningly at Christine who was busy with the Minitel keyboard. 'Shief?'

'I don't think so. Why would that thing send a minion

131

along to offer less than he has?'

'He could be testing us,' said Alec. 'Seeing if we put environmental or ideological considerations first.'

'Don't we?'

'You always have.'

Christine gave a dismissive gesture as she tapped on the keyboard. 'That stuff about soil conditioner is crap. I could smell when he was lying. Which means that someone in Avanti has leaked information or another organisation has found something out.'

'Like who?'

She was engrossed in the Minitel keyboard and screen so Alec had to repeat the question.

'The Australian government,' Christine replied. 'Their intelligence services are supposed to be the best in the southern hemisphere.'

'Honicker would make a pretty ineffectual spy,' Alec observed. 'Do spies stay at the Savoy?'

'He doesn't need to spy,' said Christine. 'He knows more about us than we do. And you're right – he'd make a lousy spy. Maybe they do stay at the Savoy, but they don't list themselves in landline telephone directories.'

'What?'

She turned the screen around so that Alec could see it. 'There's about a couple of hundred Honickers listed in the whole of Australia, with variations on his spelling,' said Christine. 'But only one W. Honicker.' She pointed to a Canberra address. 'A frightful, boring place. The only reason for living there is if you love order or you're a government employee. I suspect that with our Mr Honicker, it's both.' She gave an impish smile and touched out the number, using the telephone in hands free mode so that they both heard the giveaway tones over the speaker of a call being diverted. Then a ringing tone. Only one ring followed by a man's voice: 'Hallo?'

'Could I speak to Bill Honicker please? That's H-O-N-I-C-K-E-R initial W.'

H's office, Christine scrawled on a pad.

132

'As you're calling from England,' said the voice resignedly, 'didn't it occur to you to check the time? It's after ten. Everyone's gone home and I don't know if we have anyone of that name here.'

'All I want is for you to route this call to Bill Honicker's Iridium number,' said Christine earnestly. 'It's very urgent and to do with his mission to London. I don't want you to give me his number – just route this call through.'

'Hold on please.' The line went quiet.

'You're crazy,' Alec muttered.

'Shh!'

'Hallo?' said the voice.

'Still here,' said Christine pleasantly.

'Your name please, miss.'

'I can't say. Look, this is desperately urgent. If you don't put me through to Mr Honicker the whole thing could fall apart.'

'Hold on please.' The line went dead again, this time for two minutes. The man never came back. Instead they heard a ringing tone from the speaker at the same time as the faint trilling from outside of an Iridium Klipfone. Christine gave a little wriggle of triumph at the success of her ruse in bouncing a call around the world through several low-orbit satellites to speak to someone not twenty metres away.

'Hallo, Mr Honicker,' she said sweetly. 'Christine Rose. We've talked over your offer. Perhaps you'd like to come up now?'

Honicker entered the office looking sheepish. 'How did you find out my Iridium number?'

'Your government department in Canberra put me through,' said Christine, smiling warmly at the Australian's momentary flicker of surprise. A hopeless spy. She definitely liked him. Especially now that she had control. He even sat when she indicated the chair and waited for her to speak.

'So the Commonwealth of Australia want to buy our company? Will you forgive me, Bill – may I call you Bill? – if I say right at the outset that your story about millions of cubic metres of fertiliser is a load of fucking crap?'

Honicker looked taken back for a moment, uncertain

133

how to react until he saw the half-smile playing at the corners of Christine's mouth. He nodded in agreement and admitted that it was indeed a load of fucking crap. He was not given to swearing and had old-fashioned views about doing so in front of women, but she'd started it.

'Congratulations on finding out about us, Bill. Alec, make some coffee, we've got a lot of talking to do.'

The three talked for an hour, listening to each other's point of view with respect, each side divulging as much as they dared and offering compromises when the discussion got bogged down.

Damn Houseman and his civil servant mole-like mentality, thought Honicker when Alec and Christine expressed their mistrust of Shief. The direct approach from the outset would have saved time all round.

'You're right about Shief up to a point,' said Honicker. 'But you must remember that he's a businessman with a legal responsibility to protect his shareholders' investments. Naturally, businessmen like political stability for long-term projects involving major capital investments. Indonesia under military control offered stability for many years. Foreign investment boomed. Now the country has a creaking democracy with ten political parties vying for control. The result: inter-trade union disputes, riots, strikes, civil unrest. And the corruption that was always there, now running out of control. It's a gross simplification but those are the bald facts.'

'You sound as though you favour the return of a military dictatorship,' said Alec.

'Never,' said Honicker vehemently. 'We've done everything we can to support President Sulimann. The guy is our best hope for peace in Melanesia. He wants to pull out of south Borneo and Timor, but he can't with General Oman Putriana still in command of the armed services and just itching to get back into the presidential palace. Sulimann tried to sack him twice last year and nearly had an army uprising on his hands. Putriana is the real danger. I don't like superlatives because they tend to obscure the problem, but

134

in his case, "power-mad megalomaniac" fits extremely well. With south Borneo he was testing the mettle of the West, and the West was found wanting. He nibbles. A little bite here, a little bite there. Always testing. Next it'll be the rest of Borneo and Brunei. And then maybe a really big and bloody bite – Australia. Shief and businessmen like him have to live with realities. That's why Shief is in thick with Putriana.'

'Are you sure?' Christine interrupted.

'They're almost buddies.'

A silence followed. Christine found her wedding ring of great interest. 'Do you have proof?' she asked.

'I can get it,' Honicker replied. He met Christine's eye without flinching. 'If you wish I can supply you with video recordings of the two together on Shief's yacht in Singapore.'

'That won't be necessary,' Christine replied, making no attempt to hide her concern.

'It's not just Shief but at least twenty multinationals that are providing Putriana with tacit support. And then there's the whole of the European arms industry – particularly the British and Dutch. They continue to curry favour with Putriana because his budget is undiminished since he lost the palace. You sell your company to Shief and you strengthen Putriana's hand. If Indonesia has the potential to become the biggest oil-producing country in the world, his position would become unassailable and the West would want him to stay in power. Look at the lengths the West goes to to support corrupt and despotic regimes in the Persian Gulf.'

'Our equipment is a long way from commercial application,' said Alec.

Honicker regarded him steadily. Now he was getting to the nub of this discussion. The geo-engineer had left most of the talking to his wife, but he was the key to the whole issue.

He phrased his next question carefully. 'There's a graph that can be applied to turning any new technology into a commercial proposition. One component is time. The longer the time line, the greater the opportunities for serendipity and hard work to solve problems. The other component is money. In the case of your development' – he was careful to avoid saying 'invention' – 'would money shorten the time line?'

It was another way of asking if all the problems had been solved.

'If you're talking unlimited money then the answer's yes,' said Alec without hesitation and without looking at Christine. 'There aren't any serious design problems left with the Darwin itself. Maybe a year's work and two more field tests. But the cash injection you offered would not take our equipment to any sort of commercial potential because we've not looked at the design of free-floating deep-water production platforms.'

There aren't any serious design problems left ... Hell! Honicker's expression remained impassive. Provided he didn't have to lie, he was a better actor than he gave himself credit for. He said: 'But such platforms already exist for sea-bed manganese nodule mining. There wouldn't be any point in your working on platform design.' He picked up his untouched cup of coffee and realised that it was cold.

'The design of an existing free-floater would have to be changed quite substantially,' said Alec. 'But it wouldn't be difficult – just expensive.'

Honicker decided to play a risky card. He had intended to hold it back until he was more firmly in the Roses' confidence, but the discussion had gone surprisingly well. 'Would you let me see your Darwin?'

'Meaning that you haven't seen it, Bill?' Christine inquired archly.

'How could I have seen it?'

'We made no attempt to hide it in Darwin. What would have been the point? It was just another sediment sampler. You don't expect me to believe that you haven't unearthed a photograph or video recording from somewhere, do you?'

'We've seen some pictures,' Honicker admitted. There was no point in lying, not to Christine Rose.

Alec stood. 'You're welcome to take a look. Not that

136

you'll learn anything. The workshop is in a mess. Give me a few minutes to tidy up.'

There wasn't a sketch, model or drawing in sight when Alec and Christine showed Honicker into the workshop fifteen minutes later. The only obvious sign of activity was a block of partly machined aluminium clamped to the laser mill's bed, and the Darwin hanging like a falling bomb from its hoist in the centre of the workshop. Its covers had been bolted loosely in place. The graphic composition of the outer casing imparted a sinister black sheen.

Honicker walked around the strange device. His engineering background led to his appreciation of the painstaking love and care that had gone into its design and construction. The helical teeth on the snub boring augers, meshed together at the nose, were fine examples of perfect machining. Not a pit or blemish marred their hardened and polished surfaces. And yet the device had been in use at a depth of 10,000 metres. One atmosphere of pressure for every ten metres. Roughly 1,000 bar. Remarkable, and he said so. The geo-engineer looked pleased.

Honicker guessed that the Roses' obsession with secrecy meant that Alec had been starved of praise for his considerable achievement. 'Quite amazing, Alec,' he said. 'Is the casing pressure-moulded, spark-eroded, or machined?'

The question surprised Alec. 'Machined.'

'Not on that laser mill, surely? Those Shaeffers don't like working graphic-based materials.'

It was Christine's turn to be surprised. This Aussie was more knowledgeable than she had supposed. She began to appreciate why he had been chosen for this task.

'We had the casing made by a subcontractor,' said Alec. 'I use the Shaeffers for machining internal parts that demand an extremely high degree of precision.'

'Which I imagine is most of them,' Honicker commented. 'Those machine tools are not cheap.'

'A third of our budget over the last five years,' said Christine. 'But it brings in some subcontract work for Alec which helps pay for them.'

137

Crazy, thought Honicker. A tinpot, hopelessly under-capitalised company sitting on the most important invention of this century and they behaved like a jobbing engineering company scratching a living doing subcontract work. They didn't even employ a machinist. Amateurs. Gifted, but still amateurs. But there was a question uppermost in his mind, one that he wasn't sure he would get an answer to. He turned to Alec. 'You said that you thought there was another year's work on the Darwin?'

'About that,' Alec agreed.

'More like ten years,' said Honicker bluntly. 'You can't just scale up a mechanism from model size to commercial size. The physics doesn't work like that. You double the dimensions of an object and you increase its volume and mass eightfold, and its surface area quadruples. Design has to change with size. That's why you can't have giant ants with bodies the size of St Bernards because their legs would only be as thick as pencils and wouldn't support their weight. It's why ostriches can't fly and elephants' hooves have evolved into pads. Everything is right for its size. Your Darwin works, but a bigger one wouldn't, unless it was an entirely different machine. A commercial-size Darwin is several years away – not just one.'

The slow smile on Alec's face told Honicker that his deliberate overstating of the case was about to produce a dividend.

'It wouldn't be possible to build a really large Darwin for at least ten years – possibly more,' Alec agreed, either ignoring Christine's danger signals or not noticing them. 'The limiting factor is Plastronic hose technology. A 50-millimetre bore is the maximum possible. But my idea is to have 2,000 Darwins working from a single platform. A cluster of five such automated platforms working day and night, day in and day out, deriving all their power from the hose's thermocouple effect, would produce well over a million barrels a day. Three clusters working the trench we've earmarked would produce a billion barrels a year.'

He misread Honicker's expression as that of surprise. The

Australian was more taken aback at the frankness of Alec's answer, and even more annoyed with himself for not foreseeing it.

It was all so blindingly obvious. A thousand little springs could spawn a mighty river.

32

It was late when Honicker returned to the Savoy because he had insisted on taking the Roses out to dinner. An astute move because it had helped cement the good working relationship he was building with them. Of course, a real spy would have opted for something more exciting than a local pub, but casinos were thin on the ground around Walton and Weybridge.

He stretched out on his bed, turning over the events of the day, and decided to file a voice report to Houseman while the details were still fresh in his mind. He called Houseman's Iridium number and got straight through just as Houseman was starting work.

'Press the record button,' said Honicker. 'I've got a lot to tell you.'

'I record all calls automatically.'

Yes – you would.

Honicker talked fast.

'You identified us!' Houseman wailed in horror.

'I was tripped,' Honicker shot back. 'Check the duty officer's night log. Christine Rose is what the Americans would call a smart cookie. If you don't like it, recall me and send out a trained operative, but hear me out first.'

Houseman listened attentively to the rest of Honicker's report, interjecting only when a point needed clarification.

'So that's the final position,' Honicker concluded. 'Christine Rose wants to make direct contact with the Indonesian government first. But only with the democratic factions.'

'Well, that's something,' Houseman conceded. 'Can she

be trusted?'

'She's adamant on that and I believe her. I've said that we might be able to arrange a contact in Jakarta. That went down well with her and puts us in good light. They've agreed to stall Shief until then and they won't enter into any deal without consulting us.'

'Nothing in writing,' said Houseman icily.

'That's because I've stopped being a spy and become a diplomat,' Honicker retorted. 'You may find it hard to believe because I don't suppose you ever meet these sorts of people in your social circle, but they aren't in it solely for the money – at least, Christine Rose isn't. She's the powerhouse behind their commitment to helping Third World countries.'

'God protect us from political idealists.'

'They're decent people.' Honicker realised that the comment made him sound naïve but what the hell.

Houseman snorted. 'They've certainly put one across on you.'

'So who do we point them at in Jakarta? It's got to be someone firmly in Sulimann's camp.'

'I'll come back to you in an hour,' Houseman replied. The line went dead. Honicker watched a movie on the TV, guessing that this particular hot potato was being passed right to the top. The Klipfone trilled exactly one hour later.

'President Sulimann,' said Housemann brusquely. He heard Honicker's sharp intake of breath. 'He's the guy we want to stay in power. Our ambassador in Jakarta will fix for him to see the Roses.'

'For God's sake, they'll think we're manipulating them.'

'That's exactly what we are doing,' Houseman countered. 'We'll let the Roses play their silly game. This way at least we get to write the rules.' He added grudgingly: 'A message from the prime minister: he seems to think that you're doing a good job.'

With that Houseman ended the conversation.

33

Jez opened his eyes and stared disbelievingly at his bedroom ceiling. Outside the dawn chorus was in full avian throat to greet what promised to be another hot June day.

He had actually done it! He had managed to fall asleep on the eve of the greatest day of his life! He had gone to bed early, praying for sleep to speed the hours, and now the wonderful day had finally dawned. The weeks of calendar-watching torment were over. But there was a whole host of nagging doubts to temper his elation. He listened intently to the news. Thankfully, there were no reports of strikes or technical problems with the Eurostar services. He punched the frequency of the French FM station that he had found some weeks before. To pull in a decent signal had meant stringing a wire dipole aerial across his bedroom. His Mother had complained, of course. The station gave regular travel bulletins. Bus and train services in northern France seemed to be running normally. So far, so good.

A quick shower followed by a shave. At the beginning of the year he had needed to shave only once a week. Now it was every other day. He went quietly downstairs. If he disturbed his parents, the chances were that his mother would comment on his uncharacteristic choice of a freshly laundered shirt and clean tie. It was vital that he appeared to do nothing out of the ordinary today. He had planned everything down to the last detail. Two weeks before, he had started leaving home an hour earlier than usual, saying that he wanted to walk to school instead of using the bus now that the long hours of daylight had arrived. His mother had complained, of course. Her offspring's early starts denied her the right as a good mother to stuff a large breakfast into her growing boy's stomach every morning, even though Jez wasn't growing.

This morning all Jez could manage for breakfast was a slice of toast to keep the butterflies company. Pausing to listen for movements from upstairs, he made himself a sandwich, inexpertly hacking ragged slices off the salt beef joint he found in the refrigerator because the electric knife made such a racket. He stuffed it in his trusty old kitbag along with the Mars bars and cans of self-chilling Coke that he had been hoarding. The prices of snacks in France were ruinous, especially at Sabre Industries' tourist bars. A final check on his inventory in the security of his bedroom. He wanted to travel light, therefore much of the rubbish that had accumulated in his kitbag had been cleared out. Everything was there: money, ID card, food and drink, Eurotravel snapcard timetables, autograph book, new dark glasses, new baseball cap, pen, spare contact lenses, day excursion through ticket, and lastly, most important of all: the priceless gold-edged invitation card, now in a protective plastic sleeve.

He had deferred a decision on whether or not to take his camera. Should he or shouldn't he? If his parents ever found the resulting pictures, the two and two they would put together would add up to six – being the number of months of mass confiscation of all his treasures. But not to have a record of this wonderful event he would be witnessing today . . . It was an electronic camera that snapped instant pictures into its memory. He could always keep the images on his computer with password protection. Most of his friends stored some quite fascinating pictures in this manner. The last batch he had seen had stirred an already awakening interest in girls, but he doubted if they would ever subvert his passion for the Sabre, although of late he had often fallen asleep with a sex problem on his mind and woken up with a solution on his stomach. He had decided to acquire a girlfriend some time that year. If nothing else, to find out if they really did look like those pictures. But the spaceplane came first. The camera went into his kitbag.

His final chore was to dictate a message to the kitchen television. The sentences appeared on the screen, telling mum not to worry if he was late back from school because he was going round to John's house. He knew four Johns and could always invent a fifth if his mother took it into her head to phone them all.

He scooted out of the house just as he heard someone enter the bathroom. His next worry was the faint chance of being recognised on Richmond station. The baseball cap and dark glasses solved that because normally he never wore such absurdities. The dark glasses were a hazard because his contact lenses had darkened automatically in the bright sunlight anyway. Getting to the right platform involved frequent stops to lift the dark glasses to see where he was going. He kept them on while aboard the Waterloo train just in case one of his father's commuter friends saw him, and he was the last to leave the train on arrival in London.

The rest of the journey went without a hitch. The safety margins he had built into his schedule to cover last-minute Eurostar cancellations were not needed. He found himself in the bustle of St Omer's Gare du Nord at 11.30 a.m. – well ahead of schedule. The roll-out ceremony was due to start in three hours at 14:30.

Then disaster struck.

He stared aghast at the sign in the bus terminal. The hourly tourist bus service to Sabre Industries had been cancelled that day. The complex was closed to the public due to a special event.

How could he have been so stupid as not to have foreseen that? He frantically flexed the Eurotravel snapcard through its displays until he found the St Omer region, but its coverage of bus services was hopelessly limited. From a nearby timetable and map he learnt that there was an Abbeville bus in an hour's time that would take him to within eight kilometres of Sabre Industries, provided the driver stopped at the Fruges turn-off that led to the complex. A taxi was out of the question on his finances, so it would have to be the bus.

The bus was thirty minutes late leaving the terminal. Jez suffered agonies as it ground south, stopping and starting every hundred metres it seemed, and every new passenger bringing the driver up to date with their life history before he moved off.

The outskirts of the town thinned to countryside and the stops became less frequent. Jez didn't realise that they were at Fruges until they were leaving it, when he saw a road sign with a slashed line across it. No, the driver couldn't stop – there was no designated stop for three kilometres. Which struck Jez as unfair because he had arbitrarily stopped for just about every passenger.

It was 1.20 p.m. when the bus finally disgorged him on a lonely stretch of D road fringed with poplars and potato fields that stretched to the horizon. The roll-out was due to begin in seventy minutes and, as far as he could work out, he was at least ten kilometres from Sabre Industries. Could he walk that distance in time? Well, there was only one way to find out.

He set off back towards Fruges at a brisk pace, but after fifteen minutes the heat forced him to slow down. It was turning into a suffocatingly hot day, with the sun beating down on the road from a cloudless sky. His trainers soon got to work on establishing what promised to be painful blisters. The sporadic trucks and cars that swept by ignored his upraised thumb. He had read somewhere that France had made it illegal to pick up hitch-hikers.

He trudged on, trying to keep to the meagre shade offered by the poplars, his spirits sinking with each burning step. The frequent roar of low aircraft losing height as they passed overhead to the west, dropping into Sabre Industries, added to his mounting misery. The complex was so near and yet so far. The aircraft were a mixture – executive jets, Airbuses and light planes – all converging on the grand event that he had so looked forward to all these weeks and was now destined to miss. The whine of a bright yellow Mistral drowned the sound of the car until it was almost too late. Luckily the ancient Citroën was incapable of serious speed. The driver spotted his frenzied thumb-waving and brought the thirty-year-old 2CV Dolly to a shuddering standstill in the middle of the road.

144

Jez piled gratefully in beside her, expressing his thanks in a confused mixture of French and English. She was a large-boned, friendly brunette, wearing a short skirt rendered even shorter by the cramped seat. Her breasts strained impatiently at her blouse buttons as she cranked the awkward dashboard gear lever and the car moved off. Her smile was as wide as the bench seat was narrow. Jez guessed that she was about thirty-five, but he was not very good at judging the ages of women over fifteen. She had wide, almost almond-shaped brown eyes that complimented her generous mouth.

'I think English is better for us, yes?' she said. 'I am Louise. You must tell me what such a pretty English boy is doing here alone like this.'

'I'm going to the roll-out of the first commercial-service Sabre,' said Jez proudly. 'I have an invitation.'

'But you will be late walking!' Louise exclaimed in concern. She stirred on the seat in agitation, bringing her hip into contact with Jez's thigh and dislodging from his mind the question he was about to ask as to how she knew the time of the ceremony.

'If you could drop me at Fruges, please, I will be really grateful and should be able to make it on time.'

'It is too hot for walking,' Louise scolded jokingly, chucking him under the chin. 'You must let me take you to the Sabre front gate.'

'Oh but I couldn't let you do that,' Jez protested. 'I don't want you to go out of your way.'

Louise's answer was to put her hand on Jez's thigh and give him a friendly squeeze. Her hand remained in place for a few moments, testing its welcome. Then she slid it over his hand and guided it to the inside of her parted thigh just above the knee. Jez's first reaction was to pull away, but the touch of her bare skin was altogether too fascinating.

'The Sabre is not the only example of good Anglo-French friendship, is it not?' she said mischievously. 'What is your name?'

'Jez – short for Jeremy.' Her skin felt magically smooth.

'How old are you . . . Jez?'

'Fifteen next month.'

'Ah – fifteen,' said Louise wistfully. 'Such a lovely age.' She pointed to a copse by a stream as they passed by. 'I had my first lover there when I was fifteen. Or perhaps I was fourteen?' She laughed to herself.

Jez complimented her on her good English while wondering what to do about his left hand. His fingers were the prisoners of Louise's determined grasp.

Fruges was deserted, which was just as well because Louise's hand had marched its captives further up her thigh to the unguarded portals of her soft castle. Jez's emotions swam at the shock of this first contact, and felt her moat starting to fill.

'Look out for the signs,' sighed Louise.

'Next right,' Jez replied, his voice cracking as Louise's hand became a drill instructor in command of a platoon of not unwilling fingers. Even when she had to change gear, her charges remained on duty. 'But I can't let you take me all the way.'

'Oh, but you must . . . Ah . . .!'

They trundled along the stretch of road that led to Sabre Industries. It had once been a farm track and, unusual for a French road, meandered. A chauffeur-driven limo sidled up behind the Citroën, tooted its horn and swept past. Jez wondered what the time was but his wrist-watch was hidden between Louise's clenching thighs.

She snatched a handkerchief from between her breasts and gripped it in her teeth. '*Vitesse!*' she gasped. 'Faster, please!'

'Are we nearly there?' Jez asked.

'*Oui! Oui! Oui!*'

Jez could only wonder at her excellent control; her buttocks bounced dementedly around on the seat like eager lottery balls before selection and yet the Citroën remained unerringly on course, following the road's twists. Only once did the 2CV wobble slightly when she suddenly arched her back off the seat and gave a muffled shriek into her handkerchief. A tempting nipple popped briefly into view. An Airbus roared overhead, drowning her sobs. Horrified, Jez tried to pull his hand away but Louise's thighs locked tightly together and kept the platoon at their station.

'I've hurt you!' Jez exclaimed.

Louise relaxed and allowed the drenched soldiers to stand down. They had done their duty admirably. She stuffed the handkerchief between her breasts and slowed down to give Jez a quick kiss on the cheek. 'You are a good boy, Jez. But of course you didn't hurt me. You have your invitation? They won't let you in without it.'

Jez delved into his kitbag. His fingers, which had found out so much in the last few minutes, found the invitation. He looked up and was surprised to see the main gates of Sabre Industries straight ahead. The queue of waiting cars was being cleared quickly by security men. He looked at his watch. A little after 14:00. He was in good time and brimming with gratitude for this wonderful woman. She had further surprises in store when she turned the 2CV into the entrance and stopped at the barrier as it dropped after admitting a taxi. She showed her identity card to the security guard and clipped it to her blouse. The guard inspected Jez's invitation, gave him a sharp look, a numbered seat ticket and a programme, and raised the barrier.

'You work here?' Jez stammered as the Citroën entered the complex and turned on to the perimeter road, following the taxi.

Louise gave a little laugh. 'You are not angry with me?' she asked reproachfully.

Jez shook his head. He was about to ask which department she worked in when the apron came into sight. His heart thrilled to the magnificent spectacle. Two rows of towering flagpoles, each bearing the flag of a nation whose products had contributed to the Sabre or was proposing to buy it, bounded a red-carpeted expanse that extended across the apron, drawing the eye to the huge construction shed where Sabre 005 would soon be emerging into the bright

June sunlight. A canopied rostrum was in place at the other end of the flagged avenue like an altar at an outdoor service, and beyond that a press stand, packed with newsmen making last-minute adjustments to their equipment. Well-dressed crowds were milling around the horseshoe rows of garden tables and chairs, gossiping loudly in small groups – hardened reception attendees, not wanting to lose peer credit by actually sitting, wondering why the drinks weren't free. A few security men were doing their best to keep visitors off the expanse of red carpet. Two Autovacs were at work, while a third had been cornered by a group of giggling debs' delights whose collective IQ was on a par with the machine they were tormenting. The hapless robot cleaner kept testing escape routes while complaining loudly in French, and had to be rescued by security men.

'I will drop you here,' said Louise, stopping. 'I have to go to the staff car park.' She treated Jez to another kiss, this time on the lips, and stroked his cheek. 'You are a very nice boy, Jez. I will see you when the tea is served.'

Jez thanked her profusely and climbed stiffly from the car, his recent experience not entirely forgotten. He waved to Louise as the absurd little car rattled off, and stood drinking in the wonderful scene, holding his kitbag awkwardly in front of him. A howl of feedback and a test voice boomed from speakers, counting in French.

He decided that his baseball cap would look out of place in this smartly dressed crowd. The dark glasses alone would have to suffice for disguise. He moved towards the semi-circle of tables and chairs, keeping his face turned away from the press-stand, and was accosted by a smiling stewardess wearing a new version of the Sabre uniform. The French influence clearly apparent in a hemline a little below C-level, and a neckline like a graph plot of a stock market crash and recovery. She looked at his seat ticket and directed him to a table. Jez was disappointed that it was on the outside row. The tables were smaller, with only two chairs each. Jez guessed that they were for loners like himself. A craggy, bull-necked, stocky man with an age-lined face and broken nose was already seated at the table when Jez joined him. He was smoking a cigar and fanning himself with a fedora.

'Sure is hot,' said Joe Yavanoski genially, wondering if Jez was the harbinger of swarms of kids yet to appear.

Jez politely agreed that it was and edged his chair around so that its back was towards the massed TV cameras. The swarms of Hovercams worried him. The bloody things were everywhere and their lenses were the equal of their big brothers because they could get so close.

'You're English,' Joe stated.

'Yes, sir.'

'Guess I'm too old for this heat. One thing about being outside though – at least I can smoke.'

An Autovender stopped nearby and did some brisk business selling cans of self-chilling drinks. Jez looked at his watch. Five minutes to go. The stewardesses were ushering people to their seats. The Autovacs spied and sucked up the last fragment of litter and trundled off the carpet.

Jean Lesseps spotted Joe Yavanoski and made his way to the table. He had hoped that Joe would be alone but there was a kid with him. Joe gave the French-Canadian a cursory glance as his shadow fell across him and returned his attention to a nearby stewardess who was bending over talking to a visitor.

'I'm English,' Jez blurted nervously when the stranger spoke to him in rapid French. The man was wearing a staff badge. An icy hand stilled Jez's heart. Maybe there was a ban on kids and he was about to be evicted?

'Sorry,' drawled Lesseps, grinning down at Jez. 'My table's too near the god-damned speakers.' He gestured across the expanse of red carpet. 'Front row over there. You wanna swap?' He held out his staff ticket.

'Yes please!' said Jez eagerly. 'Thank you. Thank you very much indeed, sir!' They exchanged tickets and Jez hotfooted around the perimeter rather than risk the wrath of the security men by crossing the red carpet. He found the table without trouble and was too spellbound by its superb position to notice that it was some distance from the nearest battery of speakers.

'Polite kid,' Lesseps remarked as though striking up a conversation with a stranger as he sat in Jez's vacated chair.

'Yeah,' said Joe laconically, still ogling the stewardess.

'That's the English for you,' Lesseps commented. 'You're looking well, Joe—'

'We talk when the circus starts,' said Joe cryptically. An expectant hush fell when the limousines appeared and sidled up to the rostrum. A voice boomed from the speakers requesting everyone to remain seated. Jez sat on his kitbag so that he got a reasonable view of Paul Santos leading his colleagues and guests up the rostrum's steps. Jez recognised most of them: the entire board of Sabre Industries including Ralph Peterson, the chief designer. The faces he didn't recognise would be the Rolls-Royce team. Alan Bond was there – the man who had conceived the Hotel and Skylon projects back in the 1980s and who had persuaded Rolls-Royce to begin work developing the Synergic Air-Breathing Rocket Engine at a time when there were no customers for it.

Paul stood at the microphone and waited for total silence. He spoke very quietly, first in English and then French, but the quality of the public address system was such that every word was amplified clearly to the huge gathering. To Jez's relief the Hovercams had vanished as soon as Paul started speaking. The crowd listened attentively to his opening words and laughed at his joke about fortune favouring those who took chances with the European stock exchanges to finance such a magnificent project, and who took even bigger chances with the weather in northern France to launch such a project outdoors.

'The Sabre is the most exciting and most expensive venture that Europe has ever embarked on,' Paul continued, his soft tone scarrying immense authority that stilled the entire crowd. 'It has been born out of the confidence of seventy-five years of peace and prosperity within our borders. It is an aircraft for the people, financed by the people. Not a penny of government money has gone into it. It belongs to us – the people of Europe.'

He paused, his grave eyes seeming to look penetratingly at everyone in turn like a skilled headmaster addressing an assembly. 'It is more than an aircraft, more than a means of flying from one place to another faster than anyone has ever done before. It is so much more than that. Sabre will give ordinary men and women the opportunity to share in the spiritual adventure of going into space – to go to the very brink of the final frontier where our future lies.' He paused for effect.

'That great adventure starts on Friday, 18 December. On that day the first fare-paying passengers in history to travel into space will see our mother earth as everyone should see it – a beautiful creation drifting alone in the firmament. But those 200 men and women on that first flight will be ordinary men and women like you and me. They will not be from the privileged few. The 200 seats will be subject to a draw to be held right across Europe. Every European citizen who wishes to buy a ticket will be able to take part in that draw. Tickets will then be made available at the normal fare to the lucky names, but I stress that they won't be free. They will be sold at the first class rate.'

The news caused a stir and provoked warm applause. It electrified Jez. Would he be eligible to take part at his age? He checked himself. What was the point of worrying? He could never afford the fare.

Paul waited for silence to be restored before continuing. 'That decision was taken some weeks ago. But another important decision concerning the Sabre was decided in my office last year on the toss of a coin. The coin was tossed by the chairman of Air France, and called by the chairman of British Airways. The toss was to decide who 005 should go to and so who should have the honour of operating the very first commercial flight.' He adopted a woebegone expression which caused a ripple of laughter in anticipation at what was to come next. 'As a patriotic Frenchman, I regret to say that Air France lost the toss.' He brightened, and that produced more laughter. 'But as a good European, I'm delighted to say that the winners are the most successful

151

airline in Europe and the world! British Airways!'

Enthusiastic applause greeted Paul's diplomatic wording.

'No mention of the part that America played in making that bird a reality,' Joe muttered to Lesseps, his mild tone disguising his smouldering hatred.

'There's not much of the original SOFT design left in the Sabre now, Joe.'

'Ladies and gentlemen,' said Paul, 'I call on the gentleman who called and won that toss to present his Sabre to the world! Sir Andrew Hobson!'

Hobson was not a man given to smiling and yet not only did he do so during his short speech, but he also managed a joke, which David Morgan had written for the occasion. It wasn't a very good joke, but Hobson was no more equipped to judge humour than was a chimpanzee to summarise Proust. 'I've been told that all I have to do is press this button,' he concluded. 'So here goes – because it's a lot easier than signing cheques for the Sabres. Ladies and Gentlemen – Sabre Zero Zero Five!'

And he pressed the button.

The laughter and applause died away and an expectant hush fell. All eyes went to the construction shed's massive sliding doors. Jez wriggled on his seat as the first deep chords reverberated from the speakers, sending little shivers of anticipation racing up and down his spine. At first nothing seemed to be happening, then he saw that clouds of white vapour had begun swirling from vents set into the carpet near the mighty doors. As he watched, more of the hidden vents started emitting the strange fog until a dense white screen completely obscured the building. The chords rose to a crescendo that blended into the stirring strains of the European anthem: Beethoven's *Ode to Joy*, hijacked from his Ninth Symphony.

At that moment a projector of colossal power to make its effect visible in the strong sunlight sprang into life. The curtain of fog changed to a shimmering blue and one by one, the golden stars of the European Union formed a circle of dazzling auric light in the centre of the swirling, iridescent blue. The simple design of the European flag, shown in such awesome splendour, caused an involuntary pricking at the corners of Jez's eyes. Normally he would have dismissed such powerful emotions as frivolous patriotism but the swelling music and the stunning spectacle swept aside such reservations. He was not the only one so moved. A woman near him was actually crying, but he didn't take his eyes off the mighty, luminous flag. Something appeared in the exact centre of the circle of stars. It was like the tip of a knight's lance. It emerged slowly into the bright sunlight, steadily lengthening and increasing in diameter until the stars were shining on the polished aluminium of Sabre 005's materialising nacelle. The flush windows of the cockpit next – the projector's beam flaring on the Plasglas. Then the wings appeared, gently parting the swirling curtain and allowing it to close over and under them like a lover's embrace. Secondary jets of vapour sprang up in the path of the spaceplane, completely obscuring its undercarriage as it advanced into the light so that it appeared to be floating on a cloud. It came to a halt with the tip of its needle-like nose not twenty metres from where an entranced Jez was sitting.

Suddenly he found himself on his feet, joining in the whistles, cheers and thunderous applause until his throat and hands were sore from their rapturous acclaim. The vents stopped, the clouds dispersed quickly in the heat and the music died away.

'Sabre 005,' Paul's voice boomed above the continuing uproar. 'God's speed to all who fly in her!'

And there she stood. A shining goddess. The most wondrous, most beautiful creation that Jez had ever seen. It was so different from its three predecessors, not counting the mock-up. This was the real thing. She was ready to begin work, as was evident from the British Airways logo emblazoned on her knife-like tailplane.

Joe slumped back in his chair when the applause died down and the crowds began surging across the carpet towards the spaceplane. He had joined in the clapping to avoid drawing attention to himself. He could talk freely to

153

Lesseps now – the tables around the two men were emptying – but they kept their distance. To an observer they were strangers – a member of the staff following instructions and making a visitor feel at home.

'Quite a show,' Joe remarked grudgingly. 'That Santos guy is a helluva showman.'

'But not such a good salesman,' said Lesseps. 'You heard the news today?'

'Commonwealth have deferred a decision on their options until next year. Yeah, I heard. Still means he's got eighteen definites in the bag. And British Airways and Air France are sure to go ahead. This loan deal is a big sham.'

'The eighteen won't be enough,' said Lesseps.

Joe turned his bushy eyebrows towards the French-Canadian and jerked his thumb in the direction of the enthusiastic crowds thronging around 005. 'You know anyone here today? Any of those faces?'

Lesseps was puzzled. 'Only my colleagues.'

'They're all here!' Joe snapped. 'Everyone who's something in civil aviation is here right now. If they were half convinced by that Sydney to London fifty-nine-minute stunt, then they sure as hell are going to be knocked out by this little show.'

'Surely it doesn't work like that,' said Lesseps. 'There are accountants—'

'Bullshit. It works like Wall Street. Herd instinct. That Santos guy knows that. The airlines have got to buy airplanes to see them into the middle of the century. But which hoop do they jump through? The hoop that says bigger but safe, boring conventional jets and safe, boring conventional profits? Or the hoop that says sexy spaceplanes and profits higher than that pretty bird can fly? So what do they do? Same as on the floor of Wall Street. They hang back and keep their eyes on the pack leaders. One pack leader makes a move. That fires up the courage of another pack leader. And that triggers a couple more. And then you've got yourself a stampede, and if you ain't out in front you eat dust. Afterwards they get their accountant

154

munchkins to produce reports to kid their stockholders into thinking that they've made sober, rational decisions. That's how it works. Unless a wrench . . .' He broke off, not wanting to enter deeper water with Lesseps until he knew more about the undercurrents. He looked speculatively at the French-Canadian and found himself loathing everything about him. The sallow complexion, broad face and wide-set eyes, and that oily, lank hair falling across his eyes. 'So how're things with you?'

'Fine, Joe. Just fine. I'm really grateful to you for all you've done—'

'You've said all that.' Joe could sense that something was praying on his mind.

Lesseps gave a nervous smile. 'So what do you think of the reports I've been sending you, Joe?'

The American unwrapped a cigar and tore off the band with his teeth. Now was the time to hit this shit hard. 'What do I think of the reports you've been sending me? I'll tell you – they could earn you twenty years for industrial espionage. I fix you up with a job and in gratitude you send me information I didn't ask for. Drawings, specifications – hundreds of them. And plenty of notes in your handwriting with your fingerprints on them. Jesus Christ, you would've been in deep shit if the US postal authorities had opened them. And you sure will be if I decide to hand them over.'

The flame of raw panic in Lesseps's eyes was exactly what Joe expected and got. And even if he hadn't seen that sudden onset of terror, you could smell it. The guy had the glands of a skunk: they gave off fear. Solid waves of it you could carve your initials on.

'But . . . But . . . There are your payments when you cleared my debts—'

'Pipexed to all your debtors through several Net bureaux using cash,' said Joe cryptically. He grinned at his trembling victim. 'Whoever made those payments was careful and left no traces – as anyone buying industrial secrets would be. And then no more money came your way after you'd taken up here. Maybe whoever was paying you didn't like the

155

information you were sending them so you turned to me. And being a law-abiding citizen, I report the matter and you get twenty years in the pokey. French pokeys; British pokeys; Canadian pokeys; US pokeys – they're all pokeys.'

'Hi, Joe!'

Joe twisted in his chair and returned the friendly wave of a tall, stooped man about his own age who was trying to make headway with a stewardess half a century his junior.

'Thought you'd be here, Joe,' said the tall man. 'Great airplane, huh?'

'Great airplane, Walt,' Joe replied non-committally. 'Go easy on the girls – hard on the heart. And that airplane's gonna be real hard on cash reserves.'

The stooped man laughed and moved away with his arm around the girl, his long fingers reaching across her buttocks.

'Walter Graymond,' said Joe laconically. 'Pacific Rim Airlines. Runs a lot of long-haul routes West Coast–Asia. He'd sooner eat pussy than dust.' He chuckled at his joke, but it wasn't appreciated by Lesseps. He was still staring ashen-faced at Joe, terror and sweat oozing from every pore.

'Joe – you can't do this to me.'

'Sure I can. A lot of witnesses here, seeing you talking to me. Their evidence would back up my story that you're trying to sell me information.' Joe chuckled. 'But who said anything about doing anything? I said what those reports *could* earn you.'

'But . . .' Bafflement overlaid the fear in Lesseps' eyes. 'I don't understand . . .' He leaned forward and clutched at his antagonist's sleeve. Joe pulled smartly back. 'For God's sake, Joe. Why are you doing this?'

Joe drew on his cigar and exhaled slowly, savouring the wild look of desperation in the French-Canadian's eyes. Now to spring the trap. He tipped his fedora forward and leaned back, steepling his fingers on his stomach, regarding his victim steadily. 'If I know anything about airplane construction, that pretty bird ain't ready to go nowhere yet. That right?'

Lesseps forced himself to focus on what Joe said. He glanced at 005 and nodded, his frightened stare gling back to his antagonist. 'A lot to be done,' he muttered, half to himself.

'A lot of work that you have to do?'

'Yes.'

'I want you to make something. I'm stopping over in London for a few more days. The Savoy. Expensive, but what the hell. You come to me with a workable plan within seven days and you'll earn yourself another half a million dollars.'

'Another half a million? Make something?' Lesseps felt foolish and humiliated at this parrot-like repetition.

'My guess is that you could use another half a million dollars,' said Joe lazily. 'My guess is that you've gotten yourself along a path that gets you up to your neck again.'

Lesseps's silence answered his question. Joe fanned himself with his fedora, watching Lesseps carefully.

'So what is it that you'll want me to make?' Lesseps asked at length.

'A wrench,' said Joe simply, and chuckled at his companion's expression. 'Big enough to knock a bird off its perch come next December.'

34

On the other side of 005 Jez was confronting a problem of a different sort. Or rather, two problems. Louise, now kitted out in a Sabre uniform, had arrived to wipe the table where he was sitting alone. He had been feasting his eyes on 005 while eating his sandwich, admiring the changing light on the polished aluminium as the sun moved westward. But Louise's bosom pals were having a jostling argument and looked in danger of falling out. They held his surreptitious attention while she chatted. His dark glasses were proving their worth.

'Such an exciting day,' she was saying. 'So many new

157

experiences.' She bent lower to wipe the vacated chairs. 'Such a magnificent spectacle.'

'Yes,' Jez agreed woodenly, praying that she wouldn't want him to stand in order to wipe his chair.

'Strawberries and cream,' said Louise brightly, straightening. 'A big bowl, yes?'

'I can't afford it,' said Jez sadly, having seen stewardesses scurrying by with mouth-watering orders.

Louise's little laugh was followed by a friendly tweak of Jez's earlobe which set it on fire. 'You will be my guest,' she insisted as she moved off. She was back a few minutes later with a generous bowl of strawberries and a little jug of cream. She poured the cream and splashed some on Jez's hand. 'Oh, pardon!'

She no longer had her cloth but she did have her French resourcefulness. She put Jez's fingers in her mouth, closed her warm lips and gently withdrew his fingers. Jez thought he was going to faint. No one around them seemed to notice, but this wasn't England.

'You have such clever fingers, Jez.'

'Really?'

'How will you get back to St Omer?'

'The bus.'

'Oh, but it is so slow and such a long way to the stop! You must let me take you.'

'No – really – I couldn't.'

'But you must!' Louise insisted, pouting. 'Otherwise I will think that you no longer love me. I finish work soon. I could meet you where I dropped you in forty-five minutes.'

Jez thought quickly. A lift to St Omer would solve a worry and he would be in good time for an early train. Also, he was finding the heat wearing. He thanked Louise and gratefully accepted her offer.

Louise smiled happily. 'Wonderful. Forty-five minutes.'

She was on time. Her 2CV scooped Jez up. His eyes almost punched the lenses out of his dark glasses when he scrambled in, causing him to forget to take one last look at 005. 'You're still in your uniform,' he blurted.

'Oh . . . the changing rooms, they are so full. I would have kept you waiting.'

The Citroën's windscreen badge was enough for them to be waved through the main gate without formality. The little car accelerated along the road to all of 70 kph, although the protesting uproar from the knackered air-cooled engine spoke of double that speed.

'I've got plenty of time,' said Jez nervously.

Louise flashed him a quick smile. 'I've smuggled some food from the staff restaurant. We can have a little pique-nique. I have a favourite place . . . But of course, I have told you about it.'

Ten minutes later the Dolly bumped off the road and parked under the trees where it was hidden from the road. Louise stopped the engine and reached up to open the roof. Tree-dappled golden sunlight streamed into the little car and a pleasant breeze wafted through the open windows. The nearby stream flowed sluggish and silent.

'This is the exact place where I stopped being a virgin,' Louise announced. She laughed at Jez's expression. 'Ah, I am so sorry, my little Jez, I have shocked you.'

Jez assured her that she hadn't. An Airbus climbed away and turned towards Paris. Louise kicked off her shoes. She twisted around so that her back was resting against the driver's door and plonked her bare feet on Jez's thigh, her knees slightly parted and almost touching her chin in the confined space. He noticed, among other things, that she had surprisingly long, supple toes which she flexed enticingly as she talked. 'He was English, like you,' she said dreamily, gazing up at the overhanging branches. 'Older than me. Perhaps my age now, and I was your age . . .' She slipped a hand in her top and toyed absently with her breast. 'He was on a bicycle holiday. By himself, a loner – I think that's the word – just like you.' She took her hand away, leaving a nipple exposed, and touched Jez's temple. He sensed that she was using him in her strange, wonderful way to relive memories that had a special magic for her, but he wasn't going to complain.

159

'And he was pretty,' said Louise. 'Just like you . . . Oh – I think that is not the right word.'

Jez hardly noticed what she had said but he joined in with her infectious laughter. Her toes had walked her right foot higher up his leg as she talked and had started to work a little mischief on their own account.

'You have a camera, Jez?

''Yes – but I didn't use it. There were notices saying that I would need to buy a licence.'

Louise gave an angry little shake of her head. 'They are so mean . . . You must take some pictures of me as compensation.'

Jez said that he would love to and produced his camera. Louise's posing was skilled and completely unselfconscious. Still leaning against the driver's door, she twisted her body this way and that, going through a repertoire of provocative positions that thrilled Jez as he peered through the viewfinder and clicked the shutter. For the final shot she lifted one foot on to the dashboard and held her hair in a pile with both hands, pouting alluringly straight at the camera like a professional model. None of the pictures could be considered obscene, with the possible exception of the last one, but they would be unlikely to meet with parental approval.

'Show me,' said Louise, holding out her hand. She took the camera and looked through the viewfinder, clicking slowly through the images. 'I wanted you to have something to remember me by,' she said, returning the camera. 'I have nothing but memories of my English boy.'

'There's one I could erase,' Jez offered.

'Which one?'

'The last one.'

A teasing little smile played at the corners of her mouth. 'But why would you want to rub me out?'

Jez wished that he had kept quiet. He groped for words. 'It shows your . . . It shows . . . It shows that you are *sans lingerie*.' His voice faltered in embarrassment.

Louise gave a delighted laugh, threw her arms around him and kissed him on the cheek. 'My little Jez is already the

English gentleman. You must keep it. It is a captured moment that must live for always. Use it in your lonely moments, but you must never think badly of me.'

'I would never do that,' said Jez seriously.

She gave him a strange little half-smile and kissed his chest where his shirt was open. She undid some more buttons and her head went lower. Jez touched her hair and marvelled at its softness. A minute slipped by and he found himself cradling her head, nervously at first and then with steadily mounting gratitude at the heady contact of her lips. The moment came and fled in a heavenly instant, but leaving a burning impression on his memory that time would never fade.

She straightened and tidied him but Jez's eyes remained tightly closed.

'Is there anything else you would like me to do?' she asked.

Jez opened his eyes and focused them on her. He nodded, his thoughts still a confused whirl. 'Oh, yes . . .' It came out as a croak. He cleared his throat. 'Would you mind signing my autograph book?'

35

For three days after the fateful discussion with Joe Yavanoski at the 005 roll out, Lesseps brooded on the problem of placing a bomb aboard the spaceplane, unable to concentrate properly on his work.

But even if he were prepared to commit such a terrible act it was out of the question. Every centimetre of the 005 was checked, rechecked and checked again. Never had any aircraft been subjected to such rigorous and continuous scrutiny.

'There's got to be somewhere,' Joe had said at the roll-out.

'Joe – please believe me. She's not built in the ordinary way. All the airframe sections are machined from solid and can be unbolted. There are no hidden corners. Inside she's a mass of lightening holes. Every part of her can be inspected and is inspected before and after every flight. There's nowhere in the systems bay and nowhere in the cabin. Come and take a look inside. No lining, no seat cushions, no bar trucks – nothing.'

But Joe had refused to set foot in the hated spaceplane and would not listen to reason.

'Joe, please,' said Lesseps desperately, lowering his voice. 'Even if the Sabre were lost, would it have any effect on confidence?'

'What are the chances of bits of the spaceplane being recovered if it blew up in space?' Joe countered. 'I'll tell you because I've been reading up. None. Every bit of wreckage would be burnt up on re-entry. And no one would know what caused it. Back in the 1950s, the Brits had a big lead with their Comet – the first passenger jet. Then Comets started crashing. Metal fatigue. It took years for confidence to be restored. And when it was, it was too late for the Brits because the 707 had taken off. That's what I want to happen again.'

'But—'

'Seven days or twenty years,' were Joe's parting words.

The time passed in a torment for Lesseps. He lay awake at night and always woke in a cold sweat when he did manage to doze off. He even considered filling the Mistral with fuel and just taking off. But where could he go? The whole of Europe was in the EU. There was nowhere to hide and he certainly couldn't hide his beloved Mistral. The finance company would take it and the last of his money, and the police would hunt him down and take his freedom. Joe had him held in the jaws of a terrifying trap.

On the fourth night there was a news report on TV that rekindled his terror. A technical clerk who had passed information to a rival freezer company received a savage fifteen-year sentence in a Lille court. Fifteen years for information on industrial freezers! What would the French throw at him for passing information on their beloved

162

spaceplane to the hated Americans?

'Mr Lesseps.'

He jumped visibly, so bad were his nerves. Claudia was standing by his work station, staring down at him with those knowing eyes. He stood hurriedly. He had learnt that she liked such courtesies.

'Are you all right?' she asked.

'Yes – fine.' He managed a reassuring smile.

'Henri's doctor has called to say that he has been taken into hospital.'

'I'm sorry to hear that,' said Lesseps. Henri Broccini was preparing the documentation on the Sabre's fuel control systems. The previous week he had been complaining of stomach pains. He hadn't attended the roll-out.

She nodded, her gaze unwrapping his secrets. 'They think a month. You will have to take over his work. We are committed to delivering all the service manuals on the fuel systems by November.'

'Do you want me to start tomorrow?'

'No. You are to start now please.'

Lesseps spent the rest of the afternoon picking up the threads of the sick man's work. None of the photographs had been converted to CD-ROM images because their quality wasn't up to standard. He decided to see what the problem was at first hand and took a golf cart to construction Shed A. He was a familiar sight on the shop floor, therefore no one took much notice of him.

005 was back in a stripped-down state, having been temporarily assembled for the roll-out. Work was badly behind. He walked under the port wing and wheeled steps in position so that he could take a good look at the complex mass of liquid oxygen and liquid hydrogen pipes that fueled the engines when they were in rocket mode. The problem with the photographs was immediately self-evident: the bright lights set flush into the shed's concrete floor to provide good illumination for the men and women working on the spaceplane were not well placed to secure clear prints for conversion to illustrations, and the portable lights lacked the

power to kill unwanted shadows. A special shoot would be needed – maybe at night when the main lights wouldn't be required.

As he studied the problem, he found himself looking for a likely site to plant a bomb. There was nowhere. The huge fuel tanks were part of the wing's weight-saving monocoque construction – they were not separate tanks with plenty of dark spaces between them where a device could be hidden. Also the pipework was well spread out to provide good thermal isolation. Everything was made deliberately accessible for fast turn-round servicing. It was not only good design philosophy, but also ensured that anything there that shouldn't be there would be immediately apparent.

He dismounted from the steps and made his way towards the wing-tip where two fitters were busy positioning the power jacks that operated the ingenious wing-warping flight control system. No likely place there . . . or anywhere.

Compared with aircraft he had been used to working on, Lesseps was always amazed at how uncomplicated the spaceplane appeared to be. It was misleading, of course. Much of the apparent simplification was due to the scrapping of the old system of massive harnesses carrying thousands of separate wires. Multiplexed light signals flowing along one optical fibre could replace a thousand individual conductors. It was the CSF-Thomson 'flight-by-light' system and matched the Sabre engines for sheer design brilliance and was an approach that the Americans hadn't even considered with their ill-fated SOFT project.

He made his way back towards the wing root and studied the exposed Sabre engines. There were many likely-looking sites in the huge, now open air-intake ducts that fed the mighty engines. But Lesseps knew the engines were subjected to continuous computer monitoring when in use. The slightest obstruction would be detected by the many sensors and reported. A bomb in an engine? No – even if there were room, there was the likelihood of the explosion being premature due to the intense heat. The thought of the Sabre crashing on take-off with all the evidence of a bomb there to be found was too horrifying to contemplate.

He returned his attention to the rocket fuel systems. Liquid oxygen and liquid hydrogen ... A lethal, volatile cocktail which was why it was used. But the technology of liquid fuel rocket engines had been perfected over a period of seventy-five years – a lifetime – and they now enjoyed a remarkable safety record.

On the other hand, it wouldn't have to be a very big explosion here to produce a cataclysmic knock-on effect ... An explosion in space just before orbital injection velocity was reached was the answer. Joe was right: the wreckage would burn up on re-entry into the atmosphere. There wouldn't be a shred of evidence left, apart from the so-called 'black box' flight recorder. The bright orange egg-shaped housing which protected the recorder had been designed to withstand re-entry. But the information it stored would only point to what everyone would know anyway – that there had been an explosion. Nothing would point to him.

But how? How? How?

He ran his hand along a liquid oxygen pipe until it encountered one of the big motorised fuel regulators manufactured by Plessey. The entire regulator was enclosed in a machined aluminium body. This part of the fuel control system regulated the regenerative cooling of the rocket's main bell. Fuel pumped around the steel jacket before being fed to the engine enabled the steel jacket to contain the awesome plasma without melting, in much the same way that water in a kettle prevented it from melting when placed on a gas ring.

If that cooling effect were suddenly lost ...

At that moment the answer to the problem came to Lesseps.

It was so simple that he wondered why he hadn't thought of it before.

It would be a perfect bomb.

Part Two
Priming and Planting

1

Alec heard the detested but faint buzz of a Hovercam. He stopped hefting suitcases into the car and stared up at the night sky.

Christine used her key-ring remote control to set the house alarm systems. She turned to the car, the blazing intruder lights projecting her shadow across the lawn. 'What's the matter, Alec?'

'Shhh!'

She shushed and waited until Alec relaxed. 'What was it?'

'Hovercam.'

'Here? At night?'

'Infra-red.'

'You're hearing things.'

'That's right. One of those bloody aerial bugs.' Alec remained staring at the sky with his back to the lights.

Christine moved towards the car. She was wearing a body-hugging travel suit that accentuated her lithe figure, its conditioner whirring softly on her belt. The water-cooled garment was a present to herself – something she had promised herself for her next visit to the tropics. In a perverse way she was now looking forward to their trip to the steaming heat and humidity of Jakarta. Honicker had kept his word and fixed their appointment with, of all people, President Sulimann. Christine had read everything she could lay her hands on about the Indonesian president and was convinced that he was a man they could do business with. Sulimann had proved himself a democratic socialist prepared to wage war on his country's crippling corruption. 'Come on, Alec. We've got a flight to catch.'

169

He turned his attention to the grounds and the encircling trees. On the advice of the security firm, they had grubbed out the shrubs, but Christine had vetoed tearing up the avenue of soaring Queen Elizabeth roses. It was now July; the double row had reached nearly three metres.

'Someone's watching us,' Alec muttered. 'Now who do we know who likes Hovercams?'

'You want me to say Shief. But a Hovercam out in the open like this? The operator would have to be nearby.'

'So?'

'So let's get going.'

Alec decided against an argument. He gave one long hard stare around, taking in nothing but light and shadows, and returned to the car.

Ian Hoskyns was a hundred metres away, crouching behind the roses and cursing the Hovercam. He had hit the recall button on the remote control unit, but instead of returning, the damned bug had taken exception to the proximity of the roses and had overridden his command. It had set itself down neatly on the lawn where Alec Rose was certain to see it. It was close enough to the couple for its mike to pick up their conversation and relay it to his earphone.

'Ian!' a voice barked in his ear. 'Can you talk?' Music and laughter in the background.

'Hold on a moment, Mr Shief,' Ian whispered, probably too quietly for his throat mike to register.

There was the double slam of car doors. An engine started and the car moved off. The security lights timed out when the car was beyond the range of their infra-red sensors. Ian waited until the sound of the engine had faded into the night. Several lights had been left on in various rooms. Probably on time switches.

'They've gone, Mr Shief. They had some luggage and I think I heard the woman say something about a plane to catch.'

The news disturbed Shief. He had spoken to Christine the previous day and she had said nothing about a pending holiday or business trip. 'In that case, Ian, it would seem that your job will be even easier, since they're not in the house.'

Ian acknowledged. He activated the remote control's tiny monitor screen and saw the building from the Hovercam's point of view. My God, it had set down close to the house – a chance in a million that Rose hadn't seen it. Thankfully, the thing was smart enough always to cut its motor on touchdown, conserving the charge in its lithium-ion cells. He operated the control that sent it to twenty metres and did a low pass over the house. A skylight caught his attention. He steered the Hovercam into a close-up and chanced a high-res shot using the flash. The control unit's memory grabbed the image and enhanced it, pumping the picture to 1,024 lines – sharp enough to read a maker's label had there been one, but Ian recognised the skylight immediately: bloody Pilkington 15-mill Armorglas in a Boulton and Paul security frame.

Shit!

A sweep around the house and several more pumped images of the windows confirmed his fears. From a distance the frames looked like genuine Victorian sash jobs. Close up, they turned out to be cunning replicas: hardened steel subframes dressed up with a PVC coating to look like timber. Bloody well dressed up too. None of the clinical sharpness that usually gave away fake wooden window frames. A self-contained slave radio transmitter on permanent stand-by would be embedded in each frame. Open or tamper with a window and it squawked to a master receiver which in turn sent a fax alarm to a security company or the local plods, complete with diagram pointing out which window someone was having a go at. The doors on the converted stables were the same. Two hundred and fifty grand's worth of security. The place wasn't going to be the pushover that he had anticipated.

'Mr Shief.'

'Ian?' Laughter and music still there.

'Problems. The place is more secure than it looks.'

'As I suspected, Ian.'

'As they've left, there's no point my waiting until the small hours. But the security systems will be armed, so I'll need a casual caller.'

'Twenty minutes, Ian.'

'Thank you, sir.'

Ian used the time to stow the Hovercam in its case and unpack his tool-kit, transferring those tools he would need to a linesman's pouch belt. His climbing rope was a coil of plastic strapping attached to a grapnel, lighter and less bulky than rope. He was pulling on a balaclava helmet when a pair of headlights turned into the drive and sprayed light on the front of the house. The security lights retaliated, exploding into glaring life, trouncing the approaching car's efforts by 3000 watts.

Shief parked his Rolls-Royce near the front entrance. The car was lit up like a lone ballerina. He stepped out, blinking in the harsh glare, moved to the front door so that the CCTV camera would see him, and rang the bell. The door was fitted with a facial recognition system. It responded with: 'Sorry, Mr Shief.' It was Christine's sampled voice. 'We're not available at the moment. Please leave a voice message and we'll get back to you as soon as possible. Speak now.'

'Hallo, Chris,' said Shief genially, smiling at the smart door's logo. 'I was visiting friends nearby and saw your lights on, so I thought I'd drop by. I'll ring you in the morning.' He returned to his car and called Ian. 'I expect you noticed my arrival.'

'I certainly did, sir.'

'So how was it?'

'I'm now in position, sir.' He sounded slightly out of breath.

Shief resisted an impulse to glance up at the roof. The cameras would still be watching him. 'You're quick. Do you need me for anything else?'

'No thank you, sir. I can manage fine now.'

'What about the lights coming on when you've finished?'

'That won't be a problem, sir.'

'Don't go sabotaging anything. There must be no evidence of your visit.'

'There won't be, sir.'

Shief grunted and drove off.

Ian waited until the security lights timed out and remained motionless for a further five minutes on the roof until his night vision was back to normal. He was crouching in the valley between two steeply pitched dormer ends. The zinc rain trough he was standing on creaked as he tested the nearest row of tiles. They were modern cement pantiles, imitations of the Victorian originals on the front of the house. The first row refused to give. Nailed. He tried the lower row and was able to ease the tile from its batten without trouble.

As any decent gale knows, the greatest weakness in most houses with conventional pitched roofs is the tiles. British building practice is to nail every fifth row, relying on the weight of the tiles to keep the intervening rows in position. Owners spend considerable sums making their premises secure with alarm systems and armoured windows and yet pay scant attention to the roofs. An intruder equipped with the simplest of tools and rudimentary knowledge of building construction can gain access without trouble.

Ian had no trouble.

As a university student his vacation jobs had been labouring on building sites. He left university with a degree that was not first class, but with a knowledge of the way houses are built that certainly was. Two successful years raiding large houses without getting caught ended when he found himself confronting the business end of a shotgun in the hands of the owner of a Wimbledon mansion. Shief took a liking to Ian and offered him a job instead of handing him over to the police. The oil man needed a chauffeur – someone who was presentable, intelligent and bent. Qualities that rarely came together except in accountants. Until then the agency had been sending him either gorillas or limp young postgrads. They agreed terms, which was why Ian was now making a hole in the Roses' roof.

He used a claw hammer to lift the tiles one by one, stacking them carefully, until he had exposed half a square metre of tile battening. A few strokes with a pad saw through the wooden battens, three cuts with a Stanley knife to make a flap of the felt roof lining, and he had a hole in the roof large enough for him to wriggle through with ease. But first he checked the roof space, using an infra-red torch to sweep the dark interior. The torch's tiny screen revealed close-boarded ceiling joists piled high with ancient suitcases, old mattresses and cardboard boxes. To one side was a modern cold-water tank and header tank.

He dropped lightly into the loft and moved to the hatch – the one door into any house that was rarely fitted with a lock. It opened easily. The lights were on in the corridor. He doubted if the house was fitted with an IRIS system. The Roses probably relied on their windows rather than an Infra-Red Intruder System, but Ian was careful. He squirted some plumber's foaming polystyrene into a black plastic sack and added the catalyst. The chemicals combined, causing the bag to swell as the foam was formed. In so doing the bag gave off a considerable quantity of heat. He lowered it into the corridor and held it suspended for a few minutes – long enough for it to trigger any alarm systems. There was no sound, nor did he expect there to be; alarm systems didn't work like that. They alerted the security services but not the housebreaker. He retrieved the sack, closed the hatch and returned to the roof to wait.

He watched the lights streaming along the road. No vehicle turned into the drive. Had anyone turned up, he would have merely waited until they had checked the doors and windows and had left. He waited thirty minutes to be absolutely certain and re-entered the house. There were no locked internal doors to contend with. First job was to find the security lights control box and trip the circuit-breaker fuse. Five minutes later he was in the office over the workshop. That the lights had been left on made his job easier, but the locked steel filing cabinet that had been made doubly secure with a padlocked steel bar down the front of the draw-

174

ers was going to be a problem. He eased the cabinet away from the wall and examined the back. He counted twenty spot welds that secured the steel sheet back to the carcass.

Damn!

The trouble with spot welds was that they also spot-hardened the steel, making them a pig to drill out. Five minutes per spot if he was lucky, and if the charge in his cordless drill held out. He called Shief.

'I'm with the supplier now, sir. But I'll need at least two hours to secure a delivery.'

'So long?'

"Fraid so, sir. But it's no problem as they went off with luggage.'

'Very well. I'll stand by.'

Ian went to work with the cordless drill.

2

There was chaos around the check-in desks at Heathrow. With their customary love of secrecy, flight operations had enough information to cancel all flights to Indonesia but lacked the wit or will to tell over one thousand angry and frustrated passengers why. London Airport was an information hub: a sprawling entity tapped permanently into a global communications network, and yet all its public radio and TV station could manage were endless commercials, inane chat and reports on traffic conditions on the M25.

Alec fought his way through the mêlée to where Christine was guarding their luggage-laden trolley. 'Nothing,' he said bitterly and jabbed angrily at the insert screen on his watch which depicted a studio muppet showing viewers how to pack a suitcase. 'Nobody knows a bloody thing.'

The answer came from a worried Indonesian doctor who had called his wife on his Iridium Klipfone. 'There are tanks on the streets in Jakarta!' he announced in a half-wail. The hubbub died away. The Indonesian, now listening intently to his wife, became the focus of attention.

175

'Oh, for Christ's sake,' Christine muttered bitterly. 'That's all we want.'

'No fighting!' the Indonesian doctor announced, giving a heave of relief. 'But there are soldiers everywhere.'

'Singapore!' Christine urged Alec. 'Get our tickets changed.'

'What's the point? Everyone will have the same idea.'

'Just try! If you won't do it, look after our luggage and I'll do it!'

'Even if we get to Singapore, the chances of us—'

'Just do it!'

Alec was back a few minutes later. 'All international airports in Indonesia are closed,' he announced dejectedly.

Christine rummaged in her handbag for her Klipfone and called the presidential office in Jakarta. The answering machine detected that the call was from the United Kingdom and provided her with an English announcement to the effect that the office was unavailable until further notice. She tried Honicker's number.

'Sorry,' said the Australian's cheery voice. 'I'm at a concert and never have my phone switched on in a concert hall.'

'That's it,' said Christine dejectedly, beaten for once. 'We might as well get a refund on our tickets and go home.'

3

Ian had removed the back of the filing cabinet and was half-way through photographing the contents of the Darwin patents file when Shief called him.

'How are the negotiations proceeding, Ian?'

'I'm about half-way through the contract papers, sir.'

'Excellent. Excellent. I'm looking forward to seeing the results.'

Ian finished photographing the documents and returned the files to the drawers in exactly the same order that he had removed them. There were more papers than expected and he had used all his camera's memory cards. He Superglued the filing cabinet's back in position, confident that it would be months before his tampering was discovered, if ever, and pushed the cabinet in place against the wall. He gathered up his tools, made doubly certain that nothing in the office betrayed his visit and headed for the loft. Once on the roof, he used the same giant tube of Superglue to fix the roof felt and tile battens in place. He returned the heavy pantiles, abseiled from the roof and spent a couple of anxious minutes trying to free the grapnel. Eventually it fell at his feet. His car was parked about 500 metres away, along with several others outside a row of houses where it wouldn't attract attention.

He was stowing his equipment in the boot when, to his surprise, the Roses' car passed him and turned into their drive. He called Shief immediately with the news.

'Really, Ian? That is most curious. Are you sure you saw them leave with luggage?'

'Positive, Mr Shief. Several pieces.'

The oil man was deep in thought after he had finished talking to Ian. The news of the troubles in Jakarta had come through while Ian was in the Roses house. Flights had been cancelled and the Roses had returned home two hours later. Maybe it was just a coincidence but his instinct told him that the Roses were trying to double-cross him.

And that made him dangerous.

4

Honicker was returning to the Savoy by taxi when he remembered to switch on his Klipfone. There were several unanswered calls listed. He deemed the one from the Roses the most important and returned it, guessing that they should be well over eastern Europe by now.

'We're not,' said Christine, her voice brittle with frustration. 'We're back at home.' She told him what had happened.

'A coup!' Honicker echoed. 'So what's going on?'

'Nothing much that we can make out,' Christine answered. 'The news services here aren't very interested in Indonesia.'

Honicker promised to get back to her and called an Australian dial-up news service. The taxi driver waited patiently outside the Savoy with his meter running. Honicker was talking to Christine again five minutes later. 'An attempted coup,' he reported. 'Sulimann's still in the saddle. The air force remained loyal and took out the army's main barracks and supply depots around Jakarta. But he's suspended his entire cabinet pending an inquiry. In Indonesia that means a purge. This could be just what we want but it does mean that your meeting will have to be put on hold for the time being.'

'So what do we do now?' For once Christine sounded unsure of herself.

'Let's meet tomorrow. I'll stand you lunch here at the Savoy at one o'clock. By then we should have a clearer picture of what's happening.'

While Honicker was talking, another taxi drew up behind his. Joe Yavanoski climbed out on the side opposite the kerb to fox the doorman. Why the hell should these flunkies get a tip for opening a god-damned door? He ignored the white-gloved doorman and entered the hotel. The one thing he couldn't ignore was the pain in his knee. Christ, it was giving him hell today. Too much walking but he had enjoyed his day spent sightseeing.

His room's business terminal bleeped while he was soaking in the bathtub. He padded naked and dripping across the room. The fax machine's ID pad didn't like his wet fingerprint and refused to disgorge its message until he dried his hand. Lesseps' handwriting:

Dear Mr Yavanoski,
    The job is a great success. I've had an idea that is sure
to earn me a bonus.
    Many thanks for your help.
    Maurice Lineham.

Joe fed the sheet of paper into the thermal eraser and climbed back into the bath. He added some hot water, lit a cigar and stretched out, his stocky frame filling the tub. The heat helped his knee.

So that oily little toad had come up with an idea? He exhaled a cloud of smoke, taking care not to get the cigar wet.

About fucking time.

5

A brimming water tower dumped its icy contents on Jez's spirits when he saw the length of the registration queue outside Richmond's Going Places. His jaws froze in mid munch on a hamburger. The bits of microwaved dead cow and fried lettuce in his mouth turned to builder's sand from a council dog toilet. The travel agents had only just opened and yet the queue extended fifty metres along the pavement and, as he realised after waiting in it for ten minutes, it wasn't moving.

'Computer down,' was the rumour passed back from the authoritative head of the queue. Jez was going to be mega-late for school and bitterly wished that he had anticipated this demand. How could all these people really want to be the first fare-paying passengers in the world to go into space? With the exception of a girl in an outrageous miniskirt, they all looked so boring. He derived some comfort from the fact that the queue was steadily lengthening behind him, and that some in front got pissed off with the wait and abandoned their positions. A reporter from the local radio station appeared. Jez made himself inconspicuous – which he never found difficult – and was relieved when the man homed in on the miniskirt who was just in front of him.

'You've heard of the 5-Mile High Club?' said the girl mischievously in answer to the reporter's question. 'Well I want to be the founding member of the 200-Kilometre High Club.'

The reporter laughed and wondered whether the broadcast was too early to follow up with supplementary questions in a like vein. 'Really? What does your boy-friend think?' he asked.

'I haven't got one – I shall take pot-bellied luck with the material to hand,' the girl replied tartly.

Definitely too early. The interviewer finished off with an off-the-cuff piece into his Klipfone extension mike which Jez overheard. 'It's the same scene all over the area,' the reporter said. 'In Teddington, Hounslow, Kingston, people are queuing by the hundreds to register for seats on the first Sabre spaceplane flight, and the registration desks have been open for less than thirty minutes. It's sure to be the same picture all over the country, indeed, all over Europe. Millions of hopefuls but only 200 will be lucky. Well, maybe the odds are better than the National Lottery, but I wouldn't like to bet on it.'

His words depressed Jez even further. For a moment he was tempted to give up and go to school, but the queue started moving briskly, and the miniskirted girl was really quite fascinating. It was nearly 10.00 a.m. when he reached the woman manning the registration terminal.

'I'm very sorry, sir,' she said, 'but registration is only open to those over eighteen.'

'I'm registering for my dad,' said Jez. He gave his address.

'I've a Mr Jack Moreton on the electoral roll.'

'J. Moreton,' Jez corrected. 'He hates being called Jack.'

'A single seat or double-seat registration, sir?'

'Single,' said Jez.

The woman's fingers danced on her keyboard. 'J. Moreton it is, sir. If successful, will your father object to publicity?'

'He'd hate it,' said Jez with feeling.

'Very good, sir – no publicity.' She gave Jez a printed receipt and explained that the receipt number was the one which would go into the draw, stressing, as she was required to with every applicant, that the draw was for the chance to *buy* a ticket on the Sabre's first flight. 'If your dad wins, he'll have to buy his ticket.'

Jez said that he understood and left the travel shop clutching his receipt. He committed the number to memory: 72739.

A nasty thought. Supposing Dad tried to register? But the queue was now even longer and he realised that the unexpected popularity of the draw ought to work in his favour. The chances were that the queues would be just as long outside travel agents in London. His dad wouldn't dream of wasting his lunch-break or his money on such a frivolous venture.

Jez's step was jaunty as he set off for school and the inevitable bollocking he'd get for being late.

6

'You're late,' said Joe curtly when Lesseps sat at his table at the coffee shop on Waterloo station.

The French-Canadian placed a bulky briefcase on the table, brushed his lank hair away from his eyes and grinned sheepishly, seemingly unabashed by the abrupt opening. 'Hi, Joe. Sorry – I had trouble getting a station taxi at Fairoaks.'

'Fairoaks? What's Fairoaks?'

'A one-horse little airfield just south of London.'

Joe hooked his thumbs in the waistband of his trousers and stretched his legs out sideways to the table. He tipped his baseball cap back and unwrapped a toothpick. He went to work on his wisdom teeth. They were his own and he was proud of them. Lesseps avoided the hard stare and granite-chipped features. 'You flew here?' Joe asked casually.

Lesseps nodded. 'Sure.'

'Private?' Even more casual.

Lesseps sensed the danger in Joe's relaxed attitude and tried to talk his way around it. 'Let me take you up, Joe. It's a fantastically clear day. The whole of the English Channel is visible from the Cherbourg Peninsula to—'

The toothpick suddenly snapped in the stubby fingers.

181

'For Chrissake! The whole point of meeting here was so that you could come by train!'

'Yes, but—'

'Yes, but nothing!' Other mid-morning customers glanced at the two men. Joe lowered his voice. 'I don't suppose Europe is any different from back home. Private flights get logged. Departure and destination. If we continue to do business together you come on the train, along with hundreds of others. You go along with that or it's the deep-shit option I offered you.'

The crawling panic in the other man's eyes confirmed to Joe that his grasp on Lesseps' balls was still satisfactory. Lesseps gave a nervous smile but the look of fear lingered. A waitress took his order and returned with his coffee. He sipped it slowly, his fingers trembling, and was relieved when a spate of public address announcements emptied most of the nearby tables. Joe watched him carefully and began to question the wisdom of the whole operation. If Lesseps was nailed he had only to be gently tweaked and he'd blurt out the whole thing. But what was there to link them, apart from the fact that Joe's company had landed Lesseps his job with Sabre Industries? Nothing.

'How long will you stay in London, Joe?'

'Three weeks. It has to look like a vacation. I usually go to Hawaii, so this had better be good.'

Lesseps nodded nervously. 'It is good, Joe. Believe me.'

'So let's have some details.'

'A device as a separate entity is out of the question, Joe.'

'You mean a bomb?'

Lesseps swallowed and glanced around. 'Well . . . Yes.'

'So let's call it that.'

'There's nowhere where it could be hidden.'

The American snorted. 'So you said before. My answer's the same: crap. There must be a million and one places, especially for someone who has access to the Sabre when she's stripped down.'

'I've got plenty of pictures of the Sabre stripped down,' said Lesseps. He took a clamshell laptop computer from his briefcase and hinged it open to reveal an A4-size screen. The machine was more bulky than the increasingly popular cardboard-thin memopads, but it could send and receive faxes and provide a video link via the tiny TV camera set flush above the screen. 'Just switch it on and take a look at the "SABREPICS" menu. The first ten or so pictures are the most important.'

Joe did so. The colour images were pin-sharp – sharper than reality because the focusing ability of the human eye lacks depth of field in close-up. The deep vision 3-D effect of the digitalised photographs was such that it looked possible to reach a hand into the picture and touch the components in the fuel control system. He scrolled through the pictures one by one. Close-ups of the Sabre engines; fuel systems; fibre optic distribution boxes; fuel cells; current regulators; fire control systems. The computer's memory seemed endless. He adopted the slightly bored expression of someone called upon to look at a friend's holiday snaps, but he was impressed – not only by the quality of the photographs, but by the incredibly high standard of engineering that was so obviously going into the Sabre.

'Take a look at number four,' Lesseps invited.

Joe called up the required image – a close-up of a block of machined alloy sprouting two pairs of armoured fuel lines attached to the block by threaded couplings. Part of the Plessey designation label was just visible. 'A motorised fuel reg?' he ventured.

Lesseps nodded emphatically. 'One for each engine. They only operate when the engines are in rocket mode. Liquid hydrogen feed on the right, liquid oxygen on the left. The capsule houses the drive motors and the control circuitry.'

'So?'

'We make a substitute block. A perfect duplicate, working from the original machining drawing, only we make it from magnesium alloy instead of aluminium alloy – they look identical. Same colour. Similar hardness. But magnesium alloy weighs about thirty per cent less than aluminium.'

Joe looked at Lesseps and raised his eyebrows. 'The only

things I can remember that were made of magnesium were the old one-shot flashbulbs.'

Lesseps's Adam's apple bobbed, but other than that he was doing a good job controlling his fear. 'That's right, Joe. The stuff burns like hell. And those old flashbulbs contained only a pinch of magnesium wool – less than a gram – and the glass envelope had to be coated with a tough, clear plastic to prevent it exploding when the flash went off. A dummy regulator would consist of nearly two kilograms of magnesium.' Lesseps shed his terror and became surprisingly animated as he talked, as though he was deliberately seeing the project in terms of an engineering exercise rather than a plan to bring about the terrible death of 200 souls. 'Transfer the electric motor capsule and all the fittings – even the maker's inspection labels and serial numbers – to the magnesium block and we'd have a working fuel regulator that would look absolutely identical to the original.'

The computer sensed that there had been no activity and timed out. The screen going blank caught Joe's attention for a moment. He held up his hand. 'Now hold on. Let's not get ahead of ourselves here. I can see a whole stack of problems. First, even aluminium burns given a high enough temperature. My guess is that there's a helluva difference between getting a pinch of magnesium wool in a flashbulb to burn and getting a block of the stuff to catch.'

'You're right, Joe. The stuff used in the old flashbulbs was pure magnesium, whereas magnesium for industrial purposes is alloyed to increase its strength and ductility. It's the same with aluminium. The stuff's useless in its pure state.' He turned the computer round slightly and pointed to the motor capsule. 'A 6-mill hole bored in the main body under that cover and packed with magnesium wool with a small electric filament as an igniter ought to do the job. I'm going to have to do some experimenting.'

Joe unwrapped and lit a cigar. He was impressed but didn't show it. 'Okay, second problem. Control. How does the igniter get triggered?'

'That's easy. The regulator contains a flight-by-light logic

184

controller chip with its own built-in software – firmware. All that's needed is a few extra lines of source code to trigger the igniter on throttle-back. And throttle-back only happens once the spaceplane has reached orbital velocity.'

'And then . . .?'

'And then – bang,' said Lesseps softly.

Joe thought of the energy that was unleashed when the gram or so of magnesium in a flashbulb went off and tried to picture the explosion that would result from a block of the stuff burning – especially when it was being fed with liquid oxygen and liquid hydrogen.

'It'll be a thousand times the *Hindenburg* fireball,' said Lesseps. 'That was low-pressure gaseous hydrogen. You ever see that old black-and-white news footage?'

Joe had a vivid recollection of the newsreel – flames engulfing the mighty airship as it was docking at New York, and an even more vivid recollection of the commentator's words as he broke down in tears and yet managed to keep talking: *Please forgive me, ladies and gentlemen . . . This is terrible . . . All those people . . . Oh my God! My God!*

'It was before I was born,' said Joe laconically, shutting out the monochrome images of the blazing airship which he could see in angry crimson. He added: 'Okay. So the explosion definitely takes place in orbit?'

Lesseps nodded. 'No doubt about it. I know what you're thinking, Joe. The explosion takes place in orbit and the debris stays in orbit. A million orbits for a million bits of junk. And those that don't stay up burn up on re-entry. But a take of the fuel reg in magnesium alloy is totally obliterated within the first few milliseconds. Pretty neat, huh?'

'Pretty neat,' Joe agreed. Jesus – not only an 'invisible' bomb, but a bomb that left no trace of itself. Lesseps's fiendish scheme was more than just neat – it was fucking brilliant. 'Okay,' he said expressionlessly. 'Next problem. How do you make the reg's body?'

Lesseps produced a packet of drawings from his briefcase and partially unfolded one. It was nearly the size of the tabletop. 'One of the advantages of a fully digitalised drawing office is that it's easy to alter drawings before printing them. These are plotter outputs from the original Plessey drawing of the block but with suitable alterations before they were printed. Apart from the material spec change and removal of Plessey's name, I've changed their dimension fonts so that they don't look like Plessey drawings. Three copies, Joe. Everything you need is there. They're fully dimensioned. Tolerances, thread sizes – the works.'

'What the hell do you mean, everything *I* need?' Joe demanded, irritated by the other man's new-found confidence.

'We'll need three finished blocks, Joe. One for final testing, one to fit to the spaceplane and one back-up. You've got a decent workshop – a mill, a jig-borer, et cetera – and you know how to use them. You wouldn't have too much trouble knocking them out.'

'I don't get involved,' said Joe bluntly. '*You're* being paid to see to everything.'

'I'm no tool-maker, Joe. But it's a straightforward machining job. An angular lump of alloy – not a casting. No webs or fillets. The only difficulty I can see are those 70-millimetre coupling threads for the fuel lines, but you should be able to set your lathe up for screw-cutting. You can ignore those numbers down the side. They're the control codes for batch production of the blanks. But we only need three. Four if possible.'

Joe was anxious to reassert the control over Lesseps that he felt was slipping away. The lever was money. He pushed an envelope across the table. 'That's $50,000 in cash to cover expenses and you get half a million when the job's done. Those expenses include finding a small engineering outfit to make the bodies. *I don't get involved.*'

Lesseps ignored the envelope on the table and folded his arms. He returned Joe's hard stare without flinching. 'In that case, Joe, we don't have a deal. You'll have to go ahead and report me for industrial espionage.'

'What the fuck are you talking about?'

'I'm not taking the risk of going around to jobbing engineering companies and getting them to make those blocks. They'd all need drawings. Drawings get copied. In one, maybe two years' time, someone might see a drawing and recognise what it really is. Except that the material would be wrong.'

Joe snorted. 'Like who?'

'There're hundreds employed on the Sabre project,' said Lesseps evenly. 'Not just at St Omer, but in subcontractors all over Europe. Changing jobs – moving about. Every day would be an agony. I don't want that hanging over me for years to come.'

The blistering comment that Joe was about to voice never materialised. Despite his arrogant stubbornness, he was never totally blind to the other party's point of view when they had a valid point. Much as he disliked having to yield in negotiations, he realised on this occasion that he would have to do so. That Lesseps had tapped in to an unexpected seam of assertiveness was, in a curious way, encouraging; it meant that he wasn't so likely to panic if things went wrong. He looked at the drawing. 'I'm not used to metric dimensions.'

'Get yourself a set of digital micrometers, Joe. They're all switchable from Imperial to metric.'

'All my taps and dies are for American threads.'

'You could buy a set of metric taps and dies while you're in London,' Lesseps replied. 'A normal enough purchase for a keen model-maker.' He gave a supercilious smile, convinced that he had manoeuvred Joe into a corner.

'So what's this magnesium stuff like to work?'

It was a capitulation. Lesseps was pleased with himself. He was about to close the computer but Joe slammed the lid shut, nearly trapping his fingers. 'Careful, Joe, it's an expensive—'

'You fucking well erase what it's been recording,' said Joe softly.

The fear returned to Lesseps eyes. 'I don't know what you're—'

'This thing's been recording ever since you opened it.

Sound *and* vision.'

'Don't be silly, Joe. The activity LEDs have been blank.'

Joe kept a beefy fist planted firmly on the computer. 'You disabled the fucking lights,' he said, keeping his voice dangerously low. 'Only you made a big mistake, John. You disabled *all* the fucking lights! The stand-by light didn't come on just now when the screen blanked out.' With that Joe turned the machine over and slid the back off.

Lesseps paled. 'Joe, I've a lot of valuable data—'

'Tough,' said Joe savagely. 'You should have back-ups.' He found the memory clear button and held it down for several seconds before reassembling the machine and checking through its menus. The only software left was the memory operating system. The machine had defaulted to the manufacturer's settings. Compared with the old hard-disk-based machines, zeroing the contents of a solid state laptop was all too easy, which was why the zap button was made deliberately inaccessible. He thrust the computer into Lesseps' hands and wound up his anger, leaning across the table, his face centimetres from the other man. 'Pull another stunt like that, you little streak of rancid skunk smegma, and by Christ you're in the slammer for the next twenty years. No one shits on Joe Yavanoski. No one!'

Lesseps's new-found confidence evaporated like methylated spirits poured on a hotplate. Joe cut short the blurted apologies. He had re-established control and had Lesseps squirming – that was enough. 'Okay. Now put the god-damned thing away.'

Lesseps returned the computer to his briefcase.

'What were we talking about?' Joe demanded.

'You were wondering what magnesium alloy was like to work,' Lesseps muttered.

'So?'

The French-Canadian swallowed nervously. 'It's much the same as aluminium alloy according to the *Machinery Handbook*. Use plenty of kerosene as a lub. Back off frequently when drilling and tapping. When milling, don't try to skim more than three or four mill at a time.'

'I hate working ally.'

'I only want three. Two – minimum'

'I'm gonna have to make at least ten!' Joe snapped. 'Look at all this god-damned internal boring! I'm gonna have a helluva scrap rate!'

Lesseps was plunged into the depths of a black despair as he returned to St Omer. His trick with the laptop computer, upon which he had pinned a desperate hope of breaking Joe's terrible hold over him, had gone disastrously wrong. And now he was inextricably caught up in the whirlwind of Joe's iron will and blinding hatred, without hope of escape.

7

Paul Santos was woken by a gentle jabbing sensation on his wrist. It was the pricker alarm on his wrist-watch. For a moment he was unable to account for the quiet drone of jet engines, the darkened first class cabin and the gentle snores of slumbering fellow-passengers.

Tel Aviv, of course . . .

No . . . No . . . Monday had been Tel Aviv. Mexico City? He had a vague idea that that had been Tuesday and Wednesday. It could be Montreal because he was certain that he hadn't met Louis Canaird of Air Canada yet. Or had he? Yes, he had – the contrary bastard had continued to stall him.

His wrist-watch maintained its insistent jabbing. He cancelled the alarm and groped in his inside pocket for his Klipfone. 'Hallo, Sophia,' he said thickly, keeping his voice low to avoid disturbing other passengers, while at the same time doing his damnedest to get his brain into gear. He was in possession of sufficient reason to know that it had to be Sophia, or a call routed through her, because she was the only one who had the number of this particular telephone.

'I'm sorry to disturb you, Paul, but this is important. I've just had a call from Walter Graymond of PRA. He couldn't hold but will be calling back in three hours.'

PRA? Don't ask her what that stands for – try to sound intelligent. 'Did he say what he wanted?'

'He's interested in Pacific Rim buying four Sabres and wants to know more about ground service pooling at Singapore.'

'Thank you, Sophia. Any other calls?'

'British Airways. The first flight lottery sales desks closed at 17:00 CET today. There were over three million registrations.'

It would be another two hours and a thousand miles further from Charles de Gaulle before the detonator in that information went off. For the time being Sophia's guided missile with its warhead of shattering news went wide of the mark and fell to earth in an unregarded area of Paul's consciousness. He had a much more pressing problem to deal with: 'Thank you, Sophia . . . Er . . . Sophia?'

'Yes?'

'Who am I seeing on this trip?'

'No one, Paul.'

Now he was really confused. 'No one?' His brain swam against a turgid current of stale information. 'Then what am I doing on this plane? Where am I going?'

'The Azores. Fourteen days' reading and lazing, and eyeing half-naked females – doctor's orders. Look but don't touch – my orders.'

It all came back to him. The sharp, stabbing pains in his chest as he entered the gymnasium's changing rooms. This time he had known exactly what to do. He immediately stretched out on the floor and kept perfectly still, awaiting the thrash of the paramedics' helicopter. They got to him two minutes later, having been alerted by his underarm sensor five minutes before the pains started. And ten minutes after that he was in the hospital at St Omer receiving treatment and a stern lecture from his doctor. It was not a serious heart attack – Paul was back in his office at his usual 7.30 the next morning – but it was his third and that was enough for Sophia to have pulled the plugs on all his communication links so that his office and apartment were cut off from the outside world. Not even his intercom worked. All he had was one Klipfone and the only person he could call on that was her.

'And so it will remain for two weeks,' she had declared. 'So you might as well spend it in the Azores.'

She had packed his things, driven him to the airport and ensured that he had taken his pills before take-off.

'Paul?'

Paul forced himself to concentrate on her voice. 'Sophia?'

'I'm sorry if I disturbed you. I had hoped that the pills would've worn off by now. But it was such good news, I thought it would give you a boost to start your holiday.'

'Will you marry me, Sophia?'

'And be a widow in four years? What kind of offer is that? Ask me again when you're thinking straight.'

'Thank you, Sophia,' Paul murmured, and slid back into blissful unconsciousness.

8

Ian threaded Joshua Shief's Rolls-Royce through the evening traffic heading out of London. He picked up the A3 at Kingston Vale. With three occupants, the car was entitled to use the executive lane. It locked on to the separation control system and settled down to a steady, hands-free 110 kph, its sensors automatically maintaining a safe distance from the vehicle in front. He adjusted his mirror so that he could see Alain Colgate examining the sheaf of colour laser prints that had been produced from the photographs he had taken during his break-in of the Roses' Triton Exploration office.

'Well?' Shief demanded.

'How did you come by these, Mr Shief?'

Shief grinned wolfishly. 'Never you mind, Alain. What I want to know is just how watertight are they and can we work around them?'

'Yes and no.'

Shief's good humour went back in its cage. 'What's that

supposed to mean?'

'Yes, they're watertight, and no, we can't work around them without running the risk of a legal knee-capping by a horde of patents lawyers. Anyway, these are only patent précis. The European Patent Office now allows—'

'Précis! But they look like original applications!'

'Sorry, Mr Shief. But one of these pictures includes a safe deposit receipt. Fifty items.' He showed Shief the appropriate document. 'What's the betting that the Roses' originals are sitting in a bank vault and full copies are in another safe at the patents office in Wales?'

'Okay – a scenario for you to chew on. We go ahead anyway and get an engineering company to start making and testing Darwin systems. I don't suppose the Roses can afford decent lawyers.' Shief broke off and looked quizzically at his technical director. 'Or are you going to tell me that contingency lawyers have moved into the patents business in a big way?'

'Contingency lawyers have moved into the patent infringement business in a *very* big way.'

'Bugger.' Shief thought about that. The American contingency system was now allowed in the UK. The scheme meant that lawyers could take on strong cases on behalf of small companies or individuals for a percentage of the damages instead of a fee. He could see Christine Rose having no problems using her considerable skills to persuade a big-name bunch of legal sharks to fight her case.

'A suggestion,' said Colgate. 'One that might not appeal to the unconventional streak in your business methods, but one that might work.'

'Do I detect a veiled insult in that statement?'

'Of course. Why not up our price?'

'Alec Rose might go along with that, but we'd never get around his wife. She has a crazy notion about cheap energy for Third World countries. Even if we got total control of the company, she'd make damn sure we were hedged in by covenants. I want a free hand.'

Colgate considered. 'Okay. So she's an old-fashioned

socialist. But she's sure to have a price.'

Shief glowered at Ian's smirking expression in the mirror. 'What sort of price do you imagine is going to appeal to a woman who not only owns 10,000 hectares of Worcestershire, but two years ago set a pack of lawyers loose on her own brother when he wanted to develop a tenth of that as a new rural village. She turned down the best part of twenty million. She said that she didn't want to spoil the view of her favourite spot when she was a kid. Tell me how to deal with someone like that and I shall listen intently.'

The two men sat in silence. Ian left the A3 and headed for Colgate's home in New Malden.

Colgate cleared his throat. 'So what do we do next?'

'There's damn all we can do except play a waiting game. Indonesia's still a mess and is likely to be for some time. Maybe waiting would be the smart move. It'll make Alec Rose sweat a bit. I sense that he'd like to sell out but is scared of his wife. Maybe if he thought I was losing interest it might lead to him putting pressure on her. If they split, we win.'

Colgate was dropped outside his home. Shief politely declined an offer of hospitality and ordered Ian to Wimbledon.

'I'm not robbing a bank for you, sir,' said Ian as he reversed the Rolls into Colgate's drive to turn the car round.

The oil man smiled. 'Find a bank containing enough money to buy Christine Rose and I might insist.'

9

It was 6.00 a.m. Joe had been busy in his workshop all night – the hottest August night for twenty years according to the radio – and had got nowhere. He was exhausted, angry and frustrated, in that order, although he perceived frustration as the dominant emotion. His knee was giving him hell because he had been standing most of the night. He switched the mill off, wiped the kerosene off the block of magnesium alloy that was clamped to the mill's table and stared at the chatter marks.

Jesus Christ! A miserable fucking twenty-thou skim and he was still getting chatter marks that looked like sand ribbles after the tide had gone out. The pictures on Lesseps's computer had shown the finish on the fuel regulator block as an essay in machined perfection but this crap stuff was unworkable. He took the rotary mill off the mandrel, used a magnifying glass to examine its cutting edges and could have wept at what he saw. The alloy had heat-bonded itself to the cutters. The result was that instead of being milled away, the impossible material was being torn away. It had been much the same when he tried boring an experimental hole using his pillar drill. The twist drill's bit hadn't so much drilled into the material as ripped its way in. He had reground several of his bits, increasing the back-off angle to give the swarf a chance to clear without bonding, but without luck. Lesseps was wrong when he said that the stuff was like aluminium to work – it was a hundred times worse.

He stared at the five brick-sized billets of the alloy that he'd bought from an engineering supplies supermarket. He had used a place in Vancouver rather than risk the friendly questions of the staff at his regular supplier. He wondered what the hell he was going to do. The main trouble was the size of his machine tools – none of his kit was sufficiently rigid to withstand the rigours of working industrial-size billets of any material: chatter was inevitable. The six pages of information on the alloy that he had printed from his *Machinery Handbook* memory card stressed that laser shapers or spark mills were the best approach for high-quality work. What had surprised Joe was that the material, having fallen from favour in the last century, was becoming more widely used. Many of the latest Formula One racing cars made extensive use of magnesium alloy for structural components, and a Frenchmen held the world speed cycle record on a bicycle made almost entirely of the weird stuff.

He picked up one of the billets and hefted it. It sure was light. He turned his attention to the drawings that Lesseps

194

had given him in London and took a close look at the large screw threads for the fuel intakes and outlets. A big, six-inch lathe would do the job – they could be picked up cheap enough these days – but it would never fit into his workshop. And what the hell would a model-maker want with a six-inch lathe? Questions were sure to be asked.

Joe was forced to accept that on this occasion he had run up against an ego-bruising problem that was not going to be solved by his iron will or driving energy or bluster. For the first time in his life he was beaten before he had even started. He glanced at the time and suddenly felt his age. It was Saturday. His birthday. Seventy-six.

Seventy-six!

How many years did he have left? He was in good health apart from his damned knee. Ten years? Maybe fifteen if he was lucky and kept bucking the statistics. Even fifteen years was not long to the great accounting if there was such a thing. Joe had always scorned all religions. An atheist through and through, but of late he had often wondered if he was wrong. Shit. If he was, how was he going to account for the biggest atrocity in aviation history since Lockerbie?

Please forgive me, ladies and gentlemen ... This is terrible ... All those people ... Oh my God! My God!

It was the first time he had had doubts about the terrible road he had chosen. Hitherto his all-consuming ego, his obsession with his country's aviation industry and above all, his fixation that France had robbed the United States, had overshadowed everything.

He looked at the time. Christ! No wonder his spirits were slopping about in the bottom of the corn barrel. In six hours his family would be descending on him for the birthday cook-out. It had become a tradition that he always looked forward to but right now could do without.

He snatched four hours' fitful sleep, fully expecting his misgivings to have been banished when he woke, and found that they were looming even larger as he shaved and showered. By the time he had dragged himself down to the local mall to load up with marinated sirloins, charcoal and Bud

195

six-packs, he had decided to call the whole thing off. Lesseps wouldn't be sorry. Ought he give him a few grand? Naw – why the hell should he? The oily little shit had had enough and was holding down a better job than he deserved.

Joe loaded the car's trunk from the supermarket shopping truck and slammed it shut. He was about to open the driver's door when he caught sight of a tall, stooped figure wearing a supermarket coat that was too short for him. The guy was straining to push a train of interlocked trucks towards the supermarket and the whole caboodle was veering off-course. He stared in astonishment.

Johnny Coreba! It could only be him. The best airplane main-gear designer in the business. What in hell was he doing shunting shopping trucks?

'Hey – Johnny!'

The man was in his late fifties. He stopped struggling and looked up, puzzled at first. His lugrubious, grey expression broke into an embarrassed half-smile when he recognised Joe hurrying towards him. 'Hi, Joe. Howya doing?'

The two men smacked palms.

'Never mind how I'm doing,' said Joe as they embraced. 'What the fuck are *you* doing? Most folk are happy stealing just one truck.'

Johnny managed a hollow laugh. 'Keeps me out of the house, Joe. Gives Martha a hubby-free zone for waging war on dust.' It was said without rancour. Thirty years of marriage was long enough to adjust to a woman who cleaned the tops of doors every day and mowed the lawn with a Philishave.

'So this is a Saturday job?' Joe inquired. 'Depriving college kids of work?'

'Full time, Joe.'

Joe stared. 'Since when?'

'Since Monday.'

'You quit the plant?'

'They let me go.'

The news astonished Joe. 'But you're on the 1,000-series design-build team! Who's gonna design that bird's main-gear if you're not there, for Chrissake!'

196

Johnny shook his head. 'I don't think they're going ahead with the theatre body after all.'

It was confirmation of a rumour that Joe and his staff had been trying to pin down all week without success. If the plant was prepared to let ace designers like Johnny Coreba go – top personnel from the design-build core that the company had gone on record as saying they would hold on to – then it looked certain that the axe would be falling on the 1,000-series theatre body. If so, that meant the plant was pulling right out of the civil airplane industry altogether. It wouldn't happen overnight, but without the One-Treble-Zero series they had nothing for the future.

'For fuck's sake, Johnny, why didn't you come to me? We could've fixed you up with something better than this. We still can.'

Johnny Coreba's expression became even more downcast than normal. 'I'm fifty-seven, Joe. The pay-off was generous. I don't need a job except to keep out of Martha's war zone . . .' He hesitated, adding sheepishly, 'Sorry, Joe, but they gave me extra not to go to you. Didn't say nothing about not talking to you though. How's the *Spruce Goose* doing? Must be nearly finished by now.'

'She's looking good,' Joe replied. 'Every time I work on her I think of Howard Hughes and how we could do with guys like him around today.'

Johnny Coreba laughed. 'Yeah – but not too many of them.'

They talked for a few minutes until an assistant manager showed to find out what had happened to the supply of shopping trucks.

Joe drove slowly home, his seething thoughts at variance with the car's sedate pace. A carfax came through, echoed from his office. He ripped it from the slot and read it at the next set of red lights. An embargoed press release from Pacific Rim: Graymond had done it – the horny little Mike-Foxtrot had ordered four Sabres. Joe balled the fax in fury and risked a $1,000 fine by tossing it from the car. At that precise moment he made up his mind.

197

There would be no turning back.
His forging of the spanner would continue.

10

While Joe was entertaining his family on a hot afternoon in Seattle, on the other side of the Atlantic Jez settled down to watch the gala draw for the first seats on the Sabre. Dad was in his den playing a networked 3-D battle game against half of southern England, his mother was visiting her sister, so Jez had the big projection wall screen television in the Moreton sitting-room to himself.

The whole thing was being run like the Eurovision Song Contest with draw centres in several European capitals. The event wasbeing hosted from the Palace of Versailles by Canal Plus who had rigged up a full-size hologram of Sabre 005 so that it appeared tobe suspended, ghost-like, above a host of multi-coloured fountains. The show started with blaring music and a chorus line of about a hundred prancing girls wearing little other than projected images of 004's spectacular first arrival in Sydney. Against the backdrop of bobbing boobs and pirouetting pudenda, a well-known Parisian cabaret performer in sequinned top hat and tails had his welcoming song drowned out by the raucous music. It was all in the worst possible taste.

Howls of derisive laughter greeted the scene on the big TV in Paul's apartment at St Omer. Refreshed and invigorated after his holiday, he was hosting a small dinner party of senior management and their husbands and wives. Sophia, looking graceful and elegant in a black slip dress with a neckline and hemline best described as adventurous, moved among the dozen or so guests distributing coffee and liqueurs, arousing the interest of the men and the envy of those women younger than her who didn't have the legs to chance such a high hem. She herded them diplomatically into easy chairs to watch the strange show and sat beside

Paul. It escaped few of the women present that on this occasion Sophia had never strayed far from Paul's side and had, unusually, sat beside him at dinner. Sophia, the cool professional, unbending? It was unthinkable.

The Canal Plus spectacular went from bad to worse. First there was the draw to determine the order in which countries would make their selections. Paul was the only one present who had any idea of what was going on. Sophia had badgered an embarrassed British Airways PR office into releasing Canal Plus's format of the event.

'British Airways have made a real public relations meal of it,' Paul told his guests. 'They've allocated seats to each country based on population.'

'Three million registrations!' Claudia Picquet exclaimed. 'It doesn't seem possible.'

Paul chuckled and waved his hand at the screen. 'Dare I admit that it was my idea? Something I thought of on the spur of the moment when I was at a meeting with BA. I never thought they'd pounce on it so eagerly.'

'And they've made some serious money before they've flown a single air mile,' Ralph observed.

'And I never thought to ask for a commission,' Paul rejoined ruefully. 'I'm slipping.' He glanced at Sophia, took her hand, and added with Gallic modesty: 'But my judgement is as sound as ever in other matters. I've asked Sophia to marry me. Sadly, I can't say the same for her judgement because she's accepted.'

The television show was forgotten in the flurry of fulsome congratulations, handshakes and kisses that followed.

'Swiss prudence allied with French intransigence,' said Ralph drolly. 'A lethal cocktail. So when's the happy event?'

'Friday, 18 December in the Terminal 6 register office at Heathrow,' Paul replied. 'And a breakfast reception afterwards in the VIP lounge. You'll all be there to see off 005 on her first fare-paying flight, therefore none of you will have excuses.'

'There'll be a press call at the reception,' Sophia added. 'Good publicity for the company, therefore the company will foot the bill. Swiss prudence.'

It was the first time that the guests had heard the ever-correct Sophia utter a categoric statement *and* a joke.

'Not forgetting a honeymoon in Australia,' said Paul. 'There's a flight leaving that morning that will get us there in under two hours.'

Claudia frowned. 'You'll be flying on 005?'

'Of course,' Paul replied. 'But we will be paying for our seats.'

Ralph's laughter boomed around the room. 'So much for your loony socialist views about no VIPs on the first flight.' He nodded to the television. 'So you'll be bumping a couple of winners?'

Paul was unperturbed by the jibe. He turned his sorrowing gaze on Ralph. 'Not at all. I had held two seats back for emergencies. Now seriously, Ralph, if you were marrying Sophia, wouldn't you regard getting on honeymoon as fast as possible as an emergency?'

Even Sophia looked faintly embarrassed at the laughter that greeted Paul's comment. Ralph was tempted to make a remark about heart attacks but sensed that that might be stepping over the trip wire with Paul Santos, and quite definitely with Sophia.

'Now let's watch the show and see what manner of travelling companions we'll have,' said Paul.

Italy won the first draw. A glass booth rose out of the floor in the centre of a packed Rome Colosseum. Inside was a girl clothed in a blizzard of tickets like a kid's snowstorm shake toy. With much eye-rolling, a male presenter reached through a flap in the booth and, to a chorus of phoney squealing from the girl, seized ten tickets which he passed to a female presenter.

'This is terrible,' someone groaned. 'They've turned our spaceplane into a circus!'

Paul shrugged. 'It's publicity. Anyway, I never thought to include a "no tack" clause in BA's contract.'

Six of the lucky couples were in the audience. Spotlights swung and ushers plunged into the mob to herd the jubilant winners on to the stage. They all appeared to be overweight.

'Haven't they heard of Leptin in Italy?' Ralph moaned. 'There's at least a thousand kilos in that lot!'

Everyone laughed at his woebegone expression.

Jez was thinking much the same thing as he watched the show in Richmond. Brussels was next. Four bulky winners. Another hour dragged by. It was all very boring so he channel-hopped, managing to follow three movies simultaneously – something that he could never do with his mother present because it always drove her to distraction.

Finally it was the turn of London and the three movies were abandoned. Instead, there was a break in the Wembley Stadium pop concert and a swirl of bagpiped Highlanders around a slow-turning glass drum on the centre stage. The lights dimmed, leaving a single spotlight trained on the drum. Jez couldn't help sitting on the edge of his seat as the bagpipes died away. He knew that his feeling of anticipation was childish. There were over a quarter of a million tickets in that drum. The odds were such that he was unlikely to win, but at least he was involved in the show.

A minor Royal put an evening-gloved hand into the drum and passed the first ticket to the presenter. He read out the number and 81006 appeared on a giant screen above the audience.

'A Mr and Mrs Kenton from Hull!' The presenter announced. 'We'll be trying to get through to them in a minute! May I have the next ticket please, Your Highness.'

72803.

Jez relaxed. Well, that was it then; the number was too close to his own, 72739, for him to stand any chance of winning now.

A couple from Wales followed.

Next was a Mr Edward Lithgow from Hampton Court.

Jez decided that that definitely knocked him out of the frame. Hampton Court was only a few miles from Richmond. There wouldn't be two winners that close together.

Another ticket was passed to the presenter.

'72739!' A pause, then: 'A single seat winner who doesn't wish to be identified!'

Jez's world imploded like a star collapsing into a black hole in which time's arrow and rational thought became imprisoned by the colossal gravity. A finger, which could not possibly be his because he was suddenly gripped by a terrible paralysis, somehow managed to stab the buffer store button on the TV's remote control. A bar graph appeared at the foot of the screen showing that the television's memory was grabbing frames but Jez's vision had gone into extreme soft focus. The only information his glazed eyes were allowed to convey to his stupefied brain was the existence of a large blotch of light that marked where the wide-screen TV was fixed to the living-room wall.

Seconds passed. The TV's sound was the first to penetrate the defensive wall that his brain had erected around its external sensors: numbers being read out; cheering, clapping, congratulatory speeches. Jez forced his eyes into focus. London's turn was over; the wailing bagpipes gave way to Madrid's twanging flamenco.

Jez forced his leaden feet upstairs to his bedroom and recovered the receipt from its hiding place. There was no need for the trip because its number was burned into his memory with the permanence of a thermic lance. But there was a faint chance – so faint that he knew he was being incredibly stupid – that he had memorised the wrong number. He unfolded the receipt.

72739.

Perhaps there was another number on the receipt? He searched it carefully, even turned it over. But there was only the one number.

My number is 72739! screamed the receipt. *How many times do you have to look?*

Maybe he had misheard the number on the TV? Yes – that had to be the answer. He returned to the sitting-room and cycled back through the stored frames in the TV's video memory until he came to the presenter announcing the fateful number. Fast forward a few frames and there it was on the stadium's giant screen: 72739.

Still refusing to accept the irrefutable, Jez held the receipt against the screen and stared at the matching numbers, his eyes flicking back and forth lest he catch the digits in the act of switching around like mischievous children in a dental inspection queue.

His mother came bustling in a few minutes later. Her off-spring was sitting trance-like, staring at a muted television. She took in his deathly pallor, gathered him into loving, motherly arms and announced, more perceptively than she could have imagined, that he didn't look very well.

11

Jez's near neighbour winner, Ted Lithgow, was in a similar state of shock. Like Jez he was sitting frozen in front of the television in his tiny living room in a back street at Hampton Court.

The presenter's words penetrated the confused whirl of his thoughts. 'We can't get through to lucky Mr Lithgow, but we'll keep trying before we hand over to Madrid.'

They would never get through. The cable company had taken away the TV decoder but had left the telephone service for outgoing emergency phone calls only.

Ted's first impulse was to rush upstairs and wake Nikki to break the wonderful news. There had been little good news in the ten years since he had become unemployed. The decade had been one long, desperate struggle to hang on to their little terraced house which was all they had left. He checked himself as he was about to leave the room. What was the point of disturbing her? He had only just given her her sedatives and put her to bed. Waking her now would frighten and confuse her. It could wait until morning.

He cherished the mornings with Nikki and had even started keeping a diary – a permanent record of their conversations for him to look back on when she was gone.

Morning was the time of day when she was almost her old self, when she bustled cheerfully around the kitchen, went shopping and pottered in their handkerchief-size back garden. During afternoons the light of her wonderful reason started its cruel flickering. Yesterday afternoon Ted had found her on her knees in the middle of her vegetable plot, in tears before a heap of healthy tomato plants that she had uprooted believing them to be weeds. By late evening the light was completely extinguished, when she became restless and forgetful and – more often of late – subject to panic attacks.

Nikki's most recent phobia was that she imagined a former neighbour was intent on gassing her. He had been a gas fitter and Nikki had never really liked him. The only way of calming her sufficiently to get her to bed was to throw the bedroom windows open regardless of the weather. This had been going on for a week, causing Ted to worry about the coming winter, but the doctor had said that the phase would pass. In the morning following the first such panic attack, Nikki had been both incredulous and appalled when Ted related what had happened. That was the really terrible thing about Alzheimer's disease: in its early stages its victims knew what was happening to them. They knew that the course of the disease could not be halted – it was inexorable – that it would first rob them of their personality, before moving on systematically to close down their bodily functions. Only when it had turned its hapless victim into something barely alive that had to be washed, clothed and fed, sometimes for many months, would it finally close in for the kill and stop the heart.

And the victim knew . . .

There was now a vaccine available to prevent the disease, but its approval after several years of clinical trials had come too late to save Nikki.

That night Ted lay beside his beloved wife, listening to her breathing, kept awake by the turmoil of his thoughts. They were both sixty and had been married thirty two years. They had met in Kingston Hospital where Ted had been taken following a car crash. Nikki had been one of the nurses on duty. On the other side of the world they had four grand-children whom they had never seen, except on v-mail cards played on a friend's terminal, and had no hope of ever see-ing.

Until now . . .

But how would he raise the money? A thousand bizarre ideas stormed his mind and he eventually gave up trying to breach the ramparts of sleep that finally came to his defence.

12

Joe's birthday barbecue was not a success. He was taciturn and withdrawn, not wanting to talk about his European trip, snapping at grandchildren and having to force himself to muster meagre enthusiasm for his presents. Not only was he preoccupied by other matters, but the pleasure of having his family around reminded him of what he was depriving them of by his encashing of an insurance bond to finance this project. He apologised, saying that his knee was preventing him from sleeping properly and that he wasn't feeling too well. His family commiserated. Grandchildren were gathered up and by 4.00 p.m. he was alone.

He should've taken himself to bed but the workshop was a compulsive draw – Jesus, how he hated being defeated. He laid a sheet of emery cloth on his surface plate, oiled it and tried drawing the partly machined block of magnesium alloy back and forth in the forlorn hope of smoothing down the chatter marks. It was hopeless – a dozen strokes and the emery was clogged. In temper he tossed the block in his scrap bin and contemplated the mess in his normally immac-ulate workshop. He set about cleaning up, despite the fact that his body was crying out for sleep. The magnesium swarf gave him an idea. He crammed some of the sharp spirals into a paper bag and went into the garden. The bar-becue's charcoal bed was still glowing. He removed the grill, dumped the bag of swarf on the charcoal and stood back.

Nothing happened at first. The paper bag burned away and the swarf gradually changed colour from silver to black. He looked around for something to use as a poker when the waste metal suddenly flared into an incandescent fireball that burned with unremitting, shadow-scouring fury for some five seconds. The blaze of raw, white-hot energy died away, leaving exploding after-images dancing like dervishes on Joe's retinas.

He inspected the barbecue when his vision had returned to normal. There was no trace of the swarf — not so much as a whisker blown clear by the miniature hurricane of air that the fireball had sucked in. All was consumed in that brief but terrible furnace of destruction.

'Holy shit,' Joe muttered to himself. He remained staring at the dying barbecue for some moments before returning to the house, deep in thought. He had an idea and called Johnny Coreba, catching him as he returned home from his supermarket job.

'Wanna pick your brains, Johnny. Something I meant to mention when we were talking this morning. I'm thinking of building an all-metal replica of the *Spirit of St Louis*.'

'Sounds like fun, Joe. I've heard you can buy complete sets of airframe drawings from the Lindbergh Trust.'

'A flying model,' Joe added.

'Forget it, Joe – stick to your replicas and avoid a lot of heartbreak.'

Joe assured him that he was serious. Okay, so scaled-down propellers didn't work too well on scale models and there would be a helluva power-to-weight problem, but he wanted to give it a try. He cut short a whole list of objections from the former designer. 'The fairings were all planished ally, Johnny. They've got to look good – aluminium paint on balsa or beech looks crap. How about magnesium alloy sheet instead? And maybe I could use it for the main spar and frames?'

'You could but you'd never machine it, Joe. Mag ally may look like ordinary aluminium ally, but it's a dog to work.'

You can say that again!

206

'So I use a specialist company?'

There was a pause while Johnny Coreba turned the problem over. 'Guess there must be plenty of companies with laser shaping facilities. That's what you need, Joe, if you're prepared to spend money. Give me a coupla hours to grab something to eat and I'll fax some stuff through to you.'

The former designer was as good as his word. After twelve hours' sound sleep Joe found a stack of sheets in his fax machine's bin. Good old Johnny: he had called up engineering databases on the Net and downloaded lists of West Coast specialist engineering companies. A handwritten note said:

> *All these companies have Shaeffer shapers and mills etc. Swiss. The best machine tools for working mag. Good luck. Johnny.*

The nearest firm was fifty miles away. Joe considered e-mailing them, but realised he would be walking into the problems that Lesseps had anticipated. E-mails left trails unless he used a bureau and the right court order could make even them disgorge information on their users. Drawings got copied. They kicked around workshops. In a year's time someone might pick one up and recognise what the block was. The trails could be tracked back to his doorstep. God knows, his motives were well known. How many times had he been on the local TV networks sounding off about the munchkins who were running America's airplane business into the ground? And that pointed to another problem: if he walked into an engineering outfit off the street clutching a fistful of dollars and a drawing there was an outside chance of someone recognising him. And many of his more colourful ravings on TV had been picked up by the major networks. The whole of North America was a no-go area.

How about Europe? Language problems unless he used an English company. Now *that* was an idea. He looked at the headers and paths on Johnny's downloads to work out how he had approached his trawl of the Net. A few key search words starting with magnesium had eventually led to the sites of those companies that specialised in machining the stuff. A search refining word had been 'Shaeffer'. All Joe had to do was log on to the Net and follow Johnny's paths but broaden the global electronic yellow pages search to include the United Kingdom.

Ten minutes later Joe was sitting at his terminal examining the list that his printer had just delivered. There were about twenty specialist companies in England. A Walton-on-Thames address caught his eye. Many years before when Judith was alive, they had taken a pleasure boat trip up the Thames from Hampton Court to Windsor. They had passed through Walton-on-Thames just before reaching Runnymede. It was only a few miles outside London. He thought about telephoning them to leave a message, but people didn't like phone calls with blocked caller IDs. Faxes had to have headers by law. Using an anonymous server to send an e-mail would be sure to arouse suspicions. Nope – the best thing would be to go and see them. A businessman passing through; a frequent visitor to London, with a fistful of dollars in one hand and a drawing in the other.

He switched sites to a travel agent that his company had an account with and called up the seat plans of Monday's flights to London. Every flight packed – Monday was a popular day for business travel to Europe. Wednesday was a quiet day and it would give him two days in the office to clear his desk. He could explain yet another trip to Europe to his staff by saying that he was looking for a tie-in with a similar employment agency in London. Curiously, this was something they had suggested to him long before the Sabre business blew up. Passport cards were a problem. All entry points into Europe had turnstiles whose card scanners read all the information off the card including a string of compressed code that could be assembled into a photograph if needed.

Get a grip on yourself, he chided himself. You're seeing problems before they arise.

He mouse-clicked on a vacant exit seat in lounge class so that he could stretch his leg. Two more clicks to accept the quote and confirm the booking, and a brightly-coloured ticket hissed softly into the fax bin.

The company he had selected to machine his wrench was called Triton Exploration. Its directors were listed as Alec Rose and Christine Rose.

13

Ted Lithgow woke late. Nikki was already up. They rarely slept late now: mornings were too precious to waste in bed unless it was to make love – which they did with increasing frequency these days.

She was standing at the sink peeling potatoes, humming. He crept up behind her, slipped his arms around her waist, as always marvelling at how she had retained her youthful figure. He rested his chin on her shoulder. 'Shepherd's pie?'

'Do you mind it again?'

'Of course not.'

Nikki always prepared the evening meal in the morning – invariably something that was easy to warm up. 'Oh damn,' she said petulantly, 'I've forgotten to make tea.'

She tried to slip out of her husband's embrace but he tightened his grip.

'Tea can wait. I've got a little surprise for you.'

'Too late, you lecherous beast. I'm up and dressed. Unhand me, sir.'

'A Christmas surprise.'

She laughed. 'This from someone who always rushes about on Christmas Eve to buy presents.'

'We're going to see our grandchildren.'

Nikki turned round and stared at him, her lovely grey eyes shining with excitement. Her words came in a rush: 'They're coming to England? When? How? How can they afford it? On Lizzy's last card she said that they had had to sell the car and that their welfare was being cut!'

Ted explained about the grand draw the previous night, telling a white lie by saying that they had won the seats. Her eyes became troubled.

'But Ted – we've talked it over so many times – twenty-four hours in an aeroplane! Sinbad would take me over completely. It would be terrible – all those people staring at me.'

Sinbad was their joke name for Nikki's affliction. Neither of them could recall how it had come about but the absurdity of the nickname somehow diminished the disease, blunting the vicious sword edge of its proper name, making it a little easier to live with.

Ted stroked her hair and kissed her forehead. 'The flight will be less than two hours. Sabre – the new aeroplane that travels at twenty times the speed of ordinary aeroplanes. It takes off at ten in the morning and we'll be there about a hundred minutes later. So you'll be fine.'

'Oh, Ted! We'll be seeing them at last! I can't believe it! I'm so happy!' She threw her arms round her husband and clung tightly to him. He waited for the worries to assail her. She was living on an emotional switchback these days. He didn't have long to wait. 'But December is another four months. What will I be like then, Ted?'

'You'll be fine.' He chucked her playfully under the chin. 'And if Sinbad misbehaves we'll knock him on the head with those new patches. It won't matter if you sleep through the flight – it's getting there that matters.'

'You *are* telling me the truth, Ted? You've not done anything silly about the house?'

He was solemnly swearing that he really had won in last night's draw when there was a sharp rap on the door. The first reporter had tracked them down. Terry Warton – a local stringer hoping for a fat lineage fee from a national if he was quick.

14

Honicker breezed into Christine Rose's office unannounced, but he was always welcome, especially as he appreciated her coffee and her legs. He had expressed his feelings several times on the former, but his manners and natural reserve precluded comment on the latter. On this occasion it was nearly torpedoed by the heat and her shorts.

'You know,' he said, sipping his coffee, 'this country cheats. No one ever told me it could be so damned hot here. I expected it on occasions, but not day after day like this.'

'Surely you're used to it, Bill?'

'Never,' said Honicker emphatically. 'I looked forward to this posting because I thought that an English summer would be the equivalent of our winter.'

'It won't last now, we're into September.'

'I've been told to put pressure on you regarding our offer.'

'You're wasting your time until we have a clearer idea of what's going to happen in Indonesia.'

Honicker smiled engagingly. 'That's exactly what I said. In the meantime, we'd like to commission Triton Exploration to sample a potential trench we've identified.'

'For a fat fee that ties us to you?'

'We had in mind a fair fee,' Honicker replied.

'I thought I'd made it clear that we do no deals with anyone until we're absolutely certain that the Indonesian people benefit from our work.'

'We're talking about a straight commission for a survey, Chris. Nothing to do with buying into Triton.'

'We're expensive and we've got you over an oil barrel. So where is the survey site?'

'Can't say, Chris, because I don't know. But it's in the south – well away from Indonesia. Nothing like the commercial size of the Banda Trench but big enough to be interesting. Part of the deal would be that we provide a research ship.'

'The Darwin won't be ready until the end of the year, and we're seeing President Sulimann in January.'

'That could fit in nicely,' said Honicker. 'April will be the best time from the weather point of view.'

Their discussion of details was interrupted by the telephone. Christine took the call using the handset instead of the hands-free system. Honicker noticed from the telephone's ID display that the call was from a public telephone.

Christine listened intently for a few moments. 'Certainly, Mr Wright – we'll be only too pleased to look at your drawing and give you a quote ... Yes ... our Web pages are correct ... Yes – we have a Shaeffer, and we guarantee confidentiality ... Thirty minutes will be fine. We'll look forward to seeing you.' She gave the caller directions on how to find them and hung up. 'Sorry about that, Bill.'

'So you're still doing your jobbing engineering work?'

'Of course. It earns good money and it gives Alec a break from working on the Darwin.'

'Are you sure it'll be ready by April?'

He liked the way Christine's cheeks dimpled when she smiled. 'Alec's asked me to book the hydrostatic test tank at Teddington for November,' she replied. 'That means he's confident that he'll have cracked most of the problems by then. April will be fine. Now ... We shall want the entire fee up front. No point in having you over an oil barrel if we don't take advantage of it.'

While they were arguing, Joe drove past the entrance to the Roses' place in his rented car and parked outside a row of houses. He walked to the drive's entrance, pausing to rest his leg and mop his forehead, cursing car rental companies who wouldn't accept cash and always wanted to check passport cards. It meant that he couldn't risk taking the car up to the front entrance because its registration could be traced to him. There was nothing for it but to walk up the drive, clutching a briefcase, while giving several closed-circuit TV cameras the chance to get a good look at him. It was a risk he had accepted he would have to take. Of course, he could carry out the whole operation using the Net

212

– sending the drawings out from commercial bureaux and arranging payments through anonymous servers – but it was a complex business and would be certain to be counter-productive by drawing attention to his project.

Triton Exploration didn't give him confidence. He had expected a modern engineering plant, not a converted old mansion. He followed some signs around to the rear of the premises and was about to ring the office bell when the door opened and a couple emerged. The girl was a brunette, close-cropped hair, white shorts that accentuated her bronzed legs. Her companion was a smart business suit in his mid-thirties. Joe had an uncomfortable feeling that he had seen him before but decided that he was mistaken. The man gave him only a cursory glance as he moved to a parked car. The girl looked at Joe in surprise.

'Mr Wright?'

'At your service,' Joe replied breezily.

'I rather hope we can be at *your* service, Mr Wright. I didn't hear a taxi.'

'I left my car outside. Rented. One of those electric town cars. Haven't got the hang of the reverse switch and I wasn't sure how much room there'd be in your driveway.'

'It's usually a lever marked reverse,' said Honicker wryly as he started the engine. He smiled at Christine. 'See you and Alec tonight then. Eight o'clock.'

'We'll give your Savoy account a caning,' Christine promised.

Honicker reached the end of the drive and waited for a break in the traffic. Despite being preoccupied with the details of the coming survey that he would be thrashing out with the Roses that evening, he noticed that there were no electric cars parked in the vicinity of the house.

15

The woman in the Richmond travel agents was the same woman who had sold Jez his lucky registration. She checked the number on his receipt and gave an exclamation of pleasure. 'Oh – it was you! We knew that a number from our allocation had won. I ought to get my boss to give me a bonus.'

'Actually it's my dad who's won,' said Jez.

'And no publicity,' said the woman dolefully. 'We had to remain silent. The rules are quite strict.'

Publicity was Jez's main worry, now that he'd got over the initial shock of his win. There were a thousand and one other agonies churning in his tortured mind but publicity was the one printed in 72-point headlines.

'That's what Dad asked me to call in to check with you,' he said.

'Well he's got nothing to worry about right up to the check-in.'

'What happens then?'

The travel agent looked surprised. 'There'll be TV cameras at Terminal 6. Bound to be. The first fare-paying passengers to go into space.'

'Yes, of course.' Jez matched her smile and hesitated. 'The other thing he asked me to ask you is if there's some sort of payment scheme for the tickets – monthly or something like that?'

'Well, the seats must be paid for in full seven days before departure. If winners don't take up their purchase option by noon on 11 December, their reservations will be sold in the normal manner. But the fare is awfully expensive. Hasn't he got a charge card or credit card he could use?'

Jez mumbled his thanks and left. He went and sat by the river, plunged too far into the depths of a black despair to appreciate the girls in skimpy outfits taking advantage of the warm summer afternoon as they strolled along the towpath with their boy-friends.

214

16

'Magnesium alloy?' Alec queried, looking up from the drawing that was spread out on Christine's desk.

'Is that a problem for your machinists?' Joe asked.

Alec caught Christine's eye before replying. 'Not at all, Mr Wright. I'm just surprised, that's all.'

'It's lighter than aluminium,' said Joe, his pronunciation of aluminium as "aloominum" jarring on the English couple's ears, 'and about the same strength.'

'Control block,' Alec mused, reading the drawing's title. 'To control what, Mr Wright?'

'Does it matter?' Joe countered affably. 'Isn't everything you need on there?'

'For a one-off, this has to be the best drawing I've ever seen,' Alec replied. 'Some jobs are literally sketches on the backs of envelopes.'

'We're spending big money. We expect the best – from our designers right down to work on the shop floor.'

'Will the finished blocks be subjected to any form of testing?' Alec wanted to know. 'Pressure tests, for example?'

'I'm only the project co-ordinator,' Joe replied, drawing upon his acting skills. The timing of his hesitation before he continued was just right. 'I guess it's only fair to put you in the picture, but I want your guarantee that you'll keep this 100 per cent to yourselves.'

'I gave you that assurance on the phone, Mr Wright,' said Christine evenly.

Joe nodded. 'The group I'm involved with is going to make an attempt on the world land speed in '22. We're building virtually the entire vehicle from magnesium alloy and carbon fibre – wheels, chassis, the works. We don't want word getting out because there're other groups exploring the same idea, but we reckon we're two years ahead of the opposition, and we'd like to stay that way. Spreading the work around is costing us plenty, but no one gets an overall picture of our design. That make sense?'

'Perfect sense,' said Christine, having decided that Triton didn't need this commission. 'If you could give me your address and phone number, we'll prepare a quotation for you.'

'I need to get this job placed now,' said Joe firmly.

'We can't possibly—'

'I'm catching a flight home tonight so I want this fixed up now,' Joe insisted. He realised that he had slipped into his customary pugnaciousness – possibly a mistake with this couple but there were other companies. 'Our designer reckons around 150 hours to make four of those blocks. We'll pay the going rate at home of $500 an hour. Half now and the other half on delivery. I'll be back in this country on Monday, 2 November and I'll expect them to be ready.'

Christine was about to object but Alec got in before her. 'The blocks will be ready for collection on 2 November, Mr Wright,' he said, avoiding his wife's eye.

Joe produced an envelope and dropped it on the table. 'Fifty thousand dollars. That's more than fifty per cent. I'd like a receipt please, made out to Bob Wright.'

Five minutes later Joe left the office and strode confidently down the drive as briskly as his knee would permit, pleased with the deal. As usual, his brusqueness had paid off. They had even accepted his anger at having his hotel room robbed and his personal telephone stolen.

Alec watched the stocky figure from the window and turned to Christine, who was re-counting the contents of the envelope. 'Weird,' he muttered. 'Sorry I jumped in but I sensed you were about to turn him down. I could do with some experience working magnesium alloy. It's a material I know sod all about.'

Christine shrugged. 'I can't see you getting this Darwin finished. A hundred and fifty hours is a month's work.'

'I can do the job in a fortnight.' He pointed to the column of codes down the side of the drawing that was still spread out on the desk. 'Whoever designed this had a Shaeffer in mind. Those are Shaeffer's control codes for roughing out the blanks. And those are the codes for final machining. All I've got to do is set up the billets, key the numbers in, and three-quarters of the work is done automatically.'

17

It was on his fourth reconnaissance flight that Lesseps found the firing site for testing his bomb.

He levelled out at 2,000 feet and flew south a few kilometres before turning the Mistral north so that he would be approaching the location with the sun behind him. He banked and snapped ten high-resolution pictures into his camera's memory. It was an ideal spot in every respect: a large, worked-out clearing in the centre of a reforestation project that covered several thousand hectares. The nearest habitation was a cluster of farmhouses and a tiny village ten kilometres to the north-west. He judged the length of the track from the clearing to the Bazas–Roquefort road to be about five kilometres. It looked rough going but would be unlikely to present problems for a car unless there had been exceptionally wet weather.

The site was further south than he preferred – nearly a three-hour flight from St Omer to Bordeaux – but that couldn't be helped: it was the most remote and therefore the most suitable location he had found so far. He drew the position on his chart using a transparent overlay that could be disposed of later, and sketched in the exact position of the track. It had been a good day's work. There was nothing left to do but to reset his GPS navigation receiver to give him a course for home.

It was late afternoon; the bright sunlight threw long shadows that made every detail on the terrain below stand out in sharp relief – conditions that even the most seasoned pilot enjoyed. But Lesseps's pleasure was tempered by black thoughts that refused to be banished by the sensation of power and freedom at his fingertips. Yes, the recce had been a success, but it took him one more step along the terrifying path that Joe Yavanoski's threat of a twenty-year prison sentence was driving him.

18

Every Saturday morning Sophia's fax machine started work an hour before she did so that by the time she entered her office all the European and North American press reports that had mentioned the Sabre during the previous week were waiting for her. This week the cuttings agency had earned their retainer because the stack of clippings was formidable – the tabloids of every country in Europe had given the gala draw for tickets massive coverage.

Originally Paul had read all the Sabre cuttings but since his last heart attack Sophia had insisted on further reducing his workload by giving him a weekly résumé printed on a single sheet of paper. She waded quickly through the cuttings, her steely eye on the look-out for adverse reports in heavyweights such as the *Herald Tribune*. There was nothing of interest, so she returned to the grand draw stories with the intention of singling out two or three pieces that conveyed a flavour of the silly season spaceplane hysteria. One of her selections was the front page of the British *Daily Mail* with the headline: HEARTBREAK COUPLE'S SUPERPLANE WIN.

The story that followed was about an unnamed couple who had won an option on two seats but couldn't afford the fare. The wife was suffering the early stages of Alzheimer's disease. Sophia was about to write a covering note to Paul when he surprised her by walking into the office. It was unfortunate for Paul that none of her staff worked Saturdays because her surprise was tempered with anger and an ability to be a slightly less than a perfect secretary. Besides, Saturdays were English-speaking days, and English was an excellent language for civilised abuse when her tongue was withdrawn from its scabbard.

'You are supposed to be playing golf at ten o'clock,' was

the reproof that greeted Paul.

'The driving range isn't golf,' he protested.

'Nor is your slice.'

'Now *that* is cruel. I come seeking coffee and your delightful presence and all I get is abuse.' He sank into her chair and idly leafed through the sheaf of press cuttings while she poured.

'You're here because it's 005's final full-blown test this morning,' said Sophia sternly, setting a cup before him. 'You can stay but that gives me the right to make your life utterly miserable.'

'That is something you could never do, Sophia.'

She ran a finger along his temple. 'Would you care to chance a bet on that, Mr Santos?'

Paul laughed and tried to catch her hand but she moved away. 'Being here is less stressful than knocking balls down a fairway while worrying about the test,' he observed.

'The test will be fine. Whereas your handicap doesn't bear thinking about.'

Paul made no reply because he was studying one of the cuttings. 'This is very sad. An English couple have won joint tickets but can't afford the fare. Their grandchildren, whom they've never seen, are in Sydney, and the wife is too ill for a long flight.'

'I saw it. I was going to show it to you as an example of the week's tabloid outpourings.'

'This paper also publishes a Sunday edition.'

'So?'

'So call them please and tell them that we will pay the couple's fare.'

This was an order from the chief executive of a large public corporation. Sophia slipped into the role of secretary but there was a discernable pause that spoke other than her crisp, 'Certainly, Mr Santos.'

'You don't approve?'

'The story appeared last Monday. It is more than likely that a benefactor has come forward by now.'

'And perhaps not. Tell them that we would also like to

show the couple around the plant and offer the paper exclusive coverage. They will be certain to bite.'

'Certainly, Mr Santos.'

'And lastly, tell me the real reason why you don't approve.'

'It's cheap publicity, Paul.'

'Which is preferable to expensive publicity. Do it please, Sophia.' Paul crossed her office to the row of windows that looked down on to the floor of Shed A where a small army of technicians were working around 005 like termites attending to their queen. The partly complete 006 had been moved out of the shed on to the apron beside 004 to give them plenty of room as they wound wide strips of polythene around 005's fuselage. From this vantage point he could see the neat circle of the docking hatch cover set flush in the flight-deck roof – the NASA-inspired design modification that the Japanese had first suggested and British Airways had adopted. The hatch cover disappeared under the broad strips of polythene bandage.

The group that was gathered around the production work station near the tail included Ralph Peterson and several officials from the EAA who were to witness this crucial final test.

Sabre 005 was now complete. Every last cable and optical track had been installed, every instrument connected, every telemetry link tested. Although there was still a huge amount of service documentation to be prepared, the graceful spaceplane was ready for the final and crudest test she would ever have to face before pre-delivery flight trials could begin. All her doors and hatches would be closed and she would use her air pumps to boost her cabin air pressure to 2-bar – double atmospheric pressure. This test would be carried out with the Sabre in flight condition, therefore she was fully fuelled with kerosene, liquid oxygen and hydrogen, and resting on cradles and airbags with her main gear retracted. Unlike earlier similar tests, this time her internal air pressure would be provided by the Sabre's own systems. She would be on her own.

The purpose of the trial was to test the structural integrity of the fuselage by simulating the vacuum of space. It wasn't practical to build a vacuum chamber large enough to accommodate the Sabre, therefore the simple answer was to inflate the spaceplane to double normal atmospheric pressure. If that went well, the pressure would be increased another fifty per cent just to see what would happen. Or rather, hear what would happen. Failures were unlikely to be catastrophic during this late stage, such as a window blowing out, which would be easy to locate. More likely was a minor failure such as a rupture around an antenna seal – difficult to find but for the loud, farting noise the escaping air would make as it blew past the broad strips of polythene bound around the fuselage.

Paul turned to speak to Sophia but she was busy on the telephone to London. He entered his office and activated the wall screens that monitored the test. The main screen showed several large vibration rigs being wheeled into place around 005 and clamped to the wings and fuselage.

Lesseps was among the technicians. He now made a point of volunteering for additional weekend duties to secure the upgrading of his electronic pass to allow access to the construction shed at any time. A woman's voice rang out over the staff address system to advise that the test was about to begin. Ralph led the group behind a safety screen where the test controller was sitting at a console. She caught Ralph's nod and touched the controls that brought the Sabre's fuel cells to life. There were no umbilical cables to the spaceplane, even the data feeds were through the Sabre's normal radio telemetry links.

One of Paul's screens showed the spaceplane's internal pressure creeping towards 2-bar. Another row of gauges indicated the inevitable stretching and swelling of the fuselage, but this was normal, provided the readings returned to zero when the pressure was released.

Ten minutes passed with no failures. The pressure was increased by fifty per cent and held for the required fifteen minutes before being bled back to operating pressure. The next test was the pressure test of the flight-deck to ensure the integrity of the pressure-tight door that separated the flight-deck from the main passenger cabin. In an emergency, such as the perforation of the hull by a meteoroid, the flight-deck could be independently pressurised. One of the door's inner rubber seals failed but the outer seal held and therefore the test was deemed a success.

'We're ready to start the vibration cycles,' the test controller announced.

It was the one trial that Ralph and his designers detested because the buffeting levels set by the EAA were way above those that any Sabre would normally encounter. The pounding of the huge jack-hammer rams going about their business could be heard in Paul's office. A monitor showed the wing-tips flexing through over half a metre. In the foreground Ralph appeared to be having a heated argument with the EAA officials. He guessed that Ralph would be sounding off about the hated crease beams beneath the flight-deck floor and hoped that the chief designer wasn't being too abrasive.

All the tests were concluded and the party made their way to the boardroom where Paul greeted each official by name, accompanied by handshakes and smiles. Waitresses plied the guests with coffee and sandwiches, while Sophia laid out the licensing documents on the boardroom table. There were warm congratulations for Sophia and Paul on their engagement.

'I never thought that Paul Santos would ever do anything so conventional as to marry his secretary,' said one official, beaming.

Ralph took Paul aside while the visitors were eating and drinking. 'They won't budge on those bloody crease beams,' he muttered.

'Were you polite?'

'No.' He moved towards the buffet before all the salmon sandwiches disappeared.

Sophia, armed with a glass of water and two pills, cornered Paul.

'How about the *Daily Mail* couple?' he inquired.

'How about your pills?'

'But—'

'Pills!'

'Yes, Ma'am.' He dutifully swallowed the pills. 'Thank God the tests went well.'

Sophia regarded him steadily, her eyes dark and serious. 'And we'll have the same tests next month with 006. And 007 after that, and so on. Will you promise me that this will be the last time that you show your nose in here at weekends?'

'My heart's fine, Sophia.'

'Who said anything about your damned heart? You've got to work on your golf. If I'm going to spend the rest of my life with someone, is it asking too much to expect a decent game now and then? So promise.'

Paul gave her the assurance she wanted and inquired again about the *Daily Mail* couple.

'They're Ted and Nikki Lithgow. They've had several benefactors offering to buy their tickets, but they're all from businesses who want publicity. Mr Lithgow's refused so far because he doesn't want to subject his wife to needless stress.'

Paul gave the matter a moment's thought. 'Tell them that we'll pay and that we won't require publicity.'

'That's what I've said – that *you'll* pay.'

The news alarmed Paul. '*Me?* What me personally?'

'You can hardly expect the company to pay if it has nothing to gain.'

'But two tickets, Sophia!'

'Returns as well. It would not be fair to fly Mrs Lithgow out on Sabre and not return her in the same manner.'

'You'll bankrupt me.'

She suddenly gave one of her lovely smiles. 'Oh, yes. But I shall wait until I have a credit card in the name of Mrs Santos.'

A catering assistant wheeled in a trolley bearing a magnum of champagne. The licensing documents were duly signed and stamped, and the success of the Sabre toasted.

223

Sophia double-checked the initialling of minor amendments and handed the sheaf of papers to Paul.

'There you are, Mr Santos,' she said. 'Sabre 005 is licensed to fly.'

19

There was a glaring hole in the security at Sabre Industries that Lesseps had spotted and was now about to exploit.

Whereas vehicles leaving through the main gate were subject to frequent spot checks by the security guards, and less frequent checks were applied to vehicles entering the complex, no one ever thought to check the coming and going of the flying club's light aircraft.

On Saturdays Lesseps had established his leisure time routine by taking off in his Mistral at 8.00 a.m., an hour before any of the other pilots were stirring and planning the day's flying programme in the clubhouse. He left his flight plan on the CFI's desk and strolled to his beloved Mistral.

The complex's radar was only used for test flights of the Sabre so there was no one on the ground on this particular Saturday to notice his change of course once he was into the cloudbase. He obtained a routing to Calais and landed at the city's municipal airport fifteen minutes later. A taxi dropped him in the main shopping centre. He steeled himself with coffee and croissants, for this expedition was another step along the awesome path. He paid his bill and set off in search of the model shop that he had previously tracked down on Minitel's electronic yellow pages. He found it without trouble. A huge place that had just opened and was already filling with eager model aircraft and boat enthusiasts.

He wandered around for several minutes, admiring the beautiful models on display and rather wishing that he had time to build one. He purchased a Futuba radio control transmitter and several receiver actuators, together with batteries and a collection of model-making tools that in-

224

cluded a tiny vice, a multimeter and a gas soldering iron.

Outside the shop he checked his street map and discovered that the specialist photographic supplier was tucked away down a side street within walking distance. Electronic flashguns had supplanted the traditional magnesium flashbulbs, but there were still a few photographers who preferred the colour rendition of magnesium.

The assistant searched the stockroom and returned with several dusty boxes. 'This is the last we'll ever have, sir,' he reported. 'No one has made these things for over twenty years.'

'I'll buy the lot then,' said Lesseps.

By 10.00 a.m. every item on his shopping list had a neat tick against it. He returned to the airport where his beloved Mistral was awaiting him and flew south-west along the coast, skimming low over the water, relishing the intoxicating sensation of speed and the envious faces in sailing dinghies turning towards him and trying to follow the sleek yellow monoplane's progress. Flaps down and a tight circle around a swim raft. Naked sunbathers waving to him. A loop and a barrel roll for their benefit. Orgasmic thrills coursing through him as the Mistral responded eagerly to every touch on the controls. Power. Divine power and freedom. Power to move exactly as he pleased in three dimension; freedom from the grating harshness of Joe's voice and Claudia Picquet's dark, knowing eyes reading his secrets with the certainty and accuracy of a laser head scanning a compact disk.

But, as always, the dark thoughts at what lay ahead were of a magnitude that overcame the brief intoxication of flying. His mood was sombre when he landed at Sabre Industries. He taxied to his parking spot and sat for some moments with his hands resting on the controls. Eventually he climbed out and picketed the Mistral because a gale was forecast. He strolled with studied casualness to his apartment, his purchases stuffed in the chart case slung from his shoulder.

Once in the security of his kitchen, he laid out the items

225

on the kitchen table. The array of mundane model-maker's tools brought home to him yet again the terrible nature of what lay ahead but he rationalised his disturbed feelings by assuring himself that no engineering company would be able to duplicate the perfection of Plessey's skills. The blocks that Joe would be having made were certain to be crude and therefore unusable. Even Joe, for all his boundless aggression and pugnacity, would be forced to recognise that the operation would have to be aborted.

The thought helped Jean Lesseps live with himself.

20

It was the end of September before Alec had time to take a serious look at the drawing of the 'control block' that Mr Wright had left him. There was little work he could do on the new Darwin until a sample of the latest Plastronic hose arrived from the manufacturer, and the delivery date of 2 November he had promised Mr Wright was looming, so he decided to get the job out of the way. A simple enough job, or so he thought.

His first task was to print copies of the drawings on to a set of oil-resistant plastic cards. The cards were more manageable in the workshop than the original large sheets of paper and he would be able to return the customer's documents in their original condition. He selected the card containing the first stage, roughing out control codes and entering them on the Shaeffer's keyboard. The laser and spark erosion milling machine had a built-in computer that used the codes to generate a three-dimensional wire-frame drawing of the control block on its monitor.

Alec rotated the image to check the various dimensions. Roughing out was the initial machining process that reduced the individual billets of magnesium alloy to over-sized approximations of the control blocks before final precision machining. He entered the ISO specification for the material and was astonished when the computer reported back that roughing out would take ten hours per billet. He called up a help menu and learned that the inflammable nature of magnesium alloy was such that the spark erosion cutting heads could not be used – the entire process would be carried out using the slower gas laser milling heads at the minimum temperature settings.

He picked up the first billet of the remarkably light material and positioned it in the Schaeffer's cutting field. He initialised the machine and several jaws opened automatically to grip the block. There was a series of experimental rotations and changes of grip before the machine's monitor announced that it was ready. He closed the radiation covers and touched the key that set the machine to work. A picture of the billet appeared on the monitor. A point of intense light started tracking across a rough-sawn surface, creating a perfect flat that would serve as the datum plane for the rest of the job. The heavy filtration to protect the closed-circuit TV camera prevented him from seeing the material being boiled away but the extractor fans and air pumps cut in to transfer the noxious fumes into a reservoir. With the datum surface finished, the laser heads went to work cutting the two through bores. Sixty millimetres would be the final diameter of the holes. If the thing was a fuel regulator, a lot of liquid could be pumped through such large holes. Mr Wright's rocket car must be something.

There was little for him to do but visit the office to return the drawings and annoy Christine.

'Our Mr Wright's going to get good value for his money after all,' he announced, sauntering into her domain and flopping into a chair.

Christine looked up from the report she was reading and moved the drawings that Alec had tossed on her desk. 'Why's that?'

Alec explained about the time it was going to take to rough out the billets. 'And at least another ten hours each to finalise the machining,' he added. 'It means I'll be getting up at ungodly hours to switch jobs.'

'You took the work on,' she reproved.

He smiled. 'Oh, I'm not complaining. Learning about working magnesium alloy might come in useful and the control codes make life easy.'

Christine glanced at the columns of numbers down the side of the main drawing. 'Is that the first time we've ever had them?'

'Yes. They save a lot of work.'

'Aren't they intended for batch production runs?'

Alec shrugged. 'I suppose so.'

'Doesn't it strike you as strange that they should be provided for a one-off production run? How many of these rocket cars are they planning to build?'

'Maybe they're approaching the whole thing in a professional manner.'

Christine accepted Alec's reasoning. The matter was of little consequence; even if Alec did have to wake up at odd hours to keep the Shaeffer happy, they would still be making a handsome profit on the job.

21

The summer holidays had been a particularly miserable time for Jez without school work to take his mind off his strange combination of fortune and misfortune; fortune in his win, misfortune because he lacked the money to benefit from it.

You'll have to work for it, his voice had told him.

His response was to scour the local papers for a holiday job that paid a salary commensurate with the earnings of the chief executive of a large public company, for that was the income he would need to be able to buy his Sabre ticket in December. But Sainsbury's pay filling shelves fell very short of his needs. Indeed, he calculated that he would have to fill 2,000 kilometres of shelving with tins of baked beans to a depth of two metres in order to earn the price of his ticket; enough baked beans to fly to Australia without the aid of an aircraft.

Alone in the house one evening while his parents were

228

visiting friends, he brooded long and hard on the problem and decided that there was nothing for it but to confess everything to his dad and plead for the money as an advance coming-of-age gift.

His voice laughed and was right – the amount was too frightening. Dad could be generous on occasions, but never *that* generous.

He tried watching television but was unable to concentrate, such was his misery and the turmoil of his thoughts. Perhaps British Airways would give him credit on his junior credit card? There again, perhaps not – it was for emergencies only. And then he had an idea of such audacity that even thinking about it sent snakes of fear writhing through his stomach. But there would be no harm in checking to determine if his notion might be feasible.

He entered his father's den and hunted through the filing cabinet with trembling fingers, seeking one particular file. He opened the folder on the desk and checked the e-mail statements against the calendar for the coming December, praying that the dates wouldn't dovetail.

Please don't make them fit! It mustn't work!

But the billing dates and his father's payment dates fitted with terrifying neatness.

Horrified at the enormity of the crime that lay at the end of this path, Jez immediately resolved not to set foot on it or give it another moment's thought.

There *had* to be other ways of raising the money and he still had twelve weeks.

Tempus fugit, said his voice.

'Bugger off,' said Jez.

22

Joe was punctual to the minute, having called Triton Exploration an hour previously from a public phone box. Christine saw him walking up the drive and had a cup of coffee waiting for him when he entered her office. His knee was being particularly troublesome on this visit to England. She noticed his wince as he sat down.

'Surely you haven't rented another car with a reverse you don't understand, Mr Wright?'

Joe chuckled. 'Arthritis. God-damn knee seizes up if I don't exercise it.'

Christine made a sympathetic response and called down to Alec. He entered the office a few moments later and placed a fibre transit case before the visitor.

'There you are, Mr Wright – four of your widgets, all present and correct.'

Joe opened the box, removed the bubble plastic from one of the control blocks and used the wrapping material to handle it. In view of his own experience trying to machine magnesium alloy, the quality of the workmanship was impressive. The coupling threads were clean-cut with no chatter marks; the circles of concentric threaded holes were neatly de-burred and chamfered; and the outer surfaces were machined perfection. He held it up to the light. The walls of the through-bores were also smooth with no cutting-tool marks. The anodised finish imparted a fine semi-matt grey sheen to the entire job. It looked a perfect match with the pictures he had seen on Lesseps's laptop computer.

'Looks good,' he said.

'The envelope contains our inspection certificates,' said Alec. 'They're all within tolerance except the block marked "D". It has a couple of dimensions that are just on the tolerance. Your original drawings are also enclosed.'

'How about scrap work?' Joe asked. 'This is a highly confidential project, so I need them as well.'

'We don't produce scrap work,' said Christine before Alec had a chance to reply.

Joe was disbelieving but he suppressed his usual brusqueness. 'You get an order for a number and you cut blanks for that number?'

'That's right. And we always respect customer confidentiality.'

It was likely to be a no-win argument so Joe decided not

press the matter. 'Okay – fine. How about working copies of the drawings?'

'They will be destroyed, Mr Wright. You have our word on that.'

Joe was tempted to ask for them but that might arouse their suspicions. It would be best to settle his business and get out. He handed an envelope to Christine. 'That's the balance owing, Mrs Rose. I'd like to thank you for what appears to be first-class work.'

Christine counted the money and scribbled a receipt which Joe thrust in his pocket without looking at it.

'Good luck with the project,' said Alec. 'If you're happy with the work, we'll be pleased to quote for more.'

'Perhaps you'd like to leave a number, Mr Wright?' Christine suggested.

'The project's just about finished and I'm returning to the States,' Joe replied. He thanked them again, gathered up the box and left.

'Odd,' said Christine thoughtfully, watching the stocky figure walk down the drive. 'No contact address, no phone number. And he pays cash.'

'There's probably a lot of sponsorship money riding on their bid,' Alec commented. 'A lot of kudos attached to holding the world land speed record.'

'Possibly,' murmured Christine. 'Don't forget to destroy those drawings. Right – now that that's out of the way, we have to get down to some serious work. Bill Honicker's arriving next month and will want to see some progress on the Darwin.'

Alec looked dismayed. 'Oh, shit. When?'

Christine checked a facsimile report that had come through from Canberra during the night. 'He'll be seeing us on Thursday 17 December. You've got six weeks to finish the mods and organise some cold weather for him. The latter won't be too much of a problem just before Christmas, but I'm worried about the former.'

23

Lesseps was already in the coffee shop on Waterloo Station when Joe walked in. It was mid-morning on a Saturday, therefore the place was less crowded than usual. He sat at Lesseps's table and placed a new Samsonite briefcase on the chair between them. A waitress took his order and left. He removed his gloves and slipped them into his jacket pocket. He normally never wore them but he had to be doubly certain that there was nothing in or on the briefcase that could be linked to him. Even the bubble plastics that he had handled had been disposed of, as had all the Triton Exploration documents including the original drawings. He had even thoroughly scrubbed all four blocks inside and outside with cleaning fluid to be certain of obliterating the fingerprints of everyone at Triton who had handled them.

Lesseps's anxious gaze flickered to the briefcase and met Joe's hard stare. 'Is that . . .?'

'No. It's my fucking laundry. Four new shirts.'

'Are they any good?'

'How the hell should I know? That's your job.'

Lesseps opened his mouth to speak and shut it again when the waitress returned with Joe's coffee.

'You'd better take a look,' Joe invited in a conciliatory tone, regretting his abrasive manner — there was no point in adding to Lesseps's nervousness.

The French-Canadian paled and glanced around the crowded coffee bar. 'Here?'

'They're wrapped in handkerchiefs under a newspaper. Pretend to read it. Don't touch them.'

Lesseps placed the briefcase on his knee and slipped the catches. He pushed the newspaper to one side, holding it in one hand while picking at the new handkerchiefs with the other. His trembling fingers encountered cold metal through the handkerchief's thin fabric. He eased the material aside and what he saw unnerved him. His fervent hope that the

232

control block would be an unusable crude copy was dashed: it was as perfect as though it had just come off Plessey's production line.

'Pretty good, huh?' said Joe, watching his companion carefully.

Lesseps's sallow complexion was paler than usual as he closed the briefcase. 'Pretty good,' he muttered. 'But we won't know until I've checked them.'

'Anyone who can produce work like that ain't gonna make mistakes,' said Joe. 'So you can forget any idea of kidding me that they're shit. And with four of them to choose from when you only need one . . .' He grinned wolfishly although his gaze remained hard. 'Use the one marked "D" for testing. It's okay but only just. For Chrissake be careful how you lose the ones you don't need and don't handle any of them directly. I cleaned them with alcohol so there won't be any prints on them. Keep them like that.'

'Joe – there's a problem.'

'Isn't there always?'

Lesseps glanced around the coffee shop. No one was paying attention to them. 'Does it have to be on the first passenger flight?'

'Yes.'

A sensible man would have detected the hard emphasis in Joe's reply and realised that the matter was not negotiable, but Lesseps was tortured by too many gremlins to be sensible. 'That might not be poss—'

'*You* make it possible!' Joe snarled.

'You've got to listen to me, Joe. The way I've figured it out, the device will be activated on throttle down when the engines are in rocket mode. That means when the bird's in space and has reached orbital velocity. I've got to fit the thing some time before Sabre's delivered. Christ – I don't even know when that will be, and I've no way of knowing if there'll be a space test *after* I've installed it.'

'Why not, for fuck's sake?'

'Because Santos keeps test programme details under wraps until a few hours before they take place so he can

233

spring surprises on the press. That's been his style.'

'There can't be any surprises left,' said Joe sourly. 'The god-damn thing now holds every record going.' He adopted a more friendly tone. 'Listen, Jean – it *has* to be on the first passenger flight. That's very important and you know why. You're working in the plant and you're not stupid even if I do cuss and swear at you – that's just my way. So use a bit of that French-Canadian savvy to find out what the hell's going on and when.'

Lesseps nodded. 'Okay. I guess it won't be too hard to find out.' He paused and added: 'When do I get paid, Joe?'

Joe lit a cigar. 'So how deep is this latest financial shit you're in?' The ice was back in his voice.

'I want the balance, Joe.'

'We've got a deal.'

'We don't have any sort of deal!' Lesseps retorted, showing that occasional flash of spirit that irritated Joe. 'You're blackmailing me into this, so I don't see why—'

'That's been your trouble all your life, Jean — not seeing. Not seeing beyond the end of your stupid nose. As soon as the operation is concluded, you'll get paid.'

'Right here, in cash.'

'And what will you do when you're paid?'

'What's that got to do with you?'

Joe's hard expression suddenly softened. He smiled. 'Nothing, Jean. I was thinking of you. You take off after the accident and some people might start wondering why. They might start wondering if it really was an accident.'

'Do you really think I'm *that* stupid?'

'Frightened people do stupid things.'

'You're the only thing that frightens me, Joe. We meet here the day before – 17 December — and you pay me in cash. Used bills.'

As much as Joe disliked Lesseps giving him orders, he conceded again that the French-Canadian's underlying streak of toughness might prove an asset if the impossible happened and something went wrong. Checking his diary gave him time to consider his reaction. From now on

Lesseps was shouldering the entire operation; there seemed little point in refusing this concession but habit dictated that he negotiate the point. 'That's a Thursday,' he muttered at length. 'Would you have to take the day off from the plant?'

Lesseps nodded.

'How about the next day – Friday? Most plants allow long weekends. You could take the next day off without anyone noticing.'

'I guess so.'

'So we make it the Friday,' said Joe. He grinned. 'Friday 18 December. Our D-Day. Don't want you doing anything out of the ordinary before then, John. No throwing your job in, or anything that'll draw attention to you.'

'I won't have to, Joe,' said Lesseps listlessly. 'All I have to do is wait until they let me go, because after 18 December Sabre Industries will be finished.'

24

Despite the temptation on the train, Lesseps made no attempt to examine the control blocks until he was back in his apartment at the Sabre Industries complex. He opened the case and laid the blocks out on the kitchen table, taking care not to touch them until he had pulled on a pair of kitchen gloves, his nerves fluttering like crazed butterflies. It was still daylight and theoretically possible for anyone with powerful binoculars to see into his apartment from the distant office blocks. He jumped up and pulled the blind down, realised that he never normally closed it in the day-time, and made matters worse by promptly opening it again. Chiding his stupidity helped him get a grip on his nerves. He sat with his back to the window and called up the Plessey drawings of the fuel control block on his laptop computer. A few minutes spent checking measurements with a digital micrometer convinced him that the blocks were perfect in every respect. The only difference was his one modification: a 15-millimetre diameter blind hole in the side of the motor housing recess that would eventually accomodate the igniter. He kept the block marked with a 'D' and hid the others on top of a wardrobe.

He opened the table drawer and took out five of the magnesium flashbulbs that he had purchased on his shopping expedition to Calais. He had found that carefully heating the plastic anti-shatter coating on the bulbs in a candle flame was the easiest way of removing it. Once it was stripped from the five bulbs it was a relatively simple matter to crack the glass bulbs of four of them, using a model-maker's vice clamped to the kitchen table by its suction pad. The fluff balls of magnesium wool resembled Toy Town pan scourers. He teased them from the remains of the broken bulbs and poked them loosely into the igniter hole in the control block, taking care not to pack the tiny balls any tighter than they had been in their original glass envelopes. The kitchen gloves were clumsy; he decided to buy surgical gloves for when he assembled the real bomb. The last flash-bulb received different treatment. He broke the glass in the vice and used tweezers to remove the shards from the ball of magnesium wool, taking great care not to break the electric ignition filament that was imbedded in the centre of the ball. When he had finished, he had an intact flashbulb but minus the glass. The next stage required careful insertion of the now glassless flashbulb in the hole so that its magnesium wool was in contact with the wool from the first flashbulbs. Pushing the base of the bulb so that its skirt was flush with the bottom of the motor recess required rather more pressure than he cared to exert but an electrical continuity check with a multimeter across the flashbulb's terminals confirmed that he hadn't broken the filament. He secured the skirt with rapid-setting Araldite epoxy resin and sat back to admire his handiwork while the adhesive cured.

The next phase was testing the model aircraft radio control transmitter and the tiny, matchbox-size receiver-actuator. The actuator whirred satisfactorily when he operated the proportional control joystick on the transmitter. He removed the batteries from both units, soldered two

236

wires to the contacts on the flashbulb imbedded in the control block and the entire job was virtually done. A test firing
of an intact flashbulb with a 12-volt battery made hellish
balls of blue light dance a jig on his retinas. Five minutes
later he was finished, the remote-control receiver gaffer-
taped to the test bomb. He stuffed it and all the items he
would need for the test firing in his chart case and spent the
rest of the evening watching television while trying to ignore
the gremlins of doubt and fear that were always hovering in
the wings, awaiting their chance to move centre stage to
torment him.

25

The last person in the world that Lesseps wanted to see the
following morning was Claudia Picquet. She was wearing
an orange skin-tight Micranex jumpsuit and matching
trainers instead of her severe dealing-room gear. It was too
late to turn back – she was in a group admiring the flying
club's recently restored Alouette helicopter that was parked
near his Mistral. He resented her presence: he loved walking
up to his Mistral, savouring its fine lines as he approached,
particularly when the sun was shining, as it was this
morning, making dazzling patterns of delight on its yellow-
lacquered fairings. He felt her gaze on him — boring through
him before investigating the dark secret hidden in the chart
case dangling casually from his shoulder. That the suit cut
deep into her crotch and showed her nipples had little effect;
she was still the teacher who had caught him ejaculating
down the wall in the toilets.

You disgusting, filthy boy!

'Good morning, Mr Lesseps.'

He nodded affably to other members of her group and
returned her greeting. She joined him as he unlocked the
Mistral's door and dumped the chart case on the aft seats.

'A lovely day for flying, Mr Lesseps.'

'Indeed it is, Miss Picquet.'

She ran a manicured fingertip along the Mistral's leading edge. 'A fine aircraft. I hear that you're the envy of the flying club.'

Lesseps was sweating inwardly and could think of nothing sensible to say in reply. What the hell was she doing around at this time on a Sunday, and dressed like that? She was at least fifteen years older than him and it irritated him that he had recovered sufficiently from the shock of seeing her to find her attractive.

'I've joined the flying club,' she continued, answering his unspoken question and seemingly oblivious of his silence. 'My husband was going to teach me to fly . . . But he died before we got around to it.'

'I'm sorry.'

'It was two years ago . . . Sometimes it's been quite lonely . . .'

Lesseps was too preoccupied with his own thoughts to notice the uncharacteristic lowering of her mask. She smiled brightly. 'I've decided that I should start living again. I have my first lesson today.'

Such was Lesseps's nervousness that he nearly blurted out a joke about women pilots which would not have been well received. Miss Picquet's sense of humour was not one of her strong points. He wondered if that was her maiden name. Everyone called her 'Miss Picquet' and she didn't wear a wedding ring.

'It'll be a lesson that you'll remember all your life.'

Her eyes continued turning over his innermost secrets like a surgeon rummaging in a stomach cavity in search of a cancer. 'And where are you going today?'

'Oh – my usual Sunday cross-country.'

'A short flight?'

'I'll be away all day.'

She seemed to brace herself to say something that required a degree of courage that deserted her the moment it was mustered. 'Enjoy your flight, Mr Lesseps. But don't tire yourself too much. It's less than six weeks to the first scheduled flight. We must have all the Issue "B" document-

238

ation completed by the end of this month.'

Lesseps acknowledged and assured her that he would be working all the hours God made to meet the end of November deadline. He wished her an enjoyable first lesson and taxied to the refuelling point to tank up with a full load. Fifteen minutes later he was airborne and heading south-west, helped by a thirty-knot tail wind.

The fine weather held across central France. He made good time and, after a course diversion to check that the test site clearing he had pin-pointed was deserted, landed at Bordeaux at 10.30 a.m. Finding his way out of the unfamiliar city sprawl in his rented Forager was easy enough with the GPS TrafficMaster issuing voice commands when approaching every junction or turning, but the density of the Sunday traffic took him by surprise with the result that reaching Bazas took almost as long as the flight. Time was pressing because he wasn't licensed for night flying. It was November – every minute counted. His nerves began to fray, causing him to miss the track that led to the clearing. He'd nearly reached the outskirts of Roquefort before he realised his mistake and retraced his route, cursing himself for not taking the trouble to program the TrafficMaster properly.

He found the opening in the dense stands of conifers and turned off the main road but his relief was short-lived. The condition of the track was worse than it looked in the photographs. The four-wheel-drive Forager coped with the deep logging ruts well enough, but if anyone in authority did challenge him, they would be unlikely to accept his explanation that he had left the main road in search of somewhere to rest. The vehicle lurched through a section of mature Columbian pines. They stood like stately, silent sentinels each side of the track, dark and forbidding, shutting out the sunlight and making the forest a gloomy, brooding place which did little for his already ragged nerves. He was about to turn on the radio for company when the track suddenly widened and he came upon the clearing.

He parked under the trees, killed the engine and listened intently. Apart from the ticking of hot metal there was an

239

eerie silence. Not even birdsong or the buzz of insects. He had read somewhere that such plantations were sterile places where no undergrowth survived beneath the steady ground-poisoning rain of pine needles and cones. The pines created their own environment where only they could flourish.

There was little point in further delay. His fingers shook as he unpacked the incendiary bomb. He strode quickly the length of the clearing and found a large patch of tractor-minced bare soil where there would be no danger of starting a fire. Priming the bomb was simply a matter of fitting the batteries that would operate the radio-controlled switch and so fire the detonator flashbulb. He placed it in the middle of the patch and returned quickly to the Forager. The next task was to fit batteries into the radio control transmitter and he was ready.

He clutched the transmitter in both hands to control his trembling and stared at the distant bomb. A jet passed over-head in the direction of Bordeaux but he ignored it: all his attention was focused on the tiny package. A press on the power button caused an LED to glow. All he had to do now was push the transmitter's tiny joystick all the way - forward . . . Like so.

Nothing happened.

But before panic and alarm could set in the package became a bright point of white fire like a motor cycle's head-lamp on main beam. The light suddenly expanded into a searing ball of hellish energy like a miniature sun turning into an awesome nova. Lesseps started mentally ticking off the seconds but lost count when the fireball suddenly doubled in size as a fearsome finale that was gone almost as quickly as it had appeared.

He stood rooted and stunned while the after-images of the horror he had unleashed in the clearing died away. His expression was that of a man given a brief glimpse of Hades. His first thought was the Bordeaux-bound jet – a light like that would have been visible for miles – the crew would be certain to report it. He got a grip on himself and started walking. How many times had he seen blinding flashes from the ground of reflected sunlight and paid them no attention?

He reached the heat-greyed patch of soil and stared down. The scorched circle was about five metres in diameter and there was nothing there: no fragments of metal or bits of wire or battery – nothing. Everything had been evaporated in the terrible fireball. Even the tractor ruts that criss-crossed the patch were now hardened and drought-cracked, and the few tufts of grass had been incinerated to nothing.

He carried out a careful search of the surrounding area in case debris had been thrown clear and found nothing.

But the black cloud of depression that had been dogging him for many weeks was not swept away by the successful outcome of the test. He stared long and hard at the scorched patch, realising that his commitment to Joe's insane plan was now total.

Part Three

Fireball

1

Tuesday, 1 December
Among the many tribulations that a cruel life sought to impose on the fastidious William Honicker and his craving for order and tidiness was that the earth was unreasonably large. Much as he disliked clichés, a planet with a diameter of 12,000 kilometres was clearly over the top. A third that size would provide sufficient gravity to retain an atmosphere and would cut down on the hours of misery cooped up on flights between Sydney and London because the two cities would be that much nearer to each other.

He viewed his coming trip to London later that month with a mixture of pleasure and misgivings. Pleasure because he would be escaping the heat and humidity of Canberra and going to a country which organised its December weather in a more agreeable manner, and misgivings because the long flight, coinciding with the beginning of the Christmas holidays, would be crammed with children. He had nothing against children, other than loathing, but would have preferred it if airlines adopted a policy of stowing them in the hold in secure, sound-proof boxes for the duration of long flights. On his last visit to England, a ten-year-old, boisterous, boily boy had inflicted so much misery for several hours that he had been moved to suggest to the proud mother that she sedated her unruly offspring. To which the puzzled woman had replied that he *was* sedated.

The coming inauguration of British Airways' suborbital ninety-minute service between Sydney and London on 18 December gave him pause for thought. He was supposed to be

245

seeing Alec and Christine Rose on the seventeenth. In their last report they had said that work on the new Darwin was behind, therefore it would be sensible to delay his trip until the new year and fly to London on the suborbital Sabre service.

The thought of going into space excited Honicker and he was more than willing to make up the fare difference out of his own pocket.

His secretary made inquiries and reported that all the twice-daily Sabre flights between Sydney and London were fully-booked until May.

'You're kidding?'

'I'm sorry, Mr Honicker.'

'Maybe I ought to buy some shares in British Airways?' he mused. '*Twice* daily! Four flights every twenty-four hours. Good God – that's 50,000 miles each day! That aircraft's going to be averaging 2,000 miles per hour even when it's sitting on the ground!'

Until then Honicker had not given serious thought to the Sabre project. He had followed its development with the cursory interest of an engineer, but, despite the successful test flights and spectacular first flight to Sydney the previous year, the reality of suborbital passenger flight had always seemed such a long way off, and now it was less than three weeks to the start of a scheduled Sydney–London service.

'Or you could buy Qantas shares,' said his secretary. 'They're planning a service from October. If you don't mind, Mr Honicker, I'd rather you didn't change your plans. I've arranged to use up my leave while you're away.'

Honicker sighed and was resigning himself to twenty-four hours of having kids puke on him when his digitally encrypted direct-line telephone rang. It was Christine Rose – one of the few people who knew this number.

Her voice sounded strained – businesslike and formal. No cheerful 'Hallo, Bill'. Instead: 'I'm calling you because we did promise you not make any move without consulting you first. But Shief has been to see us again and has made an offer which is going to be difficult for us to refuse.' It came out slowly and succinctly, as though she had been rehearsing.

Honicker's pulse quickened but his voice remained outwardly calm. 'Are you free to discuss the offer?'

'No . . .' There was anguish in her voice and Honicker made no attempt to break the silence that followed. 'Oh, what the hell,' she said suddenly. 'It's a hellish complicated deal but it boils down to this: we sell out to him and he'll divert twenty-five per cent of Avanti's royalties on the oil extracted from the Banda field directly to all the major aid organisations working in Indonesia. Hospitals, village clinics, schools, water purification projects. Everything.'

The Australian thought fast. 'It'll be years before the Banda field is producing, Chris.'

'That's exactly what I said, but he's willing to set up a starter fund – a big one.'

'How big?'

'Fifty million US dollars.'

Honicker snorted. 'You know the size of Indonesia, Chris. Something like 5,000 large villages. That sort of money wouldn't keep their child welfare clinics in band aids.'

'Per annum until the field starts production.'

'It's still noth—'

'It's better than nothing!' Christine came close to shouting. 'It means that money goes directly to where it's needed and not through government ministries. That's how governments work! You give aid to one ministry which means that their budget gets cut which means that more money is available to the defence ministry to buy arms. That's been the whole history of aid to poor countries. Well this is a chance to break that mould.'

They argued for ten minutes, heatedly at times. 'Okay . . . okay,' said Honicker, realising that he was getting nowhere. 'When do you have to give Shief a decision?'

'By the end of the year. Thirty-one days.'

'No, listen, Christine. I'm seeing you on the seventeenth of this month. Don't decide anything until we've had a chance to talk.'

As soon as the conversation with Christine Rose ended Honicker called Houseman's office and got an immediate appointment to see him. Thirty minutes later he was with the mole-like private secretary, both of them listening to a recording of the telephone conversation.

'She's playing a dangerous game,' Houseman observed when the recording was over. 'Playing one off against the other. There's always a chance that one of the players might drop out.'

'This isn't a game for Christine Rose,' said Honicker evenly. 'Shief has realised what sort of deal would appeal to her and has come up with the goods.'

Houseman nodded thoughtfully. 'Perhaps one of the players ought to be neutralised.'

The enigmatic comment puzzled Honicker. 'You mean us?'

'What I mean is that it's time for us to think about fighting dirty. Provided you're up to it, of course.'

2

Wednesday, 2 December

Lesseps kept his word when he promised Claudia Picquet to work 'all the hours that God made' to complete the initial work on the Sabre 005 documentation. He became a familiar sight in Shed A, clutching his memopad, crawling in and over every centimetre of 005. His work station in the paperless office had disappeared under a mountain of drawings, change notes and test specifications. To Claudia's pleasure, he had succeeded in meeting most of his targets.

'Excellent work, Mr Lesseps,' she complimented when checking his progress report.

Lesseps thanked her. He could now meet her searching gaze without inward flinching. 'But I could work much quicker if I had full security clearance for access to the entire database,' he said. 'Having to go through different department heads for information is very time-consuming.'

'Of course, Mr Lesseps. I'll have your security status

upgraded right away.'

Lesseps smiled and gave a little bow. 'Thank you. It will be a great help.'

At the end of a further five minutes of discussion Claudia Picquet took her leave, promising Lesseps that the question of his security clearance would be attended to immediately. She kept her word. Lesseps checked his terminal two hours later and discovered that several data levels that had hitherto been greyed out were now available to him. He spent a few minutes familiarising himself with the previously closed menus and discovered that he now had access to pages of confidential reports relating to the Sabre test programme. He found what he was looking for. To his immense relief, 005's space test flights were finished – the spaceplane was fully certified to begin commercial operations.

His fingers stopped moving on the keyboard and he stared at the EAA approval certificate displayed on the monitor. So when was 005's next trip into space? The answer was obvious but he had to be certain. He called up the flight schedule page and there it was:

Friday, 18 December – the world's first fare-paying sub-orbital flight. London to Sydney. Take-off from Heathrow at 10.00 a.m. He checked the Shed A shift schedules and determined that only six instrument calibration personnel would be working on Sabre 006 between 16:00 and midnight on 10 December — the day before British Airways took delivery of 005. On that evening Shed A would be virtually deserted. It was cutting it fine, but the evening of 10 December would be the best time to drop Joe's spanner in the works.

3

Thursday, 10 December

Jez opened his eyes and stared up at the time and date that his clock projected on to his bedroom ceiling. He groaned and turned over.

Today was the day he had been dreading.

Today was D-Day.

D for December; D for Deception; D for Disgrace; D for Despair; D for Depression. There was no end to them, but by far the worst was D for the Draconian punishment that his father would be handing out when his wayward son returned from Australia. In the summer this terrible day had seemed so far off but, like a publisher's deadline, it had come upon him with the speed and certainty of an express train.

He sat on the edge of his bed. The plan was that he would tell his mother that he felt too ill to go to school this morning. He had paved the way for the deception by being a model son for several weeks – always up and off to school on time and always home on time in the evening. This had naturally provoked a motherly suspicion that he had done something quite shocking to a girl and that these were measures by her offspring to diminish parental condemnation when the awful truth emerged. Eventually she decided, with a mixture of misgivings and pride, that her son was at last living up to her assertion, frequently made to a disbelieving rabbi and equally disbelieving relatives, that he 'was a good boy'. Jez's reasoning was that after such a period of sustained goodness, which had been as big a strain for him as for his parents, his mother was unlikely to make a fuss about him taking one day off school.

And now the day had finally arrived but he wouldn't have to feign illness – he really did feel sick, so sick with fear that he was tempted simply to get up, go to school and let the

250

day slip by like any other. But the stiletto-like model of the Sabre poised on his computer monitor helped steel his nerves, although it did nothing to drain the watery contents of his stomach.

He buried himself under the duvet and turned his electric over-blanket to maximum to work up a sweat for when his mother came to investigate his delayed rising. She always laid a hand on his forehead when he complained of illness – a procedure of many years that she believed had equipped her with the medical skills to diagnose correctly all Jez's claimed complaints ranging from colds to cholera.

The ploy worked too well. She wanted to rush Jez into hospital because, as usual, he had overdone it, with the result that the loving hand informed its owner that her son was on the verge of a catastrophic metabolic breakdown. It took several anxious minutes for Jez to convince her that there was nothing wrong with him that a quiet day at home wouldn't cure.

Jez waited an hour after she had left for work, just in case she took it into her head to turn her car round and return to her stricken offspring.

He crept into his father's den and the stormtroopers of terror, doubt and guilt launched a massive assault as he contemplated the telephone. But the autumn had been kind to him by breaking his voice properly so that he no longer sounded like a kid. It gave him the necessary courage to unfold the piece of paper on which he had written his instructions. An experimental recording and playback of his voice – sounding deep and nonchalant – gave him the additional courage needed to call the travel agents who had issued his winning ticket. He thanked God that his father was sufficiently old-fashioned to have shunned a video-phone.

'Ah, Mr Moreton,' exclaimed the girl. 'We were about to e-mail you a reminder. We didn't want our only winner to lose his option by not buying his ticket.'

Staring glassy-eyed at his instructions, Jez told her that he wished to pay by credit card and provided all the details she required.

'We'll need a fingerprint authorisation, Mr Moreton.'

'It's one of the old cards. My new card doesn't come into force until next year.'

There was a pause while she verified this. She came back with: 'That's fine, Mr Moreton.' She told him how much would be debited and asked how he intended returning from Australia.

Jez's voice nearly shot up a couple of octaves to its pre-puberty pitch. 'You mean that price doesn't include the return?'

'I'm sorry, Mr Moreton, that's for the single flight only on Sabre.'

Until now Jez had considered himself in the smelly stuff merely up to his neck. He now realised that this was a serious miscalculation and that it was at least a metre over his head. He collected his thoughts and voice. It crossed his mind that they used to send criminals to Australia, therefore it might be an idea to elect to stay there.

'I can't afford the time off work,' he said gruffly. 'I'll have to come back as soon as possible that day.'

Another pause and the girl came back with his return flight information and the revised credit card debit. The astronomical figure caused the room to spin around.

One metre? cackled his voice. *More like ten metres!*

The girl was talking to him: 'Do you wish to collect the ticket or shall we—'

'Can my son collect it during his school dinner-break today, please?'

'Yes – that'll be fine if he brings an ID or passport card with him.'

Luckily Jez focused his mind on the instructions to himself. 'I loathe my first name and would like to frame the ticket counterfoil. So would it be possible to make out the ticket to Mr J. Moreton please?'

The girl laughed. 'I think BA will be issuing every passenger with a special certificate, but, yes, we've already got a note of that on our computer.'

252

'My son will be along at 1.30.'

'It'll be ready for him, Mr Moreton.'

Jez thanked her and replaced the handset, surprised that his hand wasn't shaking. He returned to his bedroom and regarded the model Sabre, deep in thought. It slowly dawned on him that all his devious scheming and dreaming had actually borne fruit. His father would receive the credit card statement showing Jez's awful crime on 21 December but the grievous punishment that would surely follow the discovery would be inflicted on him in another lifetime . . .

After he had been into space on the Sabre!

He gave a great whoop of triumph and performed an exultant somersault on his bed, banging his heels on his desk and sending the scale model of the Sabre crashing to the floor.

4

That evening, as Jez sat in his bedroom staring trance-like at his Sabre ticket, Lesseps started work on the final stage of his terrible task.

It was 19:00. Shed A was quiet. The calibration team working on Sabre 006 took no notice of the technical author as he set up his reflectors under 005's port wing. The large foil umbrellas made an effective screen. He positioned his camera and lights so that they were trained through the open inspection hatch at the fuel control system for the inboard No.2 engine. He had all the tools to hand needed for removal of the genuine fuel control block including a pair of surgical gloves that he pulled on. Over a period of several weeks he had established a penchant for wearing gloves when handling his photographic equipment.

The jaws of the compressed-air power wrench were a snug fit on the four fuel-line coupling nuts. For safety, the entire fuel system was always purged, therefore no liquid oxygen or liquid hydrogen escaped when Lesseps unscrewed all four of the large hoses and eased them clear. His arms were aching from reaching up by the time he had finished. He hid the power wrench because such tampering was strictly forbidden. Removing the regulator from the airframe was simply a matter of disconnecting the data-link and power connectors, unscrewing two self-locking bolts that passed right through the block and pulling it clear. He stuffed it into his gadget bag and closed the inspection hatch. It was unlikely that anyone would open the hatch and discover that the regulator was missing during his anticipated thirty-minute absence but as a precaution he put up a warning notice saying that the lights and camera were set up for a shoot and were not to be disturbed. The regulator was a dead, accusing weight in his gadget bag as he returned to his work station in the deserted documentation office.

He unlocked a drawer in his desk and took out the fake block, already primed with the volatile magnesium wool in exactly the same manner that he had used for the test piece. He opened the Plessey manual for the fuel regulator although he had studied the exploded drawings over several days and could probably dismantle it blindfolded. Removing the solenoid motor and multiple valve mechanism from the genuine block for transfer to the fake was fairly straightforward: it consisted of a single module designed for quick replacement by ground engineers. The only modification that Lesseps had to carry out was to solder a short length of fine wire from the contact on the ignition flashbulb to pin 22 on the controller micro-processor. This was the pin that went six volts high on throttle-back of the rocket engine that this regulator block supplied with fuel. To ensure that this vital link was correct, Lesseps referred to the manual. There was no mistake. The wire was hidden once the entire capsule was installed in its new home. The ring of fixing holes in the original cover plate lined up perfectly with the matching threaded holes in the fake block.

A door opened at the end of the office. It was Marcel – one of the security officers doing his rounds. Lesseps had been expecting his appearance.

'Good evening, Mr Lesseps. Saw you on the monitors.

They work you hard.'

Lesseps casually moved a drawing to hide what he was doing. 'They certainly do, Marcel.'

'Everything okay?'

'Fine, thank you, Marcel.'

The security officer glanced around the office and withdrew.

Alone again, Lesseps contemplated his handiwork now that assembly was virtually complete. The fake regulator block looked perfect. Now for the most awkward job of all: removal of the Plessey identification plate from the genuine block. It was a thin piece of metal foil stamped with a serial and batch number, and marked with vital identification information. It even included a tiny but complex hologram motif to deter pirate copying. The plate was bonded in place and was not meant to be removed without being damaged.

Lesseps opened the box of surgical tools he had purchased for the purpose and selected the scalpel with the thinnest blade. Taking great care not to damage or mark the label in any way, he gently teased it away from the block. It was slow work which necessitated frequent replacement of the scalpel blade. After fifteen minutes' painstaking care he was able to lift the label from the block with the aid of plastic tweezers. A coating of Superglue on the back of the label, careful positioning on the fake block and smoothing down with his gloved finger, and the entire job was complete.

In his hands was a fuel regulator block that looked indistinguishable from the original.

He cleared up, stowed the fake regulator in his gadget bag and rode a golf cart back to Shed A.

Installing the fake block in the airframe took less than ten minutes. The coupling nuts for the liquid oxygen and hydrogen lines turned easily on their new mating threads. Lesseps marvelled at the expertise of the unknown machinist whom Joe had found. He tightened the two mounting bolts, locked the data and power connectors into place, and the entire job was finished. He turned on his lights and took a photograph, dumped it into his portable computer and used a split screen to compare the 'before' and 'after' images. They were identical. There was no time to savour his pride in a job well done. He was about to return the tools to his gadget bag when a voice from the past spoke to him.

You disgusting, filthy boy!

The power wrench slipped from his fingers, he spun around, his senses reeling.

'Oh – I'm so sorry, Mr Lesseps,' said Claudia. She had merely said, 'Good evening' and was genuinely sorry to have made him jump. 'I didn't mean to startle you. Please forgive me.' She was dressed in her orange skin-tight Micranex jumpsuit with matching trainers.

Lesseps managed a rueful smile as he moved one of the reflectors aside for her. He nearly picked up the power wrench to give himself time to think but realised that the action would draw attention to it. 'You certainly did, Miss Picquet. I thought I had the place to myself.'

She returned his smile and was about say something when she saw the tools. 'Oh – you're on to the servicing tools schedules? I didn't think you were so advanced.'

'I'm not,' said Lesseps, deliberately not avoiding her eye this time and causing her to look away. If he had had a better understanding of women he would have realised that something was on her mind. 'I had hoped to include the tools illustrations but we don't have the time.'

She nodded. 'Yes – I'm sure. There're not so important . . . Marcel told me you were working late so I thought . . .' She hesitated. 'Mr Lesseps, may I ask a favour of you?'

'Er – yes – of course.'

'I would like some instrument practice. Could I accompany you on your weekend cross-countries? Not every one, of course – just now and then. I hate messing about with the computer simulators. I'd be happy to contribute towards the fuel . . .' She broke off and looked slightly embarrassed, as though the request had taken some effort.

Lesseps was too relieved to be surprised. 'Well – yes.' Hardly knowing what he was saying, he added: 'I'd be glad of the company.'

256

Claudia's worried expression gave way to a warm smile and her gaze lost its fear-inducing hardness. 'In that case you will let me buy you a drink in the clubhouse and we'll talk it over. You'll have to take those gloves off – they're intimidating to a woman.'

Lesseps was too astonished to realise that Claudia Picquet had made a joke.

5

Tuesday, 15 December
The gamble Paul took with his unexpected visit to London paid off. He had found out that Yuri Segal would be staying in his apartment above his Regent Street office and decided that if the only way of seeing him was without an appointment, then so be it. He took the first Eurostar from Paris and sent the boss of Commonwealth Air a cryptic 'I wish to see you in forty-five minutes on a very urgent matter' fax as the train was pulling into Waterloo Station.

'You may go up now, Mr Santos,' said the receptionist, somewhat sulkily because Paul had declared his intention of staying put until Yuri Segal agreed to see him.

The lift took Paul up one floor from the reception area. The doors opened directly into Segal's private office.

The burly Slav was sitting in his dressing gown before the remains of a huge breakfast spread across his desk. His florid expression broke into a beaming smile. He stood, pudgy hand outstretched. 'Paul! A pleasure! A pleasure! Come in. Coffee?'

The two men exchanged pleasantries over the strongest coffee that Paul had ever tasted since a visit to Turkish Airlines in Ankara. He took one sip and decided it was enough.

'You are lucky to find me,' Segal was saying. 'We are here two nights only. My wife wants to do some Christmas shopping.'

'I know,' said Paul. 'I hired a Moscow detective agency to report on your movements.'

Segal's smile never faltered. He had total control over his face muscles. 'A remarkable admission, Paul.'

'I had to do it, Yuri, because you're so damned elusive. And my fax just now was a big lie. I'm not passing through London. I've come specially to see you.'

The Russian suddenly threw back his head and laughed. 'I have learned that Paul Santos is at his most dangerous when he is being honest.'

Paul shook his head. 'I don't think I'm dangerous, Yuri. I certainly don't feel it. But I have come here to be honest with you. Unless you convert your options for ten Sabres to firm orders, Sabre Industries is finished. It may not sound very businesslike to admit this and it makes my position even more vulnerable than it already is, but it is the plain, unpalatable truth.' Segal was about to speak, but Paul held up his hand and continued, 'I haven't come to pressure you, Yuri,' (Ha! thought Paul) just to give you the facts. I neither expect nor demand a decision from you now, but I do want you to read this when I've left.' Paul took a single sheet of paper from his pocket and handed it to the Slav. 'It's a précis of my last medical report, Yuri. I've given my doctors permission to confirm its findings to you should you wish to verify it. I know I can trust you not divulge its contents and to destroy it when you've read it. I've got twenty months if I carry on as I am now. Twenty years – maybe much more – if I bow out of the rat race.

'As you know, I'm marrying Sophia on Friday. Twenty years or more with her is worth more to me than your ten Sabres. You going ahead with them will put Sabre Industries on a firm footing and enable me to delegate much of my workload and stay in office. If you haven't ordered by 1 January, I will resign. This I have promised Sophia so there can be no going back on my word. If that happens, Sabre Industries will complete its commitments on existing orders and fold.'

The Slav's expression became inscrutable. 'You believe

you're indispensable, Paul?'

'What do you think, Yuri? Confidence is shaky enough. The shares will collapse, the next call will be a disaster and that will be the end of your dream of Moscow as eastern Europe's hundred-minute global hub.'

'Is that my dream, Paul?'

'Yes. Why else would you want options on ten Sabres?'

Segal smiled faintly. 'It's very good of you to come all this way to advise me of my dreams.'

Paul stood and held out his hand. 'I came to be straight with you, Yuri, and I certainly wasn't expecting you to reciprocate. You will destroy that report?'

'You have my word on that, Paul,' said Segal as the two men shook hands. 'Your frankness is appreciated and congratulations on your forthcoming marriage.'

They bade each other a happy Christmas.

As Paul rode down in the lift he reflected that he had just played the biggest ace of his career. But, as usual, Yuri Segal had given away none of those tiny visual clues that years of negotiating experience had taught Paul to recognise.

He had no way of telling whether or not his ace would win the game.

6

On the other side of London, Honicker was also taking a gamble. In fact he was taking the biggest physical risk in what had been, to date, a relatively action-free spying career. It required careful timing but little more than a pedestrian employed when dodging traffic.

He stepped out in front of the slow-moving Rolls-Royce as it was turning into Canary Wharf's executive car park. But instead of jumping clear when the vehicle stopped and sounded its horn, he stood his ground.

Ian rolled down the driver's window and politely asked the smartly-dressed man holding a briefcase to move.

'I'd like to speak to Mr Joshua Shief please,' said

Honicker pleasantly. The Rolls-Royce's windows were polarised to black, preventing him seeing the rear seat's occupant.

'I'm sure if you call Mr Shief's office, his staff will be able to help you,' Ian replied easily, but he was alert. The stranger looked too well-dressed to spell trouble but one could never be sure.

'My name's William Honicker. I have an appointment to see Mr Shief in an hour's time, but I'd rather talk to him now. Out here.'

Ian opened his door and confronted Honicker, his feet slightly apart, hands loose and relaxed at his side, his general demeanour that of a useful fighter ready for trouble. Honicker read the menace in Ian's stance, as he was meant to, and decided he didn't like the physical side of the spying business.

'As I said, sir,' said Ian, measuring up Honicker's weight and likely reach, 'Mr Shief's staff—'

'Your embassy arranged for us to meet in my office in one hour, Mr Honicker,' said Shief suddenly. He had lowered a window and was staring at Honicker. 'May I inquire what is wrong with that arrangement?'

Honicker approached the Rolls, watched carefully by Ian. 'Good morning, Mr Shief. I'd prefer a man-to-man talk. Just the two of us. No recorders or any of that nonsense.' He indicated a nearby bench facing a flowerbed.

'It's cold and I don't have an overcoat.'

'This won't take ten minutes.'

Shief was about to protest but changed his mind. Ian darted forward as he opened the door and climbed out. 'Thank you, Ian. Pull the car over and then stay close please.'

Ian did as he was told and hovered out of earshot of the two men as they sat on the bench. 'Perhaps you should first examine my credentials,' said Honicker, offering his diplomatic passport.

Shief brushed the card aside. 'Just what is this play-acting about?' he demanded.

260

Honicker opened his briefcase and gave the oil man a folder. 'You may keep that, Mr Shief. A little memento of our unceasing vigilance where the peace and prosperity of our country is at stake.'

With an air of indifference Shief opened the folder. The first document was a photograph of him. He was lying on a yacht's sunbed, his arm around a naked girl.

'General Oman Putriana's yacht,' Honicker commented. 'Indonesia's commander-in-chief.'

'Having to maintain good relations with unsavoury politicians is the stock-in-trade of businessmen,' Shief commented, adding pointedly that he also had to deal with unsavoury diplomats.

'Take a look at the rest of the file,' Honicker invited.

Shief leafed through the documents, his manner casual, but what he saw appalled him: photocopies of memos; secret consultative documents; records of clandestine payments; bank statements of powerful Jakarta officials with matching sums ringed – at least a hundred damning documents. The degree to which he had underestimated the Australian security services alarmed him, but by the same token his quick-thinking mind realised that he must be frightening them if they were prepared to show their hand in this manner.

'Just a small sample,' Honicker commented.

The oil man shrugged. 'So you've shown me a sample of documents relating to normal business practices in Jakarta. So what?'

'You miss the point, Mr Sheif. Under recent legislation relating to aiding potential enemies of Australia, an immediate order could be obtained closing down *all* Avanti's activities in Australia *and* the seizure of all its assets. Refineries, depots, transport fleets – everything.'

Shief shrugged. 'I've been in this business a long time. I've had such threats before. Your country making such a move would undermine the confidence of overseas investors. Australia's economy shaky enough as it is.'

Honicker had to admire the oil man's seeming indifference.

'There's more, Mr Shief. We have enough evidence to enable President Sulimann to do something similar in Indonesia. Grabbing a foreign concern would be a popular move – particularly if it was linked to the arrest and trial of a whole host of unpopular officials on corruption charges.'

Shief closed the file and tossed it on to Honicker's lap. 'All very interesting – not to me. Maybe to our lawyers if you do anything stupid. They'd tear you apart.'

Honicker produced his Klipfone. 'They wouldn't have time. The order is on the prime minister's desk now. His office is awaiting a call from me before he signs it.' He paused. Now for the big bluff . . . 'Not only that, but a courier is standing by in Singapore waiting to deliver a similar dossier to the authorities there. The Singaporeans are very touchy about corruption and tend to shoot from the hip. *And* they have a lot of influence. Within forty-eight hours about ninety per cent of your Far East operations could be wiped out.'

A muscle in Shief's neck twitched suddenly – the only sign that Honicker's barb had gone home. Nevertheless he smiled easily. 'So let me guess – your government wants to do a deal concerning a possible offshore find in the Far East?'

'It could be a very favourable deal for you if you're sensible, Mr Shief,' Honicker replied.

7

Thursday, 17 December
Christine stared at Honicker in astonishment. She sat abruptly at her desk, too stunned to speak for a few moments, her thoughts a turmoil; she didn't know whether to be angry or elated.

Honicker eyed her anxiously. Her dark hair had grown since he had last seen her. It now fell across her face, giving her a wild, almost untamed look that was accentuated by her shapeless jeans and jersey. She looked up at him. He braced himself, expecting fire to flash suddenly in those dark eyes and for her to unleash a tirade. Christine had changed his views on women. The procession of vapid, neat and tidy secretaries he had known until then was at an end. His next girl-friend would be like her: alive, strong-willed, tempestuous – someone who could offer a relationship that was like tangoing in a minefield.

But the blast of invective never came. Instead she picked up a telephone and asked Alec to join them.

'I'm surprised he's not up here to welcome me,' said Honicker affably.

'We've got a problem with the new Darwin.' She was now watching him intently.

'Serious?'

'Could be.'

Alec entered the office. He was wearing overalls and looked exhausted, dark rings under his eyes. He shook hands with Honicker. 'I expect Chris has told you—'

'Tell Alec what you've just told me,' Christine interrupted.

Alec sensed the tense atmosphere in the room and looked from his wife to Honicker. 'You two been squabbling over fees?'

'Just sit down and listen!' Christine snapped.

Alec subsided into a chair and looked expectantly at their visitor. 'What have you been up to, Bill?'

'An Australia–Indonesia summit for early next year is being hatched in Canberra and Jakarta at the moment,' Honicker began. 'There'll be an announcement next week, but not all the agenda will be disclosed. Part of the Australian side of the package will be a substantial foreign aid deal for Indonesia.'

Alec glanced at Christine. 'Provided they do as they're told?'

'Australia will match every dollar Sulimann knocks off his defence budget with a dollar in aid. The fund will be ad-ministered by an aid agency that we'll set up in Jakarta with branches right across the country, tasked with ensuring that money goes where it's needed. The agency's director will be appointed by the Australian government. We have Christine in mind.'

There was a silence in the room.

'Good God,' Alec muttered. He looked at his wife who was staring at the wall.

'There's more . . .' she said.

Honicker regarded Alec thoughtfully. 'Avanti Oil get the Banda oilfield rights in return for a sliding royalty based on production yields. It's a complex formula, but basically it means that they get twenty per cent of the profits, the Commonwealth of Australia gets twenty per cent and Indonesia gets fifty-five per cent, of which ten goes in the aid fund. Shief's twenty is a much smaller slice of the cake than he originally wanted, but he's astute enough to know it's the best deal he's likely to get.'

Alec added up the percentages. 'And the other five per cent?'

'Goes to Triton Exploration and there will be no buy-in pressure on you from any party. The use of your Darwin patents will be a straightforward commercial contract. The huge cost of getting the field in production will be met equally by Australia and Avanti – probably through a jointly owned corporation. The whole thing will be a four-party deal which will take an army of lawyers several weeks to set up – a team of our trade experts have already spent nearly two days with Avanti to get this far – just the bare bones thrashed out.'

'And you'd do such a deal with Shief?' Alec asked.

Honicker shrugged. 'You were prepared to when he was after your company. He's not much worse than many others. Maybe Avanti's growth has outstripped most others over the past ten years because of Shief's aggressive and sometimes unconventional methods, but we need him. He's got some smart operators on his payroll and he's got much of the infrastructure already in place. And don't forget that he was the only one to back you when you were getting doors slammed in your face. He's a businessman with vision. He gets things done – it would be better to have him with us

264

than against us.'

'Clever,' said Christine at length. 'We get placated because the aid goes to the right place; Triton is no longer stalked; Sulimann's position is underpinned; Shief gets a cut; and your country gets a cut and control of the world's largest oil-field. An ingenious compromise.'

Honicker smiled, still uncertain of how Christine was going to react. 'We don't know for certain that Banda field is viable yet, Chris. The survey we've commissioned Triton to carry out will now concentrate on the Banda Trench – samples taken from all over it.' He paused and regarded Christine thoughtfully. 'And you don't have to commit your-self until the results are known.'

'We'd like to talk it over,' said Christine. 'Give us an hour.'

Honicker drove into Walton and found a café. He returned to Triton's office after ninety minutes. The atmosphere was now noticeably less tense.

'Okay,' said Christine. 'We'll go along with you on that basis.' She fixed her gaze on Honicker. 'But I shall want a clause in lights to say that our patents would be tied up.'

'That will be guaranteed, Christine.'

She looked mollified. 'But there's a problem.'

'With the Darwin?'

'The new casing failed on test at the National Physical Labs three days ago,' said Alec. 'Hairline cracks at a simu-lated depth of 7,000 metres. Water flooding in at that pressure would wreck the electrics.'

The news alarmed Honicker. 'Design fault or material fault?'

'Both. Another thirty mill on the casing wall thickness should cure the problem but it will add to her weight – destroy her twenty-kilo negative buoyancy and make her too heavy for the Plaston tubing. She has to be raised and lowered by the tubing, of course. We can't use steel cable for winching because the weight of twelve kilometres of the stuff will crucify the entire design concept – we'd never be able to use existing floating production platforms if they had to carry thousands of tonnes of steel cable. The only option is to lighten Darwin's internal mechanics to put us back to square one.'

'How much weight do you need to lose?'

'Seventy-five kilos,' Alec replied.

'Any ideas?'

Alec shook his head despondently. 'It's a helluva lot to shed.'

'Any chance of coming up with a solution by tomorrow?'

'Be reasonable, Bill,' Christine protested. 'Alec's had no sleep for two nights as it is. And now you've thrown this deal at us.'

Honicker smiled. 'You're right, Christine – my apologies. I've got an overbearing chief who'd like a report tomorrow. Time is very pressing now but he'll have to wait.'

Before returning to London Honicker extracted a solemn promise from Christine that she would call his Iridium number, no matter what the time of day, the moment Alec came up with a solution.

Such was his confidence in Alec's ability that he broke his rule and took his Klipfone with him to the opera that evening, but the only *Ring* he received came courtesy of Wagner and Covent Garden.

8

Joe Yavanoski's flight from Seattle touched down at Heathrow just as Honicker's opera was ending. The flight had been delayed several hours, putting Joe in a bad humour that gradually dissipated as he relaxed in a Ramada bathtub, smoking a cigar that had been denied him on the flight and in the taxi. On the back of the chair where he could keep it in sight was a briefcase containing Lesseps's pay-off: half a million dollars in used $100 bills. All steam-ironed flat in bundles of 500 to reduce their bulk, and not one of the bills touched by Joe without his wearing gloves. Collecting them had taken several weeks.

266

He twiddled the mixer lever with his toe. The hotter the water, the less his knee hurt. But the less his knee hurt, the more his thoughts troubled him. He had learnt to shut out the old newsreel images of the blazing *Hindenburg* by thinking of Johnny Coreba pushing a line of supermarket trucks, but the grainy black-and-white pictures of the hydrogen holocaust kept stealing up on him during reflective moments.

The bedroom TV was carrying a story about the first fare-paying flight of the Sabre. He craned his neck. A reporter was standing before the floodlit Sabre 005 saying something about Paul Santos being on tomorrow's historic flight. Hardly believing his ears, Joe scrambled out of the bath and stood naked in front of the TV. Jesus – it was true! Santos was marrying his secretary in Terminal 6 – a reception in the VIP lounge and then the couple were flying to Sydney for their honeymoon on Sabre 005!

His knee protested at the sudden movement, obliging him to sit but he hardly noticed the pain. Paul Santos – the one man who more than any other was responsible for the mess that the once mighty US civil airplane industry was in – would be on Sabre 005!

Joe gave a sudden whoop of delight and punched the air. Santos nailed! It made all the weeks of agonising worthwhile and he knew that never again would he be troubled by memories of the Hindenburg footage.

9

Friday, 18 December
Jim Curtis, Director of Terminal 6 Heathrow Plc, knew that today was going to be the busiest day of his career and it got off to a bad start. He entered his office at 05:50, beating his secretary by ten minutes. Four floors below on the apron outside, bright lights flashed around the floodlit Sabre 005 as his security team checked every centimetre of the

spaceplane. There had been a worrying number of anonymous threats – most of them traced to Luddite loonies – but
Curtis took every one seriously. Not only did he have to
contend with the Sabre's first flight, but a chartered Airbus
was bringing in 125 guests for the Santos wedding breakfast
and wedding, most of whom were senior Sabre Industries
personnel. Security was going to be a nightmare: the screen-
ing of arriving journalists had been going on all night; extra
staff would be on duty to process the 200 passengers and on
top of all that there was an e-mail on his monitor from the
insurance company saying that wedding presents on display
weren't covered, and another informing him that the huge
bouquet he was supposed to be presenting to Mrs Santos on
behalf of the British Airports Authority hadn't arrived.

He left these and a dozen similar problems for his capable
secretary to deal with and went down to sort out a dispute
between security and ground ops. The latter had a tug waiting to tow the Sabre to the liquid oxygen and hydrogen
fuelling point, and security hadn't finished their work.

His team was certainly being thorough and were even
shining endoscopes into all the fuel tanks. Every inspector
was equipped with a wide-angle Memcorder on the side of
his or her helmet. Curtis worked out a compromise with
both parties and returned to his office to learn that the
morning shift Italian air traffic controllers had just called a
snap strike over the sacking of a colleague and a charter
flight from Rome bringing in the Italian passengers probably
wouldn't get away.

'All passengers were warned to be in London last night,'
said David Morgan, speaking from the British Airways
Space Operations Room one floor below. 'We've got a window clear of space debris for take off at 10:02 and we won't
have another opening for fifty-two minutes. If they're not
here on time we go without them.'

The shape of things to come, thought Curtis when the
conversation ended. Air travel won't be ruled by the weather
in future but by space junk from thousands of defunct
satellites. Five incoming calls were queuing because his

secretary was busy. The first was a problem with the catering company providing the wedding breakfast. Two waitresses were last-minute replacements and hadn't been cleared. The next was from T3 saying that they were in possession of a large bouquet and were going to charge T6 for its storage. And there was a bleat about not enough chairs from the team setting up the dining-tables in the VIP lounge.

It's going to be one of those days, Curtis reflected gloomily as he took the fourth call. Dear God – why couldn't people stay at home? He could run his terminal like clockwork if it weren't for aeroplanes and passengers forever getting in the way.

It was as well for his state of mind that he had no inkling of just how disastrous his day was going to be.

10

The Terminal 6 security officer recognised Jez as the youngster he had rescued from a plane-spotters' scrum the year before. 'Sorry, lad,' he said sympathetically, barring Jez's entry into the terminal. 'Observation dome and lounge are closed today. Sabre's first scheduled flight and all that – a real crackdown. Ticket holders only.'

'But I've got a ticket for the Sabre flight,' said Jez proudly.

The security officer looked astounded and asked to see it. 'Well damn me!' he said, examining the ticket and returning it. 'You lucky little sod.' He was about to say something about Jez's age but he spotted a limousine heading for the set-down zone. 'Oh hell – here come some VIPs. You'd better scoot – check-in Zone D. Desk's just opened. Have a good flight.'

With his kitbag slung over his shoulder, his anorak hood pulled up and with extra soles and heels glued to the highest trainers he had, Jez passed through the automatic doors and moved towards the horde of reporters and camera crews milling around Zone D.

On this occasion their presence did not cause him undue concern because the kitchen TV at home had developed an unaccountable fault owing to his removal of its internal mains fuse the previous evening. He found the check-in desk for his flight and feasted his eyes on the overhead display:

British Airways Flight SB005A Sydney.

The 'A' suffix stood for Australia; the return flight number would be SB005B.

A party of four glum Belgians ahead of him finished their check-in formalities by swallowing their Spaceqel tablets and handing over their Klipfones for return to them in Sydney. Jez found himself on the piezo mat that clocked his weight. He remembered to stand on his toes while leaning against the desk. The girl gave him an uneasy glance and sorted through the papers in his travel wallet.

She swiped his passport card through her reader, studied the information on her screen and her expression became a worried frown. 'Mr Jeremy Moreton?'

'Yes,' said Jez nervously. This was the moment he had been dreading.

'I have your date of birth as 2005. Is that correct?'

Well of course it's correct!

'Yes.' Jez's voice was a croak. 'But the Kodastripe picture of me was taken two years ago. I was younger then.'

'Just a moment please.' She checked Jez's ticket carefully, picked up a telephone and spoke to her supervisor who requested her to patch a screen echo to his terminal.

There was a sudden commotion as the reporters spotted someone of interest. But Jez didn't hear them. All his attention was focused on the girl who was listening intently and saying: 'Yes . . . Yes . . .' into her handset. Eventually she replaced it and stared at her monitor, avoiding Jez's eye. 'I'm very sorry, Mr Moreton. But I cannot stripe a boarding validation on your card. Participants in the draw had to be over eighteen. The European Aerospace Authority aren't allowing children to fly on Sabres for the time being. I'm terribly sorry.'

The terminal building seemed to swim around Jez. He for-

270

got about standing on his toes. 'But . . . But . . . I'm *not* a child! It's all . . . It was won fair and . . . Paid for . . .' He clung to the desk to prevent his knees from giving out.

'If you go to the information desk, they'll tell you the procedure for claiming a refund. I really am very sorry about this, but I'm not allowed to give you a boarding validation. I don't know how it's happened that you've been issued with a ticket.'

Jez would have continued protesting but he turned quickly away from the desk so that the girl wouldn't see the tears in his eyes.

'One more please, Mr Santos!'

'If you would look this way, Mr Santos!' The name of the chairman of Sabre Industries cut through Jez's misery and humiliation. He saw Paul Santos being shepherded through a throng of pressmen to the VIP lounge and knew exactly what he had to do. He snatched up his travel wallet, doubled up and wormed himself through the crowd with all the determination of a greased eel while yelling 'Mr Santos! Mr Santos!' Security men tried to grab him as he burst through the mêlée and caught hold of Paul's sleeve.

'Mr Santos! It's me! Jez!' His voice was cracking in desperation. 'You remember me! A year ago! I asked you for your autograph!'

A hundred pairs of hands seized Jez and threw him to the floor before Paul had a chance to react. He was rolled on to his stomach and his hands were locked into the small of his back with such force that he cried out in pain.

'Mr Santos!' Jez sobbed.

The newsmen, with cameras perched on shoulders like pirates' parrots, closed eagerly around the scene and prevented the security men dragging Jez away.

'No! No!' Paul cried, brushing aside attempts to hustle him away. 'I know this boy! Let him go!' To the astonishment of everyone, including Jez, he helped him to his feet and recovered his kitbag, although two police officers insisted on keeping a firm grip on their captive.

'Get rid of him!' Curtis snapped, wondering how this

271

plane-spotter had got into his terminal and resolving to have many heads on many plates before the morning was out.

'Mr Santos,' Jez wept, almost hysterical. 'I've got a proper ticket but they won't let me on board!'

'We're five-minutes behind schedule, Mr Santos,' said Curtis, eyeing Jez with loathing while trying to steer his guest away. But Paul insisted on hearing Jez's sorry story of the check-in girl's refusal to give him a boarding validation.

'And the ticket is in your name, Jez?'

Jez nodded, blinking in the glare of the TV lights and praying to God that this diminutive Frenchman might be able to do something.

'Let us see what we can do,' said Paul and the entire retinue, including the news teams, bore down on the hapless check-in girl who eyed their approach with all the enthusiasm of a kidnapped virgin tied down on a Satanic altar. 'It's an EAA rule, Jez,' Paul was explaining. He treated the girl and Jim Curtis to his disarming smile. 'But I expect we can bend it a little if I take full responsibility, eh, Mr Curtis?'

Curtis checked his protests when he saw the sudden icy look in Santos's eye. He gave the hapless check-in girl a reluctant nod and told her to go ahead.

'Excellent,' said Paul, looking pleased. 'See you on board, Jez. You must excuse me now – I'm supposed to be at a wedding.'

Choking back tears of gratitude, Jez stammered his heart-felt thanks but his saviour was swept away before he could pump his hand.

11

Christine called Honicker as he was finishing his breakfast at the Savoy. 'Alec's been up since five. He thinks he may have an answer to the Darwin's weight problem.'

Honicker was delighted. 'I was confident that he would come up with something, Christine,' he said. 'I'll be with you at nine, traffic permitting.'

Apart from a hold-up on Walton Bridge, the traffic was unusually permissive, with the result that Honicker was in Triton Exploration's workshop by 8.45, listening intently to Alec. The three were contemplating the wooden mock-up of the Darwin's new gearbox and pump impeller housing. The entire assembly stood nearly two metres high.

Alec pointed to the beautifully carved mahogany patterns that would be used as foundry patterns for casting the massive sections in aluminium alloy. 'Those ally castings account for fifty per cent of the weight of the internal mechanics,' he explained. 'I've got an idea for using a lighter material from a job we did recently for an American customer.'

'So what's lighter than aluminium alloy?'

'Magnesium alloy,' Alec replied. 'The stuff can be pressure cast. We use that for all the castings and we lose sixty-five kilos. The other ten kilos can be won easily from other weight savings.'

'Magnesium alloy?' Honicker repeated thoughtfully. 'I dare say the fire risk will be minimal, but would it be strong enough?'

'Plenty strong enough.'

'How about machining it? Isn't it supposed to be a bastard?'

'We've got the Shaeffer,' said Alec, nodding to the Swiss machine. 'And I've now got some experience working the stuff.' He delved into a bin under the bench and produced a control block which he handed to Honicker. 'That's a scrap job in mag alloy.'

Honicker admired the beautifully machined block. 'Doesn't look like scrap to me,' he observed.

'I made a balls-up and cut those large threads undersize.'

'Alec!' Christine protested. 'We gave an undertaking to the customer that we'd dispose of everything relating to his job. I don't think—'

'What does it matter? We don't know who Mr Wright was and we don't know who he was working for. We didn't even have an Iridium number or an address.'

'Isn't that the guy I saw on my last visit?' Honicker queried. 'Elderly. American. Arrived here on foot.'

'He arrived on foot to collect the work as well,' Alec replied.

Honicker looked surprised. 'You mean you didn't have to make many of these things?'

'Just four,' Alec replied.

'Exactly what is it?'

'Christ knows. It says control block on the drawing.'

Honicker held the block up to the light and ran his thumbnail along the coupling threads. 'Weird thread form,' he commented. 'Asymmetric.'

'ISO buttress threads,' Alec answered. 'I had to buy a set of chasers to cut them. It's a thread form that's been developed recently for volatile gases in liquid form. Rocket fuel couplings – that sort of thing. Something to do with high axial loads having good anti-creep properties. The threads bed hard against each other.'

The Darwin was momentarily forgotten. Honicker placed the curious block on the bench and switched on a lamp. He had a bad feeling about the thing. A block made of magnesium alloy and yet possibly having to handle volatile gases just didn't seem right and he said so.

'He said that it was for a rocket-powered car,' Alec replied. 'An attempt on the world speed record.'

'And they say women gossip,' Christine muttered.

'Rocket car!' Honicker echoed in astonishment. 'What sort of rocket car? These twin bores are at least 60 mill! You could run a medium-sized power station on the amount of fuel you could pump through this thing!' He thought for a moment and turned to Christine. 'How many visitors do you have who turn up on foot?'

The question took her by surprise. 'Er . . . Well, now you mention it, none.'

'There's a gardener, but he lives nearby,' said Alec.

'Post? Deliveries?'

'Van as a rule.'

'And yet your Mr Wright came on foot. Not once, but twice. And an elderly guy at that, and Americans are not noted for walking.'

'He said he left his car out in the road,' Christine pointed out.

'And there was no car parked nearby when I saw him,' Honicker shot back. 'Do you have a cheque or credit card slip from him?'

'He paid in cash.'

'Is that usual?'

'We've done a number of one-offs for cash,' Alec observed. 'Not as much as this job, though.'

'Have you got the drawing?'

Christine gave a gesture of resignation as Alec rummaged among a pile of documents and produced a print which he unfolded in front of Honicker. One glance at the meticulous draughtsmanship and the use of metric dimensions and threads was enough to tell the Australian that something was very wrong indeed. This was not the drawing of a 'one-off' job, or even a four-off. He was unable to say why looking at the drawing should make him feel so uneasy. Nor could he account for his sense of urgency when he spoke, other than a pressing desire to get to the bottom of this mystery before giving his attention to anything else. 'Christine, you have a terminal in your office. I'd like to use it please. Right now.'

It was 09:00 – one hour to take off.

12

Paul and Sophia were married at 08:15 before 125 guests crammed into Terminal 6's register office. Sophia looked so sensational in a Christian Dior white cashmere skirt and jacket that even the polished Jim Curtis stumbled over his words when he pushed through the congratulating crowd around the happy couple and presented her with the British Airports Authority bouquet. The dazzling smile, followed by a kiss, that he received from Sophia were more than adequate compensation for the two hours of Sod's Law in overdrive that he had just been through.

'Bloody uncivilised hour to get married,' he muttered when he returned to his team of minions who were suited up as ushers.

'She's lovely,' said one of the ushers admiringly. 'I fantasise about middle-aged brunettes.'

'Fantasise about herding 'em into the lounge and getting them sat down,' Curtis retorted. 'We're ten minutes behind schedule. And if one journo gets into the boarding lounge heads will roll.' He pressed the PTT on his wrist radio and warned the caterers to get ready.

The guests were ushered into the lounge. Two Autovacs espied the offensive presence of confetti. They detached themselves from their charging points, scurried across the carpet and set to work like a pair of mechanical dung beetles.

Outside on the apron, Captain Len Allenby and First Officer Nick Rowe, looking resplendent in new zero-G-tailored uniforms, were carrying out their 'visual' – the ground inspection of Sabre 005. Allenby was one of those skippers who refused to allow the traditional walk-around to become merely a ritual and the ground crew knew this. Every inspection hatch was open and all received attention from the skipper and his powerful halogen lamp. He even put his hand over the boil-off vents to ensure that the liquid oxygen and hydrogen tanks were not pressurised, and checked that the auxiliary bowser that kept the tanks primed until push-back was doing its job. On the flight deck he paid particular attention to the circular hatch in the floor that provided access to the service bay in the lower hull, and the pressure-tight door that led to the main cabin. Should an emergency arise in space, the flight deck could be sealed off to serve as an air-lock. Last to be examined was the shuttle-compatible docking hatch in the flight-deck's roof.

Once the inspection was complete and both men had 'fingerprinted' the ground engineer's memopad, they took their seats and began working through the pre-engine start

276

check-list in response to the cue headers as they appeared on their dual screens.

Allenby had hoped that Simone Frankel would be his co-pilot but she had lost in the crewing draw that had been held for this particular flight. Nevertheless, the easy-going Nick Rowe was an excellent man to have in the right-hand seat. He was BA's third most experienced Sabre pilot, having flown thirteen circumnavigation flights from St Omer, and had carried out two EVA spacewalks to fix minor faults.

Behind them, in the main cabin, chief cabin services officer Jacky Kerr and her two stewards had nearly completed their inspection. All three were wearing smart grey trouser-suit uniforms. After an unfortunate incident on a training flight involving a shy stewardess and a not-so-shy steward, British Airways had decided that their current fashion of uniforms with short skirts was unsuitable in weightless conditions and opted for the trouser suit uniform.

'I don't think I'll ever get used to this,' Neil Burrows muttered, surveying the spartan cabin. 'Fixed seatbacks; no armrests; no bins; no burners; no food; no bar; no videos; no trays; no safety cards; no duty frees—'

'No commissions,' Billy Ryan chipped in ruefully.

'. . . No gravity; no overnight expenses,' Neil continued.

'And no overshoes under 14D,' Jacky called out.

'And no jobs soon,' Billy muttered, deep in gloom. 'Three of us for 200 passengers. Seat-belt checks carried out by the front office. Doesn't seem right. Marry me, Jacky. We could take early retirement and open a gay fish and chip shop in Bognor.'

'She's supposed to be marrying me,' Neil objected.

'Overshoes – 14D,' Jacky insisted.

Billy sighed and produced a spare pair of Velcro overshoes from a zippered compartment.

In the terminal the wedding breakfast went smoothly. The speeches were short because Curtis had managed to have a quiet word with the top table guests before they sat down. The last toast was from Heinrich Kluge, president of the European Central Enterprise Bank, who raised his glass to the happy couple and, amid laughter, wished them ungodly speed to Australia. By the time Sophia and Paul had said their farewells and were escorted into the boarding lounge, eager passengers were feeding their passport cards through the boarding turnstiles and Curtis's schedule was back on target.

It was 09:31.

Twenty-nine minutes to take-off.

13

Honicker drummed his fingers impatiently on Christine's desk while waiting for the government computer in Canberra to find the routing he wanted. Alec and Christine looked on.

'Where are you trying to get to?' Alec asked.

'The Pentagon's Supply Classification Network.'

'What's that?'

'A pompous name for an inventory. It's a development of the Federal Supply Classification system that was set up for the military in the late 1940s. Then it expanded in the 1960s and '70s to become the NATO Supply Classification system, and now it's the world inventory of government and commercial supply items. Everything from drawing-pins to anti-aircraft guns. Over two billion items five years ago, so God knows how big it is today.'

'But surely this control block won't be registered as it's a specialist item?' Christine queried.

'We won't know unless we look.'

'But you've nothing to go on. No maker. No part number. Nothing.'

'I've got enough,' was the Australian's enigmatic reply. 'It's been some months since I last used this network. Let us hope that it hasn't changed too much.'

The screen filled with a complex menu. Honicker gave a grunt of satisfaction and selected 'Hardware search'.

SEARCH BY REFERENCE.
SEARCH BY DESCRIPTION.

278

He clicked on the latter.

A questionnaire appeared on the screen.

ITEM NAME:

He answered with a question mark in the reply field.

MATERIAL:

Another question mark.

DIMENSIONAL DATA:

'Now we're getting down to it,' said Honicker. He picked up the scrap block and examined it. 'If this little gizmo is a known supply item, it has three attributes that distinguish it from all the other millions and millions of manufactured items right around the globe: it's overall dimensions. It's length, width and height. They are its unique fingerprint.'

He turned his attention to the drawing and carefully keyed in the three dimensions in the respective fields. When that was done he simply clicked on the 'search' icon and selected all countries.

You have requested a global search based on minimal information. Such a search will take a considerable time. Do you wish to continue or append more descriptive information to your search parameters?

Honicker clicked on the continue icon.

ACCESSING AFGHANISTAN – SEARCHING AFGHANISTAN – NO MATCH – ACCESSING ALBANIA – SEARCHING ALBANIA – NO MATCH . . .

'Maybe you should've deselected a few countries first?' Christine observed.

Honicker agreed that she had a point but said that there was no point in interrupting the search process now.

'Amazing,' said Alec, staring at the countries as they edged up the screen. 'You go through your computer in London, which wakes up a computer in Canberra, which then bangs on the door of a computer in Washington, which in turn kicks computers all over the world.'

The message SEARCHING BRAZIL seemed to be burning itself into the screen.

'Methinks the computer was right,' Christine commented

unhelpfully. 'This is going to take time. Are you sure we're only being charged for a call to Australia House?'

14

Joe was in an expansive mood when Lesseps arrived in the coffee shop on Waterloo Station. He even shook hands with the French-Canadian and asked how he was keeping.

'So–so,' said Lesseps, trying to avoid looking at the brief-case that Joe had on his lap.

'It's all here, John.'

'Used?'

Joe grinned. 'Dirtiest money I've ever seen.'

Lesseps didn't share the joke. He bought a cup of coffee at the bar and sat opposite Joe.

'Our last meeting, John.'

'I can't say I'm sorry.'

'Same sentiments here, John. And soon we'll know if it's been a successful partnership.' Joe held up his wrist-watch so that Lesseps could see the tiny TV screen that showed the last passenger boarding the Sabre. The picture zoomed to a close-up of Jez.

Lesseps looked startled. He half rose, so that he could see the TV behind the bar. 'I know that kid. He was at the roll-out.'

'Sit down, John.'

There was a sudden wild look in Lesseps's eye. 'But I thought they weren't allowing kids as passengers.'

Joe grabbed Lesseps's wrist. His voice was mild and dangerous. 'I said, sit down.'

The French-Canadian met Joe's steely gaze and subsided on to his chair.

'It's too late now, John . . . We're both committed . . . You try making an anonymous call from here and Waterloo Station will be sealed off by the police in two minutes. So . . . We sit and chat . . . We have some more coffee . . . And we wait . . .' Joe looked at his watch. 'Fifteen minutes

280

to take-off, and this is the best coffee in London.'

15

SEARCHING UNITED ARAB STATES – NO MATCH – ACCESSING UNITED KINGDOM – SEARCHING UNITED KINGDOM . . .

'The UK might take a while,' Honicker admitted.

MATCH FOUND

'You've got one!' Christine exclaimed.

Honicker concealed his surprise and scribbled down the UK National Item Identification Number that appeared in a window against the match. He clicked on the window but allowed the search operation to continue in the background. The system now had a definite number to process and came up with information on the possible match in a few seconds:

ITEM NAME: REGULATOR HOUSING, FUEL, MOTORISED. MANUFACTURER: PLESSEY AEROSPACE SYSTEMS PLC.

Underneath was a Plessey part number which Honicker also wrote down.

'Can we get any more than that?' Alec asked.

Honicker didn't answer but worked his way through a help menu and clicked on a response. 'I'm going through to the Plessey database web site now,' he replied. 'As this search is originating from a government agency, the chances are that they'll allow us in.'

WELCOME TO THE PLESSEY AEROSPACE SPARES DATABASE.

Honicker skimmed through several pages that detailed Plessey's spares support services, clicked on a drawing/data sheet request icon and entered the Plessey part number.

PLEASE WAIT.

The monitor glitched as it went into high-resolution mode and a third angle drawing of the control block appeared on the screen.

'Holy shit! That's it!' Alec shouted. He snatched the drawing off the desk and compared it with the drawing on the screen. 'Christ! They're both absolutely sodding identical!'

Honicker saved the image to memory and ordered a hard copy which dropped into the bin on Christine's printer. 'Not a hundred per cent identical,' he said, studying the screen. 'The original is made of EAA-spec aluminium alloy and yours is made of magnesium alloy. Also, yours has an extra hole inside the body which isn't on the Plessey drawing. But other than that they are the same item.'

Honicker returned to the regulator's main data screen and studied the information carefully. 'One of the clever things about this system is that users or buyers of any supply item can register their interest. Useful if you need supplies in an emergency and the manufacturer is out of stock.' He exited from the Plessey database and clicked on the registered users' icon. Two user codes appeared against their full names and addresses: Sabre Industries and British Airways.

At that precise, terrible moment, the same thought occurred to all three gathered around the terminal.

'May God help me,' Alec whispered, his face suddenly haggard. 'I've made someone a bomb . . .'

The time was 09:58.

16

Sabre 005 was rolling along the taxiway under its own power and Jez's thoughts were a flutter of agony and delight. There was so much to marvel at and so much to worry about. Supposing someone had told his parents that they'd seen him on TV? He fervently prayed that it was too late now to stop the Sabre and turf him off.

He had just been through an anxious five minutes trapped in one of the boarding lounge's exit turnstiles – the machine had imprisoned him when it read his age off his passport card. His yells and repeated pressing of the emergency button led to his rescue by a security officer and subsequent embarrassment when his appearance in the Sabre as the last to board was greeted by a chorus of good-natured cheers from his fellow-passengers.

Now, at long, wonderful last, he could relax and joyfully take in the many changes that his beloved spaceplane had undergone. No overhead bins like 004, just zipped compartments in soft plastic, each flap bearing four seat numbers – clever idea. One of the flaps was labelled HPCs. He knew what that stood for: hull perforation capsules. Funny plastic seats but with soft corners and flimsy-looking headrests – comfortable too. Safety instructions printed on seatbacks in three languages: dos and don'ts. Don't change seats, Klipfones banned. More don'ts than dos in the zero-G toilets. No lining panels like 004; some sort of flock material sprayed directly on to the inside of the fuselage – looked good. No reading lights, no air-conditioning vents, no trays . . . all very weird . . . bit like a school bus . . . the low seatbacks meant that it was easy to look around at other passengers . . . no one beside him – why so many empty seats? He pressed his nose to the window. Leaden sky – grey day – the polished delta-wing was the only bright object in sight.

Faint click from a hidden PA speaker: 'Good morning, ladies and gentleman. On behalf of British Airways and Captain Allenby, I'd like to welcome you aboard this Sabre 005 on its very first scheduled flight. My name is Nick Rowe. I'm your co-pilot and my contribution to the little bit of history that we're writing today is that I'll be flying you to Sydney. Terminal weather is clear with temperatures around 28–29 – so those of you I saw coming aboard wrapped up like Nanook of the North might be feeling a bit hot under the collar in a couple of hours.'

Even Allenby in the left-hand seat laughed at that. His second officer had a passenger manner that the shy and somewhat reserved senior officer admired. He liked the diplomatic way in which Nick offered congratulations to the newly married VIP couple on board. Paul and Sophia were old friends and he planned to go aft once in orbit to extend his personal congratulations. There hadn't been enough time for him to attend the wedding.

'And if you're puzzled by the number of empty seats,' Nick continued, 'we've lost a couple of parties. One due to ATC problems in Italy and the other due to an aircraft going sick in Madrid. We've 149 passengers on board instead of 200, which means that we're well under our maximum take-off weight which will make the trip a few minutes quicker. Our flight time will be eighty-five minutes. Right now we're a couple of minutes ahead of schedule so we're not in any hurry. There's a Commonwealth TU in front of us in the queue but we'll be in Sydney and refuelling for our return before he lands in Moscow. After take-off we'll be flying almost due north and passing over the North Pole. Once in orbit we'll alter course to a polar orbit which will take us over Siberia, Japan to our right, then down the Pacific towards Guam. We start our deorbit burn over Papua, and then down to Sydney. That's all for the moment. I'd better concentrate on looking for a runway. Enjoy your trip into space.'

The middle-aged couple in the row behind Jez were Ted and Nikki Lithgow, holding hands, saying little. Such was the rapport between them that Ted always knew when the little needles of fear returned to torment his sick wife; he responded by gently tightening his grip just enough to restore her confidence.

For the past few weeks Nikki's excitement at the coming trip and the prospect of seeing her grandchildren for the first time had seemed to halt the advance of her illness, but the latest brain scan had shown that her Alzheimer's condition was continuing its inexorable and deadly progress. The tranquiliser patches she now wore on her arm were proving a godsend but for the last two days the same inconsequential worries kept returning to haunt her.

'Ted . . .'

'Yes, darling?' He knew what was coming.

'We've got so few presents.'

He kissed her cheek. 'We're only allowed ten kilos each, my love. And besides, there're still plenty of shopping days until Christmas. There're lots of toy shops in Sydney. Hey, let's have a little smile then. We'll be seeing them in ninety minutes – they'll all be there to meet us.'

'So quick,' said Nikki, managing a happy smile. 'It doesn't seem possible, does it?'

Ted patted her hand. 'No, my darling, it just doesn't seem possible.'

The PA clicked on again. 'Our chief cabin services officer has just put a message on my screen,' Nick Rowe reported. 'Someone else is making history on this flight. We have a Jeremy Moreton on board. Hallo, Jeremy – congratulations – you are the youngest person ever to go into space. And underneath it says, "Don't read this out but he's probably the smallest as well." '

The announcement and laughter that followed mortified Jez, but he took it with good grace and exchanged embarrassed grins with nearby passengers.

Sabre 005 continued its leisurely taxiing for what seemed an age to Jez, before turning on asymmetric thrust and coming to rest for a few seconds. The engines suddenly opened up to a roar that drowned conversation. The gentle acceleration deteriorated into a headlong rush that thrust Jez firmly into his seat, causing it to reprofile to support his back and head. The jarring from expansion seams in the concrete runway became hammer-blows of increasing ferocity as the delta-wing hurtled down the runway.

Nose-wheel steering at 70 knots. Jet-mode thrust running up to eighty per cent. Vee One at 150 knots, rotation, the abrupt cessation of vibration and 005 was climbing steeply. Safe rate of climb established and main-gear up. Jez breathed a silent prayer of thanks and told himself for the thousandth time that this was really happening.

The time was 10:02.

17

The first consequence of Christine's emergency phone call was a tyre-squealing visit by a police car that happened to be nearest to Triton Exploration when it received the alert. Alec ran downstairs and spoke hurriedly to the police officer before he had a chance to jump out of his car. The officer immediately called his HQ to say that the callers were deadly serious and that this was no hoax as far as they were concerned. All this was accomplished before Christine had finished speaking thus was the first hurdle cleared in the emergency procedure that enabled British Airways and the Airports Police to swing into fast, efficient action. The next step was verification of the caller's information. Honicker's Iridium phone trilled a few seconds after Christine had passed his name and number.

'This is BASOR – British Airway Space Operations Room, Mr Honicker,' said a voice curtly without preamble. 'My name is David Morgan. Tell me about this suspected device. Please speak clearly. This is being recorded.'

Honicker's succinct description was enough for the chief ground engineer, who was listening in, to decide on the spot that checking the Memcorders of the Sabre inspection team would be a waste of precious minutes.

'Understood,' said Morgan, reading a message off his screen from the chief engineer. 'Listen carefully, Mr Honicker. We have to verify that the device you describe is a match with that used on the Sabre. Does your terminal have video conferencing facilities and background fax?'

Honicker glanced at the tiny TV camera set into the top of Christine's monitor but, to be certain, he relayed the question to her.

'Yes,' she replied. 'But I've never set it up.'

Morgan heard her reply and spoke quickly. 'We're going to establish a full link right now but stay on this line until it's established. When our ID comes up on your screen you'll have to give us authorisation for full control over your terminal.'

The terminal screen lit up before Honicker had a chance to reply.

18

Jez's attention kept switching between the flight information screen and his window.

Forty thousand feet . . . 60,000 feet . . . 80,000 feet . . .

Harsh glare off the wing – no clouds above us now – nothing but blackness. Space! Nearly there! Pull blind down a bit. Yes! Yes! I can see it! The curvature of the earth! Sudden whining noise. What's that? The canards, of course. We're going into ramjet mode. Three thousand knots – what was that in kilometres per hour? Give up – too excited to think straight and the display would change soon anyway . . . 3500 knots . . . 4000 knots . . . neck muscles hurting like hell from fighting the increasing acceleration in order to look out of the window.

On the flight deck Nick Rowe received the flight management system go-ahead to change to rocket mode. He glanced up at the wide-angle closed-circuit screen that showed the passengers straining to look out of the windows. All was well. He flipped the safety guards clear and touched the fuel change-over controls. The four motorised regulators whined and liquid oxygen and hydrogen flowed into the combustion chambers, causing the engine note to change to a deeper roar. The warning screens in front of both pilots remained blank. All was going smoothly as Sabre 005 began the final phase of her climb into space.

Altitude 125 kilometres. Speed 21,000 kph.

Jez wriggled in excitement when the data appeared on the flight information screen. They were nearly in orbit!

Paul and Sophia were sitting two rows in front of Jez. Paul was forgotten as Sophia drank in the wondrous spectacle of the earth's atmosphere shining like an iridescent halo in the sun's raw, untempered glare. Passing under the wing's leading edge was a huge circular storm system, throwing out glowing trails of diffuse light at its edges like a monstrous Catherine wheel. Like so many others on their first venture into space, she suddenly experienced a strange and unsettling insight into the stupendous forces that ruled the universe. She could almost feel the colossal flow of energy from the sun to the earth – she felt at one with the great forces that not only powered the earth's mighty weather engine and the awesome movements of its oceanic currents, but provided the essential warmth and light to sustain life. Physicists had reduced the eternal miracle to sets of formulae to explain the unexplainable, but she now realised that this was something more than that – something more than a mechanism that had been activated at the instant of the Creation. This was something that needed the constant and untiring will of God to sustain it.

It was a profound, magical moment of revelation that wrought a change in Sophia and brought a strange peace and an end to her years of doubt and questioning. A tenuous belief took on significant form and was suddenly and wonderfully set in concrete. She turned to Paul and drew his head close to her lips. 'I love you, Paul. Not only for what you are, but for what you've done.'

He smiled and stroked her hand. 'And what have I done?'

'You've shown me God.'

It sounded so trite. She wished that she had a better command of language and yet those four simple but heartfelt words spoke a fundamental truth that could not be expressed in any other way. She turned her attention back to the window, regretting her admission and expecting Paul to tease her. But he took her hand, pressed it to his lips and said nothing. No further communication passed between them other than warmth and understanding.

19

David Morgan's training and experience had prepared him well for this awful eventuality, but giving rational consideration to the information from Triton Exploration and the need to give a fast but correct decision with the lives of 154 souls at stake were two seemingly irreconcilable requirements.

The litany of exchanges between Len Allenby and Nick Rowe playing in his earphone, plus the telemetry data on the T6 BASOR wall display, told him that 005 was four minutes from orbital injection and engine close-down. They were already in rocket mode, so the fake regulator, *if there was one on board*, was behaving as a genuine regulator. Recalling 005 was out of the question. She was no longer an aircraft but a rocket, governed by the laws of ballistics, and possessing an enormous velocity that could be lost only by an orderly atmospheric re-entry from a stable orbit.

There was a total hush in the room. No one was speaking now – every eye was on him. All he had to do was pick up the green telephone which gave him a digitally encrypted company channel direct to Allenby.

'BASOR – we have Delta Vee Six,' said Allenby's voice, confirming the telemetry data on the wall screen.

'He's committed to orbital injection,' said Morgan with finality. 'There's no point in saying anything to them until they're in a stable orbit and the engines are closed down. Rowe will have to go EVA to identify the fake regulator. We'll need the flight profile program for a three-engine DOB and landing.'

'Triton say that they made *four* reg bodies,' someone observed. 'There might be one on each engine.'

Morgan controlled an urge to swear: he hadn't thought of that.

20

Altitude 150 kilometres. Speed 23,000 kph.

Sabre had used eighty per cent of her fuel. The reduction in her mass resulted in a rapid increase in her rate of acceleration or Delta Vee.

Speed 24,000 kph.

She had reached orbital injection velocity.

'Ladies and gentlemen,' Allenby announced over the PA. 'We are about to close down our engines. We will be experiencing weightlessness so please ensure that your seatbelts remain fastened. If you feel nauseous, just close your eyes and relax. The sensation will pass after a few seconds. Please read the safety instructions on zero-G and the use of the toilets. If you need to move about, please wear your Velcro overshoes and move very carefully.'

No detail escaped the prodigious processing power of the three flight management systems:

SEAT 22B. MR COSTELLO. SEAT-BELT NOT FASTENED.

Allenby addressed row 22 directly on the problem and the screen cleared. 'There'll always be one,' he remarked to Rowe.

THROTTLE DOWN AND ENGINE CLOSE-DOWN TEN SECONDS.

'Engine close-down ten seconds,' Allenby reported and checked that electrical power had been switched from the engine APUs to the gas fuel cells.

FIVE SECONDS.

Rowe placed his hand on the ganged throttle lever. He glanced at the status screens but they remained reassuringly blank.

THREE SECONDS . . . TWO SECONDS . . .

Rowe began drawing the lever back. The muted thunder of the engines transmitted through the airframe died away to total silence.

'Throttle down and—'

Allenby never finished the sentence because all the status screens suddenly became alive with urgent messages.

'Fire action Number Two engine!' a computer-generated voice cracked out. 'Fire action Number Two engine!' It kept repeating the message.

Rowe's hand flew up to the central fire control panel. He knocked the safety bar aside, which killed the computer voice, and gripped the red T-handle for Engine Two. 'Fire action Number Two engine – awaiting confirmation.' His voice was strangely calm.

Allenby took in the deliberately lurid graphic diagram showing crimson flames engulfing Engine Two and clamped his hand over Rowe's white knuckles. 'Number Two engine fire confirmed,' he reported.

Both men pulled the lever down together. The verification was essential to ensure that the correct engine was dealt with but another two-second delay would have resulted in the flight management systems carrying out the operation automatically. At that moment all the displays on Allenby's side went blank but he heard the faint thumps of the emergency fuel cut-off solenoids slamming shut and the sharp reports of fire extinguisher distribution heads bursting in and around the engine. His mind was involuntarily racing ahead to the operating procedures for a three-engine deorbit burn and landing when the explosion ripped through the service bay.

21

Jim Curtis reacted with commendable speed and initiative when he received news of the crisis. He realised that all Sabre Industries' top brains were in Terminal 6 and were about to board their charter Airbus to return to St Omer. He immediately put the flight's departure on hold and got a security guard to hand his mobile telephone to Ralph Peterson. The chief designer listened to Curtis' rapid outline of what was known in shocked silence and only interrupted him when he paused for breath.

'Do you have pictures or any information on this device?' he demanded.

'I have everything here right now, Mr Peterson, and I have a conference link with the company that made the dummy regulators. We don't have room for all of you in this office, so if you could pick out half a dozen of your top personnel now and accompany the police officer. We need you here to assess the device and the damage it's caused.'

'We're on our way,' said Ralph grimly.

22

Jez had no time to comprehend the significance of the explosive report beneath his feet because a fragment of debris tore through the centre aisle floor beside him and punched a ragged hole through the cabin roof. The double report was a thunderclap that set his ears ringing. His first thought was that a meteoroid or chunk of satellite debris had hit the spaceplane. A woman was screaming above the continuous howl of air voiding into space through several holes that had been simultaneously punched through the thin skin and he realised that this was not a meteoroid impact. A sudden tangle of oxygen masks appeared, waving like a forest of kelp because air blasting from holes in both hulls was acting like retro rockets, imparting a rapidly worsening tumble to the spaceplane that sent it cartwheeling along its orbital path.

'Place your oxygen mask over your face and breathe normally,' a measured recorded voice insisted. It repeated the message in French, German and Spanish. The appearance of the masks added to the pandemonium. Passengers trying to reach them released their seat-belts and their frantic grabs caused their bodies to drift into a confused tangle of desperately flailing arms and legs. Some felt themselves being sucked towards holes that had appeared and clung grimly to head-rests.

Jez had the presence of mind to realise that the immediate problem was the holes in the hull and that the pain in his ears was due to the decreasing cabin pressure. A woman near him was sobbing and clutching a blood-sodden thigh but he ignored her, released his seat-belt and used his headrest to launch himself towards the overhead storage compartment that contained the hull perforation capsules. The floor spun up to meet him, he cannoned off – receiving a fast lesson that his weightless body still possessed mass and that all movements required care. He used the head-rests to pull himself towards the storage compartment just as Jacky Kerr was yanking the zipper open. Several of the Coke-tin-size canisters tumbled out but Jez managed to grab them and stuff them in his anorak.

'Do you know how to use them?' she gasped. The falling air pressure was making her eyes bloodshot.

'Yes. Just push them against the hole and pull the trigger.'

'Do as many as you can find on your side.'

Jez found himself sucked towards the hole that had appeared in the aisle. Air mixed with fine blood droplets was roaring through it into the lower hull service bay. A corner of his mind noted that the lower hull was normally pressurised, therefore that must be holed as well. He twisted his body around, pressed the neck of a canister against the jagged rim and squeezed the trigger. Fast-setting foam boiled out of the nozzle. It flowed through the hole, solidifying around the edges. The scream of escaping air rose in note as the hole shrank rapidly, then stopped. The hole was plugged, but there were more. The blood was going every-where – a fine crimson mist that splattered across Jez's face. He wiped his eyes, tugged another canister from his anorak and plugged a second hole. Getting at it meant a brutal push to shove a thrashing passenger out of the way. He stopped his body moving in the opposite direction by hanging on to a head rest.

'Another under this seat!' Jacky panted, pointing. 'I can't get at it! You're much smaller!'

It was the seat that had been occupied by the woman with the wounded thigh. Paul Santos was easing her into an exit seat and fastening her seat-belt while Neil Burrows tried to hold himself steady with one hand and cut away her blood-soaked cashmere skirt with the other. It was a hopeless task in the wildly tumbling spaceplane, made worse by the crimson mist spurting from her damaged artery.

'Doctor needed forward!' Neil shouted. 'If there's a doctor on board, or a paramedic, please come forward!'

'I must help that poor woman,' said Nikki, lowering her oxygen mask.

Ted put his hand quickly over her seat-belt buckle when she tried to release it and pushed her mask back. 'You mustn't, darling.' She had astonished him by remaining calm which he had attributed to the patches.

'I must, Ted – she's losing a lot of blood.'

There was no arguing with her. She took a few deep gulps from the mask, pushed Ted's hand away with quiet determination and released her seat-belt. She moved past her husband, remembering to press her Velcro overshoes firmly on the floor.

Jez tried to follow Jacky's directions but his slight body protested at his exertions in the rarefied air. He felt as if a hand grenade had exploded in his brain and his aching lungs were clawing at the depleted air. Jacky yanked his head up and clamped an oxygen mask over his face. 'Two or three deep breaths,' she panted. 'You'll be okay.' Jez sucked grate-fully at the sweet-tasting gas, pushed the mask away and wriggled under the seat that had been occupied by the injured woman. The puncture was hard against the hull – an ugly gash that needed the entire contents of two canisters to close it. He emerged, grabbed a mask, took a few more lung-fuls of oxygen and set about plugging some minor holes that the less terrified passengers pointed out to him.

On the flight-deck the immediate concern of Allenby and Rowe was to do something about the Sabre's tumbling, once they had established that the cabin crew had the hull per-forations in hand. Both men had pulled on their smoke helmets and polarised the windows so that they couldn't see the crazy wheeling of the earth and moon and, more importantly, weren't dazzled by the frequent blasts of sunlight. They paid scant attention to the overhead screen that showed Jacky Kerr and her two stewards restoring order and getting passengers into their seats. A message was flashing frantically saying that the passenger cabin pressure was only forty per cent. Pressurising would have to wait; stabilising the Sabre was their main priority. The problem was similar to one that they had faced on the simulator several times, when the small manoeuvring retros had been jammed on purposely. Countering the tumble was a matter of selection of the right retros and timing the bursts of thrust, but five minutes of concentrated effort by the two men, taking it in turns to exercise their judgement, had no effect on the crazy somersaulting. Letting the flight management system try its skill only made the tumble worse.

'This is fucking useless,' said Allenby quietly. 'Stop everything and let's think.'

The two men examined their dual displays.

'The passenger cabin pressure is now holding, thank Christ,' Allenby commented. 'But still falling in the service bay. That's what's screwing us up, Nick – air blasting out of holes in all directions from the lower hull. We'll have to let it drop to a vacuum and try again.'

'Chances are the bloody computer is releasing air into the lower hold – trying to maintain pressure,' said Rowe. He called up the appropriate displays and found that to be the case. He overrode the systems management computer and closed the valves, reflecting on the irony of a computer-controlled system that aggravated their problems.

'Good thinking, Nick,' said Allenby. 'We'll let it drop to a vacuum and try again.' He looked up at the cabin monitor. Most of the passengers were now settled, holding oxygen masks to their faces. By the exit there was a huddle around Sophia Santos. He paged Jacky. She approached the camera and unhooked the handset.

'What's the situation, Jacky?'

'We've plugged twelve holes, captain. Mrs Santos has an injured thigh. We have a nurse on board. She and Neil are doing their best to make her comfortable.'

'Any other pax injuries?'

'Lots of cuts and bruises. Nothing serious. Billy's looking after them. They're all badly shaken but there's no panic.'

'You've done damn well, Jacky.'

'What happened, captain?'

'Christ knows. We lost Number Two and then there was some sort of explosion. The service bay's holed – we're waiting for it drop to a vacuum before we try to kill this tumble. Because of it, our antennae have lost all satellite locks. We've no ground comms or Satnav.' Allenby was watching the pressure drop in the lower hull as he was talking. It was now down to fifteen per cent 'Looks like I've got time for a few words to the pax.'

'It would help, captain.'

'I'll have to do it over the PA. I can't come aft because we've got a pressure differential between the flight-deck and the cabin. As soon as we're straight in here we'll drop our pressure to equal the cabin pressure, so keep everyone on oxygen for the time being.'

Neil caught Jacky's attention and said something to her. She turned to the camera after a few hurried exchanges. 'Captain, Mrs Santos is in a bad way. The nurse says she's got a partly severed artery. She's lost a lot of blood and her pulse is weakening. She needs surgery urgently.'

23

The news on the television electrified the customers in the Waterloo Station coffee shop. All conversation ceased. The manager turned up the volume. Lesseps sat frozen, his cup half-way to his lips, staring glassy eyed at Joe.

'. . . but we can confirm that all contact with the spaceplane was lost ten minutes ago,' a studio reporter was saying. 'We're going over to Mike Tribe at Heathrow's

Terminal 6 for the latest.'

A harassed-looked individual appeared on the screen against a background of frantic journalists and cameramen. 'I can't really add anything to that,' he said in answer to a question from the anchorman. 'As you can see, it's all chaos behind me. The only confirmed information we have is that the spaceplane's captain reported a fire in his Number Two engine just as they went into orbit and that all contact was lost a few seconds after that.'

'How serious is the fire?'

'We don't know. The spaceplane can re-enter and land on three engines, or even two engines in a dire emergency. What's concerning officials here is the total loss of communications with the Sabre. She has three independent satellite communication systems and a datalink system that maintains continuous ground contact throughout the flight apart from a brief blackout on re-entry. They've lost everything, so whatever has gone wrong, it does look very serious indeed.'

The picture returned to the studio. 'We'll bring you updates on that story as soon as we have more information,' said the anchorman, grim-faced.

The two conspirators sat in silence, both believing that the Sabre was a total loss, not knowing that the spaceplane's automatic fire extinguisher systems had done a better job than Lesseps had anticipated.

Joe looked at his watch. His voice was calm when he spoke. 'I've got a flight to catch this afternoon, John. I'd better be getting back to my hotel.' He rose and placed the briefcase on the chair beside Lesseps. 'I guess you've earned that.'

The French-Canadian didn't seem to hear Joe but continued staring at the television. Joe shrugged and left the coffee shop without a backward glance. He was pleased to note that the pain in his knee had gone. It made his step quite jaunty as he headed towards the taxi rank.

24

Ralph Peterson, four of his senior designers and Claudia Picquet greeted the news of the total loss of communications with the Sabre in stunned silence. They were grouped around the terminal in Jim Curtis's office, the men's smart suits and carnation buttonholes in contrast with their sombre expressions. Claudia was wearing a silk blouse with a grey skirt and jacket that she had bought for the occasion. She was strangely withdrawn but her colleagues were too preoccupied to notice.

A screen carried a picture of Honicker, Alec and Christine, also grave-faced. Alec was having trouble holding back his tears; Christine was clutching his hand tightly. On another screen there was a shirt-sleeved David Morgan in the BASOR. He took off his boom mike headset and tossed it on his desk. A speaker carried the hiss of white noise from the satellite transponder that would normally be relaying the Sabre's flight deck voice channel.

'They'd be able to make contact even if they'd suffered a total loss of power,' said Ralph slowly. 'The third system has its own integral batteries. The feeds to the satellite antenna are carried in an armoured cable.'

'So we've got an eighty per cent bomb probability,' said Morgan with finality. 'If that's so, why the fire first? We had contact with Rowe and Allenby for several seconds *after* they'd reported the fire. Do you want another replay?'

'I've read up on magnesium alloy,' said Alec, not looking up at the camera. 'The dummy reg wouldn't actually explode – it would burn. A fireball.'

'And that could have caused the explosion,' Ralph added. He picked up the drawing of the dummy regulator that had been echoed from Triton's site. 'Possibly a flashback to one of the liquid nitrogen cylinders in the service bay.'

'Bottle 6 would be nearest,' said one of the senior designers. 'And that going up would probably set off—'

298

'*Could have! Possibly! Probably!*' Morgan snapped. 'Right now we need definite answers, not supposition. Jim Curtis will tell you that 005 was under constant surveillance from the moment she arrived here. No one could have planted a device.'

'There's nothing on the recordings,' Curtis confirmed. 'The chief ground engineer's just done a fast read-through of the surveillance system memory cards. No one went near engine Two and he says that swapping regulators would take at least thirty minutes.'

'So we still don't know whether or not a device was planted,' Morgan continued. 'We're just guessing. For all we know she might've been hit by junk that DEBRA didn't know about.'

'NASA's debris alert radar has plots on even bits of wire!' Ralph answered sharply.

'But NASA don't give a one hundred per cent guarantee, Mr Peterson. DEBRA is a risk reduction system.'

'We do know that no debris could possibly knock out *all* the Sabre's comms! It just isn't possible!' Ralph was dangerously close to losing his temper.

Claudia spoke for the first time. 'A bomb *was* planted.'

There was a sudden silence in the room. Everyone stared at her. She looked utterly crushed. Silent tears coursed down her cheeks, streaking her make-up. 'It was planted at St Omer . . . And . . . And . . .' She bowed her head and groped in her handbag for a handkerchief. A colleague tried to put an arm around her but she pushed him away. She managed to compose herself and looked up at Curtis, her gaze steady. 'Number Two engine, Mr Curtis . . . It was planted the evening before you took delivery . . . And I know who planted it . . .' Her self-control dissolved and she collapsed in tears.

25

Once the lower hull had equalised to a vacuum, stabilising the somersaulting Sabre was easier than Allenby or Rowe had dared hope. A sustained firing from a tail retro lasting five minutes succeeded in killing the worst of the tumble and a further two minutes of judicious use of the wing-tip retros resulted in the spacecraft travelling tail first and inverted along her orbital trajectory. Allenby depolarised the windows and the two men saw the northernmost extremities of Japan protruding from the cloud blanket that seemed to cover all of the Chinese mainland. To the south the Pacific was clear. Another minute's jockeying and Sabre 005 was in her normal nose-front attitude.

'Makes me feel good, skipper,' said Rowe, his phlegmatic tone concealing his relief. 'Doing something better than a bloody computer for once.'

'One problem out of the way,' Allenby replied. 'Another thousand to go. Antennae locks are all to hell. If the bloody computer can't seek and lock the buggers, we have to do that ourselves as well.' He mentally ticked off his priorities: airframe integrity: passable at the moment but detailed condition unknown. Thanks to prompt action by his cabin crew the passenger compartment was holding pressure, albeit low and he wasn't going to increase it until he had had a good look at those patches. Passenger safety: one injured but being attended to. Last report – her condition poor. He called Jacky and learned that Mrs Santos's condition was now critical. He promised to be with her as soon as possible but the brutal truth was that one passenger would have to wait.

The two men worked quietly and methodically to restore communications. The satellite dishes in the nose and tail were whirring back and forth, driven by three computers that had lost their bearings and were in conflict with each other. The pilots overrode them and picked up a reference carrier from one satellite, thus providing the computers with

300

the information they needed to set about correcting dish orientation in order to re-establish ground links. In this way the two men again proved the superiority of humans over machines in crisis management.

Allenby activated the port-wing TV camera and was rewarded with a blank screen. 'Left-hand camera fucked,' he commented, not giving a damn about the cockpit voice recorder. He switched to the starboard-wing camera. It was working and showed nothing amiss, although its view of the wing's underside was restricted. Unlike 004, there was no underside tail camera – it hadn't been installed to save weight. He called for an 'all fault' printout and was alarmed by the length of the list that spooled from the printer slot. 'Bloody hell,' he muttered. 'Fuel cells two and three out; zero pressure in half the gas bottles . . . Hydraulic reservoirs three and five, no oil . . .'

'Sounds like a list of what's okay would be shorter,' Rowe observed. 'I think I can guess what's coming, skipper. EVA for yours truly.'

'A spacewalk will be a chance to stretch your legs . . . What are you like at repairing punctures? Two main-gear left tyres are reading zero pressure.'

'We haven't got a big enough bath.'

'Or a footpump.'

'Life's a bitch.'

'And then you . . .' Allenby nearly completed the saying but decided otherwise. The seemingly light-hearted exchanges cloaked their true feelings; both men had no illusions about the seriousness of their situation. Their unspoken thought was that Sabre 005 was doomed.

26

The heated dispute between Ralph Peterson and Jim Curtis came close to boiling over into a slanging match. A report had just been received from the Japanese tracking station at Tanegashima that they were tracking an echo on a 90-degree polar trajectory. The object's position — 151 east and course due south – together with its height and velocity meant that it had to be the Sabre. The Japanese were trying to radio the object on line-of-sight emergency simplex but it was not responding. As that report came in, a similar sighting was received from the US tracking station on Guam. They too were trying to make line-of-sight radio contact.

'We can't do anything here, Curtis,' Ralph was insisting, his expression thunderous. 'But we can at St Omer. We've got facilities to run simulations on what may have happened and we've got duplicate comms facilities. I don't happen to believe that 005 is a total loss, and the faster we get home the faster we can get down to work. So give our Airbus priority right now and let me and my team go.'

'Sounds a reasonable idea to me, Jim,' said Morgan, who was following the dispute on his terminal. 'We can keep a wide-band conference channel open with Sabre Industries.'

That was enough for Ralph. He turned to Morgan's screen. 'Thank you, Mr Morgan. We're going now.' He beckoned to his staff and they all filed out of the office with a few hurried goodbyes to Curtis and his people.

'He's right,' said Morgan. 'Get them boarding and away a.s.a.p. They'll be of more use to us at St Omer than getting under our feet here.'

Curtis gave the necessary orders for the chartered Airbus to receive priority treatment. Once that was dealt with he decided that his next priority was to initiate the search for and arrest of Jean Lesseps. He had the keys to Sabre Industries personnel database, therefore it was a simple matter for his staff to download all the information held on the French-Canadian, including his photograph which was part of the Kodastripe information on his passport card. A call to security at Sabre Industries established that he was not in his apartment and that he had left early that morning and not returned. A member of Curtis's staff who knew her way around the Home Office's computer systems reported that Lesseps' passport had been logged at Waterloo International that morning through the non-European national turnstiles. She implemented a block, which meant that he would be held automatically wherever he next used his passport throughout Europe.

'Excellent,' said Curtis when she reported.

Now to deal with the question of his accomplice — the mysterious 'Mr Wright' who had placed the order with Triton Exploration for the fake regulator blocks.

27

Paul's cradling of his beloved Sophia's head was hardly necessary in the weightless conditions, but holding her, talking gently to her, even though she had lost consciousness, lessened his feeling of helplessness. The nurse had snipped away all her skirt and underwear, exposing her dreadfully because the injury that she was holding a wad of paper towels against was on the inside of Sophia's thigh. Every now and then he reached out to reposition the suspended blanket that he had spread out to protect his wife from the curious stares of passengers using the toilet.

The nurse worried Paul. He had noticed the patches on her arm and wondered what her medication was. There were too many for diabetes. But she had seemed competent enough when she had applied a bandage and pad tourniquet above the injury to stem the bleeding. It was just that her movements seemed so damnably slow and she kept pausing as though even a simple job like cleaning the skin around the wound needed careful thought. But she wasn't squeamish – she had done this before.

Nikki looked up at him. 'I'm going to let the pressure off for a few seconds. I'm holding the artery closed but some blood will escape. You will have to be ready with the towels to catch it.'

'Why?' Paul demanded when her hand went to the tourniquet.

'We must allow some blood to flow to her leg, otherwise . . .' She was unable to complete the sentence coherently.

'It's just that we must. Are you ready?'

Paul spread out a paper towel above the wound. It stained red as a fine spray escaped from between Nikki's fingers when she slackened the bandage. 'For God's sake stop it!' he cried hoarsely.

Nikki tightened the bandage and the blood stopped. The wad she was holding over the wound was sodden. Paul ripped a new one from a Johnson and Johnson wound cleansing pack and handed it to her using the pack's plastic tweezers. At least she replaced the wad quickly. His arms went carefully around Sophia again and he held her gently to him. A shadow fell across them.

'Please go away!' Paul snapped at the middle-aged man who was staring anxiously down at them over the top of the suspended blanket.

'Are you all right, darling?' Ted asked his wife.

She nodded. 'Go back to your seat, Ted – I'm fine.'

'For God's sake get out!' Paul shouted, covering Sophia's nakedness with a towel.

Ted muttered an apology and moved away.

'My husband,' said Nikki slowly. 'He didn't mean—'

'I'm sorry,' said Paul abruptly, embarrassed. He managed a wan smile. 'I don't know your name.'

'Nikki Lithgow . . .' She smiled happily at Paul. 'We're going to see our grandchildren. We'll be landing soon, won't we?'

28

Four pictures of middle-aged men appeared on Christine's terminal. 'Next,' she said, not bothering to check with Alec and Honicker.

Four more pictures appeared. Like all the previous photographs, none bore the slightest resemblance to Mr Wright.

'Next.'

Curtis wondered how long this virtual identity parade would go on for. His department was feeding Triton's office with passport Kodastripe pictures of all North American males over fifty-five who had entered the United Kingdom around the times that Mr Wright had visited Triton Exploration.

'How many left?' he asked the girl sitting opposite him.

'Three thousand one hundred and fifteen, sir.'

'Hell.'

'Next,' said Christine.

'Mrs Rose, can your monitor's resolution handle eight pictures at a time?'

'Try us, Mr Curtis.'

Curtis nodded to the girl who changed the settings on her keyboard. She sent eight pictures.

'No trouble, Mr Curtis. Next.'

'They're certain he was well over sixty,' said the girl, punching a key. 'We could up the age.'

'We'll play safe for the time being,' said Curtis sourly.

'Next,' said Christine.

'I'm going to get some coffee,' said Curtis, rising.

'That's him!'

Curtis sat abruptly.

'Definitely him!' said Alec Rose's voice.

'It's him all right,' Honicker added. 'I only saw him briefly in the summer but we're all agreed.'

'Which one?'

'Number three.'

'Send them a full screen,' Curtis instructed his assistant. 'Thank you, Mrs Rose. You should be getting a full screen picture of him. Look at it carefully, please.'

'We are,' Christine answered. 'There's no doubt – that's our Mr Wright.'

Curtis studied the craggy features on his screen and closed the audio circuit to Triton so that they couldn't hear him.

'Joseph Michael Yavanoski,' said the girl. Her fingers clattered on her keyboard. There was a pause while the system sought a routing through to the United States and accessed the State Department's passport database.

PLEASE WAIT . . . said the echo on Curtis's screen.

And then it appeared: more than the basic passport details

on Yavanoski – a career profile. The guy was important. A skim through the first paragraphs was enough for Curtis.

'Jesus Christ,' he muttered. 'If this Yavanoski hasn't got a motive then no one has.'

'And he's in the country,' the girl reported. 'He arrived yesterday and hasn't left.' A telephone light flashed. She answered and listened intently for a moment before thanking the caller. She held the handset out to Curtis and reported: 'Jean Pierre Lesseps has been arrested at Waterloo International. He had half a million dollars on him.'

At that moment Curtis's eye caught a flurry of activity in the BASOR downstairs. Their big telemetry data screen didn't show up too well on his monitor but he could see that it had come to life and the world map was showing a glowing track. He snatched up a telephone and learned that Len Allenby's voice had just come through with 'Speedbird Sierra Bravo Zero Zero Fife Alpha. Good morning, BASOR. Do you copy?'

29

Antarctica's King George V Land was edging over the earth's rim – a glorious string of sparkling white diamonds shining in the low sun which were gradually hardening to an iridescent halo.

Len Allenby was too preoccupied to appreciate the breathtaking spectacle. He hated having to wear a spacesuit, but at least these new lightweight jobs were fully pressurised and used ordinary compressed-air life support – none of the long periods spent purging excess oxygen or nitrogen from the bloodstream that had been the curse of the older suits. Right now he had no choice but to wear it because the flight-deck was fully depressurised; the roof hatch open with Nick Rowe's EVA safety line disappearing through it. The slack was hanging in loose coils beside Allenby, twitching like a snake every now and then as Rowe worked his way down the side of the hull. The master screen was carrying the picture from the TV camera on the co-pilot's helmet. A smaller screen in front of Allenby showed Morgan in the BASOR ops room, looking off-camera at the same images. Rowe was keeping his movements slow and deliberate, not only because it was the safest way of moving about during EVA, but to allow for the half-second's delay in communications should Morgan want the camera to take a close look at something. Right now, all they were getting was a close-up of the Super Starlight heat shield coating.

Allenby felt that an immense burden had been lifted from his shoulders now that he had ground communications. Morgan and his team were analysing the flow of data from the Sabre's telemetry links and probably had a better idea than he did of the spaceplane's condition. The exception was the underside of the left-hand wing around Number Two engine. No one knew what state that was in, which was why Nick Rowe's spacewalk was so vital.

The picture bobbed and panned jerkily as Rowe edged cautiously down the side of the hull. His breaths were sharp rasps in Allenby's helmet speaker.

'Take it easy, Nick,' Morgan advised calmly. 'There's no hurry.'

'Tell you what,' Rowe muttered, taking a rest. 'If I had been told that working for British Airways would mean having to get out and push, I would never have signed up.'

The operations room laughter was a welcome reaction to the tension that everyone was experiencing.

The joke was heard by BA's chairman in his London office where his PR staff were thrashing out the wording of the next statement for the clamouring press crews outside. Sir Andrew Hobson chuckled. Despite his own underdeveloped sense of humour he was an astute enough manager to know its value when under stress. He mentally earmarked Nick Rowe for promotion. If he got out of this mess alive . . .

The picture in front of Allenby wobbled as Rowe started moving again. He worked his way under the hull and turned his head towards Number Two engine as soon as he was sure of his grip. At first he thought what he was seeing was a trick of the light caused by the harsh contrast between light and shadow in the vacuum of space. He moved his helmet out of the sun's glare and realised that it was not an optical illusion: the underside of the port-wing skin between the fuselage and the inboard engine looked like a sheet of cardboard that had had a fist driven through it. The once beautifully machined aluminium was torn open, the ragged edges throwing long shadows along the wing's underside like the profile of a rugged mountain range. And where the skin wasn't torn it had been melted and fused to shapeless blobs by the intense heat from the fire.

'Is everyone getting this?' Rowe asked.

'We're getting it,' Morgan's unusually subdued voice answered in his helmet. 'Hold steady a few seconds, Nick, while we record . . . Okay, left . . . slowly . . . Now right . . .'

'Do you want me to go in closer?'

'Don't take that suit a centimetre nearer that mess,' Morgan warned.

There was silence for a few seconds while men and women a hemisphere apart contemplated the terrible damage that the Sabre had sustained. There was no need for anyone to spell out what it signified. They all knew that re-entry was out of the question – without the total integrity of its Super Starlite heat shield, the spaceplane hitting the earth's atmosphere at 25,000 kilometres per hour would result in it turning into an incandescent fireball in a matter of minutes.

'It seems we have a Sierra-Delta-Sierra situation,' said Nick at length using Sabre-speak for 'serious deep shit'. This time no one laughed.

'Okay, Nick,' said Morgan. 'You'd better open the service bay door for an eyeball.'

Rowe acknowledged, gave himself some more lifeline slack and edged along the underside of the fuselage towards the two-metre-square cargo loading and service bay door. David Morgan had ruled that the main door to the service bay should be opened first and not the hatch in the flight-deck floor. The explosion and fire would have unleashed a whole host of toxic particles which would have to be flushed out before opening the flight-deck hatch could be risked. Also the internal damage could be surveyed more effectively from the big outer door without venturing inside.

Even before Rowe reached the door, Allenby and the watchers at BASOR could see the evidence of the secondary explosion that had taken place inside the service bay. There were several holes in the skin, punched through from inside. The largest was twenty centimetres across and was doubtless responsible for Sabre's tumble when escaping air had geysered out.

Rowe reached the door and saw that it had been dished outwards by the impact of something inside. He panned his helmet camera slowly across the damage.

Morgan killed his microphone. 'Oh, fuck – looks like the latches will be buggered.'

Rowe felt in his belt for the T-handle key and pushed it against the spring-loaded plunger at the side of the door. The key went home and engaged on the winding gear spline but refused to turn. Normally it required twenty turns from inside or outside to retract the eight massive pins that secured the door in its frame against its pressure seals. Only when the pins were fully withdrawn could the door be opened inwards. It was a simple and safe mechanism, and it was jammed.

He sweated and strained for two minutes, and even tried turning the key by a series of quick jerks, but getting a good purchase was virtually impossible when weightless. His suit's dehumidifier had trouble keeping up with his exertions, causing his helmet to mist up.

'Solid,' he panted. 'Can't get as much as a whisker of a turn.'

'Okay, Nick,' said Morgan. 'Take a breather and return to the flight-deck . . . Skipper.'

Allenby acknowledged.

'We've got a clearer picture on your consumables. If you approve, Nick's going to have to go into the service bay through the flight-deck hatch on this EVA session while the flight-deck is depressurised. You can't afford the compressed air to pressurise and depressurise the flight-deck if it can be avoided, so let's do it now while the flight-deck's a vacuum.'

Morgan's ruling made sense. The flight deck's atmosphere had to be bled off into space each time it was depressurised.

'Understood,' said Allenby.

Nick reached the windows. 'Looks like Antarctica coming up,' he commented, resting. 'Tell you what, skipper, I ought to get a mention in the *Guinness Book of Records* — this is one hell of an overshoot for Sydney.' He eased himself through the roof hatch and closed it. He felt better with his boots anchored to the floor and after he'd taken a sip of water from his catch tube. He tried to deal with an itch but his gauntleted hand collided with his visor. 'God, I loathe spacesuits.'

'You're not through yet,' said Allenby, releasing his harness and allowing his body to rise from his seat.

'I heard. A woman's work and all that.'

The two spacesuited men unclipped the floor hatch between their seats and opened it. What they saw caused Allenby to give vent to an uncharacteristic expletive. One of the underfloor crease beams that had been installed against the chief designer's wishes had been dislodged and was jammed half-way across the hatch's circular opening. It was a substantial aluminium girder, ripped away from its welding points, and defied their efforts to shift it. They even braced their backs against the seats and strained together, with their boots planted on the obstruction, but without success.

'Useless,' Allenby gasped after their fourth combined effort. For the first time since the disaster he was badly rattled but careful not to show it. There was no way into the service bay, therefore no way to implement an interim plan that David Morgan and his staff had worked out.

They had decided that the first priority was to connect a high-pressure hose from a bleed-off point on a right-hand engine lox tank to the life-support oxygen system that supplied the cabin. The normal cabin supply was designed

310

to last a full load of passengers six hours – about four complete orbits. It could be topped up from the engine liquid oxygen tanks but the change-over system was dead. A bypass hose would solve the problem. Several other tasks needed to be carried out in the service bay but the oxygen problem was the most pressing: it was obvious now that Sabre was going to be circling the earth for many more than four orbits.

Rowe inverted himself and discovered that there was just enough room to ease his helmet through the hatch but for the rest of his body to follow while wearing a spacesuit was out of the question, and he was slightly built.

'No one's going to get through that, skipper,' said Rowe, withdrawing his head. 'There's barely a centimetre clearance for the helmet.'

'What's going on?' Morgan asked at length. He had been patiently watching a confused blur of pictures from Rowe's camera.

'BASOR,' said Allenby wearily, 'we have a problem.'

30

Michelle Finch should have been in the T6 departure lounge waiting to leave for a well-earned holiday. Instead, as a consequence of her answering a PA call, she was in the BASOR, huddled over a monitor. The picture of the open thigh wound was wobbling. She was a practical, no-nonsense woman and decided to get one or two things straight before proceeding any further. She looked up at the big wall map of the world to give herself a few moments in which to think. The sinusoidal track showed 005 over the South Atlantic, heading north, passing over the South Sandwich Islands.

'Right. Who's holding the camera? What's your first name?'

'Paul.'

'Okay, Paul. You're the only one I can't see. Are you wearing a mask?'

'Yes.'

'Good. Tighten up and try to hold the camera absolutely steady. Use an armrest or something . . . Ah – that's much better. Hold it like that. . .'

Droplets of blood hanging in mid-air over a wound were a phenomenon wholly outside Michelle's considerable operating theatre experience. 'The first name of the woman with the wedding ring?' she demanded.

'Nikki.'

'And the unmarried hands?'

'Jacky – chief cabin services officer.'

'Jacky – you're the one who gave the patient a shot of Morfon?'

'Yes. Four cc thirty minutes ago.'

'That should be plenty. And Neil and Billy – you're my gophers.'

The stewards confirmed that they were standing by.

'Well, see if you can go for some more light.'

Some left-hand blinds were raised a little more, allowing sunlight to flood in. The passengers were tense and silent, some reading, those nearest the makeshift operating theatre doing their best to ignore what was going on.

'Much better,' said Michelle. She spent the next two minutes establishing that her remote-controlled theatre staff had everything to hand and that they were clear about their responsibilities. The one called Nikki seemed a little hesitant, unsure of herself, and would need to be treated carefully, otherwise she seemed competent enough. 'Good,' she said. 'Paul – go in close to the artery and no hand shake please.'

The picture swelled. Michelle studied the lesions to the artery carefully. *Tunica adventitia* badly shredded but was all there. *Tunica media* – the centre wall tissue – some in place. The piece of shrapnel had caused some odd delamination, but the tissue looked healthy. *Tunica intima* very iffy – a lot of dead endothelial cells. Strange how weightlessness made the arterial tissue spread out like that. Made

312

her job easier. An orbital operating theatre would be interesting.

'Right,' she said. 'Can you all hear me clearly?'

Her assistants confirmed that they could.

'Pickets in position? We don't want unwanted objects and bodies floating by.'

'We've six people ready with towels to catch anything,' said Jacky. 'All other passengers not involved are seated and belted. No one is allowed out of their seats until we've finished.'

'Good,' said Michelle briskly. 'Let's get stuck in.'

31

Joe entered the Ramada Inn lobby when the operation on Sophia was well underway. He had dined extremely well on an early lunch at Stones – English cuisine at its best – and was feeling comfortably full and well-fortified against the twelve hours of airline food to come.

Two men in well-cut suits approached him. Instead of walking around him, they stopped, blocking his way to the desk.

'Joseph Michael Yavanoski,' said the taller of the two men. It was a statement, not a question.

Joe smiled easily, not unduly concerned. 'Sure. What's the trouble?'

The speaker produced a warrant card. He didn't just flash it, but held it up so that Joe could study it if he wished. Joe didn't wish but he kept smiling, even though the other man had allowed a stunner to drop down his sleeve into his hand.

'So what's the problem, fellers?'

'No problem at all, Mr Yavanoski. Provided you agree to accompany us, that is. Or do we have to arrest you here?'

32

Ralph Peterson had been busy on the telephone throughout the flight from Heathrow to St Omer. When the Airbus touched down the partly built 006 had already been wheeled on to the apron outside Shed A and there was no sign of 004 – she was inside and being worked on in readiness for her flight. The Airbus had been fed the TV pictures from Neil Rowe's camera so Ralph knew that there was no question of 005 being able to land in her present state. He was still on his Klipfone as he went down the boarding steps three at a time and strode towards the shed, with the wedding guests and senior staff trailing behind. For a big man he could move fast. This time he was talking to David Morgan — a man who could match Ralph for bluntness any day, but the British Airways manager was choosing to remain silent because he had considerable respect for the chief designer.

'You'll be wasting your time with NASA,' Ralph was saying. 'They'll need fourteen days to get a shuttle ready even if they worked around the clock. Everyone on 005 will be dead before then. I know NASA have got ten of 'em but they're forever cannibalising nine to make one spaceworthy. There's nothing we can teach those poor buggers about working on shoestrings. And even if they could get one launched in time, how do you bring back 149 passengers and 5 crew in a shuttle's unpressurised cargo bay?'

'How would you transfer them to 004, Mr Peterson? It doesn't have a docking hatch. Could you fit one in time?'

Ralph had already given the matter much thought during the flight from Heathrow the moment he had received news that contact with 005 had been re-established. For one thing, Sabre Industries used a just-in-time ordering policy and didn't have a hatch in stock. General Dynamics, the American manufacturers, had a make-in-time policy and

314

would be unlikely to have a spare. Also the complex tests needed to ensure the safety of the hatch couldn't be skipped, especially with a rip-out-and-replace job. Ralph knew from experience that if he started cutting corners he would end up with two spaceplanes stranded in orbit.

'No,' he said in answer to Morgan's question. 'We don't have time. We don't have a hatch and we don't have a docking tube. A shirt-sleeve environment transfer is out of the question. There're three spacesuits on 005, therefore we're going to need another 151 spacesuits for the transfer plus about ten spares. Say, 160 spacesuits.'

The thought of spacewalking 149 passengers in one operation appalled Morgan and he reeled off a stream of objections.

'For Chrissake!' Ralph shouted into his Klipfone. 'What choice do we have?'

'I don't suppose there are that many spacesuits in the entire bloody world!' Morgan shot back. 'It'll have to be ten or so at a time, airlocking through the flight deck and out through the roof hatch. We should be able to get ten pax at a time suited up and squeezed into the flight deck.'

Ralph reached the shed before anyone else. He kicked a door open and backed away because of the racket inside. Serious work was underway on 004. He signalled his staff through and remained locked in argument with Morgan.

'Okay, Mr Morgan – you work on your batch transfer idea while we work on 004. Some calculations for you to get your teeth into: work out how much air will be needed to repressurise *two* flight decks fifteen times. Work out how long it's going to take to desuit each batch of pax and transfer the empty suits back from 004 to 005 *fifteen* times! You do your sums, Mr Morgan. Right now I've got a lot on my plate and so have you. Let's conference in an hour.'

33

The unseen cameraman was doing his job well. The big close up of the bindings around the artery was steady. Michelle leaned forward, studying the results. The biggest blessing had been that the packet held up before the camera for her inspection had turned out to be a full carton of 3M's latest Steri-Strips – long ribbons of tough, synthetic enzyme-impregnated fabric which bonded readily to tissue and stimulated rapid healing. Jacky had cut one strip to short lengths for Nikki to use as ties around the artery. It was a neat job and Michelle was well pleased, although she had been frustrated at times by Nikki's slowness. The Steri-Strips would eventually dissolve and, God willing, further surgery on the artery when Mrs Santos was eventually hospitalised would be unnecessary. The damaged muscle tissue was another matter, and there was always the hideous spectre of infection despite the antibiotics that had been pumped into the patient. Now to ease the tourniquet . . .

'Paul, camera back, please. Jacky, fresh swabs at the ready.'

'Ready.'

'Slacken the tourniquet one turn – no more.'

Blood filled the open wound. Jacky swabbed quickly and Michelle saw that the ties were holding. She allowed a few seconds for blood pressure to build up. 'Excellent . . . Now right off . . .'

She heard a whispered prayer in French and presumed it was the cameraman. The strips held . . . Blood was pumping through the patient's leg. She stilled the relief of her theatre assistants with a sharp word and gave them clear instructions on cleaning up, closing the wound firmly and criss-crossing it with more Steri-Strips to hold it closed. She had considered sutures but decided that her team had had enough. Besides, the strips did the job just as well and the wound would have to be reopened for work on the damaged

316

muscle tissue. The patient's pulse and respiration were as well as could be expected. A few words on post-operative care and she considered that her job was done.

'Right,' she said briskly. 'I'll leave her in your capable hands. I'm off to Barbados for a fortnight – they've very kindly held my flight so there're a couple of hundred passengers cursing me. If there are any problems, you'll be able to call me on the flight.'

'Mrs Finch,' said Paul. 'I'm the cameraman. Thank you so much for all that you've done for my wife.'

'She's your wife? Oh dear, if I'd known that I would've ordered you out of my theatre. She'll be fine, Paul. You did a splendid job. You all did. Keep her quiet and give her plenty to drink when she comes to.' Michelle was tempted to wish them success with their rescue but she had seen the grim expressions of the staff in the BASOR and decided that it would be politic to remain silent on the matter. She bade them farewell and left it at that.

Oblivious of her blood-soaked clothes, Nikki returned shakily to her seat, remembering to press her overshoes firmly on the floor. Ted helped ease her down and fastened her seat-belt. 'I did it, Ted,' she whispered. 'Sinbad left me alone.'

Ted covered her hands and said nothing because she had closed her eyes. The tension drained from her face. He allowed several minutes to pass and asked her if the patient would be okay. She turned her head and looked blankly at him.

'What patient, Ted?'

34

For the rest of their lives, two billion people would be able to recollect exactly what they were doing and where they were when they heard the news of the disaster that had overtaken Sabre 005.

The plight of flight SB005A electrified an entire planet.

From minutes after the first bald announcement, British Airways' HQ and their offices were besieged by a clamouring press tasked with feeding the endless studio discussions about the stranded spaceplane now taking place across the networks. There was plenty of vapid, verbal diarrhoea and dodgy diagram broadcasting filling the airwaves and stuffed along cables, but little in the way of hard facts.

In an age of strict privacy laws and an unusual passenger list of nationals drawn from all over Europe, BA had to tread carefully. They released recordings showing the damage that 005 had sustained; they insisted that all the crew and passengers were alive and comfortable; but they steadfastly refused to release a passenger list. Reuters and other news services did a slick job assembling and marketing a list made up from existing material relating to winners of the ticket draw but there were big gaps.

Terry Warton, the enterprising stringer who had first tracked down Ted and Nikki Lithgow after their win, put his talents into overdrive right after the first riveting announcement about the bomb. He was following a slender lead that there had been another winner on his patch. He convinced a national tabloid editor that he had something and obtained the credit wherewithal to indulge in a spot of old-fashioned bribery around those local travel agencies who had handled draw tickets. By 11.02 a.m. he had a whisper a name: Jack Moreton. No promises that it was the right name, just a whisper. By 11.05 he had a Richmond address. At 11.20 he was at the house, ringing the doorbell. No one in. Stroll around to the back of house. Models of the Sabre in an upstairs bedroom window. Jesus! – he was on to something! Back to the car to find out Jack Moreton's Iridium number. No answer. Phone call to Jack Moreton's office. Damn! He was there and not stranded in space.

Jack Moreton listened and laughed. 'Chance would be a fine thing. We're following it on the radio. No – I'm behind my desk wrestling with a mortgage mess. I promise you I'm not marooned in space.'

'I took the liberty of calling at your house, sir. I noticed a window with models of the Sabre—'

'Oh, they're my son's. Jeremy is spaceplane mad.'

Warton's heart hammered. Bloody hell! – maybe the rumours that a kid had checked-in for the flight were true. 'Does he know much about it, sir?' Voice very matter of fact.

'Good God, yes. If you want to know anything about the spaceplane, Jez is your man.'

'We desperately need experts, sir. Everyone's going crazy for information. With your permission, could I call him please? He'll be well paid, of course.'

'Don't see why not. It's the last day of term so he won't be doing any work. You'll have to call the school – they don't allow kids to have personal phones.' Jack Moreton provided Warton with the name of Jez's school.

Warton thanked him profusely and called the school.

'I'm very sorry,' said a secretary. 'Pupils are not allowed to receive calls.'

'It's extremely urgent. It's about his father. I really must speak to Jeremy Moreton.'

'Can I pass a message?'

'I'm afraid it's very personal.' A solemn note that had the right effect.

'Oh dear. Very well – I'll send for him.'

Warton spent two minutes shitting bricks. Dear God! Don't let him answer!

'Hallo?' said the secretary.

'Hallo?'

'I'm very sorry but Jeremy Moreton hasn't come in today. I do hope it's not serious.'

Warton thanked her. He needed air – he opened his car window. He needed to talk. He called the editor and had no trouble convincing him because he had always been a reliable source. They agreed a fee and top-up if Warton secured an exclusive. The fax contract rolled out of the dashboard slot and Warton was on his way, driving as fast as he dared.

Thirty minutes later he was parked near Jack Moreton's

bank and talking to him on the phone.

'Well certainly you can come and see me,' said Moreton, puzzled. 'But can't you give me an inkling of what it's about?'

Warton swallowed. It was hard to believe that he had beaten the big boys.

'Are you sitting down, sir?'

35

Sabre had completed its first orbit. It had crossed the North Pole and was now on the dark side of the earth, tracking southwards over Siberia. This time it would cross western Australia. The reason for the apparent eastward shift in its orbit was due to earth's west-to-east rotation. The space-plane was actually following a fixed polar orbit, but the earth was rotating beneath it. Another twenty-four hours and twelve orbits would have to elapse before it would be passing over western Europe again and matching its original take-off path.

Len Allenby shaved in the tiny crew toilet aft of the flight-deck. There was no water for washing because the tank had been emptied to fill the drinking bulbs. He checked his cap, tie and jacket in the stretched foil mirror before stepping into the cabin. Looking smart gave the pax confidence – God knows, they needed it and he could use some himself.

Jacky greeted him as he entered the strangely silent cabin, lit by a few emergency lights to conserve power. The air felt heavy and there was the taint of urine – the flight-deck was on an independent air-conditioning system. She and her crew had done a good job. All the oxygen masks were stowed, everything was tidy, the passengers in their seats. Expectant eyes watched him as he and Jacky conferred in low tones.

'I'm worried about drinking water, skipper. We're rationing the squeezy bulbs but they're nearly all gone. There's some condensation forming on the sides and it feels muggy so I'm assuming the dehumidifiers aren't working at maximum efficiency.'

'They're not working at all,' Allenby replied. 'We're manually bleeding in oxygen every ten minutes and flushing when the CO2 level gets high.'

Jacky nodded. 'I guessed. We've been getting headache complaints, but all the pax have been marvellous really.' She pointed to Jez who was dozing. 'That lad was wonderful. He managed to reach all the difficult holes and plug them.'

Allenby glanced at the diminutive form. 'How's Mrs Santos?'

'Still sleeping.' She hesitated, steeling herself to bring up the one subject that was uppermost on her mind.

'I'll have a word with Mr Santos,' said Allenby quickly, unwilling to deal with questions concerning their rescue. He moved along the aisle, exchanging reassuring pleasantries with passengers who were awake. He sat in the exit seat opposite Paul. Sophia was wrapped in a blanket that was held in place with tapes. Her body was hardly touching the seats. Paul was holding her hand. He glanced up at his visitor, his normally grave expression now haggard. He looked utterly crushed, like his carnation, his customary vitality extinguished.

'Hallo, captain.'

'How's the missus?'

Paul smiled at the English colloquialism. 'She woke for a few seconds just now. She said that it was the most comfortable bed she had ever slept in . . . What's the latest?'

Allenby briefed Paul on their situation who listened intently, glad of the chance to take his mind off Sophia. 'So the immediate problem is hooking up another oxygen supply?' he said when Allenby had finished.

The skipper nodded. 'We've just had another go at trying to shift the crease beam. We need a lever and there's nothing suitable.'

'Those stupid crease beams. Ralph hated them.'

'Maybe they'll listen to him now.'

Paul shrugged. 'What does it matter? Sabre Industries is

finished and so is the Sabre.'

'Forgive me, Mr Santos – but that is crap. If this were a conventional aircraft we'd all be dead now.'

'If this were a conventional aircraft those swine would not have planted their bomb . . .' Paul shook his head. 'Maybe everyone was right . . . Maybe we pushed the technology too far, too soon.'

Allenby was contemptuous. 'There's nothing wrong with the technology, and you know that, Mr Santos. But no technology can ever be loony-proof. You give in to them and they win.'

Paul thought about the victims that his blinding obsession with the spaceplane had claimed: a wrecked first marriage, two estranged sons – refusing to speak to him because of the way they believed he had treated their mother – the ten years out of his life, and now the most terrible price of all, his beloved Sophia . . .

She stirred, as though sensing that she was the intense focus of his thoughts at that moment. He brushed her hair away from her face. 'So what's the latest ground situation?' he asked at length.

'We've just had some pictures patched through showing what St Omer are doing to 004. They're gutting it. Seats, fittings – everything that's not essential. They're installing extra retro fuel tanks.'

Paul forced himself to think about the problems involved in a space rendezvous between two Sabres – something they had never been designed for. 'When do they have a take-off window?'

'Tomorrow at 13:58. That's when we'll be at three degrees west over Algeria which will take us straight up the middle of France. Simone takes off in 004 ahead of us, also heading due north, and spirals out for a rendezvous over the Bering Sea.'

Paul stroked Sophia's hand as he concentrated on the huge problems of a space meeting. Unlike aircraft which could fly towards each other and match courses, height and speed if they so wished, spacecraft were denied such free-

322

dom of movement. They were confined to their orbital trajectories by the laws of ballistics. Minor corrections could be made on final closing but that was all. The timing and course of 004's orbital injection would have to be executed with absolute precision and little margin for error. 'What will her permitted deviation be?'

'Virtually none,' Allenby replied shortly. 'She won't have the correction fuel if she's as much as a degree out. She may pass us within a kilometre but all she'd be able to do is wave, complete a circumnavigation and land back at St Omer.'

'And try again twenty-four hours later.'

'Yes,' said Allenby. 'But we don't have the oxygen for twenty-four hours later. We've hardly enough to last us until tomorrow.'

36

'But this is absurd,' said the doctor who was taking part in the video conference between the BASOR and St Omer. 'There're full bottles of oxygen in the service bay and no way of getting at them. Surely you can cut your way through the outer skin? It's only aluminium. Don't you have tools on board?'

'Yes – there're tools on board,' said Ralph, speaking from the crowded operations room at St Omer. It was 5.10 p.m. He had been up for twelve hours and his temper was fraying fast. 'A hacksaw, drills, wrenches – you name it.'

'Well then—'

Morgan sensed the coming eruption. He had tried to catch the doctor's attention but it was too late.

'*But the fucking toolbox is in the fucking service bay!*' Ralph roared.

'Well,' said the doctor huffily, 'my department has given you an opinion. With the cabin supply and the masks combined, the passengers and crew have enough oxygen for twenty hours at the very outside if they keep absolutely still.

There'll be someone on duty here if you need more information.' The screen bearing his face went blank in both
centres. For a while no one on the two teams spoke.

Morgan studied his watch. 'Twenty hours . . . Rendezvous at 14:15 tomorrow . . . Say another hour to get an
oxygen line aboard . . . Which takes us to 15.15 . . . Twenty-
one hours . . . I don't suppose the life supports in the
mobility units contain enough oxygen to last them all an
hour.'

'Not a chance,' said Ralph, catching a senior designer's
head shake. 'Those spacesuits are good for one person for
three hours. And two of them have already been used.'

Morgan shuffled some photographs and found one from
the video made when Nick Rowe had pushed a TV camera
into the service bay. The damage caused by the explosion
was considerable – burnt-out cables, heat-distorted equipment racks, a shapeless glob of lava that had once been a
fuel cell. At the aft end of the bay, furthest from the fire,
were two intact oxygen bottles strapped to their frame.
They were not ten metres from the hatch, yet the distance
might as well be ten kilometres. 'How's the work going on
004, Mr Peterson?'

'It'll be ready by 11:00 tomorrow.'

A telephone in front of Morgan flashed. He picked it up
and listened. NASA's Marshall Space Center were monitoring the conference on audio only and had something to say.
Nick listened intently. 'That's a brilliant idea!' he exclaimed.
'Why the hell didn't we think of that? . . . Yes . . . Yes . . .
God . . . Yes please . . . 160 . . . When?' He listened for
another minute while scribbling on his memopad and
thanked the caller.

'What was all that about?' Ralph asked when Morgan
replaced the handset. 'NASA have come up with a
suggestion for the pax transfer. I ought to kick myself for
not thinking of it. You will as well.' He outlined the plan.

'Bloody hell – of course,' said Ralph, thumping the arm of
his chair. 'I must be getting old.'

'We were all thinking in terms of spacesuits,' said Morgan

324

ruefully. 'They're rounding them up now. If all goes well an F-200A will leave Patrick AFB, Florida in a couple of hours. Its ETA at St Omer is around midnight.'

The meeting fell silent. The unspoken thought of all those in both centres was that the NASA plan was academic. Even if 004 did manage to rendezvous with 005 on time, it seemed inevitable that all they would have to transfer would be 154 corpses.

37

To Jack Moreton's relief and alarm, his wife took the news of Jez's escapade with uncharacteristic calmness. She sat perfectly still, hands folded on her lap, quietly answering the reporters' questions about her beloved son and his impending rescue the following day.

She continued sitting quite still when the journalists and photographers had left, taking with them photographs of Jez and other artefacts in accordance with the terms of the exclusive contract that she and her husband had signed.

They sat in silence for some minutes, staring at the muted wall screen carrying yet another interminable studio analysis of the planned rescue operation.

It was her husband's observation that the sum they would be receiving from the newspaper was nearly fifty times the amount that Jez had embezzled that snipped the lines to her hitherto remarkable and worrying self-control and sent her into a tailspin. Embezzlement was, perhaps, an unfortunate choice of word and Jack Moreton's frantic excuses that he was a banker – that such words came naturally to him – were not well received. In vain did he protest that it had just slipped out and that he wasn't treating their offspring like a criminal. But no sooner had he thought he'd got his reasoning across when she was off on another tack. According to her, it was all his fault: he had encouraged Jez's obsession with the spaceplane; he had agreed to and paid for the school trip to St Omer that had triggered his obsession; he would have to bear the awful responsibility if anything happened to him. She had done her best for Jez – always trying to keep him on the straight and narrow, always trying to break the password on his computer that she was sure would unlock pictures of the naked girls that were stunting his growth – whereas he had set a bad example as a father by never watching television.

It was then that the rage directed at her contrite husband suddenly gave way to tears. After that her emotions swung wildly between anguish at the terrible danger her boy was in and the thought that she might never see him again, and the appallingly gruesome things she proposed doing to him the instant he set foot across the threshold.

38

Saturday, 19 December
Len Allenby woke.

Darkness. His head felt as though it had been kicked by a mule. He tried to focus on the displays and gave up. What did it matter how many orbits they had completed or where they were?

A tiny point of light flashing on earth. A city switching its public lighting on and off. Several had been doing it. For a few moments his befuddled, oxygen-starved mind distorted reality and he saw the friendly gestures as beacons that were mocking him:

Hey you up there! We're all safe down here! Shucks! Yahboo!

Hell – he felt awful. Part of his early training had included sessions working in low-oxygen, high-CO_2 atmospheres, but nothing had been like this. There had never been this blinding headache and his physical condition hadn't been aggravated by hunger during the training sessions. There was no food on a Sabre and yet no one, including himself, had ever thought that crews should fast before their flight simulator sessions. Dear God, the mistakes were endless. Virtually all the eventualities planned on the simulator had been proved wrong. The Flight Management System computers were worse than useless at dealing with a crisis – thousands of lines of source code would have to be rewritten. A hundred design changes swam before him.

He forced himself to relax. Worrying about the future of the spaceplane was pointless. Paul Santos was probably right – the concept was finished. Innovative but flawed, like the mighty airships of a century ago.

Time to show the flag. He floated from his seat and gave a nudge that sent his body drifting into the dimly-lit cabin. Using the Velcros took too much effort – conserving oxygen was vital. Those passengers awake regarded him listlessly without moving. They had heeded their admonishments well and weren't even reading. The simple effort of holding a book open and in position consumed precious oxygen. The BASOR doctors had ruled that the cabin blinds should be permanently closed to maintain the illusion of a long night. His mind was too befuddled to recall the reasons. Something to do with the frequent dawns and sunsets upsetting circadian rhythms and respiratory rates. He noticed that the kid who had helped plug the cabin holes after the explosion was watching him, wide-eyed. He looked as if he wanted to say something but Allenby held a warning finger to his lips. The lad had done a good job: Nick Rowe had inspected the repairs and declared them sound.

'Anyone bigger wouldn't've been able to reach half of them,' the second officer had declared. Allenby wondered why Rowe's earlier comment should choose this moment to start playing on his mind. For God's sake – this fucking headache was preventing him from thinking straight.

There was a faint thump from below. There had been odd noises from the service bay ever since the explosion — two large nitrogen bottles drifting around, bumping into the floor every now and then under the influence of the Sabre's micro-gravity.

'Skipper . . .'

327

Allenby turned back to the flight deck. Rowe's calm tone worried him.

'Push the door to, skipper.'

Allenby closed the pressure-tight door. 'What's the prob—' But he saw the new message before he finished the sentence. 'Oh, shit.'

'That noise just now must've been the feed pipe going,' said Rowe, staring at the chilling message proclaiming that the last of their depleted oxygen was leaching away. 'Probably weakened in the fire . . . And now it's burst . . .'

39

The USAF fighter-bomber landing at St Omer woke Ralph. He had been sleeping fully clothed, too exhausted to undress when he had stumbled into his office and sprawled on the camp-bed. He pondered the roar and remembered that it was NASA's promised consignment from Florida. It was three hours late but what the hell did it matter now? He wondered whether he ought to get up but others could cope. Sleep was vital. He drifted back into a fitful slumber and was woken again by the pricker alarm on his wrist-watch. Then his Iridium was trilling.

'This had better be fucking good,' he growled into the telephone after having accidentally knocked it on to the floor.

It was the control room duty officer. He offered no apologies such was the urgency of his message.

Ralph sat up suddenly – now wide awake and alert. 'What! All of it!' he shouted. 'For Christ's sake! What's the loss rate?'

40

'Captain,' said Jez hesitantly.

Allenby and Rowe whirled around from their task of balancing the Sabre's dwindling oxygen, their faces pale and drawn from the terrible decision that fate had forced on them. They had decided to allow the oxygen to continue flowing at its present rate. It would last thirty minutes and then it would be another ten minutes before everyone would become aware of their worsening breathing difficulties. Lungs would start heaving, desperately trying to claw in non-existent. The older passengers would succumb first, hopefully drifting peacefully into death after losing consciousness. That was what the two men prayed for. The bodies of the younger ones would rebel at the summary ending. Perhaps fighting, kicking, screaming, and thus hasten the inevitable end of themselves and each other. But the truth was that the two men didn't know how they or the other 152 souls aboard Sabre 005 would perish; it hadn't been included in their training.

'Get back to your seat,' Allenby ordered, not unkindly. This tiny kid probably didn't need so much oxygen — he might be the last one alive. 'Passengers aren't allowed on the flight-deck and we're busy.'

'I overheard the stewards talking just now . . . Something about the service bay hatch being obstructed and causing—'

'You must return to your seat,' Allenby insisted.

It had taken a good deal of courage for Jez to venture onto the flight-deck and he wasn't going to be deterred now. 'But I'm fairly small. Could I try getting down there?'

The two men stopped what they were doing and gaped at Jez.

'It's a possibility,' Rowe muttered, eyeing Jez's slight build. 'By Christ — yes!'

Allenby dragged the three spacesuits from their locker. 'Have you ever worn one of these things before?' he asked.

'No – stupid question, forget it. What's your name?'

'Jeremy – people call me Jez.' He wriggled quickly through the waist opening while Allenby held the suit. Weightlessness made the manoeuvre easy but the garment hung around him in loose folds.

Five minutes later all three were suited up and Jez was listening intently to his instructions through his helmet radio. He knew exactly what he had to do and surprised the two men with his knowledge of the Sabre's workings. He told them about his models but they weren't listening.

The pressure-tight door to the main cabin was swung shut and locked against its seals. The suits pressurised. Rowe released the guard that covered the dump lever that would vent the flight deck's atmosphere into space.

'Well, Jez. If it turns out that you can't go through the hatch, the skipper and I will jump on you until you do. Once the air's gone, that's it – we don't have enough to re-pressurise the flight-deck.'

He pulled the lever all the way over for a fast dump of the flight-deck's atmosphere. There was a muted roar of escaping air. Jez felt the suit closing on him as it countered the falling pressure. It felt uncomfortable, the hardening loose folds made movement difficult, the gauntlets felt clumsy. The sound of escaping air faded to a muted hiss and finally disappeared altogether once the flight-deck was a vacuum.

Allenby opened the floor hatch.

'Right, Jez,' said Rowe's cheerful voice in Jez's helmet speaker. 'Body stiff and we'll try with your arms tucked in first.' He manipulated the folds of surplus material until the spacesuit was reasonably tight and smooth around Jez's hips.

Jez kept his legs straight, boots pointing down, as he was steered carefully through the larger of the two gaps created by the crease beam across the hatch opening. His hips went through easily enough but the folds around his chest jammed on the beam. He remembered to keep his boots clear of the ladder while Rowe turned him through a few degrees. At the same time Allenby's gauntleted fingers were busy easing the more awkward folds of fabric past the hatch rim. Jez felt a gentle pressure on his shoulders and experienced a sudden wave of panic when his helmet grated against the hatch. He was about to cry out that he would be trapped, when he realised that he was actually in the service bay, clinging to the ladder.

'It's okay, Jez,' said a jubilant Rowe. 'You won't fall.'

The obvious relief of the two men was infectious. Jez laughed at his stupidity and pushed himself cautiously to the floor.

'Catch!'

A flashlight drifted slowly down. He caught it and discovered that the slide switch was surprisingly easy to operate through the gauntlets. The powerful light illuminated the blackened interior. Allenby was watching him anxiously from the hatch and directed his own torch to the heat-blistered tool-box. There was a tense moment when Jez couldn't release the lid, but, without any prompting from Allenby, he solved the problem by hitting the catch with a long piece of aluminium that was hanging near at hand.

'Okay, Jez,' said Allenby when Jez had inspected the contents. 'Close the lid. Drifting tools are a sod to find.'

Jez did as he was told and followed the direction of Allenby's torch, taking great care to stay clear of jagged wreckage. There was much less damage further aft. The paint on the two cabin supply gas bottles, that were bigger than Jez, was badly blistered but it was possible to distinguish their respective colour-coding for liquid oxygen and liquid nitrogen.

'What colour are the neck markers, Jez?'

'Both green, skipper.' He felt very important addressing Allenby thus.

'Thank Christ for that – they're full. Nitrogen and oxygen are the two gases that flow through the mixer to make ordinary air. You see the two pipes leading from the manifold and motor valves on top? Follow them with your torch and tell me what you find.'

'Should've put a camera on his helmet,' said Rowe's voice.

331

'He's got enough to cope with.'

Jez tracked the two supply pipes with his flashlight. They ran side by side along the inside of a bracing frame, out of sight of the hatch, and ended in a fused mass of synthetic rubber and melted pipework. He described the damage.

'Bugger,' said Allenby.

'Skipper!'

'Yes, Jez? Only no need to shout.'

'The pipes are okay the other side of the mess. That must be where the gases are fed to the cabin system. There's a pipe coupler on each pipe – like those things that plumbers use to join pipes. They look like they might be the same thread size as on the bottle mixer. If I could undo them and pull the pipes away from the bulkhead, I reckon I could move both bottles across and connect the mixer straight to the pipes. That way the damaged pipes will be bypassed and that'll give a direct supply to the cabin conditioning unit. There's plenty of spanners in the tool-box.' He broke off, awed by his own audacity in venturing an opinion so confidently. He added: 'Do you think it might work?'

Allenby was not a religious man but at that moment his inclination was to believe that perhaps there was some sort of deity that had decided to send him this lad.

'Yes, Jez,' he said slowly. 'I think that might work very well indeed.'

There was no 'might' about it. After twenty minutes' sweated labour that would have been much less had his visor not kept misting, Jez succeeded in moving the bottles, steering them to their position and connecting them. When he set the regulator in accordance with Allenby's instructions and opened the valves, the liquified gases mixed together and so produced an abundance of the sweetest-smelling air that the Sabre's passengers had ever breathed in their lives.

41

At 13:58 Simone Frankel opened Sabre 004's throttles and sent the spaceplane hurtling down St Omer's main runway. The lenses of hundreds of TV cameras followed the delta-wing's progress as it lifted into the cloudbase and disappeared from view. Her co-pilot was Yves Dupont, an experienced Air France skipper who had just finished his conversion to Sabres.

Simone concentrated on flying while Yves maintained continuous contact with the St Omer control room. Hitherto no Sabre flight had been subjected to such tight controls. The flight management parameters had been set to very precise limits: Simone had to maintain superimposed crossed hairs on a graphic display instrument similar to a glidescope to ensure that her velocity, course and rate of climb were exactly right. Yves's task was to reset the instrument's way points from minute to minute as updated information was received from ground radar and the on-board computers.

Jez's remarkable efforts in the service bay had granted a reprieve, but his second reconnoitre had established that there were insufficient supplies aboard 005 to provide another twenty-four hours' air supply if this rendezvous should fail.

Behind Simone and Yves, in the cavernous, empty shell of 004's main cabin, were the passengers. They comprised Ralph and two NASA technicians who had flown from Florida in the USAF aircraft. There was also a Sabre Industries technician, a paramedic and a news cameraman. All were wearing spacesuits and sat anchored to the floor by safety harnesses. Their back support against the increasing acceleration was a mountain of what looked like giant deflated beachballs. They were made of a tough, bright orange vinyl fabric, each one bearing the NASA logo. They were all crushed flat so that they took up as little room as possible. The unlikely looking cargo was secured to the floor by netting. There were also several coils of nylon rope – all clipped and neatly stowed.

'Pressurise suits,' Yves ordered over the PA. The six men closed their visors and operated the controls on their chest panels. One by one they confirmed that their suits were sealed and functioning. The reason for their being suited up and the main cabin not being pressurised was to save time. Once rendezvous was accomplished, and the passenger transfer underway, every second was vital.

Ralph switched his suit radio to the channel that enabled him to talk to 005.

'Skipper and I are suited up,' Rowe's cheery voice confirmed in answer to Ralph's inquiry. 'Flight-deck depressurised. Roof hatch open. All pax and cabin crew secured. Skipper's half out of the hatch, hoping to spot you before I do.'

'How's Mrs Santos?'

'Awake and hungry. We all are. Did you remember the crisps?'

Ralph grunted. There had been a lengthy briefing that morning with 005 to plan the transfer. Rowe was a real professional, able to grasp things quickly, but Ralph had found his sense of humour a little jarring at times.

'Mr Peterson,' said Rowe.

'I read you.'

'Message from Mr Santos. He says he hopes that you got out of bed the right side this morning.'

Ralph could not help but smile. 'Tell Mr Santos that I never went to bed last night.'

004 reached a way point height of thirty kilometres, a few degrees west of Norway. Yves leaned forward – it took an effort against the acceleration – and stared at the radar PPI that was set to its most extreme long range. The screen was blank but he could hear the ground controller at St Omer assuring him that everything was looking good. And then he saw it: a tiny dot had appeared on the edge of the screen, trailing 1,000 kilometres behind them, on the same course,

but travelling so much faster that it looked certain to over-take.

'We have radar acquisition of 005,' he reported.

Five minutes later the dot seemed to have slowed down but this was because the rescue spaceplane had reached 15,000 kph. Both craft had crossed the Arctic Circle. Southern extremity pack ice showed through gaps in the heavy cloud cover. The US radar station at Spitzbergen confirmed that the convergence gap between the two vehicles was 200 kilometres.

Allenby heard the report and directed his gaze forward and down. Two minutes slipped by and then he saw it: a silvery flash – a huge plume of exhaust gases silhouetted against thunderheads many kilometres below, but too quick for him to be sure. A brief message came from David Morgan at BASOR to wish them all a broken leg. British Airways were acting as observers only during this operation. What Allenby really wanted to hear was Simone's voice. He was rewarded when she reported engine close down in four minutes.

'We have visual acquisition,' he heard Yves say in a deliberately matter-of-fact tone. Sounds of cheering in the background over the St Omer channel when the controller acknowledged.

'Buggered if I can see them,' Rowe muttered, his face pressed to a window as he tried to look down.

'Got them,' breathed Allenby. This time there was no mistaking the low sun catching the tiny triangle thirty kilometres below with streams of engine gases spreading out behind it.

'ECD – two minutes,' said Simone.

'Zero Zero Five. Copy?'

It was the St Omer controller calling Allenby. He acknowledged.

'There's a couple of billion people waiting for TV pictures, captain.'

It was not a frivolous request. Not only was the whole world following the dramatic operation, but valuable lessons would be learnt from the recordings which was why the crew of the rescue spaceplane included a professional cameraman. Rowe passed the TV camera through the hatch to Allenby who trained it down on the swelling triangle of the converging 004.

'Engine close down – one minute.'

Yves's attention was concentrated on the radar screen which was now switched to short range. For the first time 004 appeared to be moving fractionally faster than 005, thus edging ahead. The gap between the two vehicles was now twenty-five kilometres — most of that being height difference.

'ECD – thirty seconds.'

004 had moved ahead of 005 but Rowe still could not see anything out of the windows and had to content himself with the picture from his skipper's camera. The screen showed the huge plumes of gases from 004's engines. Anxious seconds slipped by and the image hardened sufficiently for him to make out their rescuing craft's tailplane.

Four bars of Simone's glidescope graphic display flashed. A quick check with St Omer and she closed down the engines ten seconds ahead of schedule. Behind in the main cabin Ralph and his team remained harnessed despite the onset of weightlessness – there were still many manoeuvres to be performed before they could begin work.

Allenby gave himself some safety line slack and eased himself further out of the hatch so that he could keep 004 framed. 005's sister vehicle was now about ten kilometres ahead. In his helmet he could hear the St Omer controller congratulating Yves and Simone on their near perfect 'parking'. Separation was 9,800 metres; course divergence was twenty minutes of arc – well within the mission profile.

The most difficult part of the operation was about to begin: bringing the two spaceplanes together. There would be no computers or flight management systems to help Simone and Yves during this phase – everything would be by eye and judgement, because they would be doing something

336

that the Sabre was never designed to do, which was why 004 had been fitted with additional tanks containing propellent for its retro rockets. The dynamics of weightlessness required a given amount of fuel to initiate a manoeuvre and an equal amount of fuel to cancel the manoeuvre. A series of over-corrections could easily lead to ten times the calculated amount of fuel being used for a simple reorientation. The fact that the two craft were close together was of no consequence as far as the laws of gravitation and ballistics were concerned: each spaceplane was following its own orbit, dictated by its velocity in relation to the earth.

004's first manoeuvre was simple enough and consisted of turning the spaceplane through 180 degrees so that the craft were facing each other nose to nose across a distance of nearly ten kilometres. Simone performed the reorientation with five corrections — five tiny kicks and counter kicks from the retros. The fuel used was less than she had expected.

Now to close the gap.

First a one-second burst and then careful analysis to access the implication of the brief firing. Yves called off the decreasing range while Simone watched for a course deviation, her hand resting lightly on the retro controls, ready to correct if necessary. At five kilometres she executed a quick squirt from the lateral tail retro to arrest a slight yaw tendency.

'Four thousand metres,' Yves reported.

On 005 Allenby provided a commentary for the benefit of his passengers, not realising that his voice had been patched through to the networks and was being broadcast to the whole world. The vast audience included Christine and Alec Rose, watching with Honicker in his hotel suite. A few miles away Jez's parents sat in silence, their eyes fixed on their wall screen. At St Omer all the employees of Sabre Industries were watching. They included Louise, the voluptuous waitress whose thoughts were with Jez and the pleasant interlude with him beside a stream in her battered 2CV. She offered up a special prayer for her shy English boy

337

and wondered if he ever thought of her.

Yuri Segal was back in Moscow, sitting in his office at Commonwealth Airlines' HQ. He was watching the unfolding drama with close attention, his impassive Slav features giving no indication of his thoughts.

Joe Yavanoski and Jean Lesseps were not watching; they were languishing in their respective police cells, having deliberately not been subjected to questioning, and wondering what was in store for them. There were many blanks on their charge sheets that would be filled in when the outcome of the rescue bid was known.

'Two thousand metres,' said Yves quietly.

The two spaceplanes edged closer to each other like cautious cats assessing mating possibilities.

At 1,000 metres Allenby could just make out Simone. They exchanged waves. A hundred and fifty kilometres below the two spaceplanes were the Bering Straits and the frozen wastes of Alaska.

At 500 metres the cameraman in 004 released his floor harness and pushed himself to the door to aim his camera through the window. Subsequent manoeuvres would probably lead to him suffering a few minor bumps but he decided that the risk was worth it.

Simone cancelled 004's agonisingly slow approach and talked directly to Allenby. The simplex contact meant that there were none of the annoying delays as a result of their conversation being routed through satellites. She reiterated the last phase of the flight plan – that she intended to bring 004 alongside 005, slightly above and to one side so that the left-hand passenger doors on each craft were within twenty metres of each other.

Allenby acknowledged. He remained half-way through the roof hatch and continued sending TV pictures. The network controllers on earth now had two feeds to switch between.

The retro bursts that Simone applied were so brief that viewers had to watch carefully to see that the gap between the two spaceplanes was actually closing. There was a sudden buzz of excitment from the passengers on 005's left-hand side when they saw the long, sleek nose of their rescue craft easing slowly into sight alongside them.

A tiny stab from a forward retro, a careful watch to ensure that there had been no over-correction, and the intricate rendezvous was complete. The two spaceplanes were 'parked'.

'Rendezvous achieved,' Yves reported and the world below released its breath.

The second officer's two long-awaited words were the cue for Ralph's team to begin work. The two NASA technicians were old hands in space and kept their movements un-hurried but methodical. They released their harnesses and set about unshackling the net that secured the deflated beachballs to the floor. The passenger door was opened and the cameraman allowed himself to drift out of 004 on his safety line. He was space-wise, having spent several weeks on the NASA space station.

The first piece of rescue equipment was, of all things, an item much loved by all Frenchmen – a boule. It was encased in a supermarket string bag intended for fruit and attached to a length of twine. The senior NASA technician radioed across to Allenby who replied that he was ready. The boule was launched with great care and little velocity. It travelled slowly towards Allenby who had no trouble catching it. He hauled on the twine, which gave way to a more substantial rope, and thus was a physical link established between the two spaceplanes. The rope was tied to the hatch. The tech-nician who had thrown the boule pulled himself along the tether rope, a second line clipped to his belt, and joined Allenby on 005's flight deck roof.

In 004's gutted fuselage, Ralph and the second technician carefully prepared the strange fabric bags. They were clipped to the rope at two-metre intervals with quick-release shackles. Sabre's passengers watched in fascination as a train of what looked like giant flattened oranges began journeying to their spaceplane, jerking and waving, while Allenby and the technician pulled carefully on the rope.

They knew what to expect because they had been briefed on the rescue procedure – nevertheless, it was a very strange sight.

As each bag arrived on 005's flight-deck roof, it was unclipped and passed through the hatch to Rowe who proceeded to cram them tightly into every corner of the flight-deck to make the best use of the confined space.

'That's it,' he said after thirty minutes' methodical work. 'Any more and I won't have room to work the hatches.'

'How many?' asked Ralph from 004.

'Eight-six,' Allenby replied.

'Not bad,' said Ralph. 'That's six more than we managed to pack in on the dummy run this morning.'

'I can hardly move,' Rowe complained, and belied that statement by closing the roof hatch and pressurising the flight deck. He opened the door to the main cabin the moment the pressure was equalised on both sides. Jacky, helped by Neil, Billy and Jez, started pulling the bulky bags out of the flight deck and passing them along the aisle.

'Weird things,' Billy commented.

'NASA rescue balls,' said Jez. 'Like spacesuits but without arms and legs and a helmet. They've got a built-in life-support system. Simple really.'

Once the flight-deck had been cleared of the rescue balls, Rowe closed the flight-deck door and depressurised. He opened the roof hatch and a few minutes later the task of refilling the flight deck with the rest of the curious fabric bags was resumed.

'That's it,' said Ralph as the last bag passed through 004's open door. 'Hundred and fifty-seven, which gives you a few spares. The big one coming across now is for Mrs Santos.'

The elongated rescue enclosure, designed for injured personnel, proved awkward to squeeze through 005's roof hatch but it was accomplished. The second NASA technician crossed from 004 to 005. He followed Allenby and his colleague through the hatch and closed it behind him. The flight deck was repressurised.

Once in the main cabin, Allenby, Rowe and the two technicians were able to open their visors to conserve their spacesuits' life-support systems. The senior of the two technicians went over the drill: each passenger was required to pull their ball around them in the sitting position and to zip them partially closed. He spoke with a Texan accent and had a quiet, unassuming manner that inspired confidence.

'It's exactly like getting into a sleeping bag,' he said. 'You just sit cross-legged, holding it around you. Don't use the breathing mask in each bag until we say. It doesn't matter if you drift about. The important thing is to get yourselves in and ready for us to zip you closed. Take your time. Okay – let's go.'

There was a swirl of activity in the cabin as the 149 passengers climbed into their strange, deflated beachballs. Some of the older ones needed help from the crew but generally there were no problems. Even Nikki drew the heavy fabric of her bag around her without suffering a panic attack. Jez was the only one who found that he had plenty of room in his bag.

Paul and Jacky eased Sophia into her extra-long bag with great care. Fortunately it was fitted with an internal frame that afforded protection for her injury. She was looking much recovered and actually had some colour back in her cheeks. She smiled, assured Paul that she was fine and even scolded him gently for making a fuss.

The fixed cabin camera captured the odd spectacle of 149 anxious-faced individuals sitting with their heads poking out of their bags.

'Okay,' said the technician. 'We're now going to go around to close you all in.'

The four space-suited figures set to work. They ensured that each passenger had a firm grip on his or her mask and was breathing comfortably before before pulling the material over their heads and closing the pressure zips.

Jacky and the two stewards were the last to be enclosed. The final task was to clip each bag to the original rope that had been used to transfer them to 005.

'Guess we're ready to dump,' said the senior technician.

The four men closed their visors and checked their suit controls. Allenby moved to the flight deck and opened the dump valves. This time Sabre 005's entire interior was being reduced to a vacuum, not just the flight-deck. As the cabin pressure fell, so the bags swelled to tight round balls about a metre in diameter, giving their occupants more room. They jostled against each other but care was taken to ensure that Sophia's bag was kept clear.

'Equalised,' Allenby reported.

Rowe opened the main passenger door in the side of 005's fuselage. Floodlights on 004 bathed her sister spaceplane. The two vehicles were now dark-side over the Pacific. The reaction created by the air voiding from 005 had given Simone and Yves a few orientation problems but they had coped. Getting a line between the two open passenger doors was a reversal of the process with the boule. This time Ralph, standing in the open door of the rescue craft, caught the slow-moving missile. The rope was paid across and the transfer got underway.

The cameraman thought he had seen some strange sights during his career, but for weirdness nothing matched the slow-moving procession of the now bloated rescue balls, strung out like a bizarre necklace of giant oranges between the two spaceplanes. As each ball was steered into 004's cabin, it was unhitched and guided into a 'parking' position.

The operation was completed in thirty minutes. Allenby was the last to leave his stricken command. While the transfer was taking place he had completed a few 'housekeeping' tasks such as closing down all the electrical systems. Not that it mattered much – from now on Sabre 005 would be just another number on NASA's space debris tracking system. He took hold of the line and allowed himself to be pulled across to 004. Rowe had a joke for the occasion, of course.

'You're right,' said Allenby in reply. 'I did forget to set the burglar alarm and turn the oven off.'

Ralph reported to Simone that everyone was aboard. The cabin door was closed. The rescue balls lost their swollen

342

appearance as the cabin was pressurised. As soon as the atmosphere reached normal pressure, the technicians climbed out of their spacesuits and set to work opening the rescue balls. Passengers' heads emerged, looking about them, bemused and relieved at their new surroundings.

Sophia told the paramedic and Paul that she was fine and that she hadn't been bumped once. She had to repeat the assurance before Paul accepted her word.

'We're very sorry, everyone,' said Ralph loudly. 'As you can see, we've had to strip everything out to lighten 004 and make room. We don't have seats so we're going to clip your rescue balls to the floor and hope that they'll serve you for landing if you remain sitting in them, and hold them around you as best you can during deceleration and re-entry. It's the best idea we could come up with in the time that we had. Deorbit burn in twenty minutes so we'd better get a move on.'

Five minutes later Ralph pushed himself down beside Paul and Sophia and grinned amiably at them. He was holding a telephone handset. 'A call for you, Paul. I think it may be important.'

'Right now I don't feel like talking to anyone but Sophia.'

'Yes, but—'

'*Please*, Ralph.'

'I'll take it,' said Sophia unexpectedly. Before Paul could object, she reached out and took the telephone from Ralph. 'Hallo? Mr Santos's secretary speaking . . .' She listened. 'Good afternoon, Mr Segal, or is it evening? . . . Yes – very successful . . . Well, I'm feeling a bit hazy – strong sedatives – but I'll be fine . . .' A long pause. 'Yes, he's right beside me. I'll put him on . . .' She smiled at Paul and offered him the telephone. 'Mr Segal – Commonwealth. He wants to place a firm order for twenty Sabres.'

Sabre 004 landed at St Omer at 16:40, to be greeted by the biggest battery of TV cameras and the largest army of reporters ever to be assembled in one place.

42

May

Kristy Wood's editor at *Time* magazine had sufficient influence for her to be the first journalist allowed aboard the Australian oceanographic research ship *Globewatch* two days after the joint announcement by Indonesia and Australia of the ship's stupendous find.

An Indonesian air force helicopter disgorged her on to the ship's landing platform, the downwash from its rotors failing to destroy her carefully lacquered coiffure as she shook hands with a welcoming committee consisting of the captain, an Avanti Oil executive and Christine Rose.

In the *Globewatch*'s cramped but air-conditioned canteen she sipped iced water and plied Christine and Alec Rose with questions about the Darwin's findings. There were other technicians aboard that she wanted to talk to during her permitted three-hour visit, but the Roses were her main target. Luckily the months of secrecy surrounding their work had not conditioned them into reticence – the couple were only too willing to talk while her recorder captured their answers on a memory card. She studied them carefully: Alec, the quiet one – his hawk-like features watching her with interest – the brains behind the remarkable Darwin. And Christine – the driving force behind the brains, talking enthusiastically about what the massive oil find would mean for Indonesia's millions living in grinding poverty.

'We first singled out the Banda Trench because it seemed the best place to start looking,' said Christine earnestly, leaning across the table, her hands clasped tightly together as though she were fighting a coiled-up tension. 'But there are other deep trenches that have hardly been explored – mostly in the southern hemisphere where most of the world's poor live.'

'Avanti's press office have issued a release saying that the Banda field could supply the world's entire oil needs for the

344

next fifty years,' Kristy commented cautiously. 'Would you say that's an exaggeration?'

Alec smiled. 'Perhaps not accurate, Miss Wood. We've now recovered over a hundred samples from this area and they've all turned out positive. The field is much bigger than we expected from our earlier surveys. I'd say it's big enough to supply world needs for a century.'

Kristy turned her intense green eyes on Christine. 'If that's right, Christine, in about five to ten years we'll see a catastrophic collapse in the price of oil, and we'll be right back where we started – with the world's poor countries being the source of cheap raw materials for the world's rich countries.'

'They won't be so poor by then,' Christine retorted. 'They'll be as rich as the West and bidding on equal terms. It's already happening in Vietnam, Burma, Malaysia and particularly China. Their increasing wealth will double the world's oil needs.'

Kristy arched a disbelieving eyebrow.

'I'm right!' Christine snapped. 'Alec and I have total control over the Darwin's technology. We'll be granting free licences for its use provided a percentage of the oil revenues it helps earn goes to Third World countries.'

Christine went on to outline the details of her remarkable scheme while Kristy listened in mounting amazement. She played devil's advocate by offering objections but Christine Rose had sound answers for them all.

'We've calculated that the life of patents is long enough to bring about a revolution – a permanent change in the economics of this planet,' was Christine's final comment.

There was much on Kristy's mind as she spent the rest of her allotted time on a conducted tour of the ship; nevertheless, she showed a keen interest in every aspect of the recovery and processing of sediment samples. After her profuse thanks she was about to board the helicopter when she turned to Alec and Christine to congratulate them on their role in the arrest of the Sabre 005 saboteurs. 'I met Paul Santos on a VIP Sabre flight. He's quite a guy. Will you be going to the gala dinner he's laid on at St Omer next month?'

Christine nodded. 'We have to return to London anyway for the trial.'

Kristy smiled and mounted the helicopter's boarding steps. 'See you in St Omer,' she said.

43

June
The speeches dragged on but Kristy didn't mind.

She felt especially privileged because she was the only journalist to be sitting with the guests at the gala dinner being held at St Omer. The rows of linen-covered tables were laid out in Shed B which was about to be opened to handle the increased production of Sabres. The order book now stood at fifty-three; the future of Sabre Industries and their spaceplane was assured.

The speeches by various worthies from the civil aviation world extolling the virtues of the Sabre eventually bored Kristy; she passed the time making surreptitious notes on her memopad with frequent references to her guest list and seating plan.

Virtually everyone associated with the incredible rescue of 005's crew and passengers was present. All the passengers and crew themselves, the NASA technicians and most employees of Sabre Industries. Even the waiters and waitresses were members of the staff. Nikki Lithgow was there with her husband. She was sedated but blissfully happy because her daughter, son-in-law and grandchildren had been flown to Europe by British Airways to be with her; Jim Curtis and David Morgan – clapping dutifully as each speaker finished their piece; Michelle Finch, the surgeon, talking animatedly to Jacky Kerr. All the crew of 005 and their 004 rescuers.

Kristy's cool gaze scrutinised everyone in turn. Before the guests had sat down she had renewed her acquaintance with Christine and Alec Rose – sitting opposite Paul Santos – and had been introduced to William Honicker – an Australian civil servant who she had decided would be worth cultivating, especially as he was listed as a prosecution witness in the forthcoming trial of Jean Lesseps and Joe Yavanoski.

Joe Yavanoski . . . Kristy corrected her spelling of his name. Jesus, if anyone's crazy scheme had been counter-productive, his had. For the first time in aviation history a bomb had exploded aboard a flight and everyone had survived. Sophia Santos walked with a slight limp but her physios were confident it would be gone in six months. Right now she was looking lovely, smiling up at her husband as he rose – the last speaker on the list. The young man sitting on Paul Santos's left, looking ill at ease in evening dress, was Jeremy Moreton – the guest of honour. Kristy noticed that he seemed to be coming in for a good deal of attention from a large-breasted, smiling waitress, and that every time she whispered to Jeremy the tips of his ears turned pink.

The chatter gradually died away; Kristy decided that it would be impolite to continue writing. It annoyed her that all she had was a collection of jottings and no angle for her article. The reams of sentimental copy that would be sure to flow from this gathering she would leave to others – her editor expected better than that.

As was usual with Paul Santos, he was brief and to the point. He thanked everyone concerned with the rescue operation and reserved special thanks for Jez. He went on to say that if Jez was still interested in aeronautics after school and university, then Sabre Industries would have a job for him. He paused and looked around at the glittering gathering. 'A month ago one of 006's test flights was a visit to 005, still stranded in orbit. Her payload was a party of engineers and supplies. They have been working on temporary repairs to 005 and report that she is now ready to perform a three-engine deorbit burn and return home.' A buzz of surprised comment greeted the announcement.

'Tomorrow', Paul continued, '006 will ferry a recovery air-crew up to 005. They will be Len Allenby and Nick Rowe.'

There was an outburst of applause and heads turned to

347

the two men. Allenby seemed embarrassed by the attention but Nick relished it. 'It's our responsiblity to go back!' he called out. 'We forgot to turn off the gas, cancel the newspapers, and put out the cat!'

Laughter echoed around the giant shed.

'We anticipate that full-scale refurbishing and testing of 005 will take two months,' Paul continued. 'After that she will be kept on permanent stand-by as a rescue and recovery vehicle for everyone venturing into space.'

The news was welcomed with more applause. Kristy saw that Christine Rose was paying close attention to Paul. She began scribbling again; her stylus slowed as a nebulous idea clamoured for attention.

'A philosopher once said that space is important because it's where everything is,' Paul continued. 'It's certainly where our future lies. And with vehicles such as the Sabre and others like her that will surely follow, it has already become a very safe place indeed . . . For us . . . For our children . . . And our children's children.'

The end of his speech was drowned by thunderous applause and cheering. Kristy noticed that Christine Rose's clapping was particularly enthusiastic. What a fascinating, single-minded pair they were. Two very different people driven by their dreams: Paul Santos, obsessed with shrinking the world physically; and Christine Rose, obsessed with shrinking it economically. That morning the *Wall Street Journal* had commented on the increase in investment in Third World countries over the past few weeks – particularly those countries that were potential future oil producers.

Kristy recalled Christine Rose's impassioned words to her on the *Globewatch* and realised that she had her angle. It would be a development of her first article in which she had said that the Sabre would change the world.

The Sabre would undoubtedly bring about a profound change, but it wouldn't do it alone. It would be a joint but unconscious effort by the Sabre and the Darwin working in strange harmony.

And that change had already started.